Born in the London Borough of Islington, Victor Pemberton is a successful playwright and TV producer, as well as being the author of eleven highly popular London sagas, all of which are published by Headline. His first novel, *Our Family*, was based on his highly successful trilogy of radio plays of the same name. Victor has worked with some of the great names of entertainment, including Benny Hill and Dodie Smith, had a long-standing correspondence with Stan Laurel, and scripted and produced many of the BBC's *Dr Who* series. In recent years he has worked as a producer for Jim Henson and set up his own production company, Saffron, whose first TV documentary won an Emmy Award.

The Chandler's Daughter

Victor Pemberton

headline

First published in hardback in 2004
by HEADLINE BOOK PUBLISHING

First published in paperback in 2004
by HEADLINE BOOK PUBLISHING

10 9 8 7 6 5 4 3 2 1

ISBN 0 7553 0237 0

Typeset in Plantin by Avon DataSet Ltd,
Bidford-on-Avon, Warwickshire

Printed and bound in Great Britain by
Mackays of Chatham plc, Chatham, Kent

Headline's policy is to use papers that are natural, renewable and
recyclable products and made from wood grown in sustainable
forests. The logging and manufacturing processes are expected to
conform to the environmental regulations of the country of origin.

HEADLINE BOOK PUBLISHING
A division of Hodder Headline
338 Euston Road
London NW1 3BH

www.headline.co.uk
www.hodderheadline.com

For Kathleen Hatton,
my first schoolteacher,
who helped me to understand
why English is such a
beautiful language

Chapter 1

Old Clapper was up at the crack of dawn. By the time the first rays of sunlight had filtered through the cracks of his stable door, he had finished the bucket of oats Gus had left for him overnight, and when young Grace came in to brush him down, he was as sprightly as a young foal, all bright and alert, up and ready for the long trot with his master and mistress around the cobbled backstreets of Islington.

'I don't know why everyone keeps calling you *old*,' said Grace, as she used a hard brush on Clapper's bushy white tail. 'Seems to me six years old is no age.'

Clapper snorted. By popular consensus, he was one of the most handsome dray horses around the streets of Islington, and his gleaming sandy and white coat was probably the envy of all his mates he passed during each working day.

'You know your trouble, Clapper?' Grace asked irritably.

Clapper turned round to look down at her.

'Dad spoils you,' she said, brushing and stroking him vigorously. 'I mean – just look at you. If Dad's customers go on giving you lumps of sugar, you'll be as fat as a pig!'

'Hey!' called Grace's dad, Gus Higgs, who came into the stable carrying a fresh bucket of water for Clapper. 'Mind 'ow yer go wiv that brush, Gracie gel. The poor ol' boy's got a sensitive skin. Ain't yer, Clap?' He gave the horse a gentle tap on his back, then stroked him affectionately.

Grace sighed, and gave up on the grooming. She knew it wasn't worth arguing with her father. As far as she was concerned, she could never dare say a wrong word about the creature.

Gus knew only too well that he spoilt Clapper, for he was always fussing around the animal, checking his hoofs to make sure he hadn't picked up any sharp objects on the road, peering into his ears for bugs that sometimes got lodged there, and constantly stroking his back and telling him, 'You're a good'un, Claps, that's fer sure.' In fact, Gus thought the world of Clapper; they were inseparable and, more often than not, once Grace had turned in for the night, Gus would go down to the stable to have a little good night chat with the horse, which was also a way of getting things off his chest. And he had plenty of things to get off his chest.

He was beginning to find that getting up at the crack of dawn every day to travel around the streets in all sorts of weather was wearing him down. Oh yes, he liked his work all right, the business he had built up with such meticulous care over the years selling grocery provisions from the back of his 'shop on wheels', and collecting rent from his tenants for the small terraced houses he had invested in.

Meeting his regular customers and tenants was never dull, for they always stopped for a few minutes' chat, and a grouse about something before paying their rent and buying a few bits and pieces from his mobile grocery shop. His customers were his kind of people: the rough-and-ready working-class folk of backstreet Islington, where he and his late wife, Alice, were both born, and where young Grace had been brought up and given the chance of a good education – which was something that he himself had never had – at Shelburne Road and Highbury Fields Girls' School.

Gus was a self-made man. Because he was inarticulate

and uneducated, he had learnt his job the hard way, making mistakes and putting them right, and using his common sense to fathom out how to save money in order to make more money. His motto was, and had always been: 'If yer want to get on in this world, Gus 'iggs, then yer've got ter get on an' do fings fer yerself.' However, just lately he had felt that the shine had gone out of the job, maybe because he was at last feeling his age. After all, this *was* 1937, and he was now sixty-seven years of age, which meant that he'd been working for the best part of his life. He was beginning to slow down, there was no doubt about that, and it was time to call it a day. It was not only that his tired old bones were trying to tell him something, but also the fact that at night he often lay awake thinking of that glorious life before he was married long ago, when he was a young ship's chandler in the Merchant Navy, a job he had always loved so much. 'A Life on the Ocean Wave' – ah, those were the days!

'Don't forget Mrs Jolly owes you four weeks,' Grace said, giving Clapper a final stroke.

'Four weeks, is it?' asked Gus, who, as usual, hadn't really taken in what his daughter had told him. 'Time soon goes, don't it?'

Her father's lack of concern about tenants not paying their rent on time always irritated Grace. 'You can't give that woman any more time, Dad,' she said sharply, washing her hands in an enamel wash-basin. 'Bad payers only get worse.'

'What difference does it make?' replied Gus. 'Gert Jolly's been a tenant er mine fer years. Fings ain't bin easy for 'er since poor ol' Bill died. She'll pay when she can afford it.'

Grace was incensed. 'Dad, you say that about everyone who doesn't pay up on time. You're not a philanthropist.

You can't afford to go around letting these scroungers get away with not paying their rent.'

Gus cast a brief look at her. He suddenly wondered where this daughter of his had got her frosty ways. It wasn't from him, and it certainly wasn't from her mum, who had died from consumption at such a young age. Alice had been a warm, loving person, who would never say boo to a goose. True, Grace wasn't much to look at – pint-sized, with her light brown hair tied up in a bun like a school teacher, and her back always as straight as if she was stuck to a plank of wood. Even so, he did love his little girl. It was just that she could sometimes be a bit difficult.

'Gert Jolly ain't no scrounger,' he said. 'She's as honest as the day is long. It don't matter ter me if she's a bit late payin' up 'er 'alf-crown a week. I 'ave a great deal er time fer that woman.'

'Why?'

Grace's stark question took Gus by surprise. 'I don't know *why*,' he said, collecting Clapper's bridle. 'Maybe it's 'cos I like 'er name. Jolly brings a smile ter me face.'

Grace bristled. 'I've never seen Mrs Jolly with a smile on *her* face.'

'As yer gran always used ter say, "a smile gets a smile",' said Gus, teasing her affectionately. 'Yer should try it some time. It can work miracles.'

Grace felt herself tense, but she decided not to answer him. She had learnt only too well over the years that, in his own quiet way, her dad had always managed to get in the last word. 'I'm going to get ready,' she replied, quietly going to the door.

Out of the corner of his eye, Gus watched her leave the stable. Then he turned back to Clapper, and stroked him. 'She's a real problem that one, Clapper ol' mate,' he said, with a sigh. 'Don't know wot 'er mum'd say if she was still alive. Don't know wot gets into 'er sometimes. Reckon it'll take 'er a long time ter get over all she's gone fru.'

A short while later, Higgs's grocery shop was on the move. Now fully groomed, the brass nameplates on his harness gleaming in the early morning sun, Clapper picked his way carefully out of the stable yard just behind Caledonian Road market, and headed off down towards the Nag's Head. With Gus at the reins, togged up in his usual bowler hat, dark three-piece suit and pocket watch and chain, and Grace at his side wearing one of her drab floral summer dresses, and brown straw hat, it was a journey they had all covered many times over the years, so they had grown used to the rough cobbled roads, in need of repair. Caledonian Road itself was always quite a busy thoroughfare, especially for buses, trams and lorries heading back and forth past Pentonville Prison in the direction of King's Cross, but most drivers respected the right of four-legged creatures to share the road with them, and usually kept their distance. Occasionally, however, a bunch of kids would run alongside Clapper, trying to keep up with him, but he always responded impeccably when they tried to give him a gentle pat as he trotted at a slow pace, his head and bushy mane bobbing up and down.

It wasn't long before they were passing a large, elegant new building, which looked as though it was in the final stages of completion. 'I've 'eard they're goin' ter call it the Mayfair,' Gus called to his daughter. 'Bit posh for a place like the Cally!'

'I couldn't care less what they call it,' replied Grace, with no more than a passing look at the grand façade of the cinema, with its beautiful large first-floor windows in the process of being glazed. 'I could think of a lot better things to do with my time than sit in the dark for so long.'

'Well, *I* shall give it a try,' insisted Gus. 'Your gran and granddad used ter love a pennyworth er flicks at the pitture 'ouse. They often went ter see Charlie Chaplin or Fatty Arbuckle.'

Grace hadn't the faintest idea who Fatty Arbuckle was, so she didn't reply.

'Yer know, it worries me about you, Gracie,' said Gus, his eyes concentrating on the road ahead.

Grace swung a look at him. 'What are you talking about?' she asked sharply.

'Well, the way yer never seem ter get out. I know that git Eric Tyler was enuff ter put yer off blokes fer life, but a young gel like you oughta ferget the past, an' get on wiv enjoyin' yerself.'

Grace sighed irritably, and turned away. 'Please don't go into all that again, Dad,' she said haughtily. 'We've been through it time and time again.'

'Well, it's true, ain't it?' he persisted. 'All yer do is come out wiv me on the rounds each day, then yer cook the tea, and spend the rest of the evenin' knittin' or sewin'.'

'I like knitting and sewing.' Grace was getting exasperated.

'Maybe,' said Gus. 'But who're yer knittin' *for*?'

'Well, *you* haven't done too bad for cardigans!' snapped Grace. 'And Auntie Hilda says she loves the bedspread I made for her.'

Now it was Gus's turn to sigh. *Auntie Hilda.* Even the mention of his elder sister's name made him feel like getting boozed. No wonder her own husband upped and walked out on her soon after they got married. Gus shook his head. Thank God for his younger sister, Josie. At least *she* cared for more things than money. 'Anyway, I can't see wot yer Aunt 'Ilda needs a bedspread for,' Gus said. 'She ain't got no man ter share her bed wiv 'er.'

'Really, Dad!' Grace was shocked. 'That's not a nice thing to say about someone. Especially your own sister.'

Gus turned to look at her. 'I'm not only talking about 'Ilda, Gracie,' he said pointedly.

Grace stiffened.

'What I'm talkin' about is wot yer'll do when I'm gone.'

Grace waved her hand dismissively, and turned away again.

'It's no good tryin' ter ignore the facts, gel,' he said, refusing to be ignored. 'It's the law of nature that one of these days yer'll be on yer own. 'Ow d'yer fink you're goin' ter carry on the business if yer ain't got no man at yer side?'

Again, Grace swung a look at him. 'Look, Dad,' she said indignantly, 'you're still a young man – well – relatively young. So will you please stop talking as though you're about to die?'

Gus shook his head despairingly. In the split second that he looked at his daughter, he could see the determination and obstinacy that had been the ruin of her life ever since she had been jilted by that young nutcase Eric Tyler when she wasn't even old enough to have learnt about blokes like him. It was such a shame, Gus told himself. If only she'd pull herself together, wear some nice clothes and put on a bit of make-up, she could easily find a man who'd take a shine to her. At least she had her mum's dazzling blue eyes and, in Gus's mind, they alone were worth a fortune.

'And as for having a man at my side . . .' continued Grace, clearly put out.

Gus emerged from his brief thoughts to find Grace glaring at him. 'Wot?' he mumbled. 'Wot d'yer say?'

'I said,' repeated Grace, 'as for having a man at my side, I've never heard so much nonsense in all my life. Women are perfectly capable of running a business without the help of someone else. Especially a man. But in any case, *if* anything were to happen to you – which it won't – I'm not so sure I'd *want* to carry on the business.'

Shocked, Gus gave a sudden pull on Clapper's reins, and brought him to a halt. 'Wos that?'

'I said there are other things to do in life, Dad, apart from dragging a shop around the streets day after day.'

Gus wasn't given to letting anyone get him worked up, but he was being tested to the limit by the way his own daughter was talking about the business he had built up with such hard work and perseverance over the years. 'This shop, young lady,' he said firmly, ' 'as been our lifeblood. It's a good, respectable business, and it's kept you fed and watered well enuff!'

'Oh, for goodness' sake, Dad,' replied Grace, 'the way you talk to me sometimes, you'd think I was a horse!'

'Not at all,' insisted Gus resentfully. 'An 'orse is a grateful creature. 'E appreciates what 'e gets.'

As if to agree with him, Clapper snorted impatiently.

'Look, Dad,' replied Grace, 'you love this business. You love getting up at the crack of dawn every morning, dragging all these groceries around the streets, collecting the meagre rents you get, chatting to people who have absolutely nothing in common with either you or me. But I'm not cut out for all this. I want an ordinary nine-to-five job, and a place I can come back to in the evening and really call home.'

'Before yer can 'ave an 'ome of yer own, Gracie,' said Gus, 'yer 'ave ter find someone ter share it wiv.'

Grace pursed her lips and turned away.

Realising he had upset her, Gus leant across and placed his hand over hers. 'Yer know, Gracie,' he said fondly, 'yer mum loved this ol' shop of ours. She always used ter say—'

Grace swung back to him. 'Dad,' she sighed, 'I'm *not* Mum. I never could be. I never *want* to be. Why can't you understand that?'

Now it was Gus's turn to look hurt.

'That's not to say I didn't love her,' she said, trying to mollify him. 'I loved her a lot. I loved her an awful lot. When she died, I felt as though my whole world was finished. But I'm not like her. I don't enjoy the things *she* enjoyed. I have to do the things *I* want to do.'

'So you're sayin' that when I'm gone, the business goes wiv me. Is that it?'

'All I'm saying, Dad, is that I can't be the person you want me to be.' She tried to smile at him, though she'd learnt to keep her feelings hidden these days. 'But I will promise to carry on working for you for as long as I can.'

Without replying to her, Gus gently pulled on the reins, and Clapper started to trot on. As they moved off down Caledonian Road towards Holloway Road, the long terrace of Victorian and Edwardian houses on one side of the road was suddenly flooded with a burst of stifling hot June sunshine, relieved only by a titillating breeze that sent the red, white and blue bunting, stringed down from nearly every house, fluttering with total abandonment. It was hard to believe that only a month before, the Cally, together with the rest of the entire nation, had celebrated the coronation of a new king and queen.

Gert Jolly scrubbed her front doorstep so thoroughly that it was clean enough for any toff to walk across. However, in her eyes she couldn't make a really perfect job of it because she was almost out of pumice stone, so it was a good thing Mr Higgs was coming today; he always carried plenty around in his shop.

Trouble was, it was also rent day, and Gert felt a nervous strain in her stomach, knowing that she didn't have even a tanner towards the ten-bob back rent she owed him on her terraced house. She hated being poor. She hated owing money to *anyone*, but especially to someone so good-hearted as Gus Higgs. He was a fine man all right, an understanding one too. If he knew you were in trouble, he'd never make things worse for you. Oh no. A million times Gert had told herself that if it hadn't been for Gus Higgs, she would have gone downhill, and probably ended up in the workhouse. A good, Christian man, honest as the day was long, that was Gus Higgs. Which was more than she could say for his daughter, Grace. A real madam, that one. Wouldn't give you the time of day – wouldn't give you the skin off her nose. Not a patch on her dad. Nor her mum.

The sound of Clapper's hoofs, turning the corner into Mayton Street from Hertslet Road, was the first indication that Higgs's shop on wheels had arrived. Within moments, three of Gus's regular tenants were out on their doorsteps, waiting for him with their rent books. Further down the street at the Hornsey Road end, however, Gert Jolly leapt to her feet, grabbed her bucket of water, scrubbing brush and flannel, and disappeared inside, slamming the door behind her. In her small back parlour, she quickly took off her hairnet, put a comb through her rapidly greying hair, and tidied her pinafore. By the time she heard the knock on her street door, her stomach was churning so much she just wanted to run out into the back yard and hide behind the heap of junk that had been piled out there since her husband, Bill, had died ten years before. But then she took a deep breath, and thought about Gus Higgs. He would never throw her out of the home she'd lived in for years just because she owed a measly ten bob or so. Gus was a reasonable man, a kind man. He'd understand. He always understood.

The strength began to return to her legs, and she made her way along the gloomy dark passage to the front door. By the time she had got there, she was all ready to greet Gus with a huge, brave smile. But when she opened the door, the smile disappeared immediately.

'Good morning, Mrs Jolly.'

Gert's heart sank as she found Grace Higgs standing on her newly washed doorstep.

'Twelve and sixpence this week,' said Grace, checking Gert's entry in the notebook with the black leather cover that she always referred to when collecting a tenant's rent. She looked up with a curt smile. 'May I have your rent book, please?'

Poor Gert was so completely taken aback, she didn't know what to do. 'I – I,' she stuttered, 'I wonder if yer could . . . I mean . . . if it's all right . . . I could pay next week. I – I've got some money coming back to me from the Pru. I know it's a bit late, an'—'

'Mrs Jolly,' interrupted Grace, 'up until today, you're four weeks overdue. I'm afraid my father can't continue to give credit. If he gave it to everyone, he'd have nothing left to carry out repairs. Now I'm sure you understand that – don't you?'

Gert was totally flustered. 'Yes,' she replied, biting her lip anxiously, 'I know. But yer see . . .'

' 'Allo, Gert!'

The reassuring sound of Gus's voice brought a moment of hope for Gert.

'Yer doorstep looks t'rrific, gel!' said Gus, raising his bowler hat to her as he approached up the narrow front path, carrying a large, bulging paper bag. 'But then it always does. I've always said, Gert Jolly's doorstep is so clean, yer could eat yer breakfast off it!'

Gus's hearty remark brought a grateful glimmer of a smile to Gert's face.

'Mrs Jolly doesn't appear to have the rent, Father,' said Grace sternly. 'Including today, she owes five weeks.'

'Is that so?' said Gus, looking as though he was surprised. 'Oh dear.'

Gert's moment of hope seemed dashed as Gus seemed to be giving her a scolding look.

'We'd better 'ave a little chat about this, Mrs Jolly.'

'It's twelve and six this week,' Grace said to her father, as she consulted her accounts book for the umpteenth time.

'Right yer are, Grace,' said Gus. 'Yer can leave this ter me.'

Grace darted him a look. 'But—'

'Run along now,' insisted Gus. 'Sid Wilson's across the road. 'E's waitin' ter buy 'is Woodbines.'

Grace glared at him. Slamming her book shut, she strode off back to the street.

'I'm sorry, Gus,' said Gert, as they both waited for Grace to go back to the shop. 'I *will* pay yer as soon as I can, I promise yer I will. I've 'ad so many problems just lately...'

'Take yer time, gel,' said Gus, in his usual unflustered way. 'I'm in no rush. Yer mustn't take too much notice er my Gracie. She likes ter do fings by the book. It's the only way she knows.' As he looked at Gert, he saw all the pain and anguish in her face that he had seen so many times before in the faces of his other tenants. Life amongst poor folk was always a struggle for survival – he knew that only too well from his own early days. He was only thankful that he had enough to see himself through, so why should he put the screws on people who were less fortunate than himself? People like Gert, who was standing there, looking as pretty as a picture in her clean cotton dress and pinny and tatty carpet slippers, her lovely large brown eyes protruding out of a skinny gaunt face, but not knowing from one day to the next where the next penny was coming from. It wasn't fair. It just wasn't fair. He knew damned well that Gert worked her fingers to the bone as a cleaner, scrubbing floors in local offices, doing her best to make ends meet. She deserved better. 'Oh, by the way,' he said. 'Brought yer those few fings yer asked me fer last time.' He handed her the large paper bag.

Gert looked astonished. 'Fings?' she asked, taking the bag, totally bewildered. 'Wot fings?'

'Oh, you know,' replied Gus impassively. 'Bibs and bobs.'

Gert quickly looked inside the bag. There was a loaf of bread, some spuds, a bar of soap, some dried peas, half a pound of broken biscuits *and* a lump of pumice stone. 'Gus!' she exclaimed. 'I didn't . . . I can't . . . I won't be able ter pay yer fer all this.'

'Oh, yes yer will,' insisted Gus. 'One day.' With a twinkle in the eye, and a cheeky smile, he winked at her and briefly tapped the side of his nose with his finger. 'Mum's the word,' he said. 'See yer next week, gel.' He quickly turned and went back to the street.

Clutching her bag of 'bibs and bobs', Gert watched him go in absolute stunned silence. She couldn't speak. She couldn't thank him because the words were stuck in her throat, and her eyes were welling up with tears.

By the time Gus had got back to the shop, another of his

tenants, Sid Wilson, had already paid his half-crown rent money, and Grace was just serving him with a packet of five Woodbine cigarettes, a jar of pickled onions, and a half-pint of dried peas. 'My Elsie's got a real fing about dried peas,' he was saying, an unlit fag dangling from his lips. 'Trouble is, she never soaks 'em long enuff. They're always as tough as bleedin' nails when she's cooked 'em.'

Grace carried on serving him without comment, but Gus greeted Sid with one of his usual wry remarks.

' 'Allo, mate,' he called. ' 'Ow's yer love life?'

'Better ask the missus,' Sid replied, as he took his purchases from Grace, paid for them, and climbed down the two steps from the shop on to the pavement.

'It wasn't your missus I was finkin' of,' returned Gus mischievously.

Sid panicked, and immediately swung a look over his shoulder to make sure no one had heard what Gus had said. 'Give over, Gus!' he said, voice lowered. 'Yer wanna get me 'ung, drawn, an' quartered?'

Gus laughed. 'I 'eard yer was 'avin' a nice, cosy pint up The Eaglet wiv that gel from the flower shop.'

'I don't know who told yer *that*,' protested Sid indignantly, carefully arranging the quiff in his hair to cover a bald patch in the middle of his head. 'I was merely givin' 'er some friendly advice about – about . . .'

'Life?' asked Gus, again mischievously, with a broad grin.

'About a good boardin' 'ouse ter stay in,' retorted Sid haughtily. 'Fer an 'oliday in Southend.'

'Oh, yes?' said Gus, ribbing him. He had known Sid for years, especially his lecherous ways with the girls he was always meeting in his job as a railway guard on the LNER up at Finsbury Park station. 'You'd 'ave first-'and information about a place like that, wouldn't yer, Sid?'

Even Sid had to chuckle at that. 'I tell yer, Gus,' he replied, keeping his voice down to ensure that Grace couldn't overhear him, 'this one's a real cracker. Name's Sadie. Comes from up Tottenham way.'

'You dirty ol' bugger!' retorted Gus. 'If Elsie finds out, she'll castrate yer.'

'Yer only 'ere till yer time's up,' said Sid. 'Got ter make the best of fings.'

Gus nodded in agreement. 'True.'

They both went quiet until Grace had climbed down from the shop, and moved on to collect rent at one of the other houses.

'Yer know, Gus,' said Sid, 'yer should take a leaf outer *my* book. Find yerself a nice bird or two.'

Gus laughed. 'Not at my age, Sid!'

'Give over!' said Sid. 'Yer're only a few years older than me. Yer should 'ave some fun while yer still can. Yer've bin on yer own fer too long, mate. An' yer never know . . .' he drew closer, 'yer might even find a nice little woman ter settle down wiv.'

This remark clearly stung Gus, for his mischievous smile immediately gave way to a look of pain. 'Gotta be goin', Sid,' he said, turning back towards the shop. 'See yer next week.'

Sid suddenly wished he could have bitten off his tongue. 'Din't mean no offence, Gus,' he said quickly. 'I just thought, well – it's bin a good few years since . . . well, since yer lost Alice, an'—'

Gus stopped and turned. 'No offence taken, Sid,' he said, climbing up into the shop.

'Yer need someone ter look after yer, Gus,' said Sid, only making matters worse. 'A man needs a little woman at 'is side.'

'I've *got* someone ter look after me, fanks, Sid,' returned Gus, calling from inside the shop. 'Gracie's a good gel. She does 'er best.'

Making sure that Grace couldn't hear him, Sid called up to him, 'Grace ain't a wife, mate. She's yer daughter. It's diff'rent.'

'Say 'allo ter Elsie fer me,' called Gus. He then disappeared out of sight further back into the shop.

Sid felt terrible, and turned away. But he suddenly remembered something, dug into his trouser pocket, and brought out a carrot. 'Mind if I give Clap 'is treat?' he called.

'Go ahead,' came the reply from inside the shop.

Sid went up to Clapper and held the carrot out for him to crunch, which the animal did energetically.

'We'd sooner you didn't do that, if you don't mind, Mr Wilson.'

Sid looked up to find Grace, accounts book tucked under her arm, just climbing up into the shop.

'Too many of those things are not good for his teeth,' she added.

A few minutes later, a small collection of local residents were gathered around Higgs's shop on wheels to buy the 'bibs and bobs' they hadn't thought of when they were doing their regular daily shopping. The King Edward potatoes were a great favourite, but the shelves on either side of the shop inside carried more goodies than that, and pretty soon, Gus found himself running out of shoelaces, pumice stone, and Jeyes Fluid carbolic. As usual, Grace kept out of the way whilst her father served his 'regulars'. Her job would come later that night at home, when the rent money had to be counted, and checked against the tenants' balance sheets. With the June sun now pounding down on to the roof of the shop, it was like an oven inside, and Gus finally had to discard his jacket, occasionally stopping to fan himself with his 'ol' faithful' bowler. By the time the last customer had gone and he had shut up shop, he had done his best to forget what Sid Wilson had suggested to him about finding himself a 'nice little woman' to settle down with. But it wasn't easy. Not with Grace sitting alongside him, firm and resolute as ever.

Higgs's shop on wheels pulled away from Mayton Street to head off to its next stopping place. All that was left behind in the gutter was a pile of Clapper's manure, which was always a godsend for Alf Broadway and his rosebed, round the corner in Roden Street.

Pedlar's Way seemed an appropriate place for Gus Higgs to live. Tucked discreetly behind the main thoroughfare of Caledonian Road just a stone's throw from the tube station, it had once been used as a short cut for traders and farmers doing business in the nearby Islington cattle market, which in earlier times had been known as 'thieves' market', mainly because of the many illegal hawkers and highwaymen who used to gather in the nearby Boar's Head Inn. Today, however, it was a very different place, sealed off to everyone except the people who lived there, which suited Gus very well, for he had enough space at the back of his house to keep his horse stabled, in what had once been used as a barn for pigs and hens. The house itself, known as 'The Chapel' because of its tall, arched windows and stained-glass doors, was suitable enough for a family when Gus's late wife, Alice, was alive, but was now too big for two people to share. A detached, narrow, red-brick building erected during Victorian times, it was set on three floors, with Gus, at his own request, sleeping in a converted bedroom on the ground floor next to the kitchen, so that he could get out to the stable to have a chat to Clapper whenever he couldn't sleep. The first floor was Grace's bedroom and a washroom, and the top floor and attic were unused since Alice's death more than ten years before. Grace had always hated the place, not just because it was too big, but because she was the one who had to keep it clean and do the chores. Gus, however, loved his home, and had always vowed that the only way he was ever going to leave was when they had to carry him out in his wooden box. What he really loved, of course, was the atmosphere of the place, the fact that his beloved Alice had lived there with him for so long. Many a night, when he was sitting alone smoking a fag in front of the fire in the kitchen, he could feel Alice's presence all around him. He could smell the apple pie she used to cook for him for 'afters' on a Sunday, the tinge of nutmeg she added, and the smell of her own special gravy with the roast beef and Yorkshire pud. Although Grace tried her best in the kitchen, she was no match for her mum – not that her dad ever wanted her to be. And it did leave Gus very melancholy to know that Grace didn't seem to share his love of the place.

The Chapel was bathed in the uncomfortable heat of a humid June evening. In an effort to get some cool air into the place, the kitchen door was left wide open, so that the smell of the shepherd's pie Grace had cooked for the early evening meal was no longer lingering. Whilst her dad sat smoking his fag outside the kitchen door in the back yard, Grace cleared the kitchen table, washed up, then sat down to check through the day's rent collections. It was an arduous job, one that she always resented doing, for there were the usual bad payers who made endless promises about having the cash on time the following week, and those who would clearly never pay, not until they were threatened with eviction, which was most unlikely, for she knew only too well that her dad would sooner die than call in the bailiffs on people he considered to be part of his own family.

By the time she had closed the accounts books for the day, she was in her usual despondent mood. She could see no future for the Higgs family business. She had often tried to work out how her dad managed to make any money at all. Of course she respected him for being a self-made man, having started his business by buying one small terraced house with a handful of savings, and cashing in on the property market after the war, when houses could be picked up for a song. But now, instead of building on that wonderful enterprise, he had squandered so much on people who were always taking him for a ride.

Even more important was that she had very little hope for her own future. But she blamed herself. When she had left school, over ten years before, she had allowed herself to be dragged into a business that was routine and mundane. How much longer could she go on like this, she asked herself, being at her dad's beck and call? Hadn't she a right to a life of her own, a chance to do things for herself? But then, she wondered, what *kind* of life did she really want?

She got up from the kitchen table and went outside to join her dad in the back yard. 'We're three pounds, seven and sixpence short on the rents,' she said accusingly.

'Oh?'

Her dad's predictably disinterested response always infuriated her. 'I haven't done any stocktaking. It'll have to wait until the morning.'

'Best fing,' replied Gus. 'It's Saturday. We can take our time.'

'We can't take our time, Dad,' Grace replied tersely. 'I have no idea how short we are on everything. We have to restock on Monday, otherwise we'll have nothing left to sell.'

Gus took a drag on his fag, and looked up at her in the fading light. 'You worry too much, gel,' he said. 'It'll all come right in the end.'

'What does "right" mean, Dad?' she asked. 'Just think what Mr Rumble at the bank is going to say if we keep on having a shortfall like this.'

'Stop worryin' yerself, Gracie gel,' was Gus's unfussed reply. 'I keep tellin' yer, everyfin'll sort itself out.'

'Everything will *not* sort itself out, Dad,' insisted Grace. '*I'm* the one who has to sort things out, not you. It can't go on like this for ever. We'll have nothing left.'

'Gracie,' said Gus, getting up from his chair and going back into the kitchen, 'I fink it's about time you an' me 'ad a little talk.'

Grace followed him in.

'I've bin meanin' ter ask yer this fer some time,' he said, going to the kitchen dresser to collect his pint-sized glass mug and a bottle of brown ale. 'You don't like workin' fer me, do yer, gel?'

Grace stiffened and lowered her eyes.

'Oh, it's all right,' continued Gus. 'I know. I can tell.'

'It's not that I don't like working for you, Dad,' replied Grace. 'It's just that I can't bear the way we never seem to get anywhere with the business. You work so hard, and yet we seem to have very little to show for it.'

'You don't know *wot* I've got, Gracie,' he said, pouring his drink carefully so that the froth didn't flow over the top of his glass. 'But I promise yer, there's enuff. Enuff ter see me out – and you too. Now I've always 'ad it in my mind that when I'm gone the business would automatically come ter you. After all, you're me only kiff and kin, and you're entitled to it. But . . .'

Grace was watching him closely.

Gus sat down at the kitchen table, and took a gulp of his brown ale. 'This mornin',' he said, 'you told me that when I've gone, you wouldn't want to carry on the business.'

'Dad, I did *not* say that exactly.'

'Well, it's wot yer meant – more or less.'

Grace joined him at the table. 'What I said was, I can't be the person you *want* me to be. I can't be like Mum, and carry on living and working for the same business for the rest of my life.'

'So wot *do* yer want ter do?'

Grace sat back in her chair. 'I don't know, Dad,' she sighed. 'I just don't know.'

'But yer don't want ter get married?'

She looked up with a start. 'Please don't let's go through all that again,' she snapped.

Gus leant forward in his chair, and stared at her across the table. 'Gracie,' he said softly, 'you're just comin' up ter twenty-six. Yer don't want ter end up an ol' maid – do yer? Surely yer wanna settle down wiv a nice young feller, an' 'ave kids of yer own?'

'I don't know what it is about parents,' replied Grace, without looking at him. 'All they're interested in is making sure they get grandchildren.'

Gus pulled a face at this, and sat back in his chair. 'What *I'm* interested in, Gracie,' he said, 'is makin' sure that my daughter – my Alice's daughter – don't spend the rest of her time sittin' on 'er own in front er the fire, knittin' bedspreads fer people whose only interest is ter get their 'ands on any of the pickin's that ain't due to 'em. Bein' on yer own's a terrible fing, Gracie – believe me I *do* know.'

'You're not on your own, Dad,' Gracie said immediately. 'You never have been. I've always been here whenever you've wanted me.'

Gus looked up at her, and shook his head. 'It's not the same, gel,' he said. 'It's just not the same.' He got up from the table with his glass of ale, and went to look at the small, oval-shaped framed snapshot of Alice on the top shelf of the kitchen dresser. 'But I have ter know. I have to make plans. If you don't want this business when I'm gone, yer've got to tell me now.' He turned round to look at her. 'D'yer understand wot I'm tryin' ter say, Gracie?'

Gracie thought for a moment, then got up from her place at the table. 'No, Dad,' she said firmly. 'I don't understand, and I don't *want* to understand. I won't have you talking as if you're about to die. You're not going to die, because you're not old enough to die. And in any case, for a man of your age, you're as fit as a fiddle. So please don't let's talk about this again.' She made her way to the passage door, but stopped and turned. 'I'm going to bed now,' she said, very businesslike. 'I want to forget that we ever had this conversation.' She opened the door, but again hesitated before leaving. 'As I said before, I'll go on working for you for as long as I can. But just don't expect too much of me.' She left the room, quietly closing the door behind her.

For a moment or so, Gus just stood where he was, staring at the door Grace had just closed, a little concerned about what she had said about going on working for him *for as long as she could.* Then his eyes flicked back briefly to the small snapshot of Alice. 'I know, gel,' he said, with a sigh. 'I know. Wot are we goin' ter do about 'er?' He drained his glass, left it in the old stone sink, and went outside into the back yard again. The sun had only just set, and the rooftops all around were gradually casting off its deep red glow to allow the first shadows of night. Gus closed the kitchen door behind him, and made his way to the stable.

Clapper was already settled down in his bed of straw, ready for the sleep that he had so richly earned after a long day trotting around the backstreets of Holloway. But he was not asleep. He was too used to Gus's nightly visits to close his eyes, and the moment his master appeared, he raised his head and snorted. Gus didn't light up the paraffin lamp, for he could still see the silhouette of his ol' faithful spread out on the stable floor, and he could hear the creature's soft breathing, which somehow sounded so comforting in the half-light.

'Well, there we 'ave it, Clap, ol' son,' said Gus, crouching beside what he considered to be his best mate in the whole world. 'There's nuffin' I can do about 'er. Our Gracie just don't know wot she wants.' He sighed, and gently stroked Clapper's nose. 'If only she knew wot's ahead, Clap. If only she knew wot's waitin' for 'er. But I can't tell 'er, mate. Oh no. One of these days she'll find out fer 'erself, won't she, eh? One of these days she'll find out that 'er ol' dad ain't bin 'alf the mug she finks 'e is.'

Chapter 2

The early morning sky was a riot of colour. It was as though Turner had just thrown up a pot of red paint at the massive profusion of tiny clouds, which had gathered before dawn. It was a wild and spectacular sight; even the local moggies couldn't resist a quick peek, as they made their way home after yet another night out sifting through the dustbins along the back of 'thieves' market'. The only one not to notice the wonders that nature was offering was Grace Higgs, who was far too busy brewing up a pot of Sunday morning tea for her and her dad. But then Grace never looked up at the sky unless she had a particular reason for doing so. She had better things to do with her time.

Gus Higgs loved his Sunday morning lie-ins. It was about the only day of the week when he really felt relaxed enough to sleep late, sip the cup of tea Grace had brought him in bed, and read the *Sunday Pictorial*, which was always delivered to their doorstep, come rain or shine on the dot of eight, by Jimmy, the local newsboy. However, like everything else in his life, there was always something that spoilt the complete enjoyment of his day off. Sunday was traditionally the day for the family's get-together, the time when either Gus's two sisters and the gang came to eat Sunday roast cooked by Grace, or they all went over to his younger sister, Josie, who often made Gus's favourite 'afters' – bread and butter pudding. The trouble was, with the exception of Josie, the last people Gus wanted to see on his day off were his family. They were a shifty lot, at the best of times, especially his elder sister, Hilda, a real trouble-maker, if ever there was one, who couldn't wait for him to pop off so that she could get her hands on anything he might have left behind. No, all Gus wanted to do was to lie in bed all morning, then spend the rest of the day with Clapper.

'Can't yer tell Josie 'ow much I ain't feelin' up to it terday?' he said, as Grace came into his bedroom with the tea.

'No, Dad,' replied Grace sternly. 'You know the trouble Auntie Josie takes for Sunday roast. You know how fond she is of you.'

Gus grunted miserably. 'I still don't see why we 'ave ter do this back-an'-forth fing *every* Sunday. It's a ruddy ritual. Why can't we 'ave a day off sometimes? I don't like leavin' Clapper all that time.'

'Oh, for goodness' sake, Dad,' said Grace, putting the cup of tea down on Gus's bedside cabinet, 'I'll take Clapper for a walk before we go. And, in any case, you remember what Auntie Josie said when she was here last Sunday. She's got a special reason for wanting us over at her place this week.'

And then Gus remembered. The last time he had seen Josie she had told him how she had lined up some boy for Grace to meet. God knows who he was or where he came from. All he knew was that it would be a waste of time, because Josie had tried this so many times before, and it had never worked. Grace was set in her ways and didn't want to have a boyfriend. Not after what Eric Tyler had done to her. She hated the idea of a relationship with *any* man, and Gus was convinced that there was nothing anyone was going to be able to do to change her mind.

'Ruddy little twerp!'

Grace, about to leave the room, turned with a shocked start. 'What was that?' she snapped.

Gus looked up from his newspaper. 'Not you, gel,' he replied, "*im!*' He turned his copy of the newspaper round for Grace to see. On the front page was a headline photograph of Adolf Hitler.

'Who is he?' asked Grace, peering at the photograph.

'Come off it, Grace,' said Gus. 'Don't yer *ever* read the papers?'

'Not if I can help it,' replied Grace haughtily.

'This is 'Itler,' said Gus, glaring at the image. 'This bloke who's in charge in Germany. Sounds like a real nutcase ter me. He says 'e's a Nazi – whatever *that's* s'pposed ter be. I mean, just look at that 'tache. Stupid twit! A real nutter, if yer ask me.'

'Why d'you say that?' Grace asked naïvely. 'What's he done now?'

Gus slammed down his newspaper. 'Done?' he asked uncomprehendingly. ''Onest, Grace, sometimes I wonder about you. Don't yer know wot's goin' on in the world? The Boche are on the march again. This bloke 'Itler's got 'is eyes on grabbin' as much land as 'e can lay 'is 'ands on. You mark my words, it'll end up wiv us goin' ter war wiv that lot again. That is, if ol' Chamberlain 'as any sense.'

Grace sighed, and went to the door. 'Why is it that men always want to go to war?' she said, without expecting the kind of answer she wanted. 'Haven't enough people died already fighting for lost causes?'

'Lost causes?' asked Gus despairingly. 'Would you like ter see 'Itler an' 'is army marchin' down Whitehall?'

'I would have thought that most unlikely,' replied Grace, turning at the door. 'I can't believe that anyone these days wants to go to war – whatever the reason. Now please don't lie there all day, Dad. We're due at Auntie Josie's at twelve.'

She left the room without waiting for any further comment from her father. But she paused just long enough outside to ponder over what Gus had told her about this man who was now in charge in Germany. Of course she knew who he was. It wasn't possible to walk the streets without seeing some reference on newspaper billboards about the demands he was making to other countries around Europe. But the fact was, the prospect of another war frightened her. The last time it had lasted for five years and was a great human tragedy. The next time could be a catastrophe for the entire world. But at the moment, she had more important things to think about than Adolf Hitler. Fond of her Auntie Josie as she was, she guessed only too well what she was up to.

A short time later, Grace took Clapper on his morning trot around the backstreets behind Caledonian Road, his horse-shoes tapping rhythmically on the cobblestones as he went. It was still quite early, so there was not much sound or movement coming from any of the houses they passed on the way, mainly because it was Sunday morning, and the one day of the week when people weren't pressurised by the clock. Soon, the bells of St Mary's church would be ringing out over the rooftops to call Sunday morning worshippers to prayer. Whenever Grace heard them, she tried not to feel guilty, for when she was a little girl and her mother was alive, a visit to church on Sunday mornings was a ritual that they always looked forward to, not only for the service itself, but because it gave her mother her only real chance to have a good old chinwag with her neighbours.

Grace missed her mum. Grace had been fifteen when she died, and Alice Higgs had meant a great deal to her. The two of them had been inseparable, and, when Grace was little, if ever her mum and dad had gone out to visit someone without her, Grace would wait at home with her grandmother, constantly staring out of the window until she could see her parents coming down the street. Alice was not only kind and gentle, but also practical. Grace often thought back to the time when she went out shopping with both her mum and dad, and how on one occasion her mum had seen some dresses in a shop in Camden Town that would have been suitable for Grace to wear for her first days at school. Characteristically, Gus had wanted to buy the more expensive one of the two dresses she was shown, but Alice was absolutely adamant that it was unnecessary to go to the extra expense of buying something that at that time they couldn't really afford. Grace liked to think that she had inherited her mother's ways – practical to a fault. If she couldn't afford something, she simply wouldn't buy it. In her mind, it was the same thing with their tenants. If they couldn't afford to live in the properties they were renting, they should find somewhere cheaper. As much as she loved her dad, she hated the way he behaved like a benefactor.

In Stock Orchard Crescent, Grace tugged at Clapper's halter, and brought him to a standstill beneath a huge elm tree whose great expanse of foliage provided the shade Grace was looking for. Although it was not yet eleven in the morning, the sun's rays were harsh and unrelenting, and once she had tied Clapper's halter to the tree trunk, she paused for a few minutes to wipe the perspiration from her forehead. The lush green leaves above her glistened in the bright summer sunshine, and whilst she stood there looking around the elegant crescent of Victorian houses, it crossed her mind that, after all the years she had lived in the neighbourhood, she had never ever stopped to talk to anyone there. In fact, she had no idea who any of the people in those houses were.

'Oh well,' she shrugged, 'who cares? If they're not interested in me, why should I be interested in them?' At that moment, Clapper snorted, nodded his head up and down, and emptied his bowels right there in the road beside her. 'Oh, Clapper,' sighed Grace. 'Did you have to?'

''Scuse me, miss.'

Grace turned with a start to find someone approaching her. It was a young man, probably in his mid-twenties, in flat cap, well-worn shirt, baggy trousers, and plimsolls. In his hand he carried a bucket and hand shovel.

He came to a halt and doffed his cap. 'Would yer mind if I collect the droppin's?' he asked courteously.

Grace stiffened, then looked at the pile of steaming horse dung that Clapper had just provided. Then she looked back at the young man. 'It's a public place,' she shrugged. 'If you want the stuff, take it.'

'Fank yer very much, miss,' said the man, putting his cap back on.

Grace watched him shovelling up Clapper's droppings. 'What do you want all that stuff for?' she asked somewhat critically.

He looked up. '`S marvellous manure fer the garden, miss,' he replied. 'I've got plenty er customers who pay well for soil fertiliser like this.'

'Customers?' asked Grace warily. 'D'you mean – you do this as a business?'

'Well – yes an' no. I do a little bit er this, an' a little bit er that – window cleanin', clearin' out people's drains, cuttin' the grass in their back gardens – that sort er fing. But 'orse dung – it brings in an extra bob or two. Every penny 'elps.'

Grace watched in disbelief as he shovelled up Clapper's

droppings and filled his bucket. Although she found the young man a bit grubby in appearance, she could see that he was quite good-looking in a rough kind of way, his short blond hair just visible beneath his cap, and with pale blue eyes and a fair complexion, and a blond stubble on his face and chin that looked in need of a razor.

'But – can't you get a regular job?' she asked. 'Something that brings you in a regular wage? I mean, what does your father do?'

'My ol' man ain't around no more, miss,' replied the young man. 'Died er consumption two years back. No wonder really. Used ter catch rats down the sewers.'

Taken with the young chap's enterprise, Grace went across to him. 'What about your mother?'

'The ol' lady?' he asked. 'Oh, I ain't seen 'er fer donkey's years. She run off wiv some bloke up Canning Town way – breeds pigeons or somefink.' He grinned up at Grace. 'Who knows – I've probably got some 'alf-bruvvers or 'alf-sisters runnin' round all over the place somewhere!'

Clapper joined in this cheery banter by letting out a loud snort and nodding his head up and down.

Having filled his bucket, the young man straightened up. 'Fanks a lot, mate,' he said, giving Clapper a hearty stroke on his neck. 'I'll remember you in my will!' He picked up the bucket and shovel, then turned back to Grace. 'Fank you too, miss. Most grateful.'

Grace tried to respond with a smile, but it didn't come easy.

The young man started to move off, but suddenly stopped and looked back at her. 'Oh, by the way,' he called, 'I also do boots an' shoes. Give 'em a real shine. If yer know anyone who needs somefin' done, just tell 'em Mickey Burke's their man!' With that, he was gone.

Grace watched him go with curiosity, but also with just a touch of admiration.

Although Auntie Josie's house in Stoke Newington wasn't exactly palatial, it was quite spacious, and this was because she and her husband, Stan, had knocked down a dividing wall between two rooms on the ground floor, making a large front room. The Edwardian house itself was part of a terrace of houses situated in a quiet street just off Stoke Newington Church Street. It was set on four floors, which included a basement with a coal hatch on the pavement outside. The three bedrooms were light and airy, and offered lovely views of nearby Clissold Park, which could just be seen between the semi-detacheds on the other side of the street. The only problem for Grace and her dad was that to get there they had to take a bus to Manor House underground station, then another one down Green Lanes to Church Street, which Gus, in particular, always found a bit of a chore. However, Auntie Josie was always worth a visit, for she was such a warm-hearted character, who, unlike her sister, Hilda, never had a bad word to say about anybody. Josie owed much of her contented life to her husband, Stan Cooker, who had not only given her two kids, but a fairly trouble-free life together, mainly because he had always had a good job as a foreman for a local building contractor. Therefore Josie was never happier than when she had her family around her for Sunday roast. For Gus and Grace, however, it was a different matter, especially for Grace when she arrived to find that her Auntie Josie was up to her old tricks again.

'Grace, dear,' said Auntie Josie, in her most genteel North London accent, and an absolute picture of unsubtle well-meaning, 'I want yer ter meet 'Arry Wilkins. 'Arry's the son of my best friend Ada's next-door neighbour.'

The poor young bloke being introduced to Grace could not have been more than nineteen years old, but he looked younger, with neatly parted greased brown hair, lips that looked as though they stretched from one end of his face to the other, and a two-piece navy-blue suit that was clearly only worn on high days and holidays.

'H-how d'you do, Grace?' said Harry, boiling over with embarrassment, but offering his hand. 'P-pleased ter meet yer.'

Grace could muster nothing more than the weakest of courteous smiles. 'Hallo,' she replied. But the boy's handshake was so firm, it nearly pulled her arm out of its socket.

' 'Arry's got a marvellous job, 'aven't yer, 'Arry?' said Auntie Josie, egging the poor boy on. 'Go on, tell Grace all about your job.' She turned eagerly to Grace. 'You just won't believe it, Grace.'

The rest of the family, gathered round in chairs and sofa in the front room, looked on. It was hard to know who found the whole thing more cringe-making.

'I work in – wireless communication,' said the boy falteringly.

'Oh – really?' replied Grace, without even a hint of curiosity.

'Fascinatin', in't it, Grace?' added Auntie Josie. ' 'E works up at Ally Pally. They've got studios an' fings up there. 'Arry says they're workin' on wireless wiv pictures. In't that so, 'Arry?'

'Wireless wiv pittures?' spluttered Stan, a thickset man in his fifties, who insisted on smoking his own-rolled tobacco fags. 'Impossible! Where yer goin' ter put pittures in a box like that?' He looked across at a wireless set on a table on the other side of the room. 'Stupid idea!'

'Oh, no it's not!' said Josie haughtily. 'It's goin' ter 'appen. Go on, 'Arry. Tell Grace 'ow it works.'

'Oh, I don't think so, Auntie,' said Grace, backing away tactfully. 'I'm afraid I'm not very technically minded.'

Auntie Josie was a little disappointed that Grace went to join her Aunt Hilda on the sofa, leaving her and Harry afloat in the middle of the room.

'Well, I don't fink yer can beat the pittures meself,' said Gus, filling his pipe with tobacco from a tin. 'Why sit at 'ome when yer can go out an' get a bob's worf of dark up the pitture 'ouse.'

'That's your trouble, Gus,' said Hilda, who was even more slight of build than her sister, Josie. 'You want yer entertainment laid out for yer.'

'Well, I'd much sooner go to a good football match up the Arsenal any day than sit an' watch a stupid bleedin' film,' said Reg Cooker, who, at eighteen, was Josie and Stan's youngest, and was perched on a pouffe beside the fireplace.

' 'Ear, 'ear!' agreed his dad. 'Up the Gunners!'

As if in protest, Josie immediately went and opened both bow windows to let out the stifling smell of tobacco smoke from her brother and her husband. Then she drew back the white lace curtains to let some sunshine and air into the room.

Grace looked around the room. With all her family sitting in a circle, it seemed to her more like a wake. But she was always fascinated to watch the way they made small talk out of nothing. Over the years she had heard them talking about every mundane subject so many times – the 'pictures', football, where you could buy the freshest vegetables in both Holloway and Stoke Newington, and politics – always politics. When they'd all come over to The Chapel the week before, there had been yet another row about the abdication of King Edward VIII, with everyone having different ideas about whether he would have made a good or bad king.

Although she was very fond of Auntie Josie, Grace had never had much time for her two cousins, Reg and Viv. Reg had always been a bit of a weed and a big-head, and had none of his dad's practical qualities. As for Viv, well she hardly ever contributed a word to any conversation. At twenty-one, she was the elder of Josie and Stan's two kids, but whenever Grace had managed to talk with her, her only topic was her boyfriend, Alan, whom no one had somehow ever actually seen.

Grace looked across at Aunt Hilda, who seemed to be dwarfed by the large armchair she was sitting in. There wasn't much of her, but her tongue certainly had a sting in it, and she had just a suggestion of lipstick which, with her snow-white complexion and skeleton frame, made her look like a suitable candidate for a box in the mortuary.

'All right Stan,' said Josie, bustling around the table that had already been laid at the far end of the room. 'Yer'd better give everyone a fill-up before we eat. My Yorkshire puds must be almost done.'

'Right!' called Stan, getting up from his chair by the window. 'Last orders, please, ladies an' gents!' The first person he went to was the nonplussed Harry, who gave every appearance that he didn't know what the hell he was doing there. 'Same again, son?' Stan asked.

Harry, who was sitting on a high chair between Viv and Aunt Hilda, gulped down the last of his shandy. 'Yes, please, Mr Cooker,' he replied eagerly.

Stan looked at him, sighed in deep despair, and took the boy's glass.

Seeing her Aunt Josie leaving the room, Grace found a good excuse to get away from the others. 'I'll come and help,' she called, following Josie out.

In the kitchen, the smell of roast beef, roast potatoes, and Yorkshire puddings in the oven was sending Josie's two cats into a state of ecstasy, whilst on the stove, cabbage, cauliflower, and carrots were all gently simmering in their saucepans. Grace had hardly got into the room when Josie immediately turned to her. 'So,' she asked, bursting with excitement, 'what d'yer think?'

Grace came to a sudden stop. 'What d'you mean?'

'What d'yer fink I mean?' spluttered Josie, hardly able to contain herself. ' 'Arry! What d'yer fink of 'im?'

Grace sighed. 'Oh, Auntie,' she replied in despair.

'But yer must like 'im,' persisted Josie. ' 'E's so good-lookin', an' 'e's got wonderful prospects.' She moved closer to Grace, and held her at arm's length. 'Yer must be just a *bit* interested, Grace – aren't yer?'

Grace looked into Josie's eyes. They were so blue, so warm, and even though the tight little brown, greying curls that dangled over her forehead made her look like a lampshade, Grace knew that her aunt was someone she could always trust. In fact, Auntie Josie was the kindest person Grace had ever known – honest, supportive, and so well-meaning. But being well-meaning had its drawbacks, for Josie's trying to find a prospective husband for her was rapidly becoming an irritation, and she didn't know how to tell her aunt that enough was enough. Finding a husband was the last thing on Grace's mind, and, even though it may not be what she wished for herself, if she had to go through her life an old maid, then so be it.

'Auntie,' she said, with just the faintest sign of an affectionate smile, 'I appreciate what you're trying to do, but I've told you lots of times, I'm not interested in *any* man, that is – a man to spend the rest of my life with.'

Auntie Josie was crushed with disappointment, and realised that once again her attempts to interfere in something that was none of her business had, inevitably, ended in failure. 'I'm sorry, Grace, dear,' she said, lowering her eyes guiltily. 'It was just that, when I first saw 'Arry, I thought 'e was such a nice boy, not at all pushy, an' such lovely manners. I thought 'e was definitely someone that you'd like.'

Grace was embarrassed. She had never known how to deal with situations like this. 'I *do* like him, Auntie,' she said awkwardly. 'Harry seems like a very nice person.'

For one brief moment, Josie looked at her with renewed hope.

'But I don't want him as a friend – not a *regular* friend.'

With her hopes finally dashed, Josie turned away, and went to look at the vegetables cooking on the stove.

Now realising that she had hurt her aunt's feelings, Grace followed her across and put her arms around her waist from behind. It was an unusual thing for Grace to do; she had never been one to show her own feelings. 'You mustn't feel bad about it, Auntie,' she said. 'I know you mean well, but I—'

To Grace's surprise, Josie turned round to answer her. 'It's not me I care about, Grace,' she said. 'It's yer dad.'

Grace sighed again. 'Yes, I know,' she replied, pulling her arms away from Josie's waist. 'But he'll just have to get used to the fact that I'm not the marrying kind.'

Josie looked horrified. 'Yer mean – yer don't want ter get married? Not never?'

Grace shook her head.

'But don't yer want ter 'ave kids? You're nearly twenty-six now. In a few years' time it'll be too late.'

'I don't *want* to have children, Auntie,' insisted Grace unconvincingly.

Josie's jaw dropped in astonishment. 'Yer don't want ter 'ave kids?' she asked incredulously. 'But that's not natural, Grace. Every woman wants ter 'ave kids of 'er own.'

'Not *every* woman, Auntie,' said Grace, with a weak, none-too-believable smile.

It took Josie a moment for this to sink in. Then she returned to stir the carrots on the stove behind her. 'Poor Gus,' she said, half to herself. 'No grandchildren.'

Grace shrugged. 'I'm sure Dad will get used to it,' she replied.

'I don't think 'e will,' replied Josie. 'I don't think 'e ever will.' She turned round to face her again. 'Yer don't know yer dad. I know 'e's a funny ol' devil, but 'e thinks the world er you. I'm telling yer, not 'avin' gran'children ter look forward to is goin' ter cut 'im up. 'E 'as such plans for yer.'

Grace was curious. 'Plans?'

'Oh yes,' replied Josie. 'Nothin' I know about, though – not really. 'E's a dark 'orse, yer dad. Yer think 'e doesn't care about things – but 'e does. 'E sits an' works 'em out all on 'is own. 'E was like that when we was kids tergevver. Mum always used ter say that Gus was the dark 'orse er the family. If yer ask me, 'e's got quite a few fings up 'is sleeve fer you.' She looked hard at Grace. 'One thing I do know is that if anythin' 'appens ter 'im, 'e wants you ter take over the business.'

'Yes,' said Grace wearily. 'I know he does.'

'But a word er warnin', dear,' said Josie, lowering her voice. 'Yer'll 'ave a battle on yer 'ands if yer Aunt 'Ilda 'as anythin' ter do wiv it. She's 'ad 'er eye on yer dad's business fer years. She's a sly one, is 'Ilda. It's no wonder Bert Barnet left 'er.'

Grace thought about this for a moment. She knew only too well about her Aunt Hilda. Her dad had told her lots of times about her – about how, whenever they met, she would constantly question him about how well the business was doing, and how, in the event of his death, it should be divided up equally amongst members of his family, and that clearly meant her, for after all it *was* a family business. He also told Grace about an incident when he and his two sisters were kids, about when Hilda had told her mum and dad that Gus had stolen money from her moneybox, and that if it hadn't been for Josie, who had actually seen Hilda taking the money out of the box herself and hiding it under her bed, Gus would have been punished. 'I tell yer, Grace,' her dad had always said, 'yer Aunt 'Ilda's got pounds, shillin's, and pence signs written all over 'er.' If her dad had been the dark horse of the family, then her Aunt Hilda was certainly the black sheep.

'You don't have to worry, Auntie,' said Grace. 'Nothing's going to happen to Dad for a very long time. He loves the business. It's his whole life. As long as he's still got breath in his body, Dad will hang on to it for as long as he can.'

A short while later, all the family were sitting around the dining table, tucking into Josie's roast beef and Yorkshire pudding. To Grace's great relief Harry Wilkins had merely been invited for a drink, and to his great relief, had gone back home. This left everyone free to run down other members of the family, both past and present, who, for a whole variety of disagreeable reasons, were never invited to either The Chapel or Stoke Newington. However, once that gossip was out of the way, the conversation soon reverted to the topic that was being featured daily on the wireless and in the newspapers.

'I don't see why we 'ave ter keep talkin' about Spain,' said Stan, struggling to cut an obstinate slice of beef on his plate. 'If they want ter keep scrappin' wiv each uvver, then that's up ter them.'

'It's not a case of scrappin', Dad,' retorted his son, Reg. 'It's a civil war. People are bein' gunned down all over the place. It's all the fault of those Falangists.'

'Who?' asked his dad, mouth full.

'The Falangists,' repeated Reg, stretching across the table for the gravy jug. 'Don't you ever read the papers?'

'Only the back page!' replied Stan.

'Franco!' splurted Reg, mouth full of cauliflower, pointing his fork menacingly at his dad. ' 'E's the one. Bombin' and mowin' down 'is own people, and what for? Power!'

'Wot *are* you, Reg?' asked Gus, looking up at him from the opposite side of the table. 'A Bolshie, or somefin'?'

'Look, Uncle Gus, if I'm against people bein' forced ter live in poverty just because a bunch of bleedin' capitalists want ter boss over a country, then yes – I'm a Bolshevik.'

'Stop usin' that word in front of yer mum,' Stan warned his son. 'I've told yer before, an' I won't tell yer again.'

Reg, exasperated with his dad, quickly returned to his food.

'Well, I don't like the Bolsheviks either,' said Josie, also struggling with a fatty slice of beef. 'Just think wot they did ter that poor Tsar an' 'is family. 'Orrible!'

'To 'ell wiv the Spanish Civil War,' said Gus. 'We've got quite enuff trouble comin' our way as it is.'

'What're yer talkin' about?' asked Hilda, at the far end of the table.

' 'Itler!' growled Gus. 'That little nutter in Germany. If yer talkin' about power, then 'e's the one ter watch. Both 'im *an'* 'is dago mate in Italy. I'm tellin' yer, the way they're goin', it won't be long before we'll all be back in uniform again. There's anuvver war comin', that's fer sure.'

'War!' growled Hilda. 'That's all you men can ever think about. It's time they put a few more women in Parliament. Then we'd 'ave a chance ter make a go of this country.'

'Women in Parliament!' spluttered Stan, nearly choking on the roast potato he was eating. 'A prime minister in a petticoat?' He roared with laughter. 'Now that'd really be a turn-up for the books!'

Hilda came straight back at him. 'Well, she couldn't do worse than that idiot Chamberlain. Just look at him. More like a bank clerk!'

'At least he's better than Baldwin,' added Josie. 'I never liked that man's eyes. Much too shifty.'

'I don't care wot you say,' said Reg. 'The civil war in Spain is goin' ter get worse before it gets better. Give me 'alf a chance, an' I'd be out there 'elpin' the freedom fighters.'

Josie looked up with a start. 'Wot's that?' she asked anxiously.

'Lots of blokes my age are volunteerin' ter go over there,' replied Reg. 'An' quite a lot of older people too!'

'Oh dear,' sighed Josie. 'Are they?'

'Don't listen to 'im, Jose,' said Stan. 'As long as *I'm* around, 'e ain't goin' nowhere.'

'I wouldn't be so sure if I was you,' muttered Reg under his breath.

'Wot was that?' snapped Stan.

'That's the trouble wiv this generation,' said Hilda, giving Reg a chance to avoid his dad's question. 'They think they can save the whole world by goin' off ter fight for a cause they know nuffin' about.'

'As a matter of fact, Auntie,' said Reg haughtily, 'I happen ter know quite a lot about the war in Spain.'

'Is that so?' replied Hilda, glaring at him over the top of her metal spectacles. 'Well, did yer know that countries all over the world 'ave banned any of their own people from takin' part in the Spanish war?'

'I know that,' replied Reg. 'But that wouldn't stop me from volunteerin'.'

'Oh, I do wish everyone would stop talking about war,' said Josie, putting down her knife and fork. 'It does so scare me. It was bad enuff with all our boys gettin' killed in the last war.'

'That's not the only thing,' said Hilda pointedly. 'War's always bad fer business.' She looked down the table at Gus. 'Isn't that so, Gus?'

'War's bad fer anyone,' he said, refusing to look up at her from his plate.

Grace watched Hilda carefully. She knew what was coming.

'So what would *you* do with the business, Gus,' Hilda asked artfully, 'if *we* suddenly had to go to war again?'

'Oh, I imagine Dad and I would cope,' interrupted Grace, answering the question for her father. 'Just the same as everyone else.'

Hilda snorted indignantly. 'People never 'ave much money when there's a war on. I bet you any money yer like yer'd 'ave trouble gettin' rent out er 'alf yer tenants.'

'It's not easy getting money out of tenants at the best of times, Auntie,' said Grace. 'Whether there's a war on or not.'

'Anyway,' said Gus, putting down his knife and fork and taking a gulp from his glass of brown ale, 'it won't make much diff'rence ter me an' Grace – once I've got rid of the business.'

Everyone around the table froze, and turned to look at him.

Hilda took off her spectacles. 'What're yer talkin' about?' she asked warily.

Gus put his glass down and looked at her. 'I'm sellin' up,' he said mischievously. 'Didn't I mention it to yer, 'Ilda?'

Hilda was taken aback. 'No, you didn't!' she growled, through clenched teeth.

Although what her dad had said had come as just as much of a bombshell to her as to everyone else, Grace said nothing.

'You're sellin' up, mate?' asked Stan. 'The shop an' everyfin'?'

'Why not?' replied Gus. 'I reckon I've done my bit fer long enuff.'

'Yer mean – business ain't doin' well?' pressed Stan.

'No,' replied Gus. 'Nuffin' ter do wiv that.' He flicked a quick glance across at Grace. 'I just fink it's about time me an' Grace did somefin' else wiv our lives.'

'What a stupid idea!' snapped Hilda, who was clearly very angry. 'If a business is makin' money, then wot's the use of gettin' rid of it?' She turned to Grace. 'Did *you* know about this, Grace?' she demanded.

Grace flicked a quick glance at her dad. 'Of course, I did,' she replied coolly. 'Dad never keeps anything from me.'

'If you wanna sell up an' move on,' said Stan, returning to the food on his plate, 'then I say, good luck to yer, mate. I only wish *I* could do the same fing.'

The initial air of shocked disbelief quickly passed, and gradually everyone returned to their meal. Not Hilda, however. She sat through the next hour fuming with rage, deeply resenting the fact that Gus had not confided in her, Gus – her own brother!

★ ★ ★

It was not until they were on the bus heading back along Green Lanes that Grace was finally able to have it out with her dad. 'Since when did you come to that decision?' she asked curtly.

'Decision?' he asked innocently. 'Wot decision?'

'Oh, do stop playing games with me, Dad,' she said firmly, voice lowered so that the other passengers on the bus couldn't overhear her. 'You tell everyone you're selling the business, and you don't even consult *me*.'

'No offence meant, Gracie,' said Gus, patting her hand.

'No offence!' Grace pulled her hand away from his.

'Well, let's face it,' said Gus. 'Yer've told me a million times, yer ain't got any int'rest in carryin' on the business after I've gone.'

'Why?' asked Grace, turning on him. 'Have you made up your mind on a time to die or something?'

'No – not exactly,' replied Gus, with just a faint suggestion of a smirk. 'Well – not *just* yet. But I 'ave got plans.'

Grace swung a look at him. 'Plans, plans!' she complained irritably. 'I'm sick of hearing about *plans*. Just tell me, exactly *what* plans are you talking about?'

Gus hesitated a moment before answering. 'Fer you, Gracie – *an'* fer me.'

All the rest of the way home, Grace hardly exchanged another word with her father. However, she certainly now had a great deal on her mind. By the time they got off the bus at Caledonian Road, the hot sunshine that had been streaming through Auntie Josie's front room windows all day had disappeared behind dark grey clouds.

The outlook for the weather that evening was decidedly unsettled.

Chapter 3

Gus Higgs's announcement that he was seriously considering selling the business sent shock waves around the family. Whatever his reasons, Grace was very angry that he had chosen to tell the family about such an important decision that would clearly affect her more than anyone else. As far as she was concerned, her father's talk of 'plans' was just pie in the sky. To her mind, he had never planned ahead for anything in his entire life, so why should he start doing so now? Yes, it was true that if anything were to happen to her father she wouldn't want to spend the rest of her life plodding around the streets with a horse and mobile shop, but he had no right to treat her as though the matter was of no interest to her at all. And then, of course, there was Auntie Hilda herself to cope with.

The following morning, Grace accompanied her father on his usual early Monday morning visit to the wholesale grocery provisions depot in King's Cross, where they restocked for the week on those items that they had sold out of, and collected a fresh supply of fruit and vegetables from nearby Covent Garden. By mid-morning, they were back on their rounds in the Hornsey Road area of Holloway, where Gus rented out two or three low-cost terraced properties. In Kinloch Street, Grace collected rent from Mabel Buck, who lived in the two ground-floor rooms of number 14A, and her upstairs tenants, Doris and Ted Cole, who had a grown-up daughter, and were all squeezed into two tiny rooms, and had to collect water from a tap in the back yard. Meanwhile, Gus did what he liked best, which was to serve customers in the van, despite the resentment of Charlie Brend, who ran the popular sweet shop just round the corner.

A perfectly ordinary morning, however, was soon disrupted when Grace caught sight of Auntie Hilda marching at full pelt towards her from Hornsey Road.

'Where's yer father?' demanded Hilda, before Grace even had a chance to open her mouth. 'Is he in the shop?'

Again, Grace had no chance to answer before Hilda strode off to see Gus in the mobile shop, which was parked at the kerb outside number 22.

'Are you in there, Gus?' Hilda called, as though she was a sergeant major in the army. 'Gus!'

Gus, who had just finished serving a customer, appeared at the back door of the shop. One look at his sister told all he needed to know. ' 'Allo, 'Ild,' he said, with a huge smirk. 'Now 'ere's a pleasant surprise.'

Hilda didn't care for her brother's humour. She had never cared for it, even when they were youngsters together, when he used to tell her how she was always so full of wind she would make a good airship.

Once the customer had left the shop, Hilda practically pushed her brother inside. 'What d'yer fink you're playin' at?' she growled, following him in.

'Wot's up?' asked Gus, bemused.

'Don't you wot's up me!' said Hilda. 'Wot's all this about you sellin' up? Who yer sellin' it to?'

' 'Aven't made me mind up yet,' replied Gus. 'Got one or two good offers though.'

Hilda's large billiard-ball eyes nearly burst out of the sockets of her thin, gaunt face. 'Yer've got a ruddy nerve, you 'ave, Gus 'Iggs. 'Ad it ever occurred ter you that this is a family concern? We all 'ave a right ter be consulted over *anyfin'* yer do wiv it.'

'Oh – is that a fact?' asked Gus. By now his smirk was becoming noticeable. Hilda's reaction was just what he had hoped for. He loved playing games with her and getting her agitated.

'Yer've upset everyone,' retorted Hilda. 'An' yer know it!'

'I'm sorry ter 'ear that, 'Ild,' said Gus. 'I 'ad no idea.'

'Well, you 'ave,' persisted Hilda. 'We're a family, a close family. Just remember wot Mum said before she died. Yer know very well about the arrangement we made.'

'Arrangement?'

Hilda swung round to find Grace standing behind her.

'What arrangement is that, Auntie?' Grace asked.

'That anyfin' the family 'ave should be pooled,' replied Hilda. 'All fer one, an' one fer all, Mum said.'

'That's true, 'Ild,' said Gus. 'The only fing is, the business didn't belong ter Mum *or* Dad. *I* set it up. I set it up wiv me own money.'

Hilda was fuming. 'That's got nuffin' ter do wiv it!' she snapped. 'We agreed. We *all* agreed. Whatever we 'ad – we share amongst the family. Am I lying or am I not?'

Grace swung a look at her father.

Gus hesitated only a moment before giving his reply. 'D'yer mind not sittin' on the eggs, please, 'Ild?' he said, indicating the two bowls of freshly laid eggs on sale behind her. 'We don't want 'em to 'atch.'

Hilda flicked him a look of utter contempt. 'I've told yer before, Gus,' she said. 'If you're in difficulty with runnin' the business, you should tell us about it. An' if yer can't cope, there're always people who can.'

'An' who would that be, 'Ild?' asked Gus, tidying up his sack of dried peas.

'You know very well what I'm talking about,' persisted Hilda. 'If yer let me take on the books once a month, I can always keep an eye on them.'

'I don't think that's necessary, Auntie,' said Grace, coming to her father's defence. 'I'm perfectly capable of taking care of the book-keeping.'

'Is that so?' retorted Hilda, her lips pinched together as though she'd just been stung by a wasp. 'Well, it sounds as though yer 'aven't made much of a job of it so far.'

Grace stiffened, but resisted the urge to respond. It was now clearer than ever what a thorn in her father's side the redoubtable Auntie Hilda was, and had always been. It seemed quite incomprehensible to Grace how a casual remark by her grandmother was enough for Hilda to interpret as a firm commitment.

'As it so 'appens,' said Gus, who was determined not to be intimidated by his sister, 'Gracie 'ere's bin doin' a marvellous job lookin' after fings. I don't know 'ow I'd've coped all these years wivout 'er.'

'Then *why*, Gus?' Hilda asked pointedly. 'If fings are goin' so well, why d'you 'ave ter sell up?'

Gus looked at his sister. Her expression revealed years of mistrust, years of frustration. He had always known what a sad, pathetic creature she was, unable to keep a husband because she knew no other way than her own way. But so often, her looks betrayed her. Over the years, Gus had learnt that she *did* have an ability to care about people other than herself. He had seen flashes of it: a passing look that showed she was capable of better things. So why did she conceal those better qualities, and concentrate so much on the first thing that came to her mind? It worried him. And when he remembered how Grace's attitude could be like that of her Auntie Hilda, it worried him even more.

' 'Ild,' he replied calmly, 'in case you 'aven't noticed, I'm a big boy now. I don't need ter ask anyone when I want ter do somefin'. And in any case, it may int'rest yer ter know, I've got somefin' in mind that one er these days is goin' ter make everyfin' right fer me an' Gracie.'

It took Grace several days to get over her Auntie Hilda's visit to the shop. She just couldn't believe the nerve of the woman. *All fer one, and one fer all.* How could she even say such a thing. What she really meant was, all for Hilda, and nothing for anyone else. But there was now something more for Grace to worry about. What *was* this 'somefin'' her father had in mind that one day was going to make everything right for him and her? Why does he always have to be so secretive, she asked herself. And as if she didn't have enough on her mind, when she went to return some books to the Central Library in Holloway Road, the library assistant, Pauline Betts, who was one of Grace's former classmates at Shelburne Road School, had some rather disturbing information for her.

'Eric Tyler?' Grace asked, doing her best to keep her voice to a whisper. 'You've seen him?'

'He was at this party up at Dalston,' whispered Pauline, who had a pretty rose-pink face with a small mole on her chin, and large horn-rimmed spectacles that kept slipping down her nose. 'You know – Pat Keeley's place. It was her birthday. When I saw *him* walk in I nearly had a fit!'

Grace froze, then hesitated. 'Was his wife with him?' she asked acidly.

Pauline looked around carefully before answering. Then she leant forward over the reception counter. 'Come outside for a moment,' she replied.

Grace and Pauline came out into the grey stone portico.

It was drizzling with rain, and in the road outside people were hurrying to take cover.

'He's left her,' said Pauline, lighting up a cigarette.

Grace did a double take. 'Left her?'

'Apparently they were only together for a few years,' said Pauline gleefully. 'He got the wandering eye and – well, you can imagine the rest.'

Grace didn't have to imagine. She only had to look back to what Eric Tyler had done to her to know what kind of person he was. Even so, after nearly six years, she still lay awake at nights filled with the bitterness she felt about their relationship, and especially the way Eric Tyler ended it after less than a year. Promises. That's what she remembered most. Promises of undying love, of trust, and of marriage. Oh, why had she ever felt attracted to a person like that, she had asked herself so many times before. Was it his looks that had seduced her, that long wavy brown hair, the smile that was so infectious, but which never revealed his true nature? How could she ever forget that fateful summer's night, when she sat alone with her suitcase on a bench at King's Cross railway station, waiting for him to show up, waiting for him to take her off to a new life together, a life of love and marriage, a life away from the humdrum world of a shop on wheels, and a father who thought of her as an employee, and not as a daughter? How could she ever forget watching each train disappear down the railway track, heading off without her? And how would she ever forget being told by Pauline that the boy who was going to change her whole life had disappeared with another girl, a girl of means, whom he had met and married even while he was still making empty promises to Grace? The pain was real. It would never go.

'She ran out of money,' said Pauline.

With eyes glazed, it took Grace a moment to realise that Pauline was talking to her. 'What?' she asked distantly. 'What did you say?'

'I said, the woman he married ran out of money,' replied Pauline. 'That's why Eric isn't with her. What they were saying at the party was that the girl was loaded – or at least her old man was – and that when the father got fed up with subsidising them the marriage fell apart and Eric had to go out and get a job. Must've killed him to do *that*!'

Grace took all this in impassively, and without comment.

'Trouble is,' said Pauline persistently, 'he's so good-looking. Despite what he's like, if he'd asked me to go out with him, I'd probably've ditched Dave straight away!' She turned to look at Grace, and suddenly realised how tactless she'd been. 'I'm sorry, Grace,' she said guiltily. 'I don't really mean it. What Eric did to you was unforgivable. We all said so at the party. In any case, he's lost a lot of his looks. In fact *I* think he's aged quite a bit since he went off. If you ask me, hard work doesn't suit him.'

After making a vague promise to Pauline that she would meet up with her and some of the other girls one evening, Grace quickly made her excuses, and hurried off down Holloway Road. As she went, the drizzle gradually turned to a heavy downpour, and by the time she had reached the junction of Holloway and Tollington Roads, her clothes were quite drenched. As she had not brought an umbrella with her, she took shelter in the main corner entrance of Beales restaurant. She stood there for the best part of ten minutes, waiting for the rain to subside, but as hard as she tried she couldn't help taking a look at her reflection in the restaurant window. What she saw was someone she didn't recognise, or didn't *want* to recognise. After what Pauline had told her about Eric Tyler, the missing years came rushing back at her. Why had she allowed herself to become so embittered with life, just because of one failed relationship with a man who wasn't even worth associating with? But then once again she became riddled with self-doubt. Was it really only money that had driven Eric Tyler away from her, or *was* it that he had no longer found her attractive? If so, was that *her* fault? Or was it because she took him for granted, and made no effort herself to make their relationship work? Reluctantly, she looked at her reflection in the restaurant window beside her. What she saw was a bedraggled, dour creature, impaired by the misfortunes of life, a woman whom no man would give even a second glance.

She took out her handkerchief, and wiped the rain from her face, and did her best to do the same with her hat and dress. A few minutes later, the rain had subsided enough to let her go, but as she did so, she came to a sudden halt at a tall ladder that had been propped up against the side of the restaurant. As she had never been superstitious, she boldly passed beneath it, only to be brought to another sudden halt by the sound of someone calling to her.

' 'Allo, miss!'

Grace looked up to find a young window cleaner peering down in the drizzle at her from the top of the ladder.

'Remember me, miss?' he asked cheekily. 'Up Stock Orchard Crescent the other Sunday. Long time no see!'

Grace needed no reminding of who he was. She could still recall the smell of horse dung as he shovelled up Clapper's droppings in the road. 'What are you doing up there in this weather?' she called.

'It's perfect, miss!' he replied. 'Yer don't need nearly so much water in the bucket when it's rainin'. Gets the job done in 'alf the time!'

Grace watched whilst he backed his way precariously down the steps, his head, cap, and shoulders covered with a large piece of rubber tarpaulin, which was tied with a piece of string around his neck and waist, and his grubby old dungarees soaked right through to the skin. To her, he was an odd sight.

'A good-looker like you shouldn't be out in wevver like this wivout a brolly,' said Mickey, the moment he reached the pavement. 'If yer like, yer can borrer me ol' raincoat. I know it ain't much, but it'd keep the worst off yer.'

Grace looked at the tattered rubber sheet he was untying from around his neck. It almost brought a smile to her face. 'Thank you all the same,' she replied courteously, 'but it won't take me more than a few minutes to get home.' She caught a passing glimpse at the way he was looking at her, drizzle streaming down his face, eyes glowing with perky good humour. For one very brief moment, it made her feel self-conscious. 'I hope they pay you well for this job?' she asked presumptuously.

'Well, it ain't no fortune, miss,' replied Mickey. 'But every penny 'elps. One of these days I aim ter save up enough ter get me own business goin' – I mean, a *real* business.' He grinned, revealing a full set of gleaming white teeth. 'Who knows, I'll probably end up a millionaire, like ol' Rockefeller!'

Grace found herself warming to him. It unsettled her. 'If you have determination, I imagine you can achieve anything,' she replied wryly.

'You're right there, miss,' said Mickey, taking off his flat cap and wiping his face with it. 'My ol' man always used ter say, "Fill yer mind, son, and yer fill yer pockets." I believe in workin' fings out.'

Grace was curious. 'What d'you mean?'

Mickey shrugged. 'I never do anyfin' wivout workin' fings out first,' he replied. 'I mean, yer could jump in at the deep end, couldn't yer? I'd never take on a job that I knew I couldn't do. It wouldn't be fair ter me customers, which means that in the long run, I'd lose out. Word soon gets around, don't it?'

Although she was eager to move on and get out of the drizzle, Grace was fascinated by the young man's home-spun philosophy. 'I suppose it does,' she replied. 'I must get home,' she said, turning.

'If yer ever up my way,' called Mickey, 'why don't yer pop in ter my workshop?'

Grace came to a halt and looked back at him, curious. 'Workshop?'

'It's where I make fings,' Mickey replied quickly. 'All kind er fings. Yer never know, yer might want ter buy somefin'. I'm a real bundle er talent, yer know!' He laughed at his own cheeky joke. 'No, seriously,' he said, coming across to her, 'I'd like ter show yer wot I can do. You could give me some advice. I'm not much good at sellin' me own ideas. I could do wiv someone who knows about that sort er fing.'

Grace took a long, hard look at him. There was more eagerness, more imagination in his eyes than in anyone she had ever known. None the less, he was a man, and he was probably no different to the Eric Tylers of this world. 'I'm sorry,' she found herself saying curtly. 'I'm afraid I know very little about enterprise.' She turned and started to walk away.

'I'd still like yer ter come round the workshop some time,' persisted Mickey.

This time, Grace didn't stop. She merely fluttered her hand back at him without turning to look.

'Leslie Street!' called Mickey, undaunted. 'Just behind the Cally. Ask fer Mickey. Everyone knows where ter find me.'

Grace fluttered her hand again without turning back to look at him. But she knew he was watching her. Without actually seeing him, she knew he was still there, that lively, undiminished, rain-drenched figure, perched on the edge of the pavement, bucket in hand, waiting to get on with his mission to conquer the world with initiative and imagination. She also knew that the sooner she dismissed him from her mind, the better it would be.

But just when she had crossed the main road, she suddenly became aware of how he had greeted her: *A good-looker like you shouldn't be out in wevver like this wivout a brolly.* Those words, those few words, rang out in her ears as loud as the church bells of nearby St Mary's. No one had ever said such a thing to her before, and for one fleeting moment, she felt – noticed. She had a burning desire to turn back. But she resisted the urge, and quickly made her way home.

Gus Higgs sold just about everything in his shop. And if he didn't have the particular item in stock that one of his customers had requested, then he would make a special point of ordering it. On one occasion, Jack Pertwee in Enkel Street asked him to get a tin of wintergreen ointment, which had sold out at the chemist's shop in Seven Sisters Road, and so Gus got on to a bus and went all the way to Wood Green to collect a couple of tins from a chemist's shop up there. From then on, he made quite sure he kept a regular supply of the ointment on the top shelf of his own shop. There were times, however, when the challenge was more difficult than he had anticipated, especially when a foreign customer in Drayton Park asked him for an exotic fruit called rambutan, which only came from Asia and other distant parts of the world. However, he finally found some of them lurking in a wholesalers' fruit market in the East End of London, to the absolute astonishment of his delighted customer.

Today, however, Gus was concentrating on his more conventional stocks. On one side of the shop, the top shelves were neatly stacked with dry groceries such as tinned food, jars of home-made jams, marmalade, pickles and chutneys. The lower shelves had a marble slab for cutting fresh Cheddar cheese with a thin wire, and a porcelain bowl of farm-fresh butter, which was kept cool in a larger stone bowl. Gus also sold plenty of bottles of rhubarb and elderberry wine, which was specially made for him by a woman with a small brewing business in her tiny downstairs rooms in Hackney. And his customers' kids were not forgotten either, for there was one complete shelf for jars of liquorice, humbugs, jelly babies, gob-stoppers, marsh-mallows, sherbert sticks, and wine gums. The opposite side of the shop contained sacks of dried peas, lentils, beans, and sunflower seeds, and the rest of the lower space was taken up with fresh vegetables collected from Covent Garden fruit and vegetable market. The upper shelves contained odds and bobs that Gus's 'regulars' might run out of, such as needles and cotton, starch blocks, shoe black, razor blades, toe clippers, and nose hair scissors (the latter being an absolute must for Ada Snell, who lived in a house at the top of Pakeman Street, and who was always losing hers). And then, of course, there were the fags – not only for the men, but for the ladies too. Gus prided himself on being able to provide most of the popular brands, such as the cheap five or ten in a packet Woodbines, but also Player's Weights, and the posher Craven A. Gus's shop was a veritable treasure chest on wheels, and as he cleaned the whole place out thoroughly with Lifebuoy soap and thick carbolic, he couldn't help wondering what he would do if and when he really did decide to give it all up and start a life elsewhere.

'I told you I'd do all this for you,' said Grace with a deep sigh, as she climbed up into the back of the shop, which was parked in the stable yard at the back of the house. 'Why do you have to be so obstinate?'

Gus, shirtsleeves rolled up, an unlit pipe in his mouth, and down on hands and knees scrubbing the floor, gave her no more than a passing glance.

'I'm not ailin', yer know,' he replied sniffily. 'Anyway, I like keepin' the ol' gel clean.'

For some unknown reason, it always irritated Grace when her father referred to the shop as his 'ol' gel'. She had never really understood his affection for the place, and the fact that it was one way of clinging on to his fond memories of his days as a serving petty officer chandler in the Merchant Navy.

'Well, I'm here now,' she said, taking the pin out of her hat. 'So why don't you wash up and go and give Clapper his feed?'

Like a dutiful small boy, Gus did what his daughter asked, got up, wiped his hands on an old dish cloth, and rolled down his sleeves. 'I thought I might pop in fer a quick'un down the Nag's 'Ead,' he said. 'Some er the boys are playing a game ternight.'

'By all means,' replied Grace primly. She had already taken off her hat, and was rolling up the sleeves of her dress, ready to take over. She never complained when her father announced that he was going 'fer a quick'un'. She was perfectly aware that he had a number of mates to play darts with at the pub, and it gave her the chance to spend most of the evening on her own. No, she didn't mind a bit. 'I'll leave your dinner in the oven. There's some meat pudding and mashed potato left over from last night.'

Gus nodded without replying. But as he made for the door, he stopped. 'Oh, by the way,' he said. 'I won't be 'ere fer Sunday roast this week. Fink yer can cope on yer own wiv the gang?'

Grace, wringing out the flannel in the bucket of soapy water, turned round in shock to look at him. 'You're not going to be here?' she asked.

Gus shook his head.

'But, Dad – you can't . . . you just can't . . . We never miss Sundays. Why can't you be here? Where are you going?'

Gus did his best to avoid Grace's questions. 'Got something ter do,' he replied. 'A mate er mine up Tottenham. 'E's bin a bit poorly.'

'But can't you go and see him during the week?' persisted Grace. 'You know how important Sundays are to the family.'

'*This* is important ter me too, Gracie,' replied Gus firmly. 'Josie an' the uvvers won't miss me. In fact they'll probably enjoy the roast much more!'

'But what will I tell them if they ask where you've gone?'

Gus was now a little irritated with her persistence. 'Tell 'em – just tell 'em – I've got fings ter do.'

'But, Dad—'

Gus raised his hand to silence any further protests. 'Just tell 'em, Gracie – please.' With that, he left the shop.

Grace went to the door and watched him as he crossed the yard and made his way to Clapper's stable. She still couldn't believe what he had just told her. It wasn't as though she cared much for the family, but Sundays were, after all, part of the family's tradition. The get-togethers had been taking place ever since Grandma and Granddad's time. What *was* going on, she asked herself. What *was* her dad up to?

The Nag's Head pub had been Gus's regular watering-hole since he was a lad. He had first been smuggled in to the public bar there when he was just fifteen years old, when the guv'nor there in those days, old Cyril Harris, turned a blind eye to the kid who was made to wear a battered old trilby hat that was far too big for him, but which at least helped to cover his pale-faced youth. Needless to say, Gus took to the pint of bitter habit very quickly, and by the time he was old enough to join the Merchant Navy, he could hold his own with any of his mates in the pub, or anywhere else for that matter. The pub itself was very popular amongst the large local Irish community – the 'Paddys', as they were called – and as it so happened, Gus's best mate over the years was an Irishman named Georgie O'Hara, whom Gus had first met when they'd served on the same ship together back in the times when good old Victoria – 'the Widow Queen' – was still mourning the passing of her Prince Consort. No matter how much of a rough diamond Georgie was, he was as honest as the day was long, and no matter what Gus told him, he would never divulge it to another living person. And he *did* know a lot about Gus.

'Come on, Gus, ol' mate,' croaked Georgie in his thick Irish brogue, which he had never lost despite the fact that he had left County Kildare when he was a young lad. 'There has ter be somethin' wrong with a man that's only downed one pint in the past half-hour! Out with it!'

Gus shook his head. He was determined to remain tight-lipped.

'Then it's got ter be that bloody family of yours again!' persisted Georgie, whose eyes were getting more bleary by the minute, and whose nose was beginning to match the colour of his red choker. 'Wot's that daughter of yours been up to this time?'

'It's not Gracie,' replied Gus, who looked really down in the dumps. 'It's me. I'm in such a quandary, Georgie. I've got so many decisions ter make, an' I just don't know where ter start.'

'So yer still haven't decided wot ter do about the shop then?'

'Oh, I've decided all right,' replied Gus, turning to look at him. 'But I've got ter make sure the rest er the family don't try an' carve it all up. 'Speshully my elder sister, 'Ilda.'

'That ol' cow?' spluttered Georgie, nearly choking on the remains of his fag. 'Why don't yer just tell her ter bugger off, an' get herself a feller who'd know wot ter do with her!'

'Trouble is, Georgie,' said Gus, 'there ain't a feller in the world who'd know *wot* ter do wiv 'er. That's why 'er ol' man walked out on 'er years ago. No, the fing is, I want ter 'ang on ter the shop fer as long as I can, but I can't tell Gracie too much about – well, you know . . .'

'Ah!' gasped Georgie, breathing bitter fumes and stale tobacco straight into Gus's face. 'Yer mean, yer don't want ter tell Gracie about . . . you know wot?'

Gus looked around to make sure that no one was listening. Although the bar was full and rowdy as usual, no one was taking a blind bit of notice of the two of them, propped up at one corner of the counter.

'I had a letter terday,' Gus said, puffing pipe smoke out of the corner of his mouth. 'Looks like I've got a few problems.'

Georgie's ears were now really humming. 'Wot sort er problems?' he asked sceptically.

'Can't talk about it, Georgie,' replied Gus. 'I've got ter go down an' sort it out on Sunday.'

Georgie gulped down the dregs of his bitter, and banged the glass down on the counter, which was a sign for Gladys, the barmaid, to give him a refill. 'Yer can't go on like this for ever, ol' chum,' he said, just beginning to sway on his feet. 'Take my word for it. The sooner yer get this thing off yer chest, the better. Yer can't go on keepin' that girl in the dark. If she loves yer, then she'll understand.'

Gus sighed, and drained the last of the bitter from his own glass. 'I don't fink Gracie 'as much ter do wiv love, Georgie,' he replied despondently. 'She's too much at war wiv 'erself.'

Without saying a word, Gladys collected the two glasses, and pulled a refill for each of them. Georgie waited for Gladys to return the glasses, then slapped the coins down on the counter for her. 'Yer know your trouble, Gus, ol' chum,' Georgie said, once Gladys had left them. 'Yer've got a past, an' yer don't know how ter deal wiv it. Come clean. It's the only way.'

A few minutes later, Gus went into the gents. When he'd finished, he washed his hands in cold water at the sink, and dried them on his handkerchief. Then he felt the urge to take another look at the letter he'd received that morning. He reached into his inside jacket pocket for it.

Georgie was already halfway through his next pint when Gus came rushing out of the gents, pushing his way through the crowd that was now jamming the smoke-filled bar. 'Christ, Georgie!' he blurted, his face as white as a sheet. 'I've got ter get 'ome!'

* * *

Grace finished cleaning out the shop. As always, it had been a hot job, working in such a confined space, and with so many different groceries to check and balance against the stock. The last thing she did was to tidy her hair in the tiny mirror above the cash till, which was placed away from prying eyes at the far end of the enclosed van. She moved out, and locked the shop door behind her, but just as she was about to climb down the steps into the back yard, she suddenly remembered that she hadn't checked to see if there was any loose cash left over in the cash till itself. It was something her father was prone to do, and an open invitation to any petty thief who could gain entry into both the yard and the van with very little difficulty. Quickly returning up the steps, she unlocked the door, and went in. She opened the drawer of the cash till, and found no cash left there at all. However, there was an envelope addressed to her father. She picked it up. The postmark was so indistinct, she couldn't make out where it came from. She flipped the envelope over, and saw the letter 'B' scrawled there. Curious, and seeing that the envelope was already open, she tentatively reached inside, and slowly took out the contents.

Chapter 4

Gus rushed straight to his cash till in the shop. Yes, the letter *was* still there, and his only hope was that Gracie hadn't found it. But that was something he wouldn't discover until he saw her at breakfast the following morning, for she had already turned in for the night.

When he got up the next day, he was relieved when Grace made no mention of the letter, assuming that she had not come across it. So once they had finished their breakfast, he bid a hasty retreat to the stable, where Clapper was anxiously awaiting his morning feed.

Later that morning, Grace left her father to continue his rounds, for she had made an appointment to see the bank manager, Mr Rumble. On the way, she thought about her father's letter. She thought about it a great deal, and especially the reason why she had resisted the urge to read the contents. *Honest as the day is long, that's my Gracie.* How many times had she heard her father say that over the years? Yes, he knew he could trust her not to pry into his private matters. If she had one good characteristic, it was that, no matter how curious she was, she would never read her father's mail. Just like her mother. Even so, that inscription on the back of the envelope continued to intrigue her. 'B'. No matter how hard she racked her brains, she couldn't think of any one of her father's acquaintances with that initial. Would she ask her father about it? She was learning that he was a far more secretive man than she had ever imagined.

'Nothing catastrophic, my dear Grace,' murmured Mr

Rumble, peering at Grace over the top of his metal-framed spectacles, perched on the end of his nose. 'There are still plenty of funds in the business account – well, enough to keep the books balanced, thanks to you.'

Grace liked Mr Rumble. He was a kindly, understanding man, who had always been such a staunch support of her father over the years, guiding him through the intricacies of the financial side of running the shop, something that Gus Higgs had never been comfortable with. In many ways, Mr Rumble was more like a friend of the family, for he probably knew more about them all than Grace herself.

'Things would be a lot better, Mr Rumble,' sighed Grace, on the other side of Rumble's desk, 'if it wasn't for Dad insisting on giving credit to every Tom, Dick, and Harry. Sometimes I despair at the way some of them take him for granted.'

Rumble smiled wryly. 'Well, in my book your father's generosity to others less fortunate than himself is quite a plus. And if you don't mind my saying, I wish I could say the same for one or two other members of your family. Your Aunt Hilda was in here the other day.'

Grace did a double take. 'Aunt Hilda? I didn't know she used this bank?'

Again Rumble smiled. 'She doesn't. She just wanted to have a little chat with me.'

Grace found it hard to take this in. 'You're not telling me she came to talk to you about – Father's business?'

'Let's just say she expressed some concern about him.'

'But that's outrageous!' growled Grace. 'Aunt Hilda has nothing to do with the shop. Father's told her so time and time again.'

'I wouldn't worry too much about her if I was you, my

dear,' said Rumble, holding up the palm of his hand to calm her. 'She's not a bad woman really. She just wants to make sure that the business will be kept in the family *should* anything happen to your father.'

'But how dare she?' Grace snapped. 'How dare she carry on as though something is going to happen to Dad? He's not an old man. There's nothing wrong with him. He's as healthy as you and me.'

'Oh, I'm sure she knows that,' replied Rumble reassuringly. 'I think the problem is that she's been worried by your father's talk of selling up.'

'Mr Rumble,' Grace leaned across the desk, eyes pulsating with indignation, 'whatever my father does is *his* business, and no one else's.'

'Quite so, my dear,' agreed Rumble. 'Quite so.' He got up from his desk, and went round to her. 'But just remember, your father is a lot more on the ball than you might think. He's aware of the situation with your aunt. He knows how to handle things.'

Grace got up from her chair. 'Thank you,' she said, not entirely convinced.

'Let me reassure you,' said Rumble, 'the business will survive for as long as you and your father *want* it to survive. And, in any case, whatever happens, just remember, he *does* have – well, let's just say, I'm sure your future will be taken care of more than adequately.'

As Grace left Rumble's office, his parting words stuck in her mind. What did they mean? As she made her way out of the bank, she was in such a daze, that she barged straight into a customer who was just coming in.

'Oh, I'm so sorry!' she said, flustered and embarrassed. But when she looked up, she could hardly believe who she was staring at. 'Eric,' she spluttered, feeling quite numb.

'Hallo, Grace.' The young man seemed just as embarrassed as she was.

Grace found herself backing away from him. Eric Tyler. Despite the fact that he was not as young as when she last saw him those few years ago, it was a face she could pick out anywhere. It was a face she had seen so many times in her mind's eye, as she lay awake in bed night after night. His thick, brown, over-greased hair still flopped carelessly over his forehead, and his eyelashes were as long as ever, helping to conceal dark brown eyes that had once left her limp with adoration. Eric Tyler. She felt as though she was drowning.

'How are you?' he asked sheepishly.

Grace took a moment to compose herself. She was suddenly consumed with anger to find herself confronted with the man who had once broken her heart. 'I'm fine, thank you,' she replied curtly, trying to restrain her feelings.

'I must say, you're looking well,' added Eric flatteringly. 'It's been a long time.'

'A long time?' asked Grace, only too aware how uneasy he was feeling.

'Since we last met.'

Grace shrugged. She had no intention of responding to his false compliments.

'It must be five or six years.'

'Really?' replied Grace, who was gradually easing herself away from the bank entrance. 'Time flies, doesn't it?'

Eric moved in front of her, blocking her way. 'I've done an awful lot since I last saw you,' he said. 'I've done quite a bit of investing – financial investments that is. It's taken off really well. Insurance – that sort of thing. It's *the* big business to get into. The sky's the limit. The way I'm going, I'll be a millionaire before I reach thirty.'

'How nice for you, Eric,' replied Grace, with just a touch of irony. 'For you *and* your wife. Goodbye.' She started to move off.

Totally crushed by his inability to impress her, Eric changed his approach. 'How's the shop doing?' he asked jokily. 'Is your father still making a good living out of dried peas and broken biscuits?'

Grace stopped and turned. Convinced that he was taunting her, she responded accordingly. 'The customers seem to like them,' she replied coolly. 'They like dealing with my father. They always get on well with a man they can trust.' She started to move off again.

Stung, Eric tried to put things right. 'I'm sorry, Grace,' he said, 'I didn't mean to . . . I must call on you some time.'

Again Grace came to a halt. But she did not turn to look at him.

Eric tried to engage her in a smile. 'Fill you in on all I've been doing.'

Grace called back over her shoulder, 'Goodbye, Eric.' She couldn't get away fast enough. She knew he was watching her, and all she wanted to do was to get back home as fast as her legs would carry her.

As she turned into the Caledonian Road from King's Cross, the thoughts that dominated Grace's mind were of Eric Tyler, of the pain he had caused her over the years, of the way he had just upped and left her when she was at her most vulnerable. In her mind's eye she could picture him, standing on the steps of the bank, smiling that same smile that had conquered her all those years ago, the smile that would have persuaded her to give him anything he wanted – if he had only asked for it. So he was going to be a millionaire before he was thirty was he? Insurance? Financial investments? What did it all mean? Talk. Just talk. She had heard that kind of empty boasting from people so many times before, but Eric Tyler was the kingpin of it. What did *he* know about insurance, about investments? When she knew him he could hardly do his multiplication tables, hardly put two words together. And as for that phoney smooth accent – she could see through that all right. That kind of accent didn't come naturally to the son of a Chapel Street barrow boy.

How she hated him. She hated him with every fibre in her body. He had walked out on her for someone else, and she could never forgive him for that. How many times had he told her how much he loved her? How many times had he told her that she was the only girl in the world that he wanted to spend the rest of his life with? Insurance! Investments! Rubbish! All rubbish! She came to a sudden halt at the entrance to the Caledonian Road Public Baths. She would never forgive him for what he did to her – never!

In one swift movement, she moved on. But without her realising, she came to another abrupt halt. Her legs felt like leaden weights, and she couldn't move. Again, her mind became dominated by thoughts of Eric Tyler. Why had she been so affected by this fleeting few minutes with him? What did it matter whether he wanted to be a millionaire by the time he was thirty? If someone was prepared to work hard for success, then good luck to them. What difference did it make to her? Eric Tyler was the past, and the past was dead and buried. She couldn't care less about Eric Tyler. She couldn't care less whether he lived or died. She tried to move on, but her legs refused to budge. Ahead of her was the long, straight Caledonian Road, bustling with shoppers and traders, a riot of colour and movement in the late morning sun. Oh God! What *was* the matter with her, she asked herself, hoping that no one was taking any notice of her. To hell with Eric Tyler! Why should she care about *him*? Why should she care about anything he said or did? At that moment, the life returned to her legs, and only then did she understand what had happened to her. No matter how hard she tried, she couldn't *really* hate Eric Tyler. The fact was, she was still in love with him.

Gus was out of pumice stone. It was very unlike him not to have checked his stock before he left The Chapel, but then he was beginning to notice how absent-minded he was getting these days. The week before, Old Ma Parker in Enkel Street had got quite crotchety when he forgot to bring her usual three pennyworth of white candles. He was sorry about that. Ma Parker had been a good customer over the years, and he knew how many times her gas supply had been cut because she was unable to pay the bill. Then there was Ted Jessop's ounce of baccy, Minnie Murdoch's 'strong' cough drops, and Pineapple Jack's regular tin of pineapple cubes. Forgotten. All forgotten. 'Not good enuff, old mate,' Gus said to himself. 'Must be gettin' old.'

The one person who forgave him, however, was Gert Jolly in Mayton Street. After all, for years Gus Higgs had allowed her to get away with not paying her rent. Whenever she was down and out, which was more times than not, it was always Gus who offered her a helping hand. It was thanks to him that she'd got a cleaning job at the dentist's surgery in Seven Sisters Road, all because he'd spoken up for her, and it was he who was always bringing her a 'little something extra for the larder'. Yes, Gus Higgs could do no wrong in her eyes, and when he once called her 'the prettiest little woman in 'Olloway,' he was, in her eyes, a true gent.

'Don't worry about the pumice powder, Mr 'Iggs,' she said. 'I don't get many visitors, so who cares if me doorstep ain't white and clean fer one week er the year?'

'I won't let yer down next week, Gert,' promised Gus. 'I'll bring yer a couple er tins. Yer can keep one fer free fer the inconvenience.'

'You're a good'un, Mr 'Iggs,' purred Gert. 'I don't know wot I'd do wivout yer.' She sighed. 'I only wish that daughter of yours took after yer. She's an 'ard gel, yer know.'

'Now come on, Gert,' said Gus, trying to avoid stepping on the fading white doorstep. 'Grace ain't so bad. She's got a lot er fings ter learn about life. One er these days she'll surprise the lot of yer. She'll bloom like a late flowerin' dandelion.'

'The dandelions in *my* windowbox smile at me,' returned Gert. 'I don't fink I've ever seen your Grace smile – not once. An' after all she's bin tellin' us just lately, we'll all soon be out on the street.'

Gus took off his bowler, and wiped the sweat on his forehead with the back of his hand. 'Wot d'yer mean?' he asked warily.

'About callin' in the arrears.'

Gus screwed up his face and gave her a quizzical look. 'Callin' in the arrears?'

Gert peered out to the road to make sure no one was waiting to be served at the shop parked at the kerbside. 'Come on in fer a minute.'

Curious, Gus shrugged, and followed her inside, along a narrow passage with torn dark brown linoleum on the floor, and the acrid smell of boiled greens on the hob in her scullery, biting through the stifling humidity of the cramped house. It was the first time he had actually been inside Gert's place, and when he reached the small parlour at the back of the house, it looked more like a funeral parlour, for there were old framed photos of Gert's late husband, Bill, on every wall, and the hooks on the dresser were all filled with personal mementoes, such as Bill's pocket watch and chain, his dole card, reading glasses, brown choker, and a china mug commemorating King Edward VII's coronation in 1902.

'Would yer like a cup er tea?' Gert asked eagerly. 'The kettle's only just boiled.'

'No fanks, Gert,' said Gus. 'Got ter be on me way. Now wot's this all about?'

'Your gel,' replied Gert diffidently. 'She told Maisie Broom at number seventeen that durin' the comin' weeks you're goin' ter be callin' in all the arrears that people owe yer on the rents.'

'She wot?' Gus gasped, taken aback. 'My Gracie said that? *When* did she say it?'

'Just last week,' replied Gert, wiping the sweat from her forehead with her pinny. 'It's caused quite a stir round-abouts, I can tell yer.'

Even though he knew how Gert had a habit of over-dramatising things, Gus was clearly disturbed. Calling in the arrears – it was the last thing he would *ever* think of. Grace was determined to turn the business into a paying concern, not Gus's main objective at all. The idea that people were being harassed by his overzealous daughter sent a cold shiver down his spine. These people were not just his tenants, they were his friends, and friends were there to be understood, to be taken care of in times of need.

'You're sure about this, Gert?' he asked tentatively.

'Cross me 'eart an' 'ope ter die,' replied Gert, making the sign of the cross on the wrong side of her chest. 'Honest ter God, Mr 'Iggs, if she asks me fer all me back payment, I 'aven't the faintest idea where I'm goin' ter find fifteen bob. That's a small fortune ter me.'

'Well, don't you go worryin' yerself about that, Gert,' said Gus reassuringly. 'You pay the fifteen bob whenever yer can afford it. No one's pushin' yer, yer take that from me.'

Gert's eyes lit up. 'But Grace said—'

'*I'll* tell Grace,' he replied. 'Don't you give it another thought.'

'An' wot about all the uvvers who owe yer? Does that mean—'

'Leave it ter me, Gert,' he said, putting a comforting arm around her shoulders. ' 'Aven't I always told yer that if yer ever 'ave any problems, all yer 'ave ter do is ter tell me, an' I'll sort it out?'

'Yes, I know, but—'

Gus gave her a reassuring smile and put a finger to his lips, indicating that she shouldn't give it another thought. 'I've got ter be goin',' he said, making his way back to the passage. 'See yer next week.'

Beaming, Gert called to him, 'Does your hanimal like turnips?'

Gus stopped briefly at the front door. 'Turnips?'

'I've got one left over from me scrag end stew last night,' said Gert, joining him at the door. 'It's a big one.'

'Fanks all the same, Gert,' replied Gus, 'but Clapper's stuffed full enuff fer a lifetime. In any case, I'm tryin' ter cut down a bit on 'is feed. The ol' scrounger's gettin' a bit of a belly – like me!'

Gert roared with laughter, and saw him out. As she watched him climb up on to the driver's seat of the shop, take Clapper's reins and move off down the road, she waved frantically. In her eyes, Gus Higgs was a gift from God.

* * *

It was a long walk from King's Cross back to The Chapel, but as she made her way at a brisk pace down Caledonian Road, Grace hardly noticed any of the little shops where she did so much of her weekly shopping. She quickly passed by the baked potato man, whose colourful kerb stall covered with a blue-and-white striped awning was always popular with the local shoppers, as was Betsy Ragger's mutton-and-eel pie stall at the corner of Barnsbury Street, where the addictive smell of meat, fish, and home-made gravy was drifting seductively in the midday heat, and attracting just as many summer flies as hungry passers-by. Grace, however, was so preoccupied with her own thoughts that she rushed straight past Rastus, the neighbourhood's favourite elderly Negro street entertainer, who was accompanying himself on the jew's-harp between nostalgic choruses of 'Old Mister Coon', and the cries of a distant street trader yelling, 'Come on ladies an' gents! Block er salt – three pounds fer twopence!' Once she'd cleared the junction of Offord Road and the nearby railway bridge, she hurried quickly past the gloomy stone walls of Pentonville men's prison, where, amongst so many other criminals, the notorious Dr Crippen had been executed for the murder of his wife, Cora Turner, at their home in Hilldrop Crescent, which was hardly a stone's throw away.

By the time she got home, the back of Grace's flimsy summer dress was bathed in perspiration, so she went straight to her bedroom, took off her hat, washed herself down with cold water from the jug stand, and changed into a fresh dress. When she looked out of the window into the stable yard, however, she was surprised to see that the mobile shop was there, and the stable door wide open. Fearing that something was wrong, she rushed out to find her father.

In the stable, Gus was swilling Clapper down with a large sponge and a bucket of water. Although he knew that Grace was standing in the open doorway, he didn't turn to greet her.

'You're home early, Dad,' called Grace, coming across to him. 'Is anything wrong?'

'Wrong?' replied Gus, who continued with what he was doing. 'Why should there be anyfin' wrong?'

Grace was curious. 'You don't usually finish your morning rounds until well after two.'

'I decided it was too 'ot,' he replied glumly.

Now Grace knew there was something wrong, so she made her way round the back of Clapper to face her father. 'Dad?' she asked anxiously. 'Tell me.'

Gus slowly looked up at her. 'Did you tell the tenants we're callin' in their arrears?'

Grace sighed, then stiffened. 'Yes, I did,' she replied coldly.

'Why din't yer ask me first?'

'Because I knew your answer if I had.'

She got quite a shock when he suddenly threw the sponge into the bucket, and snapped back at her, 'Those people are our friends. I've known 'em fer years. They're good, honest folk. I won't 'ave you goin' round upsettin' 'em!'

Grace was completely taken aback by her father's outburst. It was so unlike him. 'Dad,' she replied, trying to calm him, 'I went to see Mr Rumble this morning. He said we've got to keep an eye on things.'

'To 'ell with ruddy Dick Rumble!' barked Gus, glaring with anger. ' 'E ain't my boss. 'E ain't my guv'nor! 'E don't pay my bills!'

'Be sensible, Dad! We can't go on giving credit to every Tom, Dick, and Harry. If we carry on like this we'll be bankrupt.'

But Gus turned his back on her, grabbed hold of a towel, and started rubbing down Clapper's coat vigorously.

'Look, Dad,' said Grace, trying to calm the atmosphere between them. 'I'm sorry I didn't tell you about – well, about talking with the tenants. But someone had to do it. These people have to be aware that we can't go on supporting them for ever.'

'*These people*, as you keep calling them, Gracie,' said Gus, 'are 'uman beings. Sometimes I fink yer ferget that.'

Grace was stung by his remark. She was shocked by her father's attitude. Not only was it the first unpleasant quarrel they had ever had, but it was also incredibly naïve of her father to believe that he could go on providing free accommodation to his tenants for the rest of his life.

'So what do you want me to do, Father?' she asked in a voice that showed how much he had hurt her. 'Do you want me to go on keeping the books, or shall I just forget all about them, and take each day as it comes?'

Gus stopped what he was doing, and looked up at her. 'All I want *you* ter do, Gracie,' he pleaded, 'is ter be like yer mum. Loosen up a bit, an' try an' understand that runnin' a shop on wheels for poor folk ain't about big business. It's about doin' a service.'

Grace could bear to listen to no more. She lowered her eyes, turned, and made for the door.

'Gracie.'

Grace stopped and looked back at him.

'Times are movin' on,' said Gus. 'One of these days there won't be no more shops on wheels, and clumsy ol' Clappers to trot around the streets all day. But I've never known anyfin' else, Gracie. My tenants, my customers've been me 'ole life. Let's make the best of it while we can. OK?'

Grace nodded without comment, then left. Instead of going back into the house, however, she left the stable yard, and went out into the street.

One side of Pedlar's Way was bathed in radiant early afternoon sunshine, while the opposite side of the small cobbled lane was a blanket of shadow. As she hurried away from The Chapel, and headed off towards Caledonian Road, all she could think about was how ungrateful her father had been, unreasonable, so short-sighted. She was hurt, there was no doubt about that. This had already been one hell of a day for her, and it was still only early afternoon. First, that fleeting encounter with Eric Tyler, and now this. All she wanted to do was to get away from everything, from everybody. She had to have time to think, to work out what she was going to do with her life.

Without knowing which direction she was heading in, she made for the backstreets, passing a group of kids playing hopscotch on a broken pavement, some of the many in the neighbourhood who were constantly playing truant from school. One of them, a boy of no more than nine or ten years old, was smoking a fag, probably nicked from his dad. As he watched Grace pass, the boy put the remainder of the fag in his lips at a jaunty angle, which showed not only defiance of authority, but also that he was someone to be reckoned with. Grace ignored him, and went on her way. Despite the heated exchange of words with her father, her thoughts were dominated by that meeting with Eric Tyler. In her mind's eye, she could see him, dark eyes flashing in the sunshine. Oh God – *what* a face it was! Why was it that, despite all the things he had done to her, she was still drawn by that strange magnetism that emanated from every part of his being?

She came to a halt, and tried to stare up at the sky. The

sun was dazzling, and it blinded her. She shielded her eyes with one hand, and looked around for the nearest shade. In the distance, she could hear the sound of workmen on scaffolding in the Caledonian Road, putting the finishing touches to the new Mayfair Cinema. She found the sound intrusive, especially as cinemas had never played a part in her own life. Again she thought of Eric Tyler. She wondered what she would have said if he had asked to meet up with her. Would she have told him that he was disgusting, that he was a married man, that he should be ashamed of himself, and that what he had done to her once he would never have the chance to do again? Or would she have relented, and given in to those devastating eyes? She wiped the sweat from her brow. How could she possibly still love Eric Tyler?

She rubbed her eyes with both hands. When she looked up, it was as though she had just woken from a sleep. Disoriented, she looked around. Where was she? What was she doing there? And then it came back to her. All around her were the tall, elegant Victorian houses in Stock Orchard Crescent that she had seen before, and when she looked up, she found herself beneath the huge elm tree under which she had sheltered when – when what? For no reason at all, her eyes gradually turned towards the kerb nearby, and the road where Clapper had once left his droppings. She looked up with a start, half expecting, half hoping to see that same young man in flat cap, well-worn shirt, baggy trousers, and plimsolls, coming across with shovel and bucket to collect the droppings. But this time, there was no one there. She sighed, then made her way back home.

Chapter 5

Alexandra Palace was bathed in a deep, crimson sunset. It was a strange, eerie sight, as though an alien spacecraft had settled on top of the hill, spying out the land beyond the calm and peace of Alexandra Park, and the distant views of North London and its leafy suburbs. Floating in the sky above them was a long, cigar-shaped hot-air balloon advertising Ovaltine, which to some people recalled the horrors of the German passenger airship *Hindenburg*, which had burst into flames and crashed on landing in New York only a few weeks before. But after the intense heat and humidity of a late June day, the air on top of the hill was at least cool, and a perfect place to escape to in the middle of a hectic working week. That's why Grace and her old classmate Pauline Betts were there. Stretched out side by side on their backs on the grass slopes high above the racecourse, they were enjoying their first opportunity in a long time to get together, to renew what had once been a strong friendship. What Grace had to say, however, was, to Pauline, totally unexpected.

'A job?' asked Pauline, sitting bolt upright. 'You mean, you're not going to work for your dad any more?'

'I don't see the point really,' replied Grace. 'These days I only seem to irritate him. I think he'd get on far better without me.'

'Well!' gasped Pauline, looking down at her. 'This is a bit of a turn-up for the books. I thought you loved your father.'

'I *do* love him,' insisted Grace, sitting up. 'But I can't go

77

on watching him ruin his life by trying to be something to every hard-luck case he comes across.'

'What d'you mean?' asked Pauline.

'Oh, you wouldn't understand, Pauline,' replied Grace. 'All I know is that sooner or later, the shop, the business – the money's just going to run out. And I just don't want to be there when it happens.'

'But I always thought that one day you'd take over the business,' suggested Pauline. 'Your father has no one else to leave it to, does he? I mean, you're his only close relative.'

Grace's expression changed. 'There are others he can leave it to,' she replied bitterly, lying back again.

'Who?'

'He has two sisters.'

Pauline was intrigued. As she watched Grace lying on her back on the grass, staring aimlessly up at the blood-red sky, she felt a surge of protectiveness for her old friend. Even when they had been young girls together at Shelburne Road School, Pauline had always known what a hyper-sensitive person Grace could be. No matter what anyone said to her, if there were two ways to interpret a remark, she would invariably choose the negative one, as though she was being criticised. It was an emotion that had blighted her life so many times, so much so that when she had been genuinely wronged by Eric Tyler, it was naturally hard for her to recover. Most people found rejection hard to take, but for Grace the only way she could live with it was to cut off from life completely.

'What sort of work d'you want to do?' Pauline asked.

'I don't really care,' replied Grace. 'I can't type, but I can learn. Maybe something to do with book-keeping. I've had a baptism of fire doing that with the shop.'

Pauline lay back at the side of her again. 'You don't think you're overreacting, Grace?'

'Overreacting to what?' asked Grace.

'Well, if you've had some kind of a disagreement with your dad, don't you think you should just think about it for a while, then talk it over with him again?'

Grace hesitated for a moment. 'It's not just my father, Pauline,' she replied. 'It's Eric Tyler.'

Pauline turned to her with a start. 'Eric?'

'I met him just as he was going into the bank,' said Grace.

Pauline propped herself up on one elbow. 'What happened?' she asked eagerly.

'Nothing *happened*, Pauline,' said Grace. 'All he talked about was how well he's doing.'

'Did he really?' said Pauline dismissively. 'Well, that's not what *I* heard. *I* heard that despite being cut off by his father-in-law, Eric still tried to get money out of him. But he got his fingers burnt. Don't listen to a word Eric Tyler says, Grace. Take my word for it, he's absolutely skint!'

Grace didn't reply.

On the grass slopes beyond, someone had put on a gramophone record of Ambrose and his orchestra playing one of the current new hit tunes of the day, 'I've Got You under my Skin'. It was a wistful sound, which drifted through the trees in the soft evening breeze, reverberating high up into the all-embracing sunset. For the next few minutes, the two girls listened to the music, eyes closed, Pauline lying on her back again, quietly joining the vocalist Sam Browne in the chorus, and Grace, as usual, deep in thought.

'Are you still in love with him?' asked Pauline, once the music had come to an end.

Grace's eyes sprang open, and she turned with a start to look at her. 'What did you say?'

'All I mean is, d'you have anything else to tell me – about Eric?'

'Don't be so absurd, Pauline!' protested Grace, flopping back on to the grass again. 'What d'you take me for?'

'There's nothing to be ashamed of, Grace,' said Pauline. 'These things happen. You know, I read this book in the library the other day. It was about these two fellers who climbed a mountain out in India or some such place. Anyway, when they got to the top, the first thing one of them did was to shout his head off, to let the whole world know that he was there. The other feller just wanted to look and listen, to feel the silence, and the peace of that magnificent scenery all around. No matter how much you know someone, it just shows how different two people can be. I mean, if Eric Tyler had done to me what he did to you, I would have wanted to tell the whole world about it, to let everyone know what a worthless creature he is. But you're different, Grace. You cling on, hoping that things might turn out the way you always wanted them to be.'

'I'm *not* clinging on, Pauline,' Grace assured her unconvincingly. 'It was just that, when I saw Eric again – after all that time – I – well – I had this strange feeling inside that – no one can really be as bad as they seem.' She turned to look at her. 'Can they?'

Pauline hesitated. 'I'm afraid they can, Grace,' she replied with a sigh. 'I'm afraid they can.'

As she spoke, the sound of another gramophone record drifted across the grass slopes. This time it was another current new hit song, 'Thanks for the Memory'.

* * *

Grace's Sunday roast for the family turned out to be a bit of a disaster. For a start, despite Josie's help, the Yorkshire pudding refused to rise, and the roast beef was so tough, her Uncle Stan lost one of his last remaining teeth, and had to spend the rest of the meal cutting up everything small. Of course it didn't help that her father had gone off for the day to see his so-called sick mate up at Tottenham, which meant that Grace had to entertain the family single-handed, as well as cook for them.

Once the meal was over and the washing-up done, Stan and his son, Reg, were given the excuse to have their usual afternoon nap on the settee in the front parlour, which left Viv free to go off for a meeting with her boyfriend, Alan. Whilst all this was going on, Grace found enough time to go to see Clapper in his stable, but if she thought this was a good way of having a few minutes on her own, she was disappointed.

' 'Ow many times a day do you have to exercise that 'orse?' asked Aunt Hilda, who had come out into the back stable yard with Josie.

'Oh – as often as we can,' replied Grace, who was filling up a fresh bucket of water for Clapper at the tap outside. 'He gets plenty of exercise during the week when we're out on our rounds, but on Sundays I usually take him for a trot round and about.'

'I wouldn't 'ave the patience,' said Hilda, shrugging herself further into her cotton cardigan, which, despite the warm afternoon, she was wearing over her navy-blue buttoned dress. 'Too much of a liability.'

'Oh, I don't know,' said Josie, in contrast looking as pretty as a picture in her floral-patterned summer dress. 'Clapper's a lovely ol' boy. If Stan had his way, he'd fill our place wiv 'orses.'

'That's only because 'e bets on 'em,' remarked Hilda wryly.

Josie glared at her sister without comment. 'I remember the time Dad took us ter the zoo,' she said wistfully. 'It was a wonderful day. I 'ad a lovely ride on a camel.'

'Wot *are* yer goin' on about, Josie?' scolded Hilda. 'A camel's not a ruddy 'orse!'

'I know that!' replied Josie irritably. 'I was only sayin' it 'cos I love animals. They're better than a lot of people I know!'

Grace ignored her bickering aunts. She had listened to so much small talk from her family over the years, and it now went in one ear and out the other. She finished filling the bucket, and took it into the stable. Unfortunately, Hilda and Josie followed her.

'So who's this person yer farver's gone ter see terday?' asked Hilda, in her most demanding voice.

'I've no idea,' replied Grace, placing the bucket of water in front of Clapper. 'All I know is it's some old friend of his who's been taken poorly.'

'Is that so?' replied Hilda sourly. 'Must be someone special if 'e can't be 'ere fer 'is own family.'

'I wonder who it is?' asked Josie, wiping the sweat from her neck with her hanky. 'P'raps it's Jimmy Marsden from 'is ol' football club. They used ter be very close. No – it wouldn't be 'im. 'E don't live in Tottenham. 'E lives over Shoreditch way.'

'Wot does it matter *who* it is, Josie?' snapped the now irritated Hilda. 'The fact is, Gus isn't 'ere, an' 'e should be!'

'I don't see why,' insisted Josie defiantly. 'Gus 'as always bin popular. 'E's always 'ad a lot of pals. Trouble is, at our age they start dyin' off.' She sighed. 'It makes yer wonder.'

'Don't you worry, Auntie,' said Grace, turning briefly

from rubbing down Clapper. 'You're looking in the peak of health. You've got plenty of time ahead of you.'

'Oh, I don't know,' said Josie. 'I try not ter fink about it. It's not me I worry about, it's Stan. If I went first, I don't know 'ow 'e'd cope on 'is own. Men are so 'elpless alone. They rely on us women so much. Mind you, I've always liked that. I like ter do fings fer 'im. 'E loves ter be spoilt. I know it sounds a terrible fing ter say, but I 'ope 'e goes first. I wouldn't want 'im ter suffer becos er me.'

'Josie! We'll 'ave ter be goin' soon. Wot about a cuppa?' Stan's voice calling from the house brought an immediate response from Josie.

'Comin', dear!' she yelled back. 'Don't you worry, Gracie,' she said. 'I'll go an' put the kettle on.'

Hilda waited for her sister to disappear back into the house, then went to join Grace. 'She's such a stupid woman,' she said wistfully. 'But I can't 'elp lovin' 'er. I s'ppose I'm jealous of 'er really. I mean, she's 'ad someone ter love 'er most of 'er life.' She watched Grace rubbing down Clapper. 'An' wot about you, young lady?' she asked.

'What d'you mean, Auntie?' Grace replied.

'You *know* wot I mean,' persisted Hilda. 'Why aren't yer courtin'?'

Grace stopped what she was doing, and looked up. 'I do wish everyone would stop asking me that question,' she replied. 'I don't have a need to get married.'

'Nobody has a *need* to get married, Grace,' said Hilda. 'But it 'elps ter 'ave someone ter look after yer – especially in yer ol' age. That's *my* trouble. I 'ave ter fink er fings just on me own. No one ter tell me if I'm doin' the right fing or not. Even when I do the shoppin', I buy one chop or just enuff sausages fer one person. I can't pretend I like it. Still,' she found a stool and sat down on it, 'I've made up fer it in uvver ways. I've learnt 'ow ter stand on me own two feet. Yer dad's lucky. At least 'e 'ad yer mum ter care fer 'im. And then you.'

'Dad's been very good to me, Auntie,' replied Grace. 'I have no complaints.'

'I'm glad ter 'ear it,' said Hilda. ' 'Cos 'e ain't perfect, yer know.'

Grace turned to look at her again. 'What d'you mean?'

'Just wot I say. There's anuvver side ter yer dad, Grace, a side that 'e keeps ter 'imself. There are a lot of fings yer don't know about 'im.'

Grace wasn't going to encourage this discussion about her father. She knew only too well what Hilda was like, and how anything that Grace might say to her would be repeated to the rest of the family, and distorted out of all proportion. But then, she had never heard her aunt talk about herself with such frankness as she had just done. To Grace, Aunt Hilda had always been the strong member of the family, proud and independent, who had never seemed to care about being left to look after herself. In many ways, Grace felt the same way about herself. In that respect, they were disturbingly alike.

'What things, Auntie?' she asked.

'Yer'll find out one day, Grace,' replied Hilda. 'All I will tell yer is that it wasn't all plain sailin' between yer mum an' yer dad. Oh yes, they was 'appy all right – well, fer most er the time. But there were moments when – when yer dad wasn't all 'e seemed. As I told yer, there was anuvver side to 'im. An' yer mum knew it.'

Gus Higgs found a seat for himself in a second-class compartment of the *Cornish Riviera Express*. As it was a Sunday afternoon, the train was quite full of holidaymakers, returning back home to London after a sunny June fortnight by the sea. Fortunately, the window of his compartment was open, and, as it was still a stiflingly hot day, it was unlikely that any of his seven fellow travellers was going to complain about the draught. It was also a blessing in disguise that most of them looked so weary that it would not be long before they dozed off, and, as it so happened, this was the case before they had even reached the next station, which was less than ten minutes away. The route the train took was one of the most beautiful in Britain, for it skirted the seashore for miles, with distant views behind of beautiful red stone cliffs, and a strange cone-shaped rock protruding from the sea just a short way offshore. But Gus saw very little of any of it. His thoughts were still on the person he had just left behind, and the problems that had brought him on such a long day's trip. After the first stop at a small seaside resort, he settled down to a quiet, uneventful journey that would be interrupted only by brief stops at some of the bigger towns. His favourite travelling companion in the compartment was undoubtedly the small terrier dog, perched on her lady's lap, which utterly refused to go to sleep. For all of twenty minutes or so, she and Gus weighed up each other, both of them wondering what on earth they were doing in a stuffy train compartment so far from home.

Gus turned to look out of the window. The sun was dazzling, and he had partially to pull down the blind to protect his eyes. As the vast stretch of seashore gradually gave way to a scorched rural landscape of trees and bushes, rolling hills and undulating valleys, it was plain to see that the power of the sun itself was almost at its peak. It wouldn't be too long now before the shadows began, to herald the hot summer's night. But, as he intermittently caught a glimpse of his reflection in the window beside him, Gus realised only too well that the track ahead was already fraught with uncertainty.

With another interminable Sunday roast day now finally at an end, Grace felt free enough of the family to get out of the house and take Clapper for an early evening walk. In the Caledonian Road, traffic was picking up a little as people made their way home after a blistering day out in the sun. One of the favourite spots for a picnic had always been down by the Regent's Canal near King's Cross, and Grace had fond memories of when she was a child, watching the horse-drawn barges, filled with all kinds of merchandise such as coal, grain, building materials, or timber, ploughing their way gracefully through the calm, still waters, heading north up to the Midlands and beyond, leaving a gentle wash to lap against the canal bank as they went. But Clapper's favourite trot was around the backstreets near home, where he could explore the various smells in the road, and tease the stray dogs, who barked their anger at him for daring to intrude upon their pitch.

This evening, Grace headed up past the police station, where she got the customary, 'Evenin', miss,' from any of the constables who happened to be around, and who never failed to stop and have a friendly word with Grace and one of the more familiar animals in the district. After that, she turned off into Roman Way, and allowed Clapper to halt for a few moments, which gave him the chance to help himself to some cool water from the horse trough at the kerbside there.

Whilst she waited, Grace pondered over the conversation she had had with her Aunt Hilda that afternoon, and Hilda's tantalising jibes about Gus's relationship with Grace's mother.

What did Hilda mean by, 'there were moments when yer

dad wasn't all 'e seemed' and that 'there was anuvver side to 'im'? Was Hilda trying to tell Grace something about her father that she didn't know, or was her aunt just being her usual mischievous self? It left Grace in a quandary, and she didn't know *what* to believe. But then, she told herself, families everywhere had skeletons in their closets, so why should her family be any different? None the less, these past few weeks, her father had been behaving oddly, so much so that she herself was beginning to reassess her whole relationship with her mum and dad. She tried to carry her mind back to when she was a child, to remember any incident that would corroborate Aunt Hilda's suggestions that things weren't always so good between her brother and his wife. But no matter how hard Grace tried, all she could remember was the most glowing relationship between them, the way they always did things together, such as Sunday evening walks, and running the shop, and going to the pictures, and endlessly going down memory lane together. No. As far as Grace was concerned, Gus and Alice Higgs were the perfect married couple. They were an example to everyone – including Grace herself.

Once Clapper had finished his thirst-quenching drink, Grace looked around to decide which route she would take him along, to see if there was any variation from the usual she could come up with. Her eyes scanned the street ahead; she couldn't remember how many times she and Clapper had plodded wearily along there, past the same old terraced houses, the same old pub with the evening darts players in the public bar getting more and more rowdy, and the out-of-tune piano getting rough treatment from its well-oiled pianist. But just as she was about to move on, she caught a fleeting glimpse of the small street leading off. The nameplate on the corner house read 'Leslie Street', and although she had seen it before, and had probably been down there on more than one occasion, this evening it seemed to ring a bell in her mind somewhere.

Without giving too much thought to what she was doing, she found herself tugging at Clapper's halter, and making a right turn down the street. Only when she was actually there, however, did she remember what it was that had brought her there: *Leslie Street! Just behind the Cally. Ask fer Mickey. Everyone knows where ter find me.* She brought Clapper to an abrupt halt. Was she mad, she asked herself. What was it that had brought her down this street just because a cheeky young bloke had asked her to visit him in his workshop there?

Instinctively, she tugged at Clapper's halter. He refused to budge. 'Get a move on, Clapper!' she snapped irritably. She knew only too well that he had a mind of his own, and if he didn't want to move, then nothing in the world would persuade him to do so. 'If you don't get going,' she warned, 'I'll tell Dad not to let anyone feed you any more carrots!'

Grace's tone was sharp enough to persuade Clapper to move on, and a short distance further, an elderly man came up to give Clapper a pat.

'Would you know where a young man named Mickey Burke lives?' asked Grace. 'I believe he has a workshop somewhere down here?'

The old man roared with laughter. 'Mickey Burke?' he spluttered, his ill-fitting set of false teeth gleaming white in the early evening sun. 'Mad Mick, yer mean! That's 'is place – just down the end.' He indicated the corner house at the far end of the street.

Grace thanked the old boy, and led Clapper on. It was a neat and tidy street, with rows of two-up and two-down terraced houses on each side. Sundays were clearly very popular in this part of the Cally, for there was the sound of family singsongs coming from several front parlours, and in the distance she could hear the familiar sound of Jimmy Galdoni's handbell, which meant that his Italian ice-cream box was perched on his tricycle, and most probably surrounded as usual by hordes of local kids.

When she eventually found 'Mad Mick's' workshop, it turned out to be little more than an old wooden shack squeezed between houses at the corner of the street. For several minutes Grace and Clapper waited outside, listening to the tinny sound of music coming from some kind of machine inside the shack. She wondered what the hell she was doing there, and very nearly turned Clapper round to go home. But she had second thoughts. Tying Clapper's halter to the nearest gas lamppost, she slowly approached the open door of the shack. For a few moments she just stood there, hardly able to take in everything she could see there.

The place was a real mess, a veritable junk shop, full of what looked like rubbish – old rubber tyres, bicycle parts, tin cans, broken pottery, piles of books that seemed to be rotting away, electrical gadgets of every description, a horn gramophone that looked as though it would never play again, old brass statues, kids' comics scattered all over the place, a shelf full of porcelain mugs, glass sweet jars containing everything from different coloured powders to marbles, bits of broken pencils, and one huge jar crammed with the remains of bars of soap. Running around the place was a model railway track, complete with a Hornby steam engine and freight carriages, a signal box, and a scale-length passenger platform station. The walls were covered with old snapshot photos of goodness knows who, together with pin-ups from newspapers and magazines, mainly of current film stars such as Greta Garbo, Sonja Henie, and Alice Faye, and hanging from the ceiling right the way across the shack was a huge, tattered Union Jack flag.

Grace looked around the place in utter bewilderment, and it took some time before she noticed Mickey himself, his back towards her, hunched over the workbench, adjusting what looked like some kind of an old wireless set. As he worked, he joined in the song 'You are my Lucky Star', which was coming from the wireless. He had a terrible, tuneless voice, and the louder he sang the worse it got.

'I hope I'm not intruding?' Grace asked rather formally.

Mickey turned with a start. His face beamed as he saw Grace standing in the doorway. ' 'Allo, miss!' he called, absolutely delighted to see her. 'Wot a treat! Wot a real blinkin' treat!' He wiped his hands quickly on an old tea-cloth, and came across to greet her. 'Welcome ter my 'umble abode!'

'I was passing by,' said Grace, as casually as she could manage, 'so I –'

'It's marvellous!' said Mickey, grabbing a chair for her to sit on. 'Come an' sit down, then I'll give yer a grand tour.'

'I can't stay long,' replied Grace, declining the chair. 'I've got our horse outside.'

'Clap?' said Mickey. 'Yer've got ol' Clapper outside? This is my lucky day all right. I've got a lump er sugar fer him. Got ter pay 'im back fer that dump 'e gave me the uvver day.'

Even as Mickey spoke, Grace could smell the horse dung, coming from a large bucket just outside the back door of the shack.

'What do you do with all this stuff?' asked Grace, still looking around the place in absolute astonishment.

'Oh, you know,' said Mickey. 'A little bit er this, a little bit er that. I put fings back tergevver again – if yer take my meanin'. See this?' He went to his workbench and picked up a small porcelain figure of a young girl in Dutch national costume, carrying a pair of buckets on a pole across her shoulders. 'This woman up 'Ighbury give it ter me ter put tergevver again. When I got it, this little gel 'ad no 'ead, and only one arm.'

Grace took the figure from him and looked at it. It was quite beautiful. 'You mean – *you* restored this?'

Beaming, Mickey nodded enthusiastically. 'Clever ol' git, ain't I?'

Grace, clearly impressed, gave the figure back to him. As he took it from her he gave her a flashing smile that sent a shiver down her back. It was the first time she had realised just how masculine and handsome he was.

'That's wot I do, mainly,' continued Mickey. 'I put fings back tergevver again. Brings in the odd bob or two. Keeps the wolf from the door.' He moved on, picking up various objects to show her as they went. 'Sometimes I make fings out er any ol' scraps left over. This one's made er matchsticks.' He handed her the small replica of a rather grand-looking house. 'I copied that from some magazine.'

Grace took the object, admiring the astonishingly delicate work and patience that had gone into it. When she put it back on to the bench again, she noticed a huge pile of children's comics stacked high on a shelf just above. 'What on earth do you do with all *those* things?' She reached up and took one from the top of the pile. 'Aren't you a little old to read this kind of stuff?'

'Well,' said Mickey, looking over her shoulder as she scanned through the different black-and-white action strips, 'ter tell yer the trufe, I don't actually *read* 'em. I look at the pittures. Sometimes they're a bit daft, but sometimes they 'ave good stories. I do like good stories.'

Grace looked up at him. 'Did you go to school, Mickey?' she asked.

Mickey hesitated, looked embarrassed. 'Me?' he replied vaguely. 'Yeah, I went ter school – well, fer a bit anyway. See – I had to earn a livin' fer boaf me *an'* me dad. He used ter ail quite a lot. 'E wasn't able ter get a job. But it was all right. I managed ter make a few bob fer us boaf doin' odds an' ends. I even learnt 'ow ter cook. I know 'ow ter cook fried eggs. Mrs Drew just up the street 'as a coupla chickens. She sometimes gives me an egg – free, mind yer.'

Grace found it hard to believe all he was telling her. The fact that anyone could survive like this amazed her. She flicked through the pages of the comic, until Mickey stopped her at a page, and pointed to a strip cartoon that depicted a massively built hero getting into a luxurious futuristic car, whilst the villain he had just defeated was in the custody of the police in the background.

'This is one of me fav'rites,' he said, pointing to the cartoon. 'See this bloke. Look at that big cigar 'e's smokin'. That's me – or at least it will be in a few years' time. Rich an' famous!' He chuckled at his own false bravado.

Grace's face hardened. She closed the comic, and handed it back to him. 'It seems *everyone* wants to be a millionaire,' she said pointedly.

'Wot's wrong wiv that?' he asked almost brusquely. 'Everyone 'as ter 'ave an aim in life, uvverwise there ain't nuffin ter work for. Anyway, I've got a few ideas wot ter do wiv me savin's.'

Grace did a double take. 'Savings?' she asked. 'You've managed to save money from all of this?'

'Yeah – a bit,' replied Mickey. 'When I get paid fer a job I do fer someone, I keep just enuff fer me board an' nosh, an' then I put the rest in this big jar I keep.' He grinned. 'I ain't goin' ter tell yer *where* I keep it, though.'

'What are you going to do with your savings?' asked Grace, moving on to look at the rest of his work.

'Invest it,' replied Mickey confidently.

Grace came to a halt and turned to look at him. 'Invest it?'

'In somefin' better than this,' he replied, nodding to the shack. 'I mean, yer've got ter use cash ter make it, ain't yer. I rent this place from the Gremlins next door. Their real name's Hamlin, but I prefer my name for 'em. They're a really nice ol' couple – salt er the earf. But I've got ter move on eventually. I've got ter make somefin' of me life.'

Grace listened with profound interest to everything Mickey was telling her. Although his big talk about becoming a millionaire with a big cigar reminded her of Eric Tyler, this man couldn't be more different. He had such a spirit of enterprise, imagination, and determination. Most of all, he was prepared to work hard to get what he wanted.

'Tell me something,' she said, looking around the shack. 'Where do you sleep at night?'

'Ah!' said Mickey. 'Come wiv me!' He led her across to a corner of the shack that was shielded by a huge heavy carpet draped from the ceiling. He drew the carpet aside to reveal an old Put-u-up, together with a jug and wash-basin stand. 'Welcome ter Mickey Burke's private boudwar!' he announced triumphantly. 'It ain't much, but I always get a good kip 'ere. 'Cept fer the spiders, that is. I don't mind the odd mouse or two, but spiders . . .!' He shuddered. 'They give me the creeps, crawlin' all over me in the middle er the night.' He lowered the carpet again. 'Hey!' he said eagerly. 'Shall I make yer a cuppa? It won't take long ter brew up.'

Grace smiled, but shook her head. 'No, thank you, Mickey,' she replied. 'I have to get Clapper back home.' She turned, slowly made her way to the door, then stopped. 'What would *you* do,' she asked, 'if you had a business of your own, and people owed you money?'

Mickey came to a halt, and scratched his head. This was a rum old question, he reckoned. 'Well, in all trufe, I couldn't tell yer,' he replied.

Grace was disappointed. She smiled courteously, turning to leave.

'If they 'ad plenty er cash,' Mickey said, 'I'd tell 'em ter coff up, or end up in the cooler.'

'And if they didn't have much money?'

Mickey thought about this for just a brief moment. 'If they were skint, I'd tell 'em ter pay me back a bit at a time, whenever they could afford it. As long as they paid somefin', I'd know they wasn't tryin' ter dupe me.'

Grace smiled. 'Thank you, Mickey,' she said. 'Thanks for letting me visit you.'

'Any time,' he replied. He followed her out into the street. 'Oh, by the way,' he called. 'If yer feel like comin' round ter try some of me 'ome cookin' some time, yer'd be more than welcome. I've got an oven. I know 'ow ter cook bangers an' mash.'

Grace reached Clapper, and untied his halter. She turned and looked back at the young man with a smile. 'You never know,' she replied. 'I might take you up on that.'

A thick pall of black smoke drifted back from the steam engine of the *Cornish Riviera Express*, and left a trail of soot clinging to the lush summer foliage right the way along the railway track. The Great Western Railway train was now ploughing its way at speed through the Berkshire countryside, and it would not be long before it reached the stifling suburbs of West London.

Gus and the small terrier dog were now firm friends, and even though most of the other passengers in the compartment were now awake, the two carried on their flirtation. At one time during the long journey, the dog had managed to free herself of her lady owner, and make her way across to Gus at the window seat. After she had done him the great honour of allowing him to stroke her black-and-white patched coat, she then made her way back to her own place on the floor under the seat.

It was now getting very dark outside, and the passing countryside looked eerie as the lights from the train compartments cast breathless flickering shadows on to trees, grass, streams, house windows and walls, and giant advertising poster boards. Gus caught a glimpse of the first star of the night just as the train was passing through the last area of rural scenery on the outskirts of the capital. When he was a kid, his mother told him that whenever he saw the first star of the night, he should always make a wish, and that is what he was doing right now. Of course, no one was there to share it with him, but he knew that somewhere up there in that great darkening wilderness, one of the stars would be his dear, darling Alice, who had never failed to keep an eye on him all these years. None the less, he hoped his wish would be granted, for he felt nothing but anxiety after a long, difficult day's outing far away from home.

His despair was real enough. He had so much to cope with, so much to prepare for, and he didn't know which way to turn. By now, his reflection in the window beside him was becoming sharper, more into focus. He didn't like the sort of person he'd become – a man who kept so many secrets from his own daughter. But then, in his mind's eye,

Grace appeared, her face both puzzled and questioning. How much longer could he hold back from telling her all she had the right to know? It was a quandary he had to face up to.

By the time the train pulled in to the platform at Paddington station, the overhead lights seemed dazzling after the sleepy confines of the train compartment. After saying his farewell to his small terrier friend, Gus joined the crowd of other passengers filing off the train, and made his way to the ticket barrier, where he handed in his cheap day return ticket, then set off for the station exit. Although it was now late in the evening, he felt desperately in need of a pint of bitter, and wished that he could go straight to join Georgie O'Hara in the public bar at the Nag's Head for a quick pick-me-up before turning in for the night. However, as it was now past the stupid Sunday 10.30 closing time, he had to content himself with queuing for a bus that would get him back to Caledonian Road as soon as possible.

On the top deck of the bus, he managed to find a back seat where he could light up his pipe and add to the thick smoke that was already stifling the confined space up there. He lay back and closed his eyes. In his mind, he was already back home at The Chapel. Grace was waiting for him, waiting for an explanation. Where had he been today? What was he keeping from her? He was tongue-tied. He didn't know what to say to her. What *could* he say to her? His eyes sprang open again. He looked out of the bus window to the pavement below. The first thing he saw was a scribbled headline on a newspaper billboard: 'WAR IN CHINA. MOMENT OF TRUTH.'

Gus closed his eyes again. The truth of his own predicament was now burning in his soul.

Chapter 6

The 'Moment of Truth' for China came on 7 July 1937, when Japanese forces, which had already invaded the Chinese mainland after making countless territorial claims, attacked Chinese forces near Peking. Despite the condemnations of the attack coming from Foreign Minister Anthony Eden in England, and President Roosevelt in the United States, it was the start of what was to be a long and protracted war between the two Far Eastern countries. In Europe the bitter civil war in Spain, between the Popular Front Communist Party and General Franco's Falangists, claimed thousands of lives, including many young British volunteers who had gone to fight alongside their 'comrade brothers' in what they saw as a universal struggle against imperialism.

One of those volunteers was young Reg Cooker, Aunt Josie and Uncle Stan's son, who early one morning had just packed his things in a rucksack and left home. In the emotional note he had left behind for his parents on the mantelpiece in the parlour, he had referred to the war in Spain as 'everyone's war', and added that if the 'forces of evil aren't stopped now, there will be no hope left for the entire world'.

Josie was beside herself with worry, and when Gus and Grace heard what had happened, they rushed straight over to Stoke Newington after their Tuesday rounds, to see what help they could give. When they got there, they found Josie and Viv in tears, and Stan pacing up and down the room in such anger, saying that all he wanted to do was to 'throttle the silly little bugger!'

'But there must be something you can do?' insisted Grace, sitting on the sofa with the distraught Aunt Josie, trying her best to comfort her. 'Can't you complain to the police or something?'

'The coppers?' yelled Stan. 'They ain't worf the bleedin' money we pay 'em. I went down the station first fing this mornin', an' d'yer know wot they said? They said, "This is a problem we all 'ave ter face, Mr Cooker. When our kids fink they're goin' off ter save the world, what can we do about it?" '

'Well, they 'ave got a point there,' said Gus, grim-faced.

'Dad!' scolded Grace.

'Well, it's true!' insisted Gus, who was already smoking out the room with his pipe. 'These days they believe all the rubbish they read in the newspapers, then they go off an' meet up wiv their pals. That's when the trouble starts.'

'What d'yer mean?' grunted Stan.

'They want ter experiment, Stan,' replied Gus.

'Experiment?'

'Wiv life.' Gus took his pipe out of his mouth, and shook his head. 'There are so many different causes these young lads can latch on to. At Reg's age, they're ready ter listen ter any ruction that's goin' on in the country. You take ol' Mosley fer instance. Most of those troublemakers around him are young kids just like Reg. They get stars in their eyes when they get a chance ter wear those fancy black uniforms.'

Grace glared at her father. Although well intentioned, she found his remarks most unhelpful.

Stan came across to the meal table where Gus was sitting. He pointed a threatening finger at him. 'Are you sayin' my boy's a troublemaker?'

'No, Stan,' replied Gus. 'Wot I'm sayin' is that there are a lot of dangerous men around in this world – Fascists,

Bolsheviks, insurgents, mind-benders – call 'em wot yer like. But they're all just waitin' out there, waitin' ter turn the minds of young kids like Reg.'

'It's all very well fer you, Gus 'Iggs,' sniffed Josie. 'You 'aven't 'ad a boy of yer own. Yer don't know wot it's like ter sit up late night after night, wonderin' wot 'e's goin' ter do next.'

Gus flicked a quick glance at Grace. 'You're right, Jose,' he commiserated. 'I don't 'ave a boy of me own. But I *do* know wot it was like when I was Reg's age. I'd've probably done the same fing.'

'You're bonkers, mate!' croaked Stan, turning away from him. 'You running away ter join the Merchant Navy ain't nuffin' like wot Reg's done.'

'Maybe not, Stan,' replied Gus. 'But it's all about the same fing, y'know – independence.'

'Independence?'

'Doin' somefin' on yer own, wivout 'avin' yer mum or dad tellin' yer wot ter do all the time.'

Stan had no time to reply before Hilda's voice came rasping into the room. 'Wot's all this then?' she bellowed. 'Wot's that idiot son er yours been up to this time?'

Josie immediately burst into tears.

'If it's all the same ter you, 'Ilda Barnet,' growled Stan, 'I'll ask yer not ter talk about my son like that.'

'Well, 'e must be an idiot if 'e goes rushin' off ter some foreign country without a by-yer-leave!' She didn't wait for a response from anyone. She just plonked herself and her handbag down on the nearest armchair. 'So where's 'e gone?' she demanded.

'Yer *know* where 'e's gone, 'Ilda!' spluttered poor Josie between sobs. ' 'E's gone off ter fight in Spain.'

'Stupid place ter go to!' retorted Hilda. 'I thought the only fing they ever fought there were bulls!'

'Spain is a very dangerous place to go to at the moment, Auntie,' said Grace, hugging her distraught Aunt Josie. 'A lot of innocent people are getting killed.'

'The *world's* a very dangerous place,' replied Hilda pessimistically. 'China and Japan, Spain, Palestine and the Jews, trouble in Albania, 'Itler an' Mussolini gettin' tergevver again – I tell yer, everyfin's a mess!'

'Well, yer can't blame my son fer that!' insisted Stan angrily.

'Oh, yes I can!' snapped Hilda. ' 'E was always a knuckle-'ead! Always goin' on about fings that 'e knows nuffin' about. I told yer years ago, yer should've given 'im a bleedin' good cuff round 'is ear'ole!'

'Yes, 'Ilda!' retorted Stan, going for her hook, line and sinker. 'That's why it's a bleedin' good job yer never 'ad kids er yer own!'

There was a sudden hush in the room. All eyes turned towards Hilda, whose face had turned to stone. Stan's remark was just about the most cruel he could have made, for he knew only too well how much his sister-in-law had craved for children during the short period she was married to her husband, Bert Barnet. Hilda, eyes lowered, sank back into her chair, without uttering another word.

'Yer know Stan,' said Gus, breaking the icy atmosphere with a glance around the room, 'I reckon yer could do wiv some new wallpaper on these walls. It's lookin' a bit tatty, mate. I don't mind comin' over ter give yer an 'and sometime.'

'Sod the wallpaper!' growled Stan, eyes bulging with rage. Then he strode to the door, yelling behind him, 'An' sod the lot of yer!' The whole room shook as he rushed out, slamming the door behind him.

Josie clung on to Grace, and sobbed profusely into her shoulder.

'Dad – do something,' pleaded Grace. 'You can see Uncle Stan's upset.'

'It's best ter leave 'im, Gracie,' replied Gus. 'This is somefin' 'e's got ter work out fer 'imself.' Gus knew what he was saying. He and his brother-in-law had been the best of mates for years, and he knew that at this very moment Stan would be blaming himself for not having paid enough attention to his boy over the years.

'I fink the best thing everyone can do,' said Hilda, who was making an effort to recover from the hurtful remark Stan had just made to her, 'is ter keep calm, and then see if the police can trace 'im.'

'Wot good can *they* do?' asked Josie, looking up briefly from Grace's shoulder, tears streaming down her cheeks. 'By now Reg's probably 'alfway down ter Spain.'

'In case yer 'adn't realised it, Josie,' Hilda reminded her, 'the government has forbidden people to go from this country ter fight in this bleedin' war. Wot Reg is doin' is illegal. If the coppers catch up wiv 'im, they could put 'im away, an' throw away the key.'

'Reg couldn't care less about the police.'

This sudden comment by Viv took everyone by surprise. She had always been such an uncommunicative girl, whose only interests in life appeared to be her job as a clerk at the Labour Exchange and her boyfriend, Alan. It was so rare for Viv to open her mouth at all that the sound of her voice prompted everyone to turn to look at her.

'Wot was that, Viv?' asked her Uncle Gus.

'I said,' replied Viv, who was still fighting to overcome her own distress at what her brother had done, 'Reg couldn't care less about the police. In fact, he couldn't care less about what *anyone* thinks.'

'Yes,' snapped Hilda, scolding her, 'and *that's* 'is trouble!

Reg should be ashamed of 'imself, givin' all this 'assle to 'is family.'

'Hassle?' To everyone's astonishment, Viv sprang up from her chair and rushed across to stand over her aunt. 'Is that what you call it, Aunt Hilda?' she growled. Her thunderous voice was completely out of character for this wisp of a girl who had never even said boo to a goose. 'Well, you know what *I* call it? I call it getting his own back.'

'Gettin' 'is own back?' replied Hilda, completely startled and bewildered. 'Wot're yer talkin' about, child?'

'I'm *not* a child, Auntie,' snapped Viv, now highly emotional. 'And neither is Reg. D'you know *why* he's gone off to fight in Spain? He's gone because he has a mind of his own; because none of his family has ever been prepared to listen to anything he had to say.'

Hilda froze. 'I know you're upset, Viv,' she said grimly, 'but try to remember who you're talking to.'

'I *am*, Auntie, believe me I *am*! But *you* should remember –' she turned to look around at all the others in the room – 'you should *all* remember that there's something more to life than Sunday roast and family get-togethers. Things are going on in the world outside, and we just can't ignore them. Has it occurred to you that Reg might never come back from – wherever he's gone to?'

On hearing this, Josie burst into floods of tears again.

'I'm sorry, Mum,' Viv said, 'but that's a fact of life. We should all have thought about this before it happened. I reckon Reg has got real guts, but if he *doesn't* come back, then it'll be *all* our faults, because *he* cares about people – and we don't!'

When she had finished, there was a deathly silence. Suddenly aware of the impact her outburst had made, Viv calmly turned and left the room.

* * *

Eric Tyler rarely came to this part of Islington. To him, Holloway was the lower end in the class scale, which was the reason why he rarely ventured much beyond the grander climes of Canonbury. Until he moved north to Sheffield with his wife, Eric's patch had always been Kensington and Knightsbridge, not because he had any connection with either place, but because that's where the money was. In fact, ever since he was a kid, Eric had always had just one thing on his mind – money, and how to get his hands on it. He was born in Dalston, just on the border with Hackney, and until he got married his accent was as thick and fast as any East Ender's. However, as his ambition was to mix with as many well-heeled people as he possibly could, he spent a great deal of his time refining his accent. Unfortunately, the kind of well-heeled people he got to know also knew about people like him, and he found it difficult to gain their confidence. That is, until he met Jane Ruddock, who came from a family who had made a considerable amount of money out of manufacturing army uniforms for the War Office. After a brief, passionate affair, they married impulsively, but after a few years, during which time Eric extracted as much of his father-in-law's money as he could, his free ride finally came to an end and his wife realised what a huge mistake she had made, and ditched him in much the same way as he had ditched Grace. Faced with a shortage of funds, Eric had to find other ways to pursue his way of life, and if that meant having to eat humble pie, then he was prepared to do it.

Grace didn't know what to say when Eric turned up at The Chapel on Tuesday evening. Her father had gone off for his usual pint of bitter at the Nag's Head pub, so she was quite alone.

'What do you want, Eric?' she said, keeping him standing at the front door.

'A little chat, that's all,' replied Eric, who was looking cool and dapper in white shirt and grey flannel trousers. 'It was like old times, meeting you at the bank the other day. I just thought you'd like the chance to talk things over.'

'What *things*, Eric?' asked Grace, her hand firmly holding on to the door.

Eric shrugged. 'The past,' he said. 'The reason why it never worked out between us.'

Grace stiffened. 'Eric,' she replied boldly, 'I'm not interested in knowing the reason for what you did nearly six years ago. For me, the past no longer exists.'

Undeterred, Eric persisted. 'I just wanted you to know that I'm sorry for what happened,' he said, with what appeared to be genuine regret. 'I've been hoping we can put the past behind us, and get to know each other again.'

'Why, Eric?' asked Grace tersely. 'Why should you suddenly want to make friends again after so many years?'

Eric gave her a soft, caring look. 'Because I was a fool to let you go,' he replied. 'I'm ashamed of what I did.' He turned, and started to leave.

For a moment, Grace watched him make his way back to the road outside. But before he had taken more than a few steps, she called to him. 'Eric.'

He stopped and turned.

Grace was holding the door wide open.

Eric went back to her, smiled gratefully, and entered.

Gus and his mate Georgie O'Hara finished their game of 501 darts in the public bar of the Nag's Head pub, downed a couple of bitters, then strolled outside for a few minutes to cool down. July had certainly come in with a thump the week before, and the way everyone moved about like snails in the evening sunshine was proof that the summer heat was taking its toll. Across the road, queues had already formed outside the Marlborough Cinema for the final evening performance of the new Tod Slaughter horror film, *Sweeney Todd, the Demon Barber of Fleet Street*, which was in direct competition with Gary Cooper in the political drama, *Mr Deeds Goes to Town*, at the Savoy Cinema further down the road, and Charlie Chaplin's full-length talkie, *Modern Times*, at the ultra-grand Astoria up at Finsbury Park. Gus and Georgie, both in open-neck shirts and braces, stood on the edge of the kerb at the corner of the wide open space of Holloway Road, gazing up aimlessly at the thin flow of traffic heading down Parkhurst Road on its way north along Seven Sisters Road. Behind them, old Wally Peters was just packing up his busy newspaper kiosk for the night, and as the queue outside the Marlborough just opposite started to clear, the last busker, who had been deafening everyone with his tuneless banjo playing, collected his final few coins from the grudging patrons and left.

'So wot did Gracie say, ol' mate?' asked Georgie, taking off his flat cap and wiping the sweat from his face with it. 'Did yer come clean with her?'

Gus, puffing away at his pipe, shook his head. 'I din't say anyfin',' he said. 'No point really.'

'Are yer loony or somefin', Gus?' Georgie splurted, incomprehendingly. 'Yer go all that way down there, an' yer don't give Gracie any reason why?'

'Why should I?' replied Gus. 'As far as she was concerned, I went off ter spend the day wiv one of me mates who'd bin taken poorly.'

'But she must've asked questions?'

Again Gus shook his head. 'That's the funny fing about

it,' he said. 'She asked absolutely nuffin'. When I got 'ome, she'd already turned in fer the night, and the next mornin' we just went out on our rounds as usual.'

'Don't yer tink that sounds a pit – peculiar?'

'Ter tell yer the truth,' sighed Gus, 'yes I do. But my Gracie never does anyfin' that's expected of 'er. And besides, if I'd told 'er where I'd been, and why I went, she'd've probably 'ad a fit.'

'But yer'll have ter tell her sooner or later,' warned Georgie. 'After all, she *is* yer own daughter. She has a right ter know.'

'She'll know sooner or later, Georgie,' said Gus, taking off his trilby and fanning himself with it. 'But not till after I've gone.'

'Well, she'll be old and grey 'erself by that time!'

Gus grinned. 'Who knows?' he replied vacantly.

For the next minute or so, they just stood there, watching the world go by, the sun gradually disappearing over the rooftops above Woolworths and Marks and Spencer's department stores behind them. Georgie was clearly disturbed. He had known his old mate Gus for many years, but in all that time he had never known him to be in such a muddle. Gus seemed determined to live two separate lives, Georgie thought. Why didn't he just own up to Gracie about what he had done years ago, about what was waiting for her one day, and that what he was doing was ultimately for *her* benefit? Instead, he had to be so secretive about everything, as if he was afraid.

'So wot're yer goin' ter do about it?'

Gus turned to look at him. 'Wot d'yer mean?'

'You *know* what I mean, Gus.'

'There's nuffin' I *can* do, Georgie,' sighed Gus, ' 'cept ter keep as much as I can from Gracie. At least, until I've gone.'

Georgie took a fag end from behind his ear, and lit it. 'Yer know,' he proffered, in his most beguiling Irish brogue, 'it's a funny ting about women. They're wily creatures. They know a lot more than they'll ever give on. Now you take *my* missus. Before we got married, we both agreed that we'd never have more than two kids – maximum. So wot did we end up with? *Six* er the little blighters! Over halfway to a ruddy football team! No wonder I ended up penniless!'

Gus chuckled.

'It's no laughin' matter, Gus!' Georgie tried to impress on him. 'Women always get their own way, wotever the likes of you an' me have ter say. They know everytin' we're tinkin' before we even tink it ourselves. That's why I tink your Gracie knows a lot more than she's prepared ter admit.'

Gus shrugged. 'I don't know, Georgie. 'Ow can I tell?'

'By givin' her a few clues.'

Gus turned to him again. 'Clues?'

For no reason at all, Georgie lowered his voice. 'A sprat ter catch a mackerel, ol' pal. Find out how much she *really* knows, 'cos when yer do, *that's* the time you'll be able ter get the whole ting off yer chest!'

' 'Ow many times do I 'ave ter tell yer, Georgie?' replied Gus emphatically. 'I don't *want* ter get fings off me chest. I want Gracie ter find out wot's waitin' for 'er only when I'm not around no more. When she knows wot's in store for 'er, she might 'ate me fer the rest er me life.'

Georgie thought about that for a moment. 'Then you're not the man I thought yer was, Gus Higgs!' he said forlornly. 'From wot I know of that girl of yours, she's as tough as ol' nuts! Wotever yer are, wotever yer've been, it's her duty ter take yer as yer are.' Suffering from withdrawal symptoms for another pint of bitter, he turned round and hurried straight back into the pub.

Gus let him go. Gazing out aimlessly at the traffic as it flashed past, he thought a lot about what Georgie had just said. But it wasn't as simple as that. Gracie wasn't just his daughter. She was Alice's girl. And that made a lot of difference. With a sigh, he turned, and followed Georgie into the pub.

Eric Tyler followed Grace out into the stable where Clapper had just finished his evening feed. Eric had had a good look around the house, which he had never seen before, and liked what he saw. Not that there was anything to his taste there, but the house itself clearly had a lot of potential. He knew very well that if *he* lived in a house like that, he would make quite a few alterations, so that it would be a fit place to entertain the right kind of people.

Grace opened the stable door, and led Clapper out into the cool shade of the back yard. She was fully aware how Eric was carefully watching everything she did, but it didn't really bother her, for despite her feeling of guilt, she enjoyed being with him again. Of course, she had no idea how she would feel once he had left. Would she, she wondered, suddenly wake up as if from some terrible dream, realising that she had made herself look a fool again? But there was no getting away from it, feeling the warmth of his presence just behind her was enough to persuade her not to treat him with hostility.

'He's quite a horse,' said Eric, moving in to rub Clapper's nose. 'Horses and I get on really well together.' To his surprise, Clapper gently backed away from him. 'Well – most of them,' he joked. 'Jane's father kept several horses at his place just outside Sheffield. He used to race them up at Doncaster.'

Grace wasn't impressed. She just carried on with what she was doing.

'You should tell your father to do the same,' Eric continued. 'You know, buy a few horses and get them trained. With a place like this right in the middle of London, he could make a packet out of them.'

'My father doesn't like horse-racing,' replied Grace, turning only briefly to look at him. 'Clapper works hard. He's part of the family.'

'Pets can be expensive,' said Eric.

'We manage,' replied Grace coolly.

Eric smiled ingratiatingly. 'I'm sure you do,' he replied. He spent the next few moments looking through the stable door, taking in its load of straw stacked in one corner, Clapper's halter and bridle hanging on a hook near the door, and the last rays of the day's sun filtering through a small hatch door in the ceiling. 'You know something, Grace,' he said, watching her closely. 'I'm sorry we were never able to make a go of it. To tell you the truth, I've never understood why.'

Grace felt her stomach tensing. But she refused to respond.

'I suppose it was my fault really,' he continued, without expecting a reply. 'The trouble was, Jane fell for me hook, line, and sinker. It all happened so quickly.' He went across to her. 'I was never really in love with her, you know.'

Grace turned to face him. 'Does it matter now, Eric?' she replied. 'You did what you did, and that's all there is to it.'

'But I didn't *want* to do it,' he replied. 'You do understand that, don't you, Grace?'

Grace shook her head. 'No, Eric,' she replied without emotion. 'Frankly – I don't.'

Eric hadn't expected that blunt reply. It made him feel inferior and uncomfortable. 'That night,' he began, 'the night we were due to meet up at King's Cross, I went to say goodbye to Jane. I went to tell her that I didn't love her, that

I never wanted to see her again. She burst into tears. She said she'd never loved any man like she loved me, and that if I left her, she'd kill herself.'

Grace turned away. She didn't want to hear any of this.

'It's true, Grace,' insisted Eric. He gently took hold of her arm, and eased her round to face him again. 'I promise to God, it's true.'

'But she couldn't delay killing herself long enough for you to come and tell me?' asked Grace, her face fixed hard and grim. 'You were quite prepared to let me sit at that station throughout the night, not knowing whether you were alive or dead? You were quite prepared to let me believe what a stupid fool I'd been, and that I should never have got involved with you in the first place?'

'It wasn't like that, Grace,' he said earnestly, staring straight into her eyes. 'You've got to believe me. I wanted to come, but the situation with Jane was so difficult . . .'

'You don't have to explain, Eric,' said Grace, making a move to break loose from him.

'I know I don't, Grace,' he replied, his hands gently holding on to her arms. 'But I *want* to. I want you to know that I would have done anything in the world not to hurt you. I loved you, Grace. I still love you.' He moved his face forward to kiss her.

She turned her face away. 'What do you want from me, Eric?' she asked directly.

Her question stopped him dead in his tracks. 'I want to go on loving you,' he replied. 'I want us to pick up where we left off.'

Again she tried to break away from him.

'Listen to me, Grace,' he persisted. 'I know you've been hurt. There's nothing worse in the whole world than for someone to believe they've been rejected. But I want you to know that I *never* rejected you. All these years, I've never stopped thinking about you.'

'Even whilst you were married?' asked Grace tartly.

Eric pulled back from her.

'Let me tell you something, Eric,' said Grace, who now had her back to Clapper, as if using him as some kind of a protection. 'What happened between you and me happened nearly six years ago – not yesterday, or last month, or last year, but six years ago. How do you think I've felt during that time? How d'you think I've been able to cope with all the snide comments from my family, from people who know me, comments about the poor little girl who was jilted by a man who played her along? You changed my life, Eric. You changed it so much that even I don't recognise myself any more.' She eased herself away from Clapper, and went to stand in the open stable doorway. 'It's all too easy for a man,' she said, staring aimlessly out into the stable yard, her slight figure now a silhouette against the pale evening light. 'A man has the strength to move on, to put down his mistakes to bad luck, or bad judgement.' She turned round to look at him across the yard. 'But for a woman, it's different. A woman looks for love, and when she doesn't get it, she blames herself.'

Eric slowly came across to her. 'There's no need for you to blame yourself, Grace,' he assured her. '*I* was the one who made the mistake – not you. I want you to give me another chance, and I'll prove it to you.'

'Prove *what*, Eric?'

'That I love you, that I've always loved you.' He moved forward, grabbed her shoulders, and kissed her firmly on the lips.

She pushed him away. 'Please go, Eric,' she said, turning from him.

For a brief moment, Eric tried unsuccessfully to meet her eyes. He couldn't believe her reaction. Finally giving up, he left her, and made straight for the back stable yard gate.

'Eric.'

He stopped, and looked back at her.

'I need some time,' called Grace.

Eric didn't reply, but his suggestion of a smile showed that he was encouraged. Without another word, he left.

Grace watched him. Her mind, her heart was full of guilt and indecision. What had she done? How could she even contemplate being in Eric's presence, after all he had done to her, after all the pain and suffering he had caused her? Could she *really* believe what he had told her – that he had never stopped loving her? She slowly raised the fingers of her right hand, and very lightly, felt her lips. She could still feel him there. She could still feel the warmth of his breath, his face pressed against her own. She wanted to despise him, but she just couldn't. From now on, Eric Tyler was back in her life again, and there was nothing she could do about it.

Chapter 7

Gus had made up his mind. By the time he had finished his rounds at the end of the day, he would at last take Georgie's advice, and tell Grace everything. It was still, however, a matter of timing. Gus knew his daughter only too well, and if she was in the wrong kind of mood she would never forgive him. No, to tell her the truth about something that he had held tightly locked up inside him for so many years was a decision that he could not take lightly; he would do it only when he was absolutely sure that the moment was right. Fortunately, that moment came a few days later, when he and Grace were out with Clapper on their rounds.

'Wanna few words wiv yer, Gracie,' he said, as he turned the shop into Mayton Street. 'Somefin' I've bin meanin' ter tell yer fer a long time.'

Grace, sitting alongside him up front, became quite apprehensive. All the way down Caledonian Road her father had seemed restless, and he had even hinted that there was something important he wanted to get off his chest. What it was she had no idea. All she knew was that he had been keeping something from her. She realised that on the day she came across that mysterious letter in the cash till, with the initial 'B' scrawled on the back of the envelope. She was relieved that he was at last going to clear the air.

'What is it, Dad?' she asked.

'Tell yer when we get 'ome ternight, gel,' replied Gus. 'Better get the rents in first.'

He was shrewd enough to recognise that ever since he came back from his day's outing down by the sea, Grace had been unusually preoccupied. He also knew that she had had a visitor at The Chapel a couple of days after that, for there were two unwashed cups and saucers in the scullery sink when he got home. But it wasn't only that. He knew his girl well enough to notice that she had not only combed her hair in a different way, but she was also wearing just a faint touch of lipstick, a sure sign that *something* was going on. Or at least, that's what he hoped.

However, there were other matters to attend to first. After what Gert Jolly had told him about Grace wanting to call in the arrears, from now on he was determined to make sure that she was not left alone when collecting the rents, and when their morning round took them to Kinloch Street, Gus became quite concerned when Mabel Buck, who already owed over a pound in rent, asked him if she could miss a week.

'Mrs Buck,' asked Grace, before her father even had a chance to open his mouth, 'why not pay us sixpence a week until you can afford to pay the rest of your arrears?'

Mabel was dumbfounded. 'Sixpence a week?' she asked, breathlessly. She turned to Gus for some kind of an explanation. 'Would that be all right, wiv you, Mr 'Iggs?'

Gus, astonished, looked at Grace, then back to Mabel. 'Can yer afford a tanner, Mabel?' he asked.

'Well – yes, I s'ppose so,' replied Mabel. 'I fink I can.'

Gus shrugged. 'Well, if yer *can* manage it, it's all right wiv me.'

Grace exchanged another brief look with her father as Mabel, her hair covered in curlers and hairnet, dug into her purse for a sixpenny piece, and handed it over to her. 'Thank you very much, Mrs Buck,' she said, taking Mabel's rent book, and marking it up. 'Every little helps, doesn't it? A few weeks and you'll soon be up to date.'

'Where d'yer get that idea from?' asked Gus, the moment Mabel had closed her front door and gone back inside.

'Common sense,' replied Grace, climbing back up into the shop. 'As long as they pay a little something each week, at least we know they can't take us for a ride.'

Gus watched her in amazement as she disappeared inside the shop, unaware that she was only echoing some home-spun philosophy from a young man who knew how to make a living out of practically nothing.

During the course of the morning, Grace continued to collect something on account from those tenants who were 'a bit short' that week, and by the end of their rounds there were at least enough sixpenny and shilling pieces in the kitty to make rent collection day less of a farce.

During their rounds there was quite a run on groceries, and at one time, in Roden Street, a small queue had formed. Gus was feeling a bit under the weather, for there seemed to be no break in the relentless hot summer sunshine that had continued right through June into July, and so Grace took over serving the customers for a while, leaving her father free to cool off in the shade on a coping stone outside Letty and Oliver Hobbs' house nearby.

By the time the queue had cleared, Grace came to the conclusion that this was not the time to be thinking of looking for a job. These days, it was becoming more and more obvious that her father was not getting any younger, and would never be able to cope with running the business on his own. None the less, if she was going to stay on working for him, there would have to be some changes made, even if those changes were not popular with the customers. Of course, she knew that she herself was not popular with their tenants and customers, but there was nothing she could do about that; she was her own person, and they would have to take her as she came.

'I'm just makin' your dad a cup of tea,' said Letty Hobbs, the pretty, middle-aged little woman from number 13, whose husband, Oliver, who had an artificial leg, worked as a ticket-collector on the Underground, and who was also one of Gus's tenants. 'Can I make one for you too, Grace? It won't take a few minutes.'

'No, thank you, Mrs Hobbs,' replied Grace. 'We've got to get moving soon. We're getting a bit behind with our rounds.'

'If I was you, I'd let your dad rest for a little while,' said Letty. 'When you get to our age this heat does take it out of you. It feels like living in the desert.'

Grace smiled her appreciation, and whilst Letty scurried back into her house, she went across to her father. 'Are you feeling all right, Dad?' she asked, a bit concerned that he was sweating profusely.

'Yeah – I'm fine,' he replied, dabbing the sweat on his forehead with his handkerchief. 'I'll be much better when we get a drop of rain. It'll 'elp ter clear the air a bit.'

At the kerbside, Clapper was merrily depositing one of his customary piles of droppings, which would be good news for Alf Broadway and his wife in number 9.

'Perhaps you're right,' said Grace, perching on the coping stone at the side of her father. 'Perhaps it's time to call it a day, get rid of the business.'

Gus turned with a start. 'Wot're yer talkin' about?' he spluttered.

'It's all getting a bit much for you.'

Gus was deeply offended. 'Come off it, Grace!' he protested. 'I'm not made er jelly, yer know! I'm not the only one who's feelin' the 'eat.'

'It's not that, Dad,' persisted Grace. 'The business isn't what it used to be. You said yourself, at your time of life you should be thinking about having some time to relax.'

'I never said any such fing!' he snapped. 'In any case, I ain't got no creekin' bones. I've still got plenty er life left in me yet. An' wot about you? If I gave up, wot d'yer fink you'd do wiv yer life?'

'Oh, I'd think of something,' Grace assured him.

Grace's remark concerned Gus. It convinced him that it was now essential that he have that talk with her as soon as possible.

In the background, a handbell ringing in nearby Pakeman Street School signalled that it was time for the kids there to break for lunch. A cool breeze suddenly swept along the street from nowhere, and although it was a welcome relief, the sweat was still pouring down Gus's cheeks, so he took off his bowler hat and fanned himself with it. For a moment or so, he and Grace sat in silence, watching some of the residents of Roden Street go about their business, one or two of them stopping to pass the time of day with each other at their front garden gates.

Gus looked across at Clapper and, as always, his eyes lit up when he saw his head bucking up and down contentedly. How he loved that old horse, he said to himself. Clapper was his world, his main reason for wanting to get up in the morning. Clapper was someone he could talk to, to share his problems. Clapper wasn't just a horse, he was his best mate. But why wasn't Grace feeling the heat like him? He ached all over, and he kept trying to rub a persistent muscular pain away from his shoulder.

'So you like the idea, do you?'

At the sound of Grace's voice, Gus looked up at her. 'Idea?' he asked. 'What idea?'

'Collecting a little something on account from tenants in arrears?'

Gus shrugged. 'If it makes yer 'appy,' he replied.

Grace was a bit irritated. 'It's not a question of making *me* happy, Dad,' she replied tersely. 'But these people do have to make an effort. It's only fair.'

'I just wish you'd stop calling 'em *these people*,' he replied with a sigh.

Grace gave up. No matter how hard she tried, her father showed no interest in running the business in a proper way. She was therefore surprised when she suddenly felt him reach across to squeeze her hand.

'I know, Gracie,' he said, looking at her affectionately. 'I know I'm a difficult ol' cuss. But I'm very grateful fer all yer've done fer me an' yer mum. We're both proud of yer, gel.'

This remark perturbed Grace. It was the first time she had ever heard her father say such a thing.

When Grace turned up at her Aunt Josie and Uncle Stan's house in Stoke Newington that afternoon, there were signs that the weather might at last be cooling down a little, for thick grey clouds were rolling in from the east, bringing with them a sharp breeze. Grace hadn't visited her aunt and uncle since that traumatic day when her cousin Viv had lost her temper with the whole family, and now, with the family having cancelled the traditional Sunday roasts, she felt duty-bound to find out what news there was of her cousin Reg.

'We've had a letter from him!' squealed Josie, bristling with excitement. ' 'E's enrolled in some Spanish regiment. 'E's fighting alongside a lot of other foreigners. Apparently they're all very nice, an' get on ever so well together.'

Grace, who had very little respect for what her cousin

had done, was relieved to know that he had at least had the decency to make contact with his mum and dad. 'But how did he manage to get a letter to you?' she asked.

' 'E gave it ter someone who was comin' back ter England,' explained Stan. 'The envelope's got a Surrey postmark. But there was no address.'

'Does he say anything about where they're fighting?' asked Grace. 'I mean, if you could find out the name of this regiment, maybe you could get the authorities to track him down?'

'It's not a regiment,' said Stan, who was sitting at the scullery table, sifting through every bit of information about the war in Spain that he could find in the newspaper. 'It's a battalion.'

'Battalion?' persisted Grace. 'Has it got a name?'

' 'Aven't the faintest idea,' replied Stan, without even looking up.

'Saklatvala.'

Grace turned from her cup of tea at the table with Josie, to find her cousin Viv just arriving home from work. 'What was that, Viv?' Grace asked.

'Reg's battalion,' she said, taking off her headscarf. 'It's called Saklatvala. It's named after the first British Communist Member of Parliament.'

'Doesn't sound very British ter me,' said Josie.

'He was an Indian,' said Viv, going to the table to pour herself a cup of tea. 'Died a year or so ago, before the war in Spain started.'

Stan glanced over the top of his specs at her. ' 'Ow come you know so much about it, young lady?' he asked.

'Reg told me,' she replied. 'We often used to discuss politics, especially the war in Spain. Reg knew a lot about everything.'

'You might have told us,' Stan said bitterly.

'Not much point,' she replied. 'You wouldn't have been interested.'

Josie knew Stan wanted to go for her, so she quickly changed the subject. 'I'm sorry yer dad's not feelin' too special, Grace,' she said. 'Is 'e goin' ter see the doctor?'

'No,' replied Grace quickly. 'He's not ill or anything, Auntie. It's all this hot weather we've been having. It's just beginning to get him down.'

'Well, let's 'ope we 'ave some rain soon,' said Josie. 'It'll clear the air a bit.'

Bored by the small talk, Viv took her cup and saucer, and left the room.

'She's got too big fer 'er own shoes, that one!' snapped Stan, after his daughter had gone. 'She and Reg make a fine pair.'

'Yer mustn't go for 'er, though, Stan,' pleaded Josie. 'She's always bin very close ter Reg, yer know she 'as. She was just as upset as all of us when 'e left.'

Stan ignored her, and carried on reading his newspaper. Since the morning when his son had disappeared so suddenly, he had virtually withdrawn into his shell. What his family didn't realise, however, was that he was blaming himself for what had happened. After all, Reg was his son, a son that he had always wanted, a son that should have been a companion for him, but never was.

'By the way, Uncle,' said Grace. 'Dad says if you do want to do up your front parlour any time, his offer still stands. He's more than willing to come over and give you a hand.'

Stan peered only briefly over his specs. 'Fanks,' was all he would reply, before looking down at his newspaper again.

Grace felt very downhearted. The atmosphere in the house had changed so dramatically since Reg had gone away. Somehow the life had gone out of the place, as though there had been a death in the family. As for Viv, well – she just didn't recognise her as the girl who, for as long as she could remember, had sat in a chair in the corner without ever opening her mouth to anyone.

'I think I'll go out and have a few words with Viv,' she said, getting up from the table.

'Thank you, dear,' said Josie. 'I think that's a good idea.'

In the passage outside, Grace was surprised to find Viv just leaving the house by the front door. 'Viv?' she called, going to her. 'Are you going somewhere?'

Viv stopped and turned. 'It's too close in this house,' she said pointedly. 'I'm going out to the park for some fresh air.'

'Mind if I join you?' she asked. 'I've never seen Clissold Park before.'

A few minutes later, they were strolling in the gathering breeze down by the geranium beds in the park. The flowers were in full bloom, a riot of colour, mainly red, swaying to and fro like guardsmen on duty outside Buckingham Palace. A group of small children were chasing two large hoops, which were being bowled along the path at enormous speed, and in danger of ending up in the nearby lake. Everywhere, families were spread out on the grass, finishing off the remains of their picnics, and relishing the cooler fresh air.

'It's different from Finsbury Park,' suggested Grace, as she and Viv strolled at a leisurely pace.

'Really?' replied Viv, with little enthusiasm. 'All parks look the same to me.'

'Oh, no,' insisted Grace. 'This is certainly different. Not so formal. It's got a lovely atmosphere, and I love those huge trees over there by the lake.'

Viv wasn't really taking much notice of what her cousin was saying. To her, Grace was just another member of the family, a family she had grown to resent. However, it had been different when the two of them were children. They had often ganged up on Reg, who was usually too rowdy for them to play with. But even in those days, Viv had shown that she preferred her own company to anyone else's. But after Viv's outburst on the day Reg had left home, Grace had a new-found respect for her.

'How long d'you think this war in Spain will go on?' she asked, as they strolled.

'Your guess is as good as mine,' replied Viv. It was a typically vague response from her, offering no sense of thought or discussion.

'What did Reg think?' persisted Grace. 'Did *he* think it would go on a long time?'

'I don't *know* what Reg thought,' replied Viv. 'He never discussed things like that with me.'

Grace was puzzled. 'But you said that you and Reg often used to discuss things.'

'I only said that for Mum and Dad's benefit,' replied Viv. 'I wanted them to think I know much more than I do. Reg and I only ever talked about what was happening in Spain when he saw something in the newspaper that upset him. He used to say that the press in this country was always full of lies.'

'Did you believe him?'

'I wouldn't know,' replied Viv. 'I don't read newspapers. I leave that to Dad. That's where he gets all his opinions from – once he manages to get past the sports pages.'

Viv's acid remark disturbed Grace. Her brother's sudden departure had, for Viv, clearly brought years of bitterness to the surface, and now it was as though she was trying to tell Grace everything that she had never been able to tell her own parents.

They reached the shores of the lake, where, despite the stiffening breeze, children were paddling, and sailing their home-made boats. Grace and Viv stopped to watch them, but Viv had difficulty in controlling her unruly flock of light brown hair, which she had allowed to grow to shoulder length. She eventually tied it back with the ribbon that had come loose, and for several minutes she looked quite lovely, with her cheeks flushed, and her flimsy cotton dress fluttering in the breeze.

'Tell me about Alan,' asked Grace, as they stood there looking out across the lake.

'Who?' asked Viv, as if she had never heard of such a person.

'Your boyfriend? He *is* your boyfriend, isn't he?'

'Who told you that?'

'You did.'

'Well, there's nothing to tell.'

'I'm sorry, Viv. I didn't mean to—'

'As it so happens, Alan *is* my boyfriend,' said Viv. 'But he's not a boy. He's twenty years older than me.'

Grace was quite taken aback by Viv's candour.

'It's all right,' Viv continued. 'You can be shocked if you want.'

'I'm not shocked,' replied Grace. 'As long as you love each other.'

'I *don't* love him. But we do talk to each other. We talk about all kinds of things together. He's taught me a lot. I wish he could take me away from all this.'

'You mean – get married?'

Viv shook her head. 'He already has a wife – and two kids.'

Now Grace really *was* shocked.

'But if he asked me,' continued Viv, turning to look

straight at Grace, 'I'd go like a shot. Mum and Dad would hate it, of course. But I don't care. They've had their chance. Nothing they could say would make any difference to me now. You're lucky. You've got a father who's different. I've always admired him. Mum's often told me about the time when he was a chandler in the Merchant Navy. He loved the life, the freedom of doing what he wanted to do. She said that he had so many tales to tell about the people he met in different countries, the way he coped with all the trouble he used to get into.'

All this came as an absolute revelation to Grace. 'Trouble?' she asked. 'What *trouble*?'

'Oh, I don't know,' replied Viv. 'All sorts of things – you know what sailors are. They all have a past. They all know how to live life to the full. From what I've heard about Uncle Gus, I only wish I'd had *him* for a dad. Things would have been so different for *me* – and for Reg.'

By the time Grace got back home, the heavens had opened up and it was bucketing down with rain. Mercifully, Gus was looking much recovered from his early attack of fatigue, so much so that he was getting himself ready to go off to join Georgie for his usual evening pint of bitter.

'Somebody left yer a letter,' said Gus, whilst Grace was taking off her drenched hat. 'I found it on the doormat when I got 'ome. I've left it on the parlour table.'

Grace rushed into the parlour and collected the letter. On the envelope was printed in capital letters simply 'Grace Higgs', but as she didn't recognise the writing, she took it up to her bedroom with her whilst she changed out of her wet dress. Once she had done so, and dried her hair, she sat on the edge of her bed, and opened the envelope. The note inside was brief: 'Grace. Got to see you. It's really important.

Meet me outside the new cinema in Caledonian Road at 8 o'clock. Don't let me down. You won't regret it. Love, Eric.'

Grace put the note down. She found it hard to believe. What had she done, what had she said to give Eric the impression that he could make contact with her again so soon? But the longer she thought about it, the more intrigued she became. Why did he want to see her so urgently? *You won't regret it* – what the hell did he mean by that? Her first reaction was to ignore the note and throw it away, but curiosity got the better of her. She looked at her wristwatch. It was five minutes to eight. She rushed downstairs, collected her raincoat and an umbrella, tied a scarf over her head, and went back into the kitchen to see her father.

'I've got to pop out for a few minutes,' she said. 'I'll get your supper as soon as I get back.'

'No rush,' said Gus, who had lit up his pipe and put his feet up to rest on a chair. 'I'm goin' off ter meet up wiv Georgie later, but don't ferget I wanna 'ave a little talk wiv yer before I go!'

Grace heard what he said, but was already halfway out the front door.

'An', Grace!' called Gus. 'Don't ferget ter remind me ter take Gert Jolly 'er pumice stone termorrer. I promised 'er!'

The rain was now pelting down, so before putting up her umbrella, Grace pulled up the collar of her raincoat, adjusted her headscarf, and hurried out into Pedlar's Way. The new cinema Eric mentioned in his note was less than five minutes' walk around the corner in Caledonian Road, but with wind and rain driving against her, it was a real struggle to keep on the move. As the cinema's exterior construction was still not complete, the place was covered in scaffolding. But the huge illuminated sign showing that the name of the cinema was going to be the 'Mayfair' was already in place high above what would shortly be the foyer entrance.

'Grace!'

Eric's voice calling to her through wind and rain brought her to a temporary halt. But the moment she saw him, in trilby hat and raincoat, sheltering from the rain in the half-completed foyer entrance, she hurried straight to him.

'Oh, Grace!' he spluttered, immediately hugging her. 'Thanks so much for coming. I needed to see you so badly.'

'What's this all about?' Grace asked, easing herself away from him. 'You said it was important.'

'It is, Grace, it is!' he said, clearly deliriously happy. 'She's letting me go. I wanted you to be the first to know.'

Grace was utterly bewildered. 'What are you talking about?'

'Jane,' said Eric. 'My wife – my *former* wife. She's agreed to a divorce.'

Grace stared at him long and hard. She was completely taken aback by his audacity.

'Don't you understand?' Eric continued. 'It means you and me are free to get together again. I can't tell you how happy that makes me.'

Grace was in such a shock of disbelief, she turned round and started to go out into the rain again.

Eric immediately grabbed hold of her. 'Grace!' he pleaded.

Grace swung round on him. 'For God's sake, Eric!' she shouted through the sound of rain hammering down on the pavement all around them. 'Are you out of your mind? What do you take me for? I haven't said or done anything to give you reason to think I want to go back with you again. I couldn't care less about your wife. I couldn't care less that you're getting divorced. She has nothing to do with me, and neither have you!'

With rain pelting down on both of them, Eric grabbed hold of her, and held her at arm's length. 'That's not true, Grace, and you know it!' he insisted. 'The moment we met, we knew we were right for each other. I want you, Grace. I want you more than anything in the whole damned world!'

'You never thought about that the night you left me stranded on King's Cross station.'

'We've been through all that, Grace!' protested Eric, raising his voice above the swirling wind. 'I've told you I'll make it up to you. I've told you I'll never let anything like that happen to you again. So help me God!'

Torn by indecision, Grace slowly looked up at him. Rainwater was dripping off the brim of his hat and streaming down his cheeks, and his eyes were gleaming in the light from the gas lamp at the corner of the road. He had never looked more handsome, more inviting. 'I told you to give me time,' she pleaded.

'*This* is the time, Grace!' he insisted. '*Now!* This very minute. If we don't grab this chance, it may never come again. I love you, and I know you love me, so please – Grace! Please, let's start again.' He leaned forward, and kissed her.

Gradually, only gradually, she responded. Now totally drenched, it was several moments before their lips parted.

'I have to get back home,' said Grace. 'My father's got something to tell me, something important. I have to go.'

She started to pull away, but he held on to her. 'Don't worry,' said Eric. 'Your father knows all about me.'

Grace looked up with a start. 'My father?' she asked. 'You've *met* him?'

'Of course!' replied Eric, beaming and holding on to her.

'He answered the door when I left my letter. We had a good chat. We got on really well together . . . Grace! Where are you going? Come back, Grace! Come back!'

Grace could still hear his voice as she rushed into the rain, heading back home along the Caledonian Road. The pavements were getting more slippery by the minute, and rainwater was flooding the gutters, and gushing down into the drains. In Pedlar's Way, she made one last dash to reach the front door of The Chapel, but in her anxiety to get home to see her father, she missed her footing and fell flat on her face on the cobbled surface. Groaning with pain, she slowly managed to pick herself up, and get into the house.

'Dad!' she yelled, the moment she had opened the front door. 'Dad! Where are you?'

She threw her umbrella down on the hall floor, and rushed straight into the kitchen. Her father's pipe was still smouldering in his ashtray tin, so she knew he was somewhere in the house. She was so angry. Why hadn't her father told her that Eric had called at the house? He knew what Eric had done to her all those years ago. He knew how much she had been hurt.

'Dad!' she yelled, throwing open his bedroom door. Still no sign of him.

Clapper. That's where he was. Every time he wanted to have a quiet moment alone, it was always that stupid animal he went to. She rushed out through the back door into the stable yard. The rain was now torrential, and once again she got absolutely drenched through to the skin just getting across to the stable. 'Dad!' she yelled, as she pulled open the twin stable doors.

Although the paraffin lamp was on above the stack of straw where Clapper slept at night, there was still no sign of her father. Could it be that he had abandoned his idea of having a talk with her that night, and just gone off to join his pals down at the pub? It was just the kind of thing he'd do, she reminded herself.

'Dad!' she called yet again, but with still no response. 'Clapper, you fool!' she snapped. 'Where *is* he?' Angry and frustrated, she turned to leave, but just as she was doing so, she noticed that Clapper was agitated, nodding his head up and down and snorting. She could sense that something was wrong. 'What is it, Clapper?' she asked, slowly approaching the animal. 'What is it, boy? Where *is* he?' She looked down – and gasped.

Gus was lying flat on his stomach in the straw at the side of Clapper, arms outstretched, and with no sign of movement.

'Dad!' Grace sank to her knees and, with great difficulty, turned him over. His lips were blue, his eyes like glass, and fixed wide open. 'Oh, Dad!' she cried, hugging him. 'Dad . . .!'

Chapter 8

'One-eyed Max' had had a busy morning. On a normal day he would have collected no more than maybe five or six dog-ends, but today was different, for there was a funeral taking place, and the Caledonian Road was ripe pickings for not only fag dog-ends, but cigar butts too. Nobody quite knew how old Max was or where he came from, but he was as regular a sight up and down Holloway as the rag-and-bottle collector, or the Irish toffee-apple seller, or Big Tim and his dancing dogs. Some said that Max lost his eye in the military during the Crimean War, others less generous said the eye was poked out when he looked through one keyhole too many. Whatever they said, on most days, Max was a happy and contented old codger. But not today. Today they were burying 'Gus the sailor', and that made him just as sad as everyone else who knew the popular local chandler.

All morning, family mourners and friends had been arriving at The Chapel to say their last farewells to Gus, whose death from a sudden massive stroke had come as a huge shock. Dressed in black from head to toe, Josie was utterly distraught. Losing her brother in such a way had been so unexpected that, for one short period of time, she had put behind her the distress she felt at her son Reg's disappearance. Stan Cooker, who was having to wear a tie for only the second time in his life, found Gus's death hard to come to terms with. They had been mates ever since he and Josie had got married, and the fact that Gus wasn't going to be around any more seemed to him totally unacceptable. Gus's elder sister, Hilda Barnet, refused to dress entirely in black, opting for a navy-blue summer dress and close-fitting hat, and although she too found it hard to believe the news about Gus, her thoughts were already directed to what was going to happen to what she still insisted was 'the family business'.

Oddly enough, Josie's daughter, Viv, was the person who gave Grace the greatest support. As soon as she had heard the news of her Uncle Gus's passing, she left her desk at the Labour Exchange and went straight down to Holloway to help Grace prepare for the funeral.

Gus's old drinking partner, Georgie O'Hara, turned up with his missus just before the cortège left the house, but he was too upset to talk to anyone, and spent most of the time dabbing the tears away from his eyes. For him, he had not just lost a long-standing mate, but also a huge part of his own life.

Grace herself was just too numb to think about anything until she had buried her father. The shock of finding him stretched out dead in the stable still hadn't fully sunk in, and when the autopsy had revealed a history of high blood pressure and a build-up of fat around his heart, she blamed herself for not forcing him to see a doctor whenever he felt unwell. But as the mourners gathered at the house, waiting for the undertakers to attach Clapper's bridle to the hearse that would carry his master on his last journey to Finchley cemetery, Grace felt no emotion. She knew that the only way she was going to get through this day was to be as practical as possible. Once the funeral was over, that would be the time when everything would come into focus; that would be the time when she would have to face up to the consequences and reality of her father's untimely death.

In the cobbled Pedlar's Way outside, a large group of

Gus's tenants, customers and neighbours had gathered to bid him farewell. Most of them were wearing at least something black, such as a hat, or, in the case of the men, an armband, and all of them were subdued and really quite sad. They had memories of Gus – of his kindness, and his understanding – and remembered the wonderful service he had provided them with over the years, always managing to obtain some small item that they were unable to find in the shops. To them, Gus was a giant of a person, who would be sorely missed. However, their feeling of warmth towards Gus did not, as yet, extend to his daughter.

'I bet there're no tears from that one,' sniffed Gert Jolly, whose hair curlers were carefully concealed beneath a black and grey headscarf.

'She wouldn't know 'ow,' added Mabel Buck from Kinloch Street. 'The only thing that'd bring tears ter that one's eyes is if she couldn't collect the rent on time.'

'Now poor ol' Gus 'as gone,' said Jack Pertwee, in dark brown trilby hat and white shirt, and reeking of the wintergreen ointment Gus always got for him, 'd'yer fink madam'll keep on the business?'

'Well, someone's goin' ter 'ave ter collect the rent,' said Gert.

'Unless she sells up,' proffered Sid Wilson, who was there in his LNER uniform and cap.

Sid's suggestion sent a ripple of concern amongst the tenants.

'She wouldn't do that – would she?' asked Mabel anxiously. 'I mean, she wouldn't sell up an' kick us all out?'

'I wouldn't put anyfin' past Grace 'Iggs!' said Doris Cole, who lived upstairs in Mabel Buck's place. 'She ain't a patch on 'er dad.'

'Gus was a true gent!' said Sid.

'One in a million!' added Mabel.

Firm murmurs of agreement from everyone. But they were suddenly plunged into silence as two funeral cars turned into the tiny backstreet from Caledonian Road. After taking up position just outside the front entrance of the house, the back gates of the stable yard were opened, and Gus's hearse appeared, drawn by Clapper at a sombre, majestic pace.

As Grace and the family filed out of the house into the cars, the men in the group waiting outside doffed their caps, and the women bowed their heads in respect.

'Gord bless yer, Gus!' Gert Jolly whispered to herself. 'Fanks fer everyfin'.'

A short while later, after a funeral service in St Mary's church just across the road, where Gus and his late wife, Alice, had been married so many years before, the cortège headed at a snail's pace along Holloway Road, holding up the traffic as it went, Clapper taking the lead with his precious load, two funeral cars with Grace and the family just behind, followed by another car carrying the undertaker, his pall bearers, and the vicar of St Mary's church. As the procession headed north towards Archway, and then Finchley, many heads stopped and turned to watch Clapper, trotting slowly, delicately, along the great main highway, his great bush of a tail swishing to and fro in the gentle breeze, his fine sandy and white coat glistening like a bright new pin. This was a proud moment for him, his last chance to serve the friend who had loved and cared for him ever since he was a young foal.

Waiting at the gates of Finchley cemetery were a group of costermonger pearly kings and queens, resplendent in their traditional dark clothes covered in colourful pearl buttons, all of them there to pay a final tribute to their old mate Gus, who had always been one of the first to help them out when they wanted to raise funds for any good causes. And when the cortège finally reached its destination after a long, sad journey, a Scottish piper, inevitably known as Jock, who was one of the Nag's Head pub's regular customers, was waiting by the graveside to sound the last farewell. Eric Tyler was also there, keeping a discreet distance from the proceedings to show his support for Grace after being one of the last people to see her father alive.

Under heavy grey skies that promised more rain, and watched by Grace, family and friends, the vicar of St Mary's church conducted a final short service of committal at the graveside. To the accompaniment of Jock puffing and blowing on his bagpipes, the air was filled with a poignant lament, as Gus's coffin was solemnly lowered into his last resting place. At the conclusion of the service, Grace, pale, drawn, numb, and wearing a black dress and hat, threw a handful of soil on to her father's coffin. This was followed by other members of the family, including Josie, who was so tearful that she had to be comforted by both Stan and Viv. However, last to leave the graveside was Hilda, who stared down stony-faced at her brother's coffin, a look that tried very hard to disguise the memories that were flooding through her mind.

As the last mourners left the cemetery, the threatening clouds kept their promise, and a steady drizzle gradually fluttered down on to the mound of heavy thick clay that would soon cover the chandler's coffin for the last time.

Nearby, Clapper waited for the horse-van that would carry him home. But he was in no hurry to go.

* * *

Prior to the funeral, Grace and Viv had prepared sandwiches and cakes for the snack everyone was only too grateful to get when they returned from the cemetery. Cups of tea were particularly acceptable, especially for Josie, who remained quite inconsolable. Grace was very grateful that Georgie O'Hara and his missus turned up for the funeral, for she didn't really know him very well, and it gave her a chance to ask him about a part of her dad's life she knew little about.

'Sure it beats me, Grace,' said Georgie, his mouth full of rock cake, eyes still red raw from tears, and voice croaking with emotion. 'As far as *I* can recall, yer dad never had a day's illness in his life. How could he just pop off like that, without a by-yer-leave?'

'Your guess is as good as mine, Mr O'Hara,' replied Grace, who was sipping tea with his missus, a sweet-natured little woman, with an Irish name that no one could ever pronounce. 'The trouble was, Dad was always so obstinate. If I asked him to do something, chances were he would always do the opposite.'

'Oh, I know,' said Georgie's missus, in her soft Irish brogue, shaking her head. 'Men're like that, that's fer sure. They wait till they're so ill they can hardly move, *then* they go ter the doctor an' expect him ter work miracles.'

Georgie ignored her scolding, and bit another huge chunk off his rock cake.

'Mr O'Hara,' asked Grace softly, drawing close to him, after taking a quick glance over her shoulder to make sure that none of her family could hear, 'on the day Dad died, he said he wanted to talk to me about something. Would you have any idea at all what it was about?'

'*Me?*' asked Georgie nervously.

'You were his closest friend,' said Grace. 'He always maintained that you were one of the only people he could

135

confide in, that you would never discuss what he told you with anyone else.'

Georgie's face crunched up, and he was close to tears again.

'You see,' persisted Grace, taking another quick glance over her shoulder, 'I know what he was going to tell me must have been important, because it had clearly been on his mind for quite a time. If you have any idea, any idea at all what it was about, I'd be so grateful. It's so frustrating not to know.'

Georgie was now very uncomfortable. He knew what Grace was saying was right, but if he said anything, if he told her anything about Gus and his past, and about everything that had happened over the years, would he be betraying the confidence Gus had always had in him? 'Yes,' replied Georgie falteringly. 'I *did* know that he had *somethin'* on his mind, but he was a pretty secretive feller, yer dad. He kept tings ter himself, yer know.'

Grace was disappointed. 'Yes, I do know,' she sighed.

'Have yer decided what you're goin' ter do about the business, Miss Higgs?' asked Georgie's missus.

'No, Mrs O'Hara,' replied Grace. 'It's too early to think about that just yet.'

'Of course it is,' said Georgie's missus. 'Yer need time ter grieve. Time's the only ting that can heal.'

'Excuse me, Grace.'

Grace turned to find her Aunt Hilda standing behind her.

'Could I have a few words with you, please?' she asked, forcing a smile towards Georgie and his missus. 'In private.'

Reluctantly, Grace allowed her aunt to lead her off to a quiet corner of the room. Behind them, Josie and Viv were busily serving cups of tea and refreshments to the other friends and neighbours who had turned up for the funeral. 'So 'ave yer made yer mind up yet?' asked Hilda, with practicality that had quickly taken over from grief.

'What about, Auntie?' asked Grace, who knew only too well what to expect.

'What d'yer fink wot about?' replied Hilda, with a quick scornful glance at the other guests nearby. 'The shop! The business! What're yer goin' ter do wiv it now?'

Grace's expression showed that she despised her aunt's lack of tact. 'I haven't decided, Aunt Hilda,' she replied coldly. 'It's far too early.'

'Yer can't leave it too long,' persisted Hilda. 'All those rents 'ave ter be collected, yer grocery stocks—'

'I shall manage, Auntie,' insisted Grace firmly.

' 'Ow?' snapped Hilda, pressing her. ' 'Ow're yer goin' ter manage just on yer own? You *are* on yer own now, yer know. Yer've got no one ter fall back on. Fer a start, 'ow're yer goin' ter lift all that stuff up at Covent Garden each day, then go out on yer rounds? Yer won't last a week. It'll kill yer off.'

'I said, I'll manage, Auntie,' repeated Grace, who was thoroughly put out by her aunt's bullying.

Realising that she had perhaps been too quick off the mark, Hilda tried to show more concern. 'I'm only finkin' of *you*, child,' she said appeasingly. 'I don't want yer ter wear yerself out. Yer poor ol' dad would turn in 'is grave.'

'Excuse me, Auntie,' said Grace, turning to go. 'I must go and talk to some of our neighbours.'

'Grace.' Grace felt Hilda's hand gripping hold of her arm. 'If yer need 'elp,' she said drily, 'yer know yer can count on me. That's wot relatives are for. Don't worry, gel, I'll keep in touch.'

With a forced smile, Grace tried to ignore her aunt's ominous remark, then gently eased herself away and retreated to the kitchen.

Viv watched her go, and followed her. 'Anything I can do to help?' she asked caringly.

Grace, her head feeling as though it was about to burst open, looked round with a start. 'You could start by doing away with Aunt Hilda,' she replied, only half joking.

'With pleasure!' replied Viv. She went to her. 'This is all terrible. You should get rid of all this lot and go straight to bed.'

'Unfortunately, I wouldn't sleep, Viv,' replied Grace. 'Too many things to think about.' She sat down at the kitchen table, which was overcrowded with dirty cups and plates. 'I don't really know where to start.'

Viv sat opposite her. 'My advice is don't let Auntie Hilda bully you,' she said. 'She's an old dragon. If she can, she'll twist you round her little finger.'

'I'll never let her do that, Viv,' replied Grace. 'I'll never let her get her hands on something that doesn't belong to her.'

'It won't stop her trying. It's funny, isn't it?' said Viv, leaning her elbows on the table. 'Aunt Hilda is nothing like Mum *or* Uncle Gus. It's hard to believe she even came from the same womb.'

'It often happens in families, Viv,' said Grace. 'There's always one fly in the ointment.'

'I wonder what Grandma and Granddad made of her.'

'Dad told me once that they often found her impossible to talk to. As a child, Auntie Hilda had a will of iron.'

'She hasn't changed a bit.' Viv sat back in her chair. 'I wish I'd known Grandma and Granddad. I wonder what they were like.'

'From what I remember,' said Grace, 'they were just like

Dad – they lived from hand to mouth each day, never stopping to wonder what would happen if the money ran out. Thank God it never did. Different from Mum's side. They were as tight as drums. Mum never got on with them.'

In a brief moment of silence between them, they could hear the hushed voices of the others coming from the front parlour. It was a curious, almost eerie sound, as though everyone was whispering behind closed doors.

'What *are* you going to do about the business, Grace?' Viv asked. 'You don't have to answer if you don't want to.'

'I really don't know,' replied Grace. 'At the moment I'm just starting to come to terms with the fact that Dad isn't going to be around any more. But I imagine I'll probably sell up – *if* I can find a buyer. I don't think I have the heart to carry on on my own.'

'Had you thought about getting someone in to help you?'

'Like Auntie Hilda, you mean?'

Viv sighed. 'No,' she replied. 'I wouldn't wish her on my worst enemy! I was thinking more of – employing someone, at least to do the hard manual stuff.'

Grace shrugged.

Viv hesitated. 'There's no one else in your life then?' she asked tentatively.

Grace looked at her.

'A relationship or anything?'

For one brief moment, Grace had to think about this. *Was* there anyone in her life? The first person she thought of was Eric Tyler. Now that his wife was divorcing him, was *he* someone she could embrace in a relationship, someone she could spend the rest of her life with? Yes, it was true that since she met him again at the bank that day, he had rekindled *something* inside her, but she didn't know whether it was love on her part, or a desperate need to be wanted.

'There's no one, Viv,' she replied dismissively. 'I'd better get back to the others,' she added, getting up from the table.

'Listen, Grace,' said Viv. 'I know you'll get fed up with people saying this to you, but if you ever need any help – I mean, if you ever need anyone to talk to – you will get in touch with me, won't you?'

Grace smiled her gratitude, and gave Viv a gentle hug. 'Thank you, Viv,' she replied. 'I'll remember that.'

A short while later, after most of the mourners had left, Georgie O'Hara came back briefly to have a last few words with Grace. 'I just wanted yer ter know that yer dad *did* have somethin' important ter tell yer,' he said, his voice almost a whisper. 'But it can't be me who tells yer. It's something yer'll have ter find out fer yerself.'

'But how will I do that, Mr O'Hara?' asked Grace intently.

Georgie shook his head. 'Keep lookin', Grace,' he replied. 'That's all I can say to yer. Just keep lookin'.'

Before Grace had the chance to ask him what he meant, Georgie was already halfway along the front entrance path. 'God in heaven bless yer, Grace!' he called back, raising his flat cap, and then replacing it.

Grace watched him go, then quietly closed the door behind him. She turned round. For the first time that day, the house was completely empty. For a brief moment, she just stood there, with her back to the door, eyes closed, taking in the silence. She could still smell the thick palls of cigarette smoke, which had stifled the parlour all afternoon, and for one split second she thought she recognised the smell of her father's pipe smouldering in his tin ashtray.

She opened her eyes, and went into the parlour. Between them, Josie, Viv, and some of the other guests had cleared away the dirty crockery, and tidied the place up so much that she had virtually nothing to do.

She went back into the hall, and was about to go upstairs to her own bedroom, when she suddenly stopped, turned, and made her way into her dad's bedroom. Everything was there intact, just as he had left it. Even a half-read copy of the *Sunday Pictorial* was spread out on the floor at the side of his bed, and in pride of place on his bedside cabinet there were small framed photographs of his wife, Alice, and Grace as a young schoolgirl, and an unframed snapshot of him and Clapper when Clapper was still a foal. She stood there awash with memories, looking around the room, at her dad's bed, and tried to imagine what life was going to be like without him. No more tea in bed on Sunday mornings, no more nagging him for not collecting arrears from his tenants, and no more just being with him – on the daily rounds, at the family's Sunday roasts, and in the stable with Clapper. It was a bleak outlook, and as she stood there in a cloud of unreality, she wondered how she was going to face up to the future.

She left the room as she had found it, and closed the door behind her, but when she was halfway up the stairs, there was a rat-a-tat-tat on the front door knocker. Her heart sank, because the first person she thought of who might try to call on her that evening was Eric Tyler. Her first instinct was to ignore the knocking, and go up to her room. But when the knocking was repeated more vigorously, she changed her mind, and went down to see who was there.

'Who is it?' she called, without opening the door. There was no reply. 'Who's there?' she called again. Still no reply. She opened the door. There was no one there. But on the doorstep was a small posy of flowers, tied together with a piece of rough string. Attached was a scrawled note which read:

Dear miss

I was realy sorri to ear about yer dad. I saw you in that car behind his coffin when you was goin up the cemmetary. I wish I could do something ter help but anyway heres hopin these flowers will cheer you up. I got them out the Gremlins garden but they said they didn't mind at all.

All the best
Mickey (Burke)

Grace folded up the note, and looked at the flowers, a carefully arranged bunch of dandelions, white daisies, and two red roses. She took them inside, closed the door, and leaned her back against it. She smelt the flowers. To her, they were the sweetest she had ever known. She clasped them to her chest. Tears welled up in her eyes, and started to trickle down her cheeks. It was the kindest thing anyone had ever done for her.

'I'm sorry I couldn't get to your father's funeral,' said Dick Rumble sombrely. 'I'm afraid there was quite a lot going on here, and I just couldn't get away.'

Grace had waited for several days after the funeral before going to see her father's friend and bank manager, but if she was going to start making decisions, it was time to get things sorted out.

'I can hardly believe what's happened,' continued Rumble with a sigh, sitting back in his chair. 'Gus was such a lively man. I really thought he was the kind of person who was going to live to a ripe old age.'

Grace sat back in her chair, eyes lowered.

Rumble sighed again. 'Oh well,' he said, 'I suppose in life we're all in the midst of death.' He leaned forward, linked his hands together, rested them on the desk in front of him, and looked across at Grace. 'So what now, my dear?'

'I think I've decided to sell up,' she replied. 'I don't have either the will or the energy to carry on.'

'What's happened to the shop now?' asked Rumble.

'I'm leaving it in the yard until I find a buyer,' she replied. 'And I don't intend to renew any of the stock. As far as the rents are concerned, I'll carry on collecting them until I can sell off the properties.'

Rumble's expression changed. 'Yes,' he said glumly. 'I wanted to talk to you about that.'

Grace looked concerned. 'Why? Is something wrong?'

'Well,' said Rumble, getting up from his desk and going to his filing cabinet, 'the fact is, Grace, none of those properties actually belongs to your father. They haven't for quite a few years.'

'What!'

'There was a time when your father was seriously short of funds,' continued Rumble. 'So – I arranged for him to take out a loan. I'm afraid it was rather a large one.'

Grace could hardly believe what she was hearing. 'But – if the houses don't belong to us, who *do* they belong to?'

Rumble hesitated before answering. 'To *us*, Grace,' he replied, taking a file out of the cabinet. 'To the bank.'

Grace felt as though she'd been struck by lightning. 'The bank – owns *all* the houses?' she asked.

'Yes, Grace,' replied Rumble. 'All fifteen of them. Your father originally bought them on a mortgage, which he was still paying back.' He handed her the file. 'You'll find details of all the transactions here. Have a quick look through it.'

Grace nervously took the thick file from him, put it on the edge of the desk in front of her, and opened it. Rumble watched, whilst she flicked through, stopping briefly to look at letters, statements, and agreements. 'You mean, we've been collecting rents all these years, and the revenue has been paid to the bank?'

'A percentage of it, Grace,' replied Rumble, sitting at his desk opposite her again. 'Your father was left just enough to carry on the business. Unfortunately, as you know, he was quite a generous man. The monthly payments into the bank weren't all that they should have been.'

Grace found it hard to take in what she was looking through in the file, especially the letter from her father, promising to bring the loan payments up to date as soon as possible, and guaranteeing, in his own words, 'It won't be long before the business picks up again. Then I'll pay off the whole account once and for all.' Thoroughly distressed, Grace closed the file and handed it back to Rumble.

'I'm sorry to be the bearer of bad news, Grace,' said Rumble. 'But that's the way it is. I wanted to tell you about this a long time ago, but customer confidentiality prevented me from doing so.'

Grace flopped back into her chair again. 'But with respect, Mr Rumble,' she said, 'what I don't understand is, the last time I saw you, you said there were still plenty of funds in the business account, enough to keep the books balanced.'

'There were, my dear,' replied Rumble. 'Unfortunately, upon your father's death, those funds were confiscated by the bank to help pay off the loan. There's nothing I can do about that.'

Grace was now beside herself with worry. 'I also seem to remember your saying something about the fact that my future will be taken care of "adequately". What did you mean by that?'

Rumble leant forward across his desk again. 'Grace,' he

said solemnly, 'I think you're probably aware that your father never made a will? God knows, over the years I tried to persuade him to do so.'

Grace shook her head. 'He never discussed things like that with me,' she replied.

'However,' continued Rumble, 'apart from your own house, he did have *something* to leave. What it is, I can't actually tell you. But he left this for you.' He got up from his seat, and stretched across to a large cash box on one side of his desk. 'We've kept it in the bank's vaults for him for some years.' He placed the box on the edge of his desk in front of her. 'The only problem is that I don't have the key.'

Grace looked at the battered old box. 'Well, how do I open it?' she asked.

'He kept the key somewhere at home,' replied Rumble evasively. 'Where exactly, I have no idea. All I can tell you is that I promised not to discuss the matter with you whilst he was still alive.'

Grace was baffled. 'Why all the secrecy?' she asked, staring at the box.

Rumble shrugged. 'You know your father,' he replied. 'He was a man of many parts. But I've at least carried out his wish, Grace. The box is now yours.' He came round to her from behind his desk. 'What I suggest you do is to take it home with you. If you will allow me, I'd like to pay for you to take a taxi.'

A few minutes later, Grace, her father's cash box on the seat beside her, made her way home in a taxi. Her meeting with Mr Rumble had been so utterly distressing, she hadn't the faintest idea how she was going to cope with things. Over and over again, she asked herself how her father could have kept so much from her over the years, so much that would affect both their lives. And how *could* he have just sold off those houses to the bank without ever telling her? It was so thoughtless of him, so terribly unfair. Now she was in a real panic. Despite Mr Rumble's assurance that the bank would not press for an immediate repayment of the loan, how on earth would she ever be able to pay it off? What it meant, of course, was that the decision to sell up the business had now been made for her. There was no way she could keep it on, nor indeed The Chapel itself. The days of living in the clouds were over. This was a time for practicality, for reality. If everything had to be sold, then so be it.

But then her heart sank. Clapper. What would she do about Clapper? Unconsciously, she thumped her father's cash box with her fist.

As soon as she got home, she took the box straight to her father's bedroom and put it down on his bed. For a moment, she just stood there, staring at it. What was in it, she wondered. It was heavy, so it probably meant that it was full of junk. How stupid of her father not to say where he kept the key! It was so typical of him, so frustrating not to know. She casually looked around the room. If the key was anywhere, it was more than likely to be right here. But where? First thing in the morning she would start the search. But not now. Too much to do.

In the stable, Clapper ignored the bucket of oats Grace had put down for him. It was a worry, for the poor creature had not been eating well since Gus had passed away. Grace was in a quandary. As she replaced the old straw for him, all sorts of ghastly thoughts came to mind. What could she do with Clapper? Thanks to what her father had done, there was no way she could keep him now. But who would buy a six-year-old horse that had been trained for nothing other than to trot around the streets of Islington, pulling a mobile shop behind him?

'You're a problem, Clapper,' she said, giving him a comfortable rub behind the ear. 'What are we going to do with you?'

Clapper did not respond. He just stood there quite motionless. Grace looked at him. She had a nagging feeling in her stomach. Clapper was just one of the many problems she was going to have to face up to. She feared the worst.

Chapter 9

During the following week, Grace made strenuous efforts to find the key to her father's cash box, searching every part of his bedroom over and over again. It was a harrowing task, going through the clothes in his wardrobe, for there were so many personal things in his pockets that reminded her of him – small, insignificant things such as a rolled-up tobacco packet, his old penknife, which he had had since his Merchant Navy days, various scraps of paper to remind him of things he needed to get for his customers, and even lumps of sugar for Clapper. However, no matter how hard she tried, she could not find the elusive key.

Gus's tenants and customers felt his loss acutely, and when word got around that Grace had decided to sell the business, the tenants felt it imperative to know what the future would now hold for them. With this in mind, Sid Wilson from Mayton Street was sent along as a kind of representative of all the residents, to see Grace at The Chapel.

'It's not that we're tryin' ter pry inter yer business, Miss 'Iggs,' said Sid, sitting uneasily on an armchair in the front parlour with a cup of tea balanced precariously on his knee, his black, carefully greased-down quiff looking like a question mark on top of his head, 'it's just that we're all a bit nervous about what'll happen to us if we get a new landlord.'

Grace sat back in her own armchair, and did her best not to notice the bare patch in the middle of Sid's head, which the quiff was supposed to cover. 'I imagine things will carry on much the same, Mr Wilson,' she replied. 'The only difference might be that the new owner wouldn't want to carry on with the shop.'

'Oh dear,' said Sid with a sigh. 'That's a terrible shame. Seein' Gus in that ol' van 'as bin such a part of our lives over the years. It won't be the same without 'im an' ol' Clapper any more.' He suddenly looked up. A terrible thought had just occurred to him. 'That's a point,' he said anxiously. 'What *are* yer goin' ter do about Clapper?'

Grace put her own cup and saucer down on a small table beside her. 'At the moment, Mr Wilson,' she replied awkwardly, 'I really couldn't say. I'm afraid it wouldn't be easy for me to look after him single-handed.'

Sid's eyes widened. 'But yer – yer wouldn't—' he spluttered.

Grace averted her look. 'I – don't know, Mr Wilson,' she replied with difficulty.

Sid bit his lip anxiously. The thought that Grace might be considering having Clapper put down horrified Sid. Clapper had become just as much a part of Gus Higgs's weekly rounds as Gus himself, and the idea that the horse might have to be got rid of just because Grace couldn't look after him sent a cold shiver up and down Sid's spine.

'Oh dear,' he sighed, putting his own cup and saucer down on the table at his side.

'Mr Wilson,' said Grace formally, 'I'll let you know when I've made any firm decisions about what I'm going to do with the properties, but I do think you should warn the other tenants about the arrears.'

Sid, alarmed, looked up at her. 'Arrears?' he asked.

'The outstanding arrears,' replied Grace. 'A future owner might not be quite so – shall we say – *understanding* as my father has been. I will, of course, suggest to whoever takes over that tenants who *are* in arrears should be given the chance to continue to pay them off in small payments on account each week, but I just want everyone to know that once the properties are out of my hands, I won't have any further say in how the business is run.'

Sid looked thunderstruck. Grace's cool appraisal of the situation, and the way she had passed the information on to him, confirmed her reputation for being as hard as nails.

'I'd better be on me way,' he said, getting up from the chair.

'Thank you for coming,' Grace said, showing him to the door. 'If there's anything else you want to know, please don't hesitate to come and see me.'

'Right you are,' replied Sid, without really taking in what she had said. 'It's a funny fing, ain't it?' he said, stopping at the parlour door. 'I'm goin' ter be sixty-five years old in a few months' time. That means I 'ave ter retire from the railways. They say they're goin' ter give me a gold watch.' He grunted ironically. 'Don't seem much for forty years er service, do it? Forty years er gettin' up at the crack er dawn one week, an' forty years er gettin' ter bed in the middle of the night anuvver week. Dedication an' 'ard work don't mean nuffin' ter no one these days, Miss 'Iggs. As far as the new generation're concerned, you're just a spent force.'

Grace was no fool. She knew what he was trying to say to her.

Sid followed her to the front door. 'Oh, by the way,' he said, as she opened the door for him. 'Everyone asked me ter say 'ow sorry they are – about yer farvver, that is. 'E was a good man, that's fer sure. We're all goin' ter miss 'im.'

'Thank you, Mr Wilson.'

'Fank *you*, Miss 'Iggs,' replied Sid, putting on his cap. He left the house, and made his way to the road outside without once turning to look back at her.

A short while later, Grace went into the stable to feed Clapper, but, as she expected, he still hadn't touched the oats she had put into his trough early that morning. When she entered the stable, she found him stretched out on the straw, dozing. He hardly seemed to have enough energy even to raise his head to look up at her. Now really concerned, Grace knelt down alongside him, only too aware that he was pining so much for Gus that he was beginning to lose weight. What she hadn't realised, however, was that she had taken to talking to Clapper as though he could understand her, just like her father had done for years.

'This is no good, Clapper,' she said, gently stroking his coat, which had lost much of its fine lustre. 'This is not what Dad would have wanted. We've got to face up to this, Clapper. We can't ignore what's happened.' She drew closer. 'Yes, I know,' she continued, gently rubbing her fingers behind his ear. 'I miss him too. Despite his stupidity, despite the mess he's left us in, I *do* miss him. But we have to go on, Clapper. We can't just stop living because—'

She stopped what she was saying. After the impression she had given to Sid Wilson about Clapper's future, it seemed so heartless to talk to this poor creature about a future life, for even if she *could* give Clapper the will to live, she would never be able to find enough money to hold on to him. She changed the way she was sitting, and squatted alongside Clapper. She felt in the depths of despair. Leaning her head on Clapper's side, she closed her eyes. Although she had never done such a thing before, feeling Clapper's heartbeat somehow made her feel close to her father again.

Oh Dad, her mind was asking him, why have you done this to me? You've got to help me. You've got to tell me how I can get out of this mess.

At that moment, she felt Clapper move. Her eyes sprang open to find his head raised, and turning to look at her. 'What is it, Clapper? What is it, boy?' Her instinct told her to look above her. A tiny shadow was moving back and forth in the streak of sunlight filtering through the stable door. And then she saw what it was. Hanging from a hook on a timber beam just above where Clapper always slept was a small key. Immediately alert, Grace sprang to her feet, stared in disbelief at the key, then grabbed it. As she did so, a voice called to her from just behind.

'Grace?'

She swung with a start to find Eric Tyler standing with her.

'Oh, darling,' he said, moving close, 'I've been so worried about you.' Without invitation, he threw his arms around her and kissed her long and hard.

Grace did not resist. Despite the misgivings she still had about Eric, she needed contact with someone – anyone – someone to hold her, to love her, to tell her that everything was going to be all right.

'Eric,' she said, gently pulling away, 'you shouldn't have come here. If anyone saw you . . .'

'What difference does it make if anyone sees us together?' he replied. 'I won't allow you to be on your own any more. *I'm* here now, and from now on I'm going to take care of you.'

Clapper's head flopped back on to the straw again.

Grace shook her head. 'No, Eric,' she said.

'What d'you mean, "no"?' he asked, perplexed. 'You *do* love me, don't you?'

'Yes, but—'

'Then that's settled,' insisted Eric, breaking loose from her, and taking in the stable energetically. 'The first thing I'm going to do is to move in and help you to get on your feet again – help us *both* to get on our feet again. Together we can make something of this place – until you decide what you're going to do.'

'I've already decided what I'm going to do,' said Grace.

Eric swung round with a start. 'You *have*?'

'I'm selling the business, Eric,' continued Grace. 'I'm selling the business *and* this house.'

It took Eric just a split second to take this in. His first reaction was panic, but then his face lit up again, and he went back to her. 'I don't blame you, Grace,' he said. 'I don't blame you at all. A complete change, a new life – that's what you need.' He put his arms around her again, and hugged her. 'You've suffered long enough, my darling,' he said quietly, gently kissing her ear. 'You're free now. Free of all the pressures you've had on you for so many years. I know it's a terrible time for you, believe me I *do* know. Losing one's parent is something that takes a long time to come to terms with. But *I'm* here now. You don't have to face up to things on your own any more.'

'There's no money left, Eric,' said Grace. 'My father left massive debts. I have to sell up to pay them off.'

Eric's expression changed immediately. This had clearly come as a complete bombshell to him, and it took him a moment to take it in. But he quickly composed himself, and by the time he was looking into her face again, he had a warm, sympathetic smile on his face. 'You poor darling,' he said, giving her a quick, gentle kiss on the lips. 'This is so unfair on you. But it doesn't matter. We'll cope somehow.'

Grace's hands were tucked behind her. In one hand she tightly squeezed the key she had just found hanging above Clapper's head.

It took Grace several attempts to get her father's cash box open. Every time she put the small, rusty key into the lock, it just turned all the way round without actually doing anything. In her frustration, she was tempted to take a hammer to the wretched thing, but just as she was on the verge of going out to the stable to find one, the lock suddenly clicked, and the lid of the box sprang open. As she suspected, the box was full of old junk, so she tipped all the contents on to her father's bed, and sat there sorting them all through. Inside, she found one or two playing cards, a rusty padlock and chain, a pair of rolled gold cufflinks, some old coins, and one of Gus's Merchant Navy ribbons, which contained two of his service medals. There were also several small snapshot photographs, which Gus had clearly kept for years. Most of them were of Alice, one of them taken on holiday on a beach somewhere; another of Gus with Josie in the back garden when they were young; one of Alice nursing Grace in her arms when Grace was a baby; another of Gus, Alice, and Grace laughing happily together, and another of a very young Clapper, all spruced up in halter and brass-plate for an appearance in the annual Easter 'Drayhorse of the Year' competition on Hampstead Heath.

The last item she came across was an envelope addressed simply to 'Grace'. When she opened the envelope she found a roughly scrawled letter from her father inside. In his time, Gus had never been much of a letter writer, so she found a lot of it difficult to unravel.

10/10/31

Dear Gracie,

By the time you read this I'll be well and truly pushing up daisies, and despite old Rumble going on at me over the years, I have no intention of making a will. That's why I'm writing this. It's the only way I know how to say sorry for all the hurt I've caused you over the years, the only way I know how to make up for things I've done to both you and your mum. There are many things I meant to tell you, but somehow never had the nerve to do so. Mind you, before you get the chance to open this letter, maybe I'll have taken the plunge and told you everything, so you can just throw this rubbish away and forget all about it. Trouble is, I'm a bit of a coward at heart. If I can avoid trouble, I'll go out of my way to do so. Anyway, just in case you haven't read this until after I kick the bucket, there's something I want you to do.

Enclosed with this you'll find a key. I won't tell you what it's for, that's for you to find out. But to find out what it fits, I'm afraid you've got a bit of a journey ahead of you. This is the address you have to go to:

The House on the Hill
Dawlish, Devon

You have to take a train from Paddington, and it takes about five or six hours to get there. So take a couple of days off. You'll need it.

Why all the mystery? Well, once you've been down to Devon, you'll get all the answers you need – at least, I hope you will. There's someone I want you to meet down there, someone who's played a big part in my life, someone I've always been very fond of. I just hope you understand, and know why I've been how I've been all these years. But I hope what you find down there in Devon will help to make up for things, and give you the chance to have a better life than I've ever given either you – or your mum.

You're a good girl, Gracie – one of the best. But I hope that one of these days you'll start to enjoy yourself – I mean *really* enjoy yourself. Find yourself a decent bloke, not someone like that Tyler rag, someone who you can settle down with and have as many kids as you want. Believe me Gracie, there's a heck of a lot of life out there, but you've got to go out to find it.

Goodbye, my girl. Take care of yourself, and if Clapper's still around by the time you read this, please take care of him too.

God bless you.

Love from Dad

Grace put the letter down. She wanted to cry, but she was far too dazed and bewildered by what it said. She felt in the envelope and brought out the key her father had mentioned. She held it up, and for several moments just stared at it. By its shape and size, it was clearly some kind of door key. She picked up the letter again, and read out loud the address of the place her father had asked her to go to: 'The House on the Hill, Dawlish, Devon.' What did it mean? What *was* this secret her father had kept from both her and her mum all these years? She put the key and the letter back into the envelope again, and tucked it into her dress pocket. Then she took one last look at the snapshot photographs that were spread out on the bed. For one brief moment, they brought back a ray of hope.

She got up and left the room. Devon seemed a million miles away, but whatever happened, it was a journey she was clearly going to have to make.

Hilda Barnet rarely called on her younger sister Josie, especially during the week, but today she had a particular reason for doing so.

'Eric Tyler?' asked Josie, who was in the middle of preparing a toad-in-the-hole for the evening meal. 'I've never 'eard of 'im. Who is 'e?'

'Don't be so stupid, Josie!' growled Hilda irritably. 'Yer know very well 'e's the one who ditched Grace and ran off wiv some uvver woman.'

'Oh – '*im*!' replied Josie, mixing up a batter of flour, milk and eggs in a bowl at the scullery table.

'Yes – '*im*!' snorted Hilda, who had plonked herself down at the table, watching Josie. 'Well 'e's turned up again, an' if yer ask me, 'e's up ter no good.'

'Wot d'yer mean?' asked Josie, who was more interested in what she was doing than listening to Hilda's paranoia.

' 'E's bin sleepin' wiv Grace.'

Josie looked up with a horrified start. 'Wot?'

'Yes!' replied Hilda. 'That's our nice little niece for yer. 'Er poor ol' dad 'ardly cold in 'is coffin, an' she's got a man friend livin' under the same roof wiv 'er.'

' 'Ow d'yer know all this?' asked Josie. ' 'Ave yer seen 'er since Gus died?'

'I don't '*ave* ter see Grace 'Iggs ter know wot she's gettin' up to,' replied Hilda, sternly. 'I 'eard all this from Sid Wilson, one of Gus's tenants. 'E told me 'e'd just bin ter see Grace on business, when 'e saw this bloke goin' in the stable yard at the back. Sid waited fer over an hour, but the bloke didn't come out.'

Josie gasped. But then she thought twice about it. 'Still, it doesn't really matter – does it?' she asked. 'I mean, Grace ain't a kid no more, is she? It's about time she 'ad a bloke of 'er own an' settled down. 'Specially now poor old Gus's gone.'

'You're missin' the point, Josie!' snapped Hilda. 'This bloke is a crook. Everyone knows that 'e's only out fer wot 'e can get. 'E ditched Grace 'cos 'e got on to somefin' better. D'yer understand wot I'm sayin', Josie? Do yer?'

Josie shook her head, and started separating the sausages she had set out on a plate. 'Can't say I do,' she replied naïvely.

' 'E's come back,' said Hilda, grabbing hold of Josie's wrist and shaking it, ' 'cos 'e reckons that now Gus's gone, 'e could be on to a good fing. An' yer know wot *that* means?'

Again Josie shook her head.

'It means, Josie,' said Hilda, 'that the family business won't belong to us any more.'

Josie pulled her wrist away. 'It never 'as, 'Ilda!' she said forcibly. 'Whatever Gus's left belongs ter Gracie, not us.'

Hilda stiffened, and sat upright in her chair. 'So that's it, is it?' she asked coldly. 'You're just goin' ter let this bloke get away wiv everyfin', twist Grace round 'is little finger and deprive us of wot Mum an' Dad intended fer all of us?'

' 'Ilda,' said Josie, ' 'ow many times do yer 'ave ter be told that Mum an' Dad *never* intended Gus's business ter be part of the family. Gus set it up on 'is own. It 'ad nothin' ter do wiv Mum or Dad or any of us. Wot Grace does wiv the business now is up to 'er.'

'Is it now?' said Hilda icily, getting up from her chair. 'Well, we'll soon see about *that*!'

* * *

Mickey Burke was a bit knackered after getting home from his evening job. Three hours down the sewers catching rats and wringing their necks with his bare hands was pretty tiring work, apart from the constant distress of having to take a creature's life just because it was considered a health risk. However, once he'd had a good wash down from a bucket of cold water, he felt freshened up, and he quickly set off to get himself some fish and chips in the Caledonian Road. So it turned out to be a real bonus for him when, just as he was turning out of Stock Orchard Crescent, he saw Grace, with Clapper in tow, coming straight towards him.

'Blimey!' he exclaimed, face beaming. 'This is a real treat! 'Ow are yer, miss? Fings calmin' down a bit now, are they?'

'I'm fine, thank you, Mickey,' she replied.

'An' wot about you, ol' Clap?' he said, stepping off the kerb to rub his fingers gently up the ridge of Clapper's nose. 'Yer don't look too sparky ternight.'

'He's still a bit down, I'm afraid,' said Grace. 'He misses my father.'

' 'Course yer do, mate,' said Mickey, rubbing Clapper's coat. 'You're only 'uman, ain't yer – well, yer know wot I mean, don't yer?'

Clapper immediately responded to Mickey's attention, nodding his head up and down, and flicking his tail energetically.

'So, miss,' said Mickey, turning to Grace, 'just out fer an evenin' stroll?'

'No,' replied Grace. 'As a matter of fact, Mickey, I was on my way round to see you. I wanted to thank you for that lovely bunch of flowers you left on my doorstep the day of my father's funeral.'

'No need ter fank me, miss,' replied Mickey dismissively. 'It was just a thought, that's all.'

'It was a very caring thought,' said Grace, 'and I want you to know how much I appreciated it.'

Clearly delighted to see her, Mickey stepped back on to the pavement again to talk with her. 'Look,' he said eagerly. 'I don't know wevver you like to eat in the evenin's, but I'm just goin' off ter get some fish 'n' chips up the Cally. Feel like joinin' me?'

Grace felt awkward, and reluctantly shook her head. 'Thank you all the same, Mickey,' she started.

'It's *my* treat,' he assured her. 'I just got paid fer me evenin' job, so I've got money.'

Grace was still floundering. 'I've got to get Clapper back,' she said, looking for an excuse.

'Well, why can't Clapper come along too?' he asked. 'After all, 'e's one er the family, ain't yer, boy?'

Clapper perked up, leaned his nose forward, and nudged Mickey in the back.

'See!' said Mickey, delighted. 'Clapper's all for it.'

Mickey's infectious good humour brought a rare smile to Grace's face. 'Well, we'll join you for the walk,' she said haltingly.

Mickey's face lit up.

A short while later, with Clapper's reins tied to a rusting bench seat down by the canal, Grace and Mickey feasted on cod and chips out of newspapers. For Grace, the meal tasted really good, and she hadn't felt so relaxed since before her father had died. Mickey sat beside her, beaming with pleasure, turning every so often to watch her, then stretching out a hand to stroke Clapper's chest. 'Sorry yer don't like fish 'n' chips, mate,' he said. 'You come down my place some time, and I'll make yer a nice carrot puddin'!'

This brought another smile to Grace's face.

Mickey saw this and froze. He thought she was the most beautiful girl he'd ever seen. 'Yer should do that more often,' he said.

'What?' asked Grace, turning to look at him.

'Smile,' said Mickey. 'Yer've got luvely teef. I envy anyone wiv luvely teef. The way I'm goin', I'll probably lose all mine before I get ter firty.'

'I don't think that's likely,' said Grace, giving him a cursory look, before breaking off a piece of cod with her fingers. 'They look in pretty good shape to me.'

Mickey liked what she had said. In fact he liked 'miss' quite a lot. She was so different from most of his customers, not at all toffee-nosed, easy to talk to, someone who didn't look down at him. If she wasn't who she was, he would love to put his arms around her. 'I fawt about you that night,' he said. 'That night after yer dad's funeral. I knew wot yer must've bin goin' fru.' He swallowed his chip, but kept his attention focused on the canal in front of them. 'Did yer get on well wiv 'im? Yer dad, I mean.'

Grace took a brief moment before answering. 'Yes, I did,' she replied. 'He was the most disorganised man I ever knew, but he was a man of honour. I only wish I could have taken after him.'

Mickey turned to look at her. 'I reckon yer *do* take after 'im,' he said. 'After all, yer worked wiv 'im, din't yer? That's why yer 'ad such a good business all these years.'

Grace turned away. A coal barge was just cutting a smooth passage through the calm water of the canal, its horse tugging the heavy weight along the tow path on the opposite bank. Grace waited for it to disappear into the nearby tunnel.

'Mickey,' she said, turning back to him, 'I think you should know that I'm selling the business.'

Mickey was really taken aback. 'Sellin' it! Yer mean – the shop an' all that?'

'The house too,' said Grace. 'We've been having quite a few money problems, and now my father's gone, I can't afford to hold out much longer.'

'Blimey!' gasped Mickey. 'That's terrible.' He quickly swung a look at Clapper. 'But wot about ol' Clap 'ere? Wot 'appens ter 'im?'

Grace lowered her eyes and turned away again.

'Hey, wait a minute!' he said anxiously. 'Yer don't mean – you're not goin' ter send 'im up the knacker's yard, are yer?'

Grace sighed.

Mickey leapt to his feet, dropped what was left of his fish and chips on to the bench at the side of him, and immediately went to Clapper to put his arms around the creature's neck. 'Yer can't do a fing like that to ol' Clap, miss!' he pleaded. 'Not Clap! 'E's too special. 'E's one of us – ain't yer ol' feller?'

Clapper nuzzled up to him.

'If you send 'im up that place, miss,' said Mickey, truly upset, 'I'd – I'd – I'd kidnap 'im from yer first. I'd look after 'im. I don't know 'ow, but I'd find a way.'

'Actually, Mickey,' said Grace, 'I have a confession to make. I didn't just come to see you tonight to thank you for the flowers. I wanted to ask you if you could do me a favour.'

Resisting the urge to look at her, Mickey hugged Clapper around his neck as tight as he could.

Grace rolled up her fish and chips newspaper, and went to him. 'I have to go away for a couple of days,' she said, 'and I wondered . . .'

Mickey immediately turned to look at her.

'. . . I wondered if you could look after Clapper for me?' She felt nervous and uneasy. It seemed extraordinary to her

162

that she had been talking to him about her selling up the business, personal matters that under normal circumstances she would not divulge to anyone outside the family. But the fact was, she trusted him. She didn't know why, because he was someone who had never had a secure job in his life, and could easily take advantage of her. But she *did* trust him. 'You see, you seem to be the only person Clapper wants to know. There's no one else. No one he'd take his feed from. If you felt you could, I mean – if you could manage to – you could sleep in the stable with him, or even in the house if you'd prefer . . .'

'Fanks, miss,' replied Mickey, a huge smile of relief on his face. 'There's nuffin' I'd like better than ter kip down wiv ol' Clap. 'Im an' me know each uvver now – don't we, mate?' Clapper snorted gustily in reply. Mickey hugged him.

'I'll pay you, of course,' continued Grace. 'It can't be very much, I'm afraid, but—'

Mickey shook his head. 'Don't you go worryin' about that, miss. I don't need no money ter look after Clap. We'll be all right. 'E ain't goin' ter no knacker's yard – not now, not never!'

Grace looked at them both, Mickey rubbing and stroking Clapper, and Clapper moving his front hoofs up and down with obvious delight. She felt as though her father was trying to tell her something.

Chapter 10

Thick black smoke gushed from the funnel of the Great Western Railway train as it sped along the track through rural Wiltshire, the smart green and white livery of its passenger compartments glistening in the hot morning sun. To Grace, the rich fresh greenery of the countryside was like another world after the heat and grime of London Town. In the distance she could just catch a passing glimpse of small villages, with thatched cottages and gardens bulging with spectacularly coloured summer flowers, and trees so tall it seemed as though they would never stop growing until they reached the sky.

As it was Friday afternoon, the train was crowded with both weekenders and holidaymakers, all making for the cool beaches of Somerset, Devon, and Cornwall. The train corridor was practically impassable, making it a test of endurance for anyone who wanted to use the toilets. Grace shared her second-class compartment with seven other people, including a young family of four, who had not stopped eating since they left Paddington station. She thought it a great imposition to have to pay seven shillings and sixpence for a weekend return ticket, and for such an uncomfortable journey, and as she had arrived at the station too late to get a window seat, it meant that for the entire journey she was squeezed between a rather buxom middle-aged woman, who smelt of onion from the cheese and onion sandwich she had just eaten, and who had the irritating habit of scratching her knee cap at least a dozen times every few minutes, and a small boy, who, convinced that Grace was taking up more room that she was entitled to, kept pushing against her.

She wished she had brought a book with her, or anything that she could read to pass the time away, but she hadn't read a book or even a newspaper in years, mainly because she could never seem to concentrate for long enough. But for much of the journey her attention was focused on the man sitting opposite, who had several times read through his copy of the *Daily Sketch*, especially the cover page, which carried banner headlines about the fighting in Spain. Grace thought about Auntie Josie and Uncle Stan, about what they must be going through, knowing that their own son was somewhere out there in the middle of all that bloodshed.

For part of the journey, Grace did manage to nod off for a while. It wasn't a deep sleep, for her mind was too full of everything that had happened to her during the past few weeks. She was also preoccupied with what lay ahead. Since opening her father's letter, she had started to imagine all kinds of things. What *was* this house he was sending her to? Was she mad, coming all this way on what could easily turn out to be a wild-goose chase? She reached into her handbag for her father's letter, and read it again for the umpteenth time. The part that still disturbed her most was: 'There's someone I want you to meet down there, someone who's played a big part in my life, someone I've always been very fond of.' She folded up the letter again, put it back into the envelope, and returned it to her handbag. She was full of misgivings.

The train stopped briefly at Exeter station, but once it was on its way again, the scenery changed dramatically, for the route it took followed the coastline, with ravishing views of long sandy beaches, and red stone cliffs that seemed to tumble into the sea. For Grace, it was easy to see why so many people loved the West Country, for she found the views not only spectacular and beautiful, but also quite mesmeric, as though they were drawing you into their own inner world.

A short while later, Grace's long journey came to an end at Dawlish railway station. Even as she stepped off the train, she could immediately hear the sound of the tide gently lapping against the shoreline, for the platform itself overlooked the beach and the hundreds of deliriously happy holidaymakers who were still basking in the late afternoon sun. Joining the other passengers leaving the train, Grace found her way down to the station entrance, where many more people were milling around, checking on train departure and arrival times, some with small children looking bronzed and fit, and devouring inviting-looking ice-cream cones. But then, she came to a halt. Where to go from here? The address in her father's letter said only 'The House on the Hill, Dawlish, Devon', but outside the station she could see quite a sizeable little town, so where would she find such a house?

' 'Ouse on the 'Ill?' The ticket collector at the platform barrier replied with a lovely Devon burr, but he clearly didn't have much of a clue what Grace was looking for. 'Which 'ouse, and which 'ill? We've got plenty of both down 'ere, y'know. Just depends which one.'

Grace looked bewildered. She was hot and tired after the journey, and she didn't feel like carrying her small holdall very far in the early evening sun.

' 'Course,' continued the ticket collector, 'yer could always try Mrs Wippit in the post office. She knows everythin' and everyone round Dawlish. Only thing is by this time of day, post office's closed.'

Grace's hopes were raised and dashed in record time.

'No,' said the ticket collector, scratching his head, and putting the rest of the tickets in his jacket pocket. 'I reckon yer best bet's Ted Gilbert up Smugglers' Inn. I wouldn't mind bettin' your 'Ouse on the 'Ill is up there somewhere.'

'How far is Smugglers' Inn?' asked Grace.

'Oh, just up the 'ill outside the station,' replied the ticket collector brightly. 'Ten minutes' walk at the most.'

Grace soon discovered that a country person's idea of ten minutes was somewhat optimistic. After struggling up the main road of a steep hill that eventually led to Teignmouth, half an hour later, and utterly exhausted, she caught a glimpse of Smugglers' Inn, a beautiful, well-preserved pub, surrounded by a plethora of trees, shrubs and flowers, and set in a spectacular elevated position overlooking the sea. But when she entered the saloon bar of the pub, she was not expecting the kind of attention she got from the customers, who, with one or two exceptions, were all male.

' 'Ouse on what 'ill?' asked Ted, the landlord, a tall, burly man, who had to bend his head down every time he walked under any of the old oak beams that supported the very low ceiling. 'We got millions er 'ouses on top of 'ills round these parts,' he sniffed haughtily.

Grace didn't really know how to answer him, and suspected that the reason he was so off with her was because, like in many pubs in London, unaccompanied young women were always suspect. 'I'm terribly sorry,' she replied wearily. 'I'm afraid I just don't know. I just have an address of The House on the Hill, Dawlish, Devon.'

'Can't 'elp yer – sorry.' The landlord went off to serve one of his regular customers further along the counter.

Feeling decidedly uncomfortable, Grace picked up her holdall; with a bar full of heads turning to watch her go, she left the pub. Outside, families were sitting at tables in the hot sunshine, sipping drinks, and sharing packets of crisps and small cheese biscuit sandwiches. Grace couldn't wait to get away from such a hostile place, but just as she was about to reach the road outside again, a voice called to her.

' 'Scuse me, miss.'

Grace turned to find a handsome, middle-aged woman in a pretty floral summer dress hurrying to catch up with her.

'I heard you talkin' ter my husband,' she said, with just the faintest West Country burr. 'You mustn't take no notice of him. It's just that he ain't got no time fer anyone 'cept his customers. It's a very closed community round here. Anyone further than Teignmouth is a foreigner. My name's Jackie.' She held out her hand to Grace.

Grace smiled, and shook hands. 'I'm pleased to meet you,' she replied. 'I'm—'

'You wouldn't be Gus 'Iggs's girl by any chance – would you?'

Grace was thunderstruck. 'Why-y – yes,' she faltered, completely taken aback. 'Yes, I am.'

'I thought as much!' said Jackie triumphantly. 'The moment I saw you walk in, I could tell. You look *so* like him. He's a fine man, your dad. Always comes into the inn when he's down here.'

'You *knew* my father?' asked Grace, utterly bewildered.

''Course I know him,' replied Jackie, with a broad grin. 'Everyone round 'ere knows ol' Gus. As a matter of fact, he was in here one Sunday just a few weeks back. Just for a quick pint, nothing—' She stopped. 'Did you say – is your dad all right?'

Grace found it difficult to answer. 'I'm afraid he passed away, about two weeks ago.'

Jackie clasped her hand to her mouth. She was truly shocked. 'Oh my G— not Gus, not ol' Gus? But he was as fit as a fiddle. How come?'

Grace shrugged. 'It was a shock to all of us,' she replied. 'It was a stroke. Totally unexpected.'

'Oh Lord,' sighed Jackie, her face crumpled up with distress. 'Wait till I tell Ted. He'll be heartbroken. We all will. I'm so sorry, Grace my dear.' She gave her a warm, sympathetic smile. 'It *is* Grace, isn't it?'

Grace nodded.

'Your dad talked so much about you,' said Jackie, gently pushing away a blonde curl that had flopped down across her forehead. 'He idolised you. I often used to ask him why he'd never brought you down here, but he always had some excuse or other. I expect you'll be wanting to go up to the house?'

Grace did a double take. 'The House on the Hill? You know where it is?'

'Of course,' replied Jackie, turning to look out to sea. 'It's just over the top of the cliff there. You can't see it from here, but if you haven't got a vehicle, the best way to get there is to go down Smugglers' Lane to the old cove. When you get there, you'll be right on the sea front by the railway line. Go along the sea wall for about two hundred yards till you get to a rusty ol' gate. It isn't marked, and it's never locked, but you can't miss it 'cos there's a small stone statue of a dog in front of a big chestnut tree there.'

'A dog?'

'They say it belonged to a smuggler in the eighteenth century,' said Jackie. 'Got shot by the law tryin' to save his master. It's probably an old wives' tale, but it does warm the cockles of yer heart.' Her face crumpled up again. 'How long are you staying here, m'dear?' she asked.

'Just for the weekend,' replied Grace. 'I've got several things to sort out,' she added evasively.

'Well, if you need any help,' said Jackie, 'please come back to the pub any time. I promise you won't get such a hostile welcome next time.' She slowly shook her head. 'Poor ol' Gus. It's hard to believe.' She started to walk away.

'Jackie,' called Grace.

Jackie came to a halt, and turned to look back.

'Is there someone up at the house I should be asking for?'

'Not really,' Jackie called back. 'As far as I know, there's only the Frenchy.'

'The Frenchy?'

Before Grace had the chance to ask her more, the landlord's wife had disappeared back into the pub.

Smugglers' Lane turned out to be a narrow, downhill path bordered on both sides by tall elm and chestnut trees, which gave it plenty of cool shade, and Grace found it intoxicating to smell salt and seaweed in the air, combined with the pungent aroma of rich foliage. As she made her way down to the railway track, she could hear not only the sound of the sea gently rolling on to the shore, but also a faint trickle of water down alongside the path, which seemed to be coming from a nearby stream. She tried to imagine what it was like when, long ago, thieves and vagabonds must have smuggled their contraband into the country from across the English Channel, and the risks they would have taken each night to moor their small boats in the well-hidden cove, whilst under cover of dark they stored the stuff in the old cave close to the water's edge. It was a romantic thought, but Grace found it just a little unsettling walking alone in such a place.

By this time, she was feeling so tired and exhausted, she wished she had found somewhere to stay before embarking on her journey to the mysterious House on the Hill, but as soon as she had crossed a tiny footbridge over the mouth of the cove, she found that she had reached the shoreline, and the exhilarating, gentle sea breeze soon helped to cool her down. She put down her holdall and paused to rest for a moment or so. Her feet were almost touching the railway track, which ran right the way along the front at the side of the sea-wall footpath. Out and beyond, shimmering in all its magnificence, was the sea, stretching for as far as the eye could see, the thin line of its horizon clear and straight against a gradually dipping sun. And just offshore was the extraordinary sight of a towering, scarlet-coloured rock, looking like some strange creature that had just risen up from the sea. Yet it was curiously beautiful, a huge cone that matched the colour of the high, steep cliffs bordering the footpath and railway track.

Once she had got her breath back, she moved on. Eventually, she found the rusting gate Jackie had told her about, and nearby, barely visible from the footpath, was the small stone statue of the smuggler's dog. Surprisingly, the gate opened quite easily, but just as she was going through, she was suddenly overwhelmed by the roar of a railway train, rushing out from the nearby tunnel, rumbling off at speed towards Teignmouth in the distance, leaving behind a trail of thick black smoke. It took a moment or two for Grace's heart to stop pounding, but once the train had finally passed, she crossed over the railway track and found the path that would, she hoped, guide her to the place she was looking for.

On the way, she took a cursory look at the smuggler's stone dog. It was a poignant sight, sitting up on all fours, peering out to sea, endlessly waiting for his master who never came.

The footpath up the cliff was a perilous climb, and quite slippery after what must have been a recent fall of rain. It also didn't help that it was badly overgrown with wild shrubs and weeds that seemed to be just waiting to entangle themselves around Grace's legs. She stopped only once, to take in the views out to sea. It was truly spectacular, with the air fresh and seductive. But as she turned and continued on her way, there was still no sign of the elusive House on the Hill. This was mainly because the path was winding, and ended up in a small copse, which had somehow managed to grow on the slopes of the red sandstone cliffs. But once she had emerged from the thick foliage, she found that she had reached the lower slopes of extensive green, well-kept lawns. She paused for a moment, her heart now beginning to thump, not only with exhaustion, but anticipation. A few steps on, and she saw it. There it was, The House on the Hill, and it really was what it claimed to be, perched at the pinnacle of the cliff, grey stone and arched windows, a bevy of chimneypots that were black from soot around the ridges, and, on the red tiled roof, a weathervane cockerel, which turned with the breeze.

Now, more intrigued than excited, Grace moved on to the house itself. What she was looking at was the back of what must have been a large country house, with upstairs windows that obviously had magnificent views of the sea. Trying gradually to take it all in, she slowly found her way to the front of the house, and it was here that her breath was really taken away. Although not a house on a grand scale, the front revealed a beautiful entrance door, flanked on either side by white stone columns, and matching stone steps, which led down to a large flower garden. In the near distance beyond, she could see huge iron entrance gates to the property, which led out on to the main road, and the approach to the house was a long, straight path of tiny shingle. She went straight to the impressive, heavy timber front door, put down her holdall, and pulled the bell clanger. Again, her heart was thumping. But when there was no reply after several attempts, she tried the iron door-knocker. With still no response, and with no sight or sound of any activity inside, she opened and searched around her hand-bag, and brought out the key her father had enclosed with his letter. Taking a deep, uneasy breath, she put the key into the lock. To her dismay, there was no match. The key just didn't fit the lock. She was suddenly confronted with a worrying situation. 'Oh, Dad!' she cried aloud. 'Why have you brought me here?'

Mickey Burke was as happy as a sandboy. To be doing a job he loved, and for someone he was becoming more and more attached to, was more than he had ever dared hope for. That's why he was determined that, by the time 'miss' had returned from her weekend in the country, Clapper would be looking better groomed than he had ever been before. And he would also make sure that he ate his meals and put on some weight. The first thing he did once 'miss' had left the house was to take Clapper for an early morning trot around the backstreets. It had been a bright, sunny morning, and Clapper had shown that, in Mickey's com-pany, he was prepared to do his best to cheer up. During the course of the day, Mickey had cleaned out the stable from top to bottom, changed Clapper's water, refilled his oats trough and hay net, and renewed the straw where he slept. Now it was early evening, and Mickey was eagerly looking forward to spending his first night in the barn, only hoping that he wouldn't keep poor old Clapper awake with his snoring.

However, at about seven o'clock in the evening, he heard a loud banging on the stable gates, and a man's voice calling from the road outside. 'Grace! Are you in there?' The banging became impatient and bad-tempered. 'Grace! Where the devil are you?'

Mickey rushed across to open the gates. 'Can I 'elp yer, sir?' he asked politely.

Standing there was Eric Tyler. 'Who are *you*?' he demanded, walking straight past Mickey into the yard. 'What are you doing here?'

'I'm lookin' after the lady's 'orse, sir,' Mickey replied. 'Just fer the weekend.'

'Looking after the horse?' asked Eric, incongruous in the yard in his soft trilby hat, open-necked shirt, and white cricket flannels. 'Where's Miss Higgs?'

'Gone away, sir,' replied Mickey.

'What are you talking about?' Eric snapped brusquely. 'Gone away? Gone away where?'

'Couldn't say, sir,' replied Mickey obediently. 'Country-side somewhere, I seem to think.'

Eric stared him out, wondering who the hell he was, and where Grace had got him from. 'Do you have the keys to the house?'

'No, sir,' replied Mickey, who wondered the same about him. 'The lady wanted to give them to me, but I said it wasn't necessary. My work's wiv Clapper out 'ere in the stable. I don't need ter go in the 'ouse.'

Eric had no option but to believe what the man had said. But he didn't like it. He didn't like it at all. The fellow was older than he looked, and was obviously a real scruff. After taking a slow, suspicious look around the yard, Eric moved off back to the gates.

'What's your name?' he called back over his shoulder.

'Burke, sir!' replied Mickey. 'Mickey Burke, at your service!'

Eric stopped briefly at the gates, and turned to look at him one last time. 'I shall remember you – Mickey Burke.'

As he left, Clapper trotted out from the stable.

'Yeah, I know, mate,' said Mickey, going to him. 'Yer know somefin'? I don't fink that bloke likes me very much!'

Grace wandered around the outside of the house, desperately looking for a door that would fit the key her father had enclosed with his letter, but, try as she may, the only door she could find was at the front main entrance. Eventually, she decided to give up, and see if she could find anyone in the surrounding area who might be able to shed some light on the place. Picking up her holdall, she made her way to the back of the house again to retrace her steps down to the shoreline footpath. But just as she was going, she suddenly noticed a timber door, which was partly obscured by a hanging vine, but which was clearly an alternative access to the house. Putting down her holdall again, she quickly retrieved the key from her handbag, slipped it into the lock, and turned it. The door opened effortlessly. With immense trepidation, she picked up her holdall, and went in.

As she had suspected, this was the kitchen entrance. It was a very grand kitchen, very unlike the scullery she had back at The Chapel, with an extensive flagstone floor, and high plastered walls – a cook's paradise. What was interesting, however, was that the house must have been recently still in use, for there were pots and pans hanging on hooks around the walls, an ancient, but perfectly operable oven range, a pine table and chairs in the middle of the room, a stone sink, and several built-in kitchen cabinets. She put her holdall down on to the table, and went to investigate the rest of the house.

The hall outside took her breath away. It wasn't grand as in the magazine photos she had seen of royal country homes, but it did have a magnificent stone staircase, which curved up to the first floor. She wanted to call out to see if anyone was there, but the sound of her own shoes, tapping on the stone floors as she walked, cut through the silence and echoed around the house. Finally, however, she plucked up courage, and called: 'Hallo. Is anyone there?' She did the same thing several times, but without response, so she quietly looked around, taking in the elegant hall stand, the draped curtains at the arched windows on either side of the main entrance, and the rotund glass chandelier dangling graciously from the middle of the hall ceiling. There were two further doors leading off from the hall. She went through one of them.

Here she found what was obviously a dining room, for its centrepiece was a long, oval-shaped, highly polished dining table with eight elegant chairs to match. Nearby was an antique serving table, which contained silver platters and dishes, and when she looked into the drawers, she found them bulging with shining silver cutlery. What fascinated her most, however, were the arched stained-glass windows, depicting Victorian country scenes, which were clearly of some significance. On the walls were several ornately framed portraits of Victorians which meant nothing to Grace, except for one over the mantelpiece above the fireplace, which was sweet and gentle, showing a mother nursing a small child in the garden, with a child's swing in the background.

She left the room, and crossed the hall to the room on the opposite side. This was the sitting room, elegant in every way, with studded leather furniture, heavy velvet draped curtains held back at more stained-glass windows with thick coloured cords, a tall, polished portmanteau alongside a red leather-covered Victorian desk, and several little side tables with cut-glass ashtrays. Her feet practically sank into the red Persian carpet, which although now worn, showed signs of better days. For a moment or so, Grace just stood there, looking around the sheer elegance and dignity of the room, until her eyes came to rest on the mantelpiece above the open fireplace, where there were several silver-framed photographs. She casually strolled across to take a look at them, but she was truly shocked when she picked up the first sepia photograph. It was of her mother, Alice Higgs, beautiful in a cotton dress and close-fitting hat, laughing happily in what was clearly a reluctant pose. Grace couldn't believe her eyes. She had seen many photographs of her mother like this before, but why here? What was it doing in a place like this? She replaced the photograph, and picked up another. She was shocked again. This time it was of herself, as a young child at Shelburne Road School.

'Grace?'

Grace swung round with a start. The woman calling her name was standing in the open hall doorway.

'It *is* Grace – isn't it?' said the middle-aged woman, slowly coming across to her. 'Yes.' She smiled. 'I knew it was you.'

Grace, her back to the fireplace, was too taken aback to answer her. Is this the mysterious 'Frenchy', she asked herself.

'He's gone, isn't he?' asked the woman, who spoke with the slight suggestion of a French accent. 'Your father – Gus – he's gone? I knew it had happened the moment I saw you coming up the hill.'

'I – I don't understand,' said Grace falteringly. 'What's this all about? Who are you?'

'All in good time, child,' said the woman. 'All in good time. You've only just arrived. It's a long journey. You must be tired. Let me show you to your room.'

Grace wanted to object, but the woman went to the door, and waited for her to follow her.

'My name is Bernice,' said the woman, as she led the way upstairs. 'Bernice Laurier. I think you may have guessed that I come from France. But that was a long time ago.'

'Is this *your* house?' Grace asked coldly.

Bernice stopped briefly and turned. She had a mischievous smile on her face. 'Oh, no,' she replied. 'This is not *my* house. I live in a cottage on the other side of the garden. That's how I saw you coming up the hill.'

Grace was now thoroughly bewildered, and desperate for some explanations. The bedroom she was shown into was utterly delightful, tastefully decorated in pale yellow, with curtains to match, and from the window she had magnificent views of the sea, especially the strange-shaped red sandstone rock just offshore. But she was desperate for answers, and could wait no longer.

'What am I doing here?' she demanded impatiently. 'Why did my father want me to come here?'

Bernice joined her at the window. 'Because he loved you,' she replied.

Grace turned to look at her. She found this woman to be one of the most beautiful creatures she had ever seen. With the evening sun throwing a golden glow on to her greying hair, the sea reflected in her violet-coloured eyes, and her milky white complexion untouched by the lines of age, she looked almost ethereal.

'If he loved me,' Grace asked, 'why did he keep so much from me?'

Bernice hesitated before answering. 'Your father was an

exceptional man, Grace,' she replied, her soft French accent clear and articulate. 'He had a vision of the future, his own future – and yours. I loved him . . . We loved each other – a great deal – a long time ago. But he wasn't for me. There were only two people in his life – your mother – and you. You'll find this house will prove what I've said.' Clearly distressed, she turned away from the window. 'It's hard to believe he'll never be here again.' She quickly composed herself. 'But then, he never liked this place. That's why he rarely came here. He said it was a house and not a home.' She went to the door. 'I'm going back to my cottage to get some food. I'll cook something for us to eat.' She opened the door, and turned. 'Tell me one thing, Grace,' she asked. 'When he – when it happened, was it quick?'

Grace took a moment to answer. 'He had a stroke,' she replied. 'Yes, it was quick.'

A faint smile of relief played across the French woman's face. 'Thank God,' she replied. 'That's how it should be. That's what he would have wanted.' She turned to go.

'Bernice.'

Bernice looked back at her.

'If this house isn't yours,' asked Grace, '*who* does it belong to?'

Bernice smiled back at her. 'To you, my dear,' she replied simply. 'To you.' She left the room, and closed the door behind her.

Chapter 11

Bernice Laurier was an excellent cook – or at least that's what Grace imagined whilst she had a cool bath in a bathroom next to her own room, for the seductive smell of meat and onions coming from the kitchen was beginning to make her feel hungry. But during the short time that Grace had now been in The House on the Hill, the shocks were coming fast and furious. To be told that her father had had an affair with this woman, albeit a long time ago, unsettled her. All her life, Grace had been brought up to believe that her parents were devoted to each other, that they had eyes only for each other, so how did all this happen? And yet in some ways, she could see why her father would have been so infatuated with such a person. Bernice was a beautiful middle-aged French woman; Grace could only imagine that she was quite stunning to look at when she was young. And graceful too; Bernice moved like a fawn, delicately, as if she was walking on air.

But the real bombshell had come with those few words that told Grace that The House on the Hill belonged to her. It was so unreal, so absurd. How could her father have owned such a property all these years without telling her? Even more bewildering was the question that if her father *did* own such a property, why had he got into so much debt with the business back home in Islington? Her mind was racing. So many questions to be answered, so much to discover, so many decisions to be made.

As soon as she had changed, she found her way down to

the kitchen where Bernice was calmly preparing a meal at the oven range. Grace was also relieved to see that the table there had been set for the two of them. Eating alone in the lavish dining room would have made her feel decidedly uneasy.

'I hope you like lamb's liver?' asked Bernice, the moment Grace came into the room. 'In France it's a bit of a delicacy – well, at least the way *we* do it.'

A few minutes later, the two women were sitting opposite each other at the table. The lamb's liver, cooked in a lovely butter sauce, was so tender it seemed to melt in Grace's mouth. And there was a bottle of red wine too, something Grace had never tasted before in her life. However, despite the French woman's culinary skills, Grace still had reservations about her connections with her father, and what she was doing looking after the house for him.

'So how long have you been in England?' she asked guardedly, taking a quick sly glance up at Bernice whilst she delicately tackled a slice of liver on her plate.

Bernice looked up with a faint smile of resignation. 'Oh – a long time,' she replied. 'I've been back home to see my mother a few times, but since she died two years ago, I haven't really bothered.' She paused just long enough to make an effect. 'But I'm thinking of going back for good.'

'To France?'

'Why not?' shrugged Bernice. 'After all, my work here is done.'

Grace put down her knife and fork, and looked at her. 'What work is that, Bernice?'

'Looking after your father's house,' she replied. '*Your* house.'

'I think it's about time you told me everything,' said Grace. 'In my father's letter, he mentioned someone he wanted me to meet down here. I presume it was you?'

'Yes, it was,' replied Bernice, sipping her glass of wine. 'So – where shall I start?' She put down her glass. 'I first met your father nearly forty years ago, when he was a young man in the Merchant Navy, a "ship's chandler" he was called.' She smiled inwardly. 'He was very proud of that title. Anyway –' she sat back in her chair – 'we met when his ship called briefly at Le Havre on a return trip to Gibraltar. One of his friends on the ship was taken ill with appendicitis, and he was assigned to accompany him to the hospital where I worked. I was a nurse in those days. Your father and I talked a lot, we got to know each other quite well – too well, I suppose. He wasn't married then, of course.' She looked across at Grace. 'But *I* was. I was what was known as a child bride. It was my father's way of getting me off his hands as soon as possible. However, I didn't see your father again for many years, not until just before the war, when his ship anchored in Le Havre. By then he was married too – with a child of his own.' She smiled naughtily. 'You were quite a late child, you know.'

Grace didn't react.

'I also had two children of my own – a boy and a girl – Gerard and Michelle. They're both married with their own families now.' She picked up her glass, and took another sip of wine. 'What happened was that – we got together again.'

'Just like that?' asked Grace cuttingly.

Bernice shrugged. 'Just like that,' she replied. 'But it wasn't physical. It never was – really. I just adored your father. He was the husband I always wished I'd had – caring, thoughtful – and loving. It was an emotional relationship, Grace. But he never shared me in any way with his wife, your mother. He loved the two of you too much for that.' She put down her glass, and carried on eating her meal.

Grace watched her carefully. Only now did she realise what a difference there was between the two of them. On one side of the table was a completely ill-at-ease twenty-six-year-old from the backstreets of Islington, no sophisticated idea of what life was all about, and on the other side of the table was this worldly French woman, calm, serene, beautiful, who knew about love and loving and being loved.

'So how did this all come about?' asked Grace, putting down her knife and fork. 'How did my father get this house?'

'He won it.'

Bernice's immediate, unruffled response took Grace completely by surprise. '*Won* it?'

'*Mais oui!*' replied Bernice. 'Your father was quite a gambler. Didn't you know?'

'No – I didn't know,' replied Grace, staring at her in disbelief.

'I say a gambler,' continued Bernice, 'but it wasn't quite that. He was always making bets. What happened was remarkable, and yet quite simple.' She dabbed her lips on her linen table napkin. 'He had a friend on board the same ship. His name was Percy. Gus called him his shipmate, but he knew very little about him, about his family or home life. Well – the two of them were always taking on bets with each other, and, as Gus told me, on one occasion they bet everything they had in the world on a wager that this country would go to war with the Kaiser. Percy said it wouldn't, your father said it would. Well, we all know what happened. The following year, in nineteen fourteen, war broke out, and Percy transferred to active service in the Royal Navy. Unfortunately, he was killed in the Battle of Jutland two years later. Your father thought no more about the wager until one day, he received a letter.'

'Letter?' asked Grace.

'From the solicitor,' continued Bernice. 'It appears that your father's old shipmate wasn't all he appeared to be. Able Seaman Percy Watkins was in fact a very rich young man, with a country house in Devon, and assets of over fifty thousand pounds. And to your father's complete surprise, Percy did not forget the wager he had lost for he had made a will bequeathing everything in the world he had to your father. Amazingly, he only had one relative – a male cousin whom he never got on with. Needless to say, this cousin did everything in his power to contest the will, but Percy's instructions were so firm, clear, and determined, the law ruled against the man.'

Grace was in a state of total shock.

'This house,' continued Bernice, 'was part of that bequest. Everything in the world Percy had went to your father – including a great deal of money. Percy kept his promise.'

For a moment, Grace just sat back in her chair staring at her plate, deep in thought. It was all too much to take in.

'So you see, Grace,' continued Bernice with calm deliberation, 'what your father inherited is now for you.'

Grace sighed. She didn't know whether to laugh or to cry. She got up from the table, went to the back door, opened it, and stared out at the lengthening shadows on the lawns outside. 'Why didn't he tell me?' she asked, a question she was almost addressing to herself. 'Why did he have to keep all this to himself?'

Bernice thought carefully before replying. 'Because – he wanted this to be your future – *after* he'd gone.'

'For God's sake, Bernice!' Grace snapped, turning back to her. 'He left enormous debts for me to cope with – our business back home is on the brink of ruin. The moment my father died I started making plans to sell up! If I'd known all this was waiting for me, I wouldn't have had to make any dramatic decisions. Now – I'm so confused, I don't know what to do.'

Bernice quietly got up from her chair, and went to her. 'You know, my dear,' she said, gently easing her arm around Grace's waist, 'sometimes it isn't easy to understand those to whom we are closest.' She calmly led Grace out into the garden. 'A long time ago, when my husband died, Gus wrote to me and asked if I would like to come to England to look after this house. At first I said no. I felt it was wrong to be a part of his secret. After all, he had a wife and child of his own to consider.' She brought them to a halt. 'But when I came over to see him, I began to understand.' She smiled, and looked around the gardens, which were bursting with multicoloured hollyhocks and different shades of blue delphiniums. 'You see, Grace,' she continued, 'Gus was afraid that you were not living your life to the full. He felt that you were missing out on so much. Your father wanted you to stand on your own two feet. His idea was that when he died, you could sell all this, pay off the debts he owed, and start a new life of your own. This was *his* way of letting you know that he would always be there to help you.' She paused. 'That's why I agreed to come here. After all, I had nothing to lose – my husband had gone, my children were grown up. I also needed to start a life of my own.' She turned to Grace. 'But I agreed to come only on one condition. I told him I would never live in this house, and I wanted no part of anything to do with his inheritance. That was for you, and you alone.'

For some extraordinary reason, this last remark stung Grace. 'And what about my mother?' she asked critically.

Bernice thought carefully before answering. 'Your mother wanted nothing,' she replied. She casually moved on.

Again taken aback, Grace followed her. 'Are you saying my mother *knew* about all this?'

'Oh yes,' replied Bernice, coming to a halt again. 'She knew right from the time the solicitor wrote that letter. She agreed with everything your father wanted to do. She knew about me too.' She moved on again, her tall, wispy figure floating across the crimson shadows of an approaching sunset.

Grace watched her go. She was finding it almost impossible to grasp everything she had heard.

Bernice stopped and turned. Behind her, the changing colours of the sea in the distance were rippling, undulating in the evening light. 'I met her – just the once. Gus asked her to come down here to see me. He had told her everything about us, about how he felt, and how things could never make any difference to the way he felt about her. She was a lovely woman, so beautiful, so – undemanding. I told her that I wouldn't stay in this place a minute longer if she didn't want me to. She said, "If Gus wants you to stay, so do I." ' There was emotion in her voice as she spoke. 'I wish I could have got to know her more. She was – quite special.' She quickly composed herself, and turned to Grace. 'But now, my dear,' she said, her French accent becoming prominent again, 'it's up to you.'

'What do you mean?' asked Grace.

'I mean that, from now on, you have to make your own decisions, about what you do with this place, about what you want to do with your own life. That's what Gus wished.'

Grace, perplexed, went to her. 'But what about you?' she asked.

'I'm leaving here.'

'*Leaving?*' asked Grace anxiously.

'It's time to go home,' said Bernice, with a wistful smile. 'Now that Gus is gone, my work is done. I wrote and told him so a few weeks ago, but he came down here and talked me out of it. I always said that I would look after this house until he died. But I changed my mind, my seeds have been nagging away at me. I'm beginning to dream of who I am and where I came from. You know,' she chuckled, 'in many ways, the English and the French have much in common – they yearn for the past, always the past – but they would sooner die than admit it.'

Gert Jolly was feeling rich. Friday being pensions day, earlier that morning she had collected her weekly ten shillings widow's pension, which meant that she could afford her usual jug of stout. Her house in Mayton Street was just a stone's throw from The Eaglet pub on the corner of Seven Sisters and Hornsey Roads, so on the dot of eight o'clock that evening, she took off her pinny, tucked her mass of curlers under her hairnet, collected her toby jug from the dresser in her parlour, and, still wearing her tattered house-slippers, tottered off.

The old arthritis in her left hip had been playing her up quite a bit just lately, so it took her a long time to reach the pub. When she finally got there, she found the public bar full of the usual crowd, mainly building navvies and brickies who were working on the demolition of the old Pykes Cinema on the corner of Devonshire Road. They were a rowdy lot, and as this was their pay day too, they looked as though they had already spent the bulk of their week's wages. Undeterred, Gert and her jug pushed their way through the bar to the counter, cursing anyone who dared tread on her toes as she went.

'Fill up, Jim!' she yelled to The Eaglet's guv'nor, plonking her prized jug down on to the counter.

'Be right with yer, Ma!' returned Jim, as he pulled up

pint after pint of brown and bitter for the endless flow of navvies demanding to be served.

Gert was not amused. She jutted her jaw, stiffened her back, and glared at the boozy crowd at the side of her. 'It's time I took me custom elsewhere!' she snorted indignantly. 'It's no way ter treat a lady!' She repeated her protest. 'I said,' she shouted, 'it's no way ter treat a lady!'

'That's right, Gert. You tell 'im!'

Gert swung round to find Georgie O'Hara, empty pint glass in hand, swaying precariously to and fro on his feet. 'Yer can't get no respect in pubs these days.'

'Wot you doin' 'ere, Georgie?' growled Gert, who had seen him and Gus Higgs drinking together many a time. 'I fawt your drinkin' 'ole was up the Nag's 'Ead?'

Georgie shook his head. He had to shout to be heard. 'Not any more, Gert, me ol' darlin'. Not now Gus ain't around ter keep me company no more. The place'll never be the same fer me. In fact, me life'll never be the same again.'

'It won't be if yer fill up any more!' Gert scolded, aware that he was not only slurring his words, but had to hold on to the counter to keep his balance. 'The sooner you get back to yer missus, the better!'

'Now that's the shame of it!' returned Georgie. 'I was just about ter offer you one fer the road.'

Gert's eyes lit up. She hadn't had an offer like that for years. The chance of a free short perked her up no end. 'Well – if yer insist!' she replied.

A few minutes later, her jug filled to the brim with stout, and a glass of 'mother's ruin' gradually trickling down her throat at the far end of the counter, Gert was already beginning to forget all about her arthritis.

'A saint!' she spluttered, wiping her lips with the back of one hand. 'That's wot dear ol' 'Iggs was!'

'One of the best!' agreed Georgie. 'That's fer sure!'

'More than yer can say fer that bleedin' madam of 'is!'

'Wot was that yer said, Gert?' asked Georgie, downing his pint of bitter like there was no tomorrow.

'I said,' Gert shouted back over the rowdy chatter and laughter all around them, 'it's more than that bleedin' madam of 'is! That daughter!'

'Ah!' said Georgie. 'That'll be our Gracie you're referrin' to? A little darlin' if ever I saw one.'

'A little darlin', my arse!' blurted Gert, instantly downing the rest of her G and T. 'She's a real toerag that one! Couldn't care a bugger fer anyone. If she 'as 'er way, she'll kick out all 'er dad's tenants!'

'Oh – I doubt that, me fair lady!' said Georgie, whose vision was clearly now decidedly blurred. 'Not now that tings're lookin' up for 'er.'

Gert shot him a penetrating look. 'Wot's that yer say?' she asked.

'I said – tings're lookin' up fer our Gracie girl. She won't 'ave ter throw no one out on the streets, not after wot 'er dad's left 'er.'

Gert's eyes were gleaming like a hawk's. She pressed closer. 'Wot *as* 'e left 'er?' she asked.

Georgie, now no longer in charge of his actions, winked, and touched his nose lightly on one side with his finger. 'More than the likes of you and me'll ever get our hands on,' he replied.

Gert was riveted. ' 'Ow come?' she asked eagerly. '*I* 'eard 'is gel's 'avin' ter sell up. So wot's goin' on?'

Georgie had a broad grin on his face. 'Yer know wot, Gert, me darlin'?' he said, taking her empty glass. 'I tink you an' me need another lil' fill-up!'

Gert couldn't have agreed more.

* * *

Grace strolled around the gardens by moonlight. Although it had been one of the most tiring days of her life, she knew there was no point in going to bed. After Bernice had said good night and returned to her own cottage, Grace's thoughts were racing. After several long hours talking with the extraordinary French woman, her mind was battered and bewildered. Everything her father had done seemed totally incomprehensible to her. *Gus was afraid you were not living your life to the full. He felt that you were missing out on so much.* Over and over again those words preyed on her mind. Was it true – all those things Bernice had told her? Did her father really tell her that? *Your father wanted you to stand on your own two feet.* How could he say such a thing? Hadn't she always *had* to stand on her own two feet? For as long as she could remember, *she* had always been the only practical one out of the two of them, always struggling to balance the books, always trying to help maintain some kind of relationship with the rest of the family, running the house and home, doing all the things her mother would have done if she had been alive.

And what of her mother? Was it possible, *really* possible that she accepted Gus's relationship with the French woman? Yes, in some strange way, Grace could believe that; her mother was exceptional. She understood her husband better than anyone in the whole wide world. But why did she let her father keep so many secrets from their daughter? It didn't make sense. It didn't make sense at all. Weren't families supposed to share their problems, their anxieties with each other?

As she strolled, an owl hooted from a nearby tree. At first it alarmed Grace, but then she decided it was only a friendly call, so she decided to answer it. For a moment or so, the owl, suspicious of a sound that it didn't entirely recognise, didn't respond, but eventually it gave a long hoot back that echoed across the gardens and way up into the night air over the distant sea.

Grace moved on and, with her mind still on other things, she drifted into the copse that she had emerged from on her arrival. Despite the dark, and the eerie beams of moonlight that were filtering through the tall chestnut trees, she continued on down the slope until she emerged from the copse at the further side. From there she had a wonderful view of the sea, which seemed to stretch out from one side of the world to the next. She found it an awesome experience to stand there, with the cool evening breeze caressing her face, so much so that she felt free enough to undo the clip holding her hair behind her head. She shook it out, and the breeze helped it to flutter recklessly. In the far distance, she could see the lights of Teignmouth town, flickering like the cavalcade of stars crowding the clear sky above. Far below, the tide was drifting in, and a calm sea was rolling over on to the rocky beach. She took a deep breath. Her lungs filled with fresh salt air. And then she exhaled. She felt good, but still couldn't understand why.

Further down the slope, she stopped at the statue of the smuggler's dog, still staring out to sea, still waiting and hoping. She crouched down to take a closer look. The moon picked out the dog's face, an anxious, but kindly face, destined to remain where he was until eternity. She put her arm around the dog's neck, and snuggled up to him. 'I bet *you* could tell a tale or two,' she told him in a hushed voice. 'Couldn't you, old chap?'

' 'Is name's Josh.'

As she heard the voice, Grace's blood chilled. Someone was standing there, in the shadows, a slight figure, but in the dark, eerie and unreal. 'Wh-who are you?' she asked falteringly, her voice barely audible.

' 'Is name's Josh,' repeated the voice. It was a child's voice, small, tinny, and with a strong Devon accent. ' 'E belonged ter Mister Pete. 'E used ter smuggle – down there in the cove.' The figure emerged from the shadows, and in the full moonlight, Grace saw that he was a boy aged no more than about twelve years. 'When the police got there, Josh barked out loud so Pete could get away. They killed Josh.' He went up to the statue, and stroked Josh's head. 'My name's Billy,' he said, without turning to Grace.

Still unsure that the figure she was seeing was real, Grace asked, 'What are you doing here so late? Shouldn't you be at home in bed?'

'I come here nearly every night,' replied the boy. 'Mum an' Dad think I'm asleep, but I'm not. I brought my sister here once. She's eight. Her name's Maggs. She thought I was mad. She says it's only an old stone dog – but you aren't, are you, boy?'

Grace watched the boy carefully as he crouched down in front of the dog and stroked its head as if it were real. The moon picked out the boy's flock of blond hair and turned it white, and his face looked almost luminous. He was only a child, but in the dark and in the moonlight, his presence in such a place unnerved her.

'In the old days,' said Billy, 'they all came here – pirates, smugglers, spies. It was really dangerous to be here on yer own, 'cos they 'ad lookouts everywhere. If they caught any strangers, chances are they'd slit their throats, take 'em out ter sea, and then dump 'em. They say there're loads er ghosts out there. I can 'ear 'em callin' out sometimes. I can 'ear Josh too – can't I, boy?'

Grace got up and looked out towards the sea; her

imagination was working overtime, and for one chilling moment, she thought she could hear voices calling out in the dark.

The boy got up. 'I'm going home now,' he announced unceremoniously.

'Why do you come here?' asked Grace, before he turned to go.

'I come ter see Josh,' he replied. 'He's my friend. Dad says yer can't make friends with somethin' that ain't alive, but yer can. I don't believe wot a lot er people say. When they say yer can't do somethin', it always means yer can.' He turned and started to go. ''Night, Josh!' he called, giving the stone dog a last pat as he went.

Grace watched him scrambling down the slope towards the railway footpath below. 'Where do you live?' she called.

'Other end of the tunnel,' Billy called back.

'Isn't it dangerous?'

'Not fer me!'

Grace held her breath nervously as she watched the boy negotiate the lower slopes of the cliff, pass through the old rusty gate on to the railway track, and disappear into the dimly lit railway tunnel that led back to Dawlish town.

Gert and Georgie O'Hara left The Eaglet together. It was well after closing time, for Jim had called, 'Time gentlemen – please!' at least half a dozen times before any of his customers took any notice. By now, Georgie was well away, and all he wanted to do was to sing. 'Show me the way to go home!' was every pub customer's favourite, and Georgie and Gert's voices practically lifted the rooftops as they belted it out along Hornsey Road. At the corner of Mayton Street, they went their separate ways, Gert carrying her jug of stout, which was now flat and spilling all over the pavement, and

Georgie attempting a jig as he continued off down lower Hornsey Road to the strains of 'When Irish Eyes Are Smilin' '.

Once in Mayton Street, Gert felt decidedly wobbly on her feet, so the minute she reached the gates of her own place, she placed her jug of stout down on the coping stone outside, and sat there herself to get her breath back. Although her mind was fuzzed from the many G and Ts Georgie had bought her, it was clear and sharp enough to mull over all the information she had pumped out of him in the stifling, smoke-filled atmosphere of the pub. So – our Gracie was going to be a rich girl, was she? Well now, that was a turn-up for the books. Fancy old Gus having all that money left to him, and a big house too. But she didn't begrudge him – oh no, far from it. Gus Higgs was one of the best, and he deserved all he got. Which was more than his girl deserved. Trust her to fall on her feet. You could bet your life it wouldn't make any difference to the way *she* treated her tenants. She'd sell up to whoever offered the most cash, then leave everyone in the lurch and go off and enjoy herself. Gus must be turning in his grave. Above Gert, an almost full moon was turning the long terrace of working people's houses into a vision of pure luxury. She hiccuped, struggled to her feet, and picked up her jug. After a quick gulp of stout, she wiped her mouth with the back of her hand. She felt good. After all, she knew something that nobody else knew. Good old Georgie! She retrieved her front door key from her dress pocket, opened the crumbling wooden gate, tottered unsteadily to her front door, and went in.

In lower Hornsey Road, Georgie O'Hara jigged his way towards home to the strains of an obscure Irish ditty, but although he lived no more than a few houses further along the road, he was finding it a real struggle to keep on his feet. He came to an abrupt halt. He was burning hot with booze, so he took off his flat cap and fanned himself with it. Although everything was blurred, he could just make out the black moggie who was sneaking along the coping stones at his side.

'Top er the evenin' to yer, blackie!' he blurted, slurring like mad. 'Don't ferget ter bring ol' Georgie some good luck!' He chuckled to himself, then moved on. But he suddenly came to another abrupt halt. Despite his clouded vision, despite his fuzzed brain, a horrifying thought had just occurred to him. 'Jesus!' he cried, clapping his hands over his ears. 'Wot have I done?'

Grace returned to the house by the kitchen door, which she locked behind her. Before she had gone back to her own cottage, Bernice had told her where to find everything, so all Grace was left to do was to turn off the gas lamps in the kitchen and the hall, and make her way upstairs using the torch Bernice had left for her.

In her bedroom, she found a box of matches on the mantelpiece above the open fireplace, and lit just one of the gas lamps on the wall. Whilst she undressed, she wondered how long it might be before the luxury of electricity reached the house, for she was not comfortable with the sinister shadows cast by the flickering gas mantle. Once she had turned off the gas again, she got into bed, and snuggled up. The sheets were fresh and clean, as Bernice had made the bed soon after Grace arrived. But they were cool, cool as the night itself. So she pulled the eiderdown up so that it covered her shoulders. She closed her eyes, but opened them almost immediately. She felt uneasy about lying in a strange bed, in a large house that now belonged to her, with a cascade of memories to flood her mind. The moon emerged from behind one obstinate night cloud, so the room was suddenly flooded with a cold white light. Her mind was racing again.

After talking with Bernice, Grace now knew who it was who had written that letter to her father, which she had found in the cash till back at the shop. It prompted her to read it as soon as she got back home. Then she thought about Billy, the boy who had befriended a smuggler's stone dog. Was he real, or was he just a figment of her imagination? But what he said was real enough: *I don't believe wot a lot er people say. When they say yer can't do somethin', it always means yer can.* She tossed and turned, and finally got out of bed.

At the window, she looked out on to the back lawns, which in the bright moonlight had turned into a sheet of white. For one scary moment, she thought she saw Billy, standing out there, looking up at her. But she quickly dismissed that thought from her mind.

She turned around. The room was gleaming white. It was trying to tell her something, to tell her that the house was there to help her all she wanted. After all, that was what her father had left it to her for, was what people would expect her to do – sell up and pay off all the debts – an easy way out of all her difficulties. But there was something more than that to consider. Her father loved his shop, loved his business, loved his tenants and customers. 'Your father wanted you to stand on your own two feet,' Bernice had told her.

She turned around and drew the heavy curtains. The room was immediately plunged into darkness. She found her way back to bed again, and covered herself with the sheets, blanket, and eiderdown.

For several minutes, she lay there with her eyes closed, but with a firm determination and a clear vision of what she wanted, what she intended to do. Yes, she would stand on her own two feet, but she would do it her own way, and with no one's help. And as much as she'd loved her father, she would have to learn how to do it without him too.

Chapter 12

Young Billy was no ghost. Not that Grace ever seriously believed that he was, but his shadowy appearance when she was with Josh, the stone dog, had been very nerve-racking. In fact Bernice had roared with laughter when Grace told her what had happened the night before; it seemed that Billy had a certain reputation for frightening off visitors to the area with his tales of smugglers and pirates. However, one thing about him had turned out to be true. Billy *did* live with his family in a house on the seafront at the opposite end of the tunnel, and he was always getting into trouble with the Great Western Railway officials for walking alongside the track inside the tunnel, a dangerous thing to do at any time, let alone after dark.

Grace's weekend at The House on the Hill had been a complete revelation to her. She had spent most of her time talking to Bernice about Gus, about the house, and what she, Grace, was going to do with it. That was a very good point. Now that Bernice had indicated her intention of going back home to France, what *was* she going to do with a huge house that needed so much care and attention? One thing she was absolutely determined not to do, however, was to sell the place in order to prop up her father's run-down business.

Grace spent most of Saturday in Dawlish. Despite the influx of holidaymakers from other parts of the country at that time of year, she found the town a delightful little place, with a small stream running right through the centre, and lots of lovely shops to roam around, selling local produce and handicrafts such as Devon pottery and cream, two or three small cafés for afternoon tea and scones, and there was even a backstreet cinema, which was currently drawing queues of locals and holidaymakers to a daily showing of *Victoria the Great* with Anna Neagle. However, she used the bulk of her time to try to find out more about her father's activities down there, and was fascinated to come across local people who had known and liked him during his frequent visits to The House on the Hill when Grace had been a youngster. At lunch time she returned to the Smugglers' Inn pub, where she was received with more courtesy and sympathy by Ted, the landlord, and his customers than when she had first arrived, and his wife, Jackie, showed that the two of them were prepared to be as good friends to Grace as they had been to her father.

By the time she left the house on Sunday morning, Grace was a different person. Bernice had taught her so much – about herself, and about her father. She had learnt that her father had not only loved her, but had also been very proud of her. But the revelation that Gus had left her a rich woman was a prospect she found daunting – and challenging. Saying farewell to Bernice had been difficult, and she hoped and prayed they would never lose touch. During the short time she had been with the elegant and charming French woman, she had come to like and even admire her. Grace could see that Bernice was a person of great integrity, someone whom her father had placed so much trust in over the years. It was not going to be easy to maintain The House on the Hill without her.

When she arrived back at The Chapel, Grace couldn't believe the transformation that had taken place in Clapper's stable. Not only had Mickey cleaned and tidied the place, but he had shifted things around so that Clapper could have more space, something she had been begging her father to do for years.

Most important of all, however, was the appearance of Clapper himself. Apart from looking spruce from the grooming Mickey had obviously given him, the moment Grace had walked through the door the animal trotted across to her, and nudged her in her stomach playfully with his nose.

'That's more like it, boy,' said Grace, giving him an affectionate stroke on his nose, something she had not very often done herself. 'Looks like you've found yourself a new friend.' Clapper snorted, and nodded his head vigorously up and down. Grace turned to Mickey. 'Thank you,' she said, with a warm smile. 'I think you've given Clapper a new lease of life.'

Mickey beamed, and stroked Clapper behind the ear. 'We've 'ad a good time tergevver, ain't we, mate?'

Again Clapper responded with a snort.

The mood changed, however, when Mickey became aware that Grace was watching him closely in an odd sort of way. It made him feel a bit uneasy.

'Well – better be off, miss,' he said, collecting his cap from a hook behind the stable door. 'Reckon yer'll be wantin' ter get some kip. Be seein' yer then.' He put on his cap, and made for the door. But he stopped a moment. 'Oh – by the way,' he said, 'someone called on yer. After yer'd gone on Friday I fink it was. Young bloke.'

Grace's bright expression changed. 'Did he say who he was?' she asked warily.

Mickey shook his head. 'Don't fink 'e wanted ter pass the time er day wiv someone like me.'

Grace had a nagging feeling inside her stomach.

'See yer then,' called Mickey from the door.

'Mickey.'

He swung round to look back at her.

'Would you like a job?'

This being Monday, for Gus's tenants in the region of the Nag's Head it was also rent day. However, circumstances had changed somewhat for them all in the past few weeks, for not only had poor old Gus passed away, but no one had been round to collect the rents for the last two Mondays. None the less, there was still an air of anxiety amongst the tenants as Gert Jolly in Mayton Street, Mabel Buck in Kinloch Street, and old wintergreen ointment himself, Jack Pertwee, stood waiting at their front doors to see if the new owners of Gus's business were coming round to catch up with them.

Gert's eyes in particular were glued to the end of the street. After the information she had pumped out of poor old Georgie O'Hara, she was now convinced that with her new-found fortune, Grace Higgs would no longer be around to harass them for their weekly rent. Good riddance too, she told herself. Grace Higgs had never done anyone any favours, so the sooner she went off with her fancy man, and left the good, honest working-class people of Holloway alone to struggle on as best they could, the better it would be for everyone. But she still had the new owners to worry about.

'I've 'eard she's sold it all ter the bank,' said Gert, to her next-door neighbour, Molly Tebbit, who had spent the last half-hour in her front porch listening to Gert holding forth about all she knew that nobody else knew.

'The bank?' asked Molly sceptically. 'Wot's a bank got ter do wiv runnin' people's property?'

'Yer'd be surprised!' retorted Gert, arms crossed defiantly.

'Money always makes more money fer people like that. Yer can bet yer life Grace 'Iggs got a good price fer the likes of you an' me!'

'Come off it, Gert,' returned Molly, a pretty little middle-aged woman who always wore a scarf around her head to disguise the fact that she had lost most of her hair. 'They're buyin' the business – not us!'

'Don't you believe it!' insisted Gert. 'They're all out ter drain the last drop er blood out of us!'

As she spoke, there was a flurry of activity at the end of the street. All along the terrace of houses, upstairs windows and front doors were opening, indicating that something or somebody was about to turn into Mayton Street from Hertslet Road.

Gert and Molly craned their necks to see what was going on. What they didn't expect to see was Gus Higgs's mobile shop, pulled by Clapper, trotting at a very sprightly pace towards them. But what took them completely by surprise was to see Grace at the reins, with a flat-capped young bloke at her side.

'Blimey!' gasped Molly. 'Am I seein' fings?'

Gert, too astonished to hang around, quickly disappeared back inside her house and shut the door.

A few minutes later, a queue had formed at the back entrance to the mobile shop, with customers delighted to be able once again to buy grocery provisions that would not only save them popping round to the shops, but also give them a chance to satisfy their curiosity about what Gus Higgs's daughter was up to. They were especially interested in the good-looking young man in working clothes who was helping her, lifting heavy sacks, assisting elderly customers to get up and down the two steps to the van. They were also fascinated to see the way he was looking after Gus's horse,

Clapper, and hear him talking to the animal as though it was his old mate.

When the shop moved on further down the street, Molly Tebbit, rent book in hand, was waiting at her front gate.

'Good morning, Mrs Tebbit!' called Grace brightly, as she climbed down to greet her. 'It's nice to see you again.'

Molly's eyes bulged as Grace took her rent book and money. She couldn't understand what had happened to Grace, for she looked so composed.

'Oh – this is Mickey,' continued Grace, nodding towards him, whilst marking up Molly's rent book. 'From now on, he's going to be helping me out.'

' 'Allo, darlin'!' said Mickey, doffing his cap to a mesmerised Molly. 'Luvely day fer a picnic!'

'Thank you very much, Mrs Tebbit,' said Grace, thoroughly enjoying the look of shock on Molly's face. 'See you next week.' She handed Molly back her rent book, and moved on to Gert Jolly's place. But the moment she reached the front door, she had no need to knock, for Gert opened it immediately.

'Ah – there you are, Mrs Jolly!' said Grace, greeting her with a warm smile. 'How nice to see you again.'

Gert was too thunderstruck to answer. Grace had never greeted her in such a way before.

'So – how are we off this week?' asked Grace, taking Gert's rent book from her, and flicking through it. 'How much can you afford to put down?' She looked up to find Gert's eyes fixed on Mickey, who was leaning on her garden gate. 'Oh – by the way,' said Grace, with a huge smile. 'That's Mickey. He's going to be helping me from now on.'

Mickey waved to Gert. ' 'Allo, darlin'!' he called. 'Anyfin' yer want, just give me a yell!'

'A shilling then?' asked Grace. 'It's not much off your pension, is it? But you can pay less if you prefer.'

'What?' Gert snapped out of her gaze. 'Oh – no – make it a bob.'

'A bob it shall be,' said Grace, marking up Gert's rent book, before handing it back. 'There we are.'

Gert reluctantly handed over her shilling towards the rent.

'And incidentally,' continued Grace, 'I've got something for you.' She turned and signalled to Mickey, who came up the front garden path carrying a brown paper bag. Grace took it from him, and handed it over to Gert. 'It's some pumice stone Dad promised you,' she said. 'I'm afraid I couldn't get the powder. Our stockist says there's been a run on it.'

Gert was speechless.

'No charge, Mrs Jolly,' said Grace, amused by Gert's bewildered expression. 'Consider it a little treat from Dad. See you next week!' She turned to leave.

'I fawt yer was s'pposed ter be sellin' up?' asked Gert, totally disoriented.

'Good gracious no,' Grace called back. 'Whatever gave you *that* idea?'

Mickey wiggled his fingers in a cheeky farewell to Gert. 'Bye-bye, darlin'!' he said, before following Grace back to the shop.

As Clapper trotted off, with Grace at the reins and Mickey by her side, Gert was still at her front door, watching them go in total amazement. In fact, she wasn't the only one. The residents of Mayton Street were all eyes.

These days, Eric Tyler had plenty of time on his hands. He had never really had a secure job, for he was usually too preoccupied with playing games with money to actually get up each morning and go to work. The trouble was, the money had belonged mostly to his father-in-law, who thought he was helping his daughter by handing over fairly substantial sums to her new husband so that he could 'play the market' and invest them in any wild financial venture he had got involved in. Unfortunately for Eric *and* his father-in-law, there had never been any return on the investments, and relations between them had eventually turned very sour. Eric's marriage went exactly the same way; it soon became evident that it was little more than a marriage of convenience, for Eric had somehow repeatedly avoided giving his wife Jane a child, which, once he had made his millions, would have tied him down to her just a little more than he had ever intended. Therefore, once he'd been kicked out of the family home, he was faced with the dilemma of how to make ends meet.

Eric's own family were no help at all. His father had more or less made a living all his life as a rag-and-bone man in the East End, and his mother was a cleaner up at the Blue Hall Cinema at the Angel in Islington, so it was no wonder they had very little spare cash for their son to play around with. Meeting Grace Higgs, therefore, had been a real stroke of luck – or that's what he'd thought the first time he'd set eyes on her. A chandler's daughter, who would one day inherit all of her father's properties that, when sold, would bring in a tidy sum, was like a dream come true. But when a better prospect had come along, such as helping his wife to share a sizeable income from an extremely wealthy father, neither love nor loyalty played any part in his calculations. Eric was no crook, just misguided. He dreamt of wealth and position, but without having to go out to do an honest day's work to achieve it. Eric's real downfall, however, were his striking good looks. Many a girl had fallen for him in his time; ever since his school days in the East End, he could have had his pick. But good looks alone were not enough. Although one part of him craved real love, his alter ego rejected it in favour of personal ambition. And that was why his current circumstances were, to say the least, precarious. He was getting desperate. Unfortunately, his new-found relationship with Grace was not going entirely to plan. In some ways, he did feel something for her, but she was so dowdy, so set in her ways, and, if it was true that she really was having to sell up because of her father's death, then he saw very little point in pursuing her.

None the less, he *was* intrigued as to the reasons why Grace had gone off somewhere for the weekend. As far as he remembered, that was something she rarely did, for she hardly ever left her father's side for a single minute. Where did she go to? Also, who was that character looking after the horse whilst she was away? Something funny was going on somewhere, and he was curious to know what. That's why he turned to someone who might be able to answer a few questions.

'I haven't the faintest idea,' replied Pauline Betts, Grace's best friend. 'Why shouldn't she get someone to work for her now that her dad's gone? After all, there's no way she can manage on her own. I don't see that it makes any difference who the bloke is. If she likes him – good luck to her, I say.'

Eric was not amused. He had deliberately waited outside the library where Pauline worked, knowing what time she usually came out for lunch. 'I hadn't realised she was so well off,' he remarked acidly, as they strolled together up towards Highbury Corner.

'Well off?' replied Pauline dismissively. 'With all those debts her father left her?'

'But she can afford to hire casual labour?'

Pauline shrugged. 'Honestly, Eric,' she replied, 'I've no idea *what* Grace can or cannot do. All I know is she's going through a very tough time.'

They walked on. As they reached Highbury tube station, Pauline crossed to the other side of the road, making for the café she used for lunch every day. Eric went with her.

'I hear she went away for the weekend,' he said, lighting up a cigarette as they went.

'Really?' asked Pauline, with very little interest. 'I hope she had a good time. God knows, she needs it.'

Highbury Corner was brimming with people, most of them office workers out for the lunch-time break. On the other side of the road, Highbury Fields was full of them, eating their sandwiches, and basking in the early afternoon sun. A newspaper vendor was shouting out the day's headlines about yet another civil war battle raging in Spain, and a meeting between the German and Italian dictators, Hitler and Mussolini. But nobody seemed to take any notice. At this moment, the only thing that was important to most people as they rushed about their business was how soon they could get their lunch and get back to work on time.

'But where did she go to?' asked Eric, as he followed Pauline at a lively pace towards her café.

'Where did who go?' she asked emptily.

'Grace,' persisted Eric, who had taken off his trilby hat to allow his thick flock of greased brown hair the freedom to get some fresh air. 'The weekend?'

'Haven't the faintest,' replied Pauline. She came to a halt outside the café, and turned to him. 'Eric,' she asked sceptically, 'why this sudden interest in Grace? She can't mean anything to you after the way you treated her?'

'It's not that I'm *interested* in her,' protested Eric. 'I'm just concerned for her, that's all. As you say, she's going through a very tough time. If I can help in any way . . .'

'Leave her alone, Eric,' said Pauline. 'Grace has been hurt enough as it is.' She started to go into the café.

'You've been a good friend to her, Pauline,' Eric called. 'I admire you for it.'

Pauline stopped and turned back to him.

'As a matter of fact I've always admired you,' said Eric with a knowing look. 'I've always thought what an attractive girl you are. You're really quite special.'

For one brief moment, they just stared at each other, exchanging intimate, suggestive looks. Then Pauline turned, and went into the café. She held the door open for Eric to join her.

If it had been a long day for Grace, it had been quite an illuminating one for Gus's tenants and customers. Since Gus's death, the prospect of 'business as usual' hadn't occurred to them, especially after all the rumours that had been flying around about his daughter's intention to sell up and throw them all out on to the streets. But the sight of Clapper, trotting down their roads with the shop in tow, Grace at the reins, and Mickey at her side, had caused great excitement – and speculation. And even more intriguing for them all was the way Grace had treated them. Gone was her brusque and off-hand manner. What they now saw was someone who was beginning to treat them more like human beings, who was showing that she was at least prepared to listen to their problems. In return, instead of shutting their doors the moment they had paid their rents, they took time to stop and talk to her for a few moments, and ask her how she was coping after the passing of her much-loved dad. Thanks to Mickey, Grace was a very different person from who she had been during the past few years. Mickey had given her the confidence to make her own decisions, and to be a warm and loving woman.

Despite all this, however, by the time Clapper had drawn the shop back into the stable yard at The Chapel that afternoon, Grace still wasn't sure how she was going to get the business into a viable position again without having to draw on the vast amount of money her father had left her in that bank account in Devon. It was one thing to have a grand vision of doing things *her* way, of paying off her father's debts by balancing the books, but if people were slow to pay off their arrears, then it was going to be an uphill struggle.

'Did I do all right then, miss?' asked Mickey anxiously, once he'd closed the stable gates, removed Clapper's bridle, reins, and tow bar.

'You did wonderfully well, thank you, Mickey,' replied Grace, who, when they first set out on the day's rounds, had been none too sure how Mickey's bright and cheeky personality would go down with the tenants and customers. 'You must have seen how much they liked you?'

'Well now, miss,' said Mickey uncertainly, 'I ain't so sure about *that*! Ol' Ma Jolly looked like she was goin' ter 'ave a stroke when she first saw me.'

Grace laughed. 'That's not the only thing Gert Jolly's going to have to get used to!' she replied. 'In fact, if I'm going to keep the business going, she and all the tenants are going to have to be fair. The first thing they're going to have to learn is that you *have* to pay for what you get. Gert Jolly probably gets around ten shillings a week on her widow's pension. She'll have to realise that part of that has to go on everyday living expenses, and not just a daily jug of stout.'

'Ain't it a bit late ter teach ol' dogs new tricks?' warned Mickey.

'We'll see,' said Grace. She followed Mickey as he led

Clapper into the stable. 'And what about you, Mickey?' she asked. 'Did you enjoy the day?'

Mickey swung round to look at her. His usual grin was now an affectionate smile. 'Oh yes,' he replied pointedly. 'You bet.'

'So how do you feel about working for me on a permanent basis?'

Mickey didn't quite follow her. 'Miss?'

'A regular job, Mickey,' said Grace. 'Every day – except Sundays, of course. I can't afford to pay you much, but at least it'll keep you going and help to pay your rent round the corner. And if you want to do the odd job elsewhere from time to time, I won't mind a bit – as long as it doesn't stop you from looking after Clapper.'

Mickey looked up at Clapper. 'Fat chance er that, eh, mate?' He picked up a cloth, and started to rub Clapper down.

'So is that a yes?' asked Grace anxiously. 'Would you like to go on working for me?'

' 'Course, miss!' he replied.

'*Of* course.'

Puzzled, he turned to look at her. 'Miss?'

'You say *of* course, Mickey,' she replied. 'Not just 'course.'

He took a moment to realise that he was being corrected, but then understood. 'Oh – right yer are, miss – 'course – I mean – *of* course.'

Grace grinned and went to the stable door. 'When you've finished, come in to the house and I'll make us both a cup of tea.'

Mickey briefly stopped what he was doing, and turned an anxious look at her. 'If it's all the same ter you, miss,' he said, 'would it be all right if we talked out 'ere? I don't like goin' in people's 'ouses unless I know them really well, or I'm doin' a job in there for 'em.'

'But you *are* doing a job for me,' Grace replied, a little baffled.

'It's not the same, miss,' said Mickey. 'It's – 'ow can I say? – the way I am.'

Puzzled though she was, Grace accepted what he asked. 'Of course, Mickey,' she said. She stayed just long enough to watch him rubbing down Clapper, then left him, and went off into the house. Whilst she was in there, she thought a lot about what Mickey had said. In fact she thought a lot about the kind of person he was, totally uneducated, lacking in any real social grace, but with an instinct and a sense of pride that gave him an inner dignity, and put him in a class of his own. He was unlike any man – young or old – that she had ever met before.

A short while later, she returned to the stable with two cups of tea. For a brief moment, she held on outside whilst she listened to Mickey talking to Clapper.

'So just you remember, mate,' he was saying, 'fings ain't goin' ter be easy round 'ere. You an' me've got ter do all we can ter 'elp our lil' lady.'

After waiting, Grace came in with the two cups, and gave one of them to Mickey. 'Fanks a lot, miss,' he said, taking one of the cups. He was now using a pitchfork to refresh the straw where Clapper slept. 'Yer've saved me life. Just wot I needed ter wet me whistle!'

'I think I ought to be straight with you, Mickey,' said Grace, perching on a stool. 'About the future, I mean – what I'm going to do – what I'm going to *try* to do.'

Mickey stopped what he was doing, and turned to listen to her. 'Miss?'

'My father was virtually bankrupt when he died,' continued Grace. 'He left me with an enormous amount of debts, which, somehow, I've got to pay off. I think you know the position I'm in with some of our tenants; it's going to take all my ingenuity to get them to bring their payments up to date. The trouble is that although they all loved my father, none of them really like *me*. It's my fault – I know that. I've always treated them with a certain amount of disdain – I don't know why. It's like *you* said, it's just the way I am, I suppose. Anyway, somehow I've got to find a way of gaining their trust. You see, Mickey, I want to restore this business to the way it used to be, the way my father would have wanted it to be. But I want to do it in a credible way, without having to – to borrow money to pay back money. Can you understand what I'm saying?' She looked across at him. His face was a picture of determined concentration.

'Yes, miss,' he returned quietly.

'D'you think you could help me to do that?' asked Grace.

'I'd like to, miss,' he replied.

'Then let me tell you what I have in mind.' She got up from her stool, and started to pace the stable. 'I want to start by making the shop more efficient. I've always said it's silly to try to compete with all the big shops that are just around the corner. Where Dad always did best was with the things that people either forget when they're out shopping, or with people who just can't be bothered to go out. That means trying to pinpoint the type of things they need on the spur of the moment, like soap or matches or candles or – I don't know – all sorts of things. That doesn't mean we have to abandon the traditional groceries like fresh vegetables, dried peas, or beans, but we need to be more imaginative, more sensitive to people's needs. D'you know what I mean?' She turned to look at Mickey.

'Yes, miss,' he replied. He was mesmerised.

It suddenly occurred to Grace that she was really talking aloud, and couldn't understand why she was sharing all this with a man she hardly knew, a man who knew nothing about the intricacies of running a business. And yet, there was something about him that made her want to tell him anything she was thinking. 'I'm sorry, Mickey,' she said. 'I shouldn't really be loading all my troubles on to you. It's just that – well, you've been so good today, I'd love you to carry on working for me, if you feel you'd like to.'

Mickey looked back at her and smiled. 'There's nuffin' I'd like better, miss,' he replied.

For one split second, their eyes met. It embarrassed both of them, so Grace quickly looked away. 'Good, then that's settled,' she said. 'From now on, I want to take the shop around the Nag's Head area at least twice a week. If I can make a go of it, I could maybe increase that to three times a week later on. Tomorrow morning, I'll go up to Covent Garden and have a word with our wholesalers, see if they can give me a little credit. After all, they liked my dad, they respected him. Then I'll do the same with all our other stockists.'

'Anyfin' I can do ter 'elp, miss,' said Mickey, 'just name it.'

Grace turned to him again. Only then did she realise what a sweet, vulnerable face he had. 'Thank you, Mickey,' she replied. 'I'm very grateful.' She started to move around again. 'Five shillings a week.' She flicked him a quick glance. 'I'm afraid that's all I can manage at the moment, Mickey,' she said guiltily. 'All I can promise is that I'll do my best to pay more if and when the business picks up again.' She paused uneasily. 'How do you feel about that?'

Mickey grinned back at her. 'Five bob'll do me fine, miss,' he replied. 'As long as I don't 'ave ter share any of ol' Clapper's dinner wiv 'im!'

They both laughed.

'What's the joke?'

They both turned with a start to find Eric Tyler standing in the open doorway. 'I trust I'm not interrupting anything?'

Unconsciously, Grace straightened her hair and dress with both hands. 'Eric,' she said, going to him. 'How nice to see you.'

To Grace's intense embarrassment Eric immediately took her in his arms and kissed her.

Mickey lowered his eyes, and carried on forking straw.

'Can we go inside?' Eric asked.

Grace took a quick, uncomfortable glance over her shoulder to Mickey. 'Yes, of course,' she replied uneasily. She made for the door. 'Let me know when you're leaving, Mickey,' she called anxiously as she went.

Mickey merely nodded and carried on with what he was doing.

Eric stopped briefly to give Mickey a passing, dismissive look. Then he followed Grace through the back door of the house.

It was nearly dark when Mickey took his leave of Clapper, and locked him up for the night. Ever since Grace had taken Eric off to the house earlier in the evening, he had spent most of his time sitting with Clapper, and taking uncomfortable looks at the back door every time he thought he heard Eric's voice. It had been a wonderful day, one of the best he had had in a long time. But now he felt a bit low. He didn't quite know why, but he did.

He crossed the stable yard, and paused just long enough to take one last, lingering look at the back door of the house. Inside the lights were on, but there was no sign of anyone. He left the yard, and quietly locked the gates behind him.

Chapter 13

The following two months proved to be quite a testing period for Grace. Although she was succeeding in gaining the confidence of the tenants, and even persuading the slow payers to bring their arrears up to date, her determination to put her father's business on an even keel was proving more difficult than she had imagined. Fortunately, all the wholesalers she dealt with were willing to give her credit, mainly because of her father's record of complete honesty, but that was not a situation that could remain for too long. After hours of sitting alone in the parlour, working on the petty cash books, scanning through endless bank statements, and checking stock lists, she reluctantly came to the conclusion that, if she was going to make a clean start with the business, she would have to fall back on at least part of the collateral her father had bequeathed her down in Devon. However, she was as determined as ever that The House on the Hill would remain her property, at least until she had decided what to do with it.

Her other problem was Eric Tyler. She was in a real quandary about what to do, for he was now a regular visitor to The Chapel, much to the obvious regret of Mickey Burke, who had turned out to be the real driving force behind the gradual rejuvenation of the shop on wheels. Time and time again, Grace asked herself if she could really love Eric again. She knew he loved *her*, or at least he said he did, but in her heart of hearts she couldn't be absolutely sure whether he had some ulterior motive. None the less, she did find him irresistibly handsome, and the worrying thing was that the more she was with him, the more he regained her trust. On the other hand, Eric *was* responsible for her change in appearance, making her feel good every time she tried something different. In place of the long brown hair tied together with a pin behind her head, she now sported a snazzy new shoulder-length style, which had taken a lot of painful decision-making at Annette's hairdressing salon in Caledonian Road. She had also started wearing just a faint touch of make-up, and although she had very little money with which to buy new clothes, Mickey Burke had been a surprising support, praising her to the hilt when she tried adapting the clothes she had had for years, using a scarf to set off a dress she had transformed on her sewing machine from long to short sleeves. On one occasion when they were out on the day's rounds, she even wore trousers, which caused a sensation amongst the tenants and customers, and quite a few admiring wolf whistles from some navvies on a building site.

By the end of September, she had paid two more visits to Dawlish, where, following Bernice's departure, she had managed to hire a local property company to manage the house in her absence. However, keeping all this from her family and friends was a great strain, and she was gradually understanding what her father must have gone through all those years. Her next problem was Aunt Hilda.

Aunt Hilda was determined to know what was going on. It had been more than two months since Gus had died, but she had still had no word from Grace about what she intended to do with what she, Hilda, insisted was the 'family' business. In her frustration, she made several attempts to see Gus's bank manager, Dick Rumble, but on each occasion was given the excuse that he was too busy. Mindful of this,

Grace decided to organise another Sunday family get-together at The Chapel.

'I fink you're a very brave gel, Grace,' said Josie, who was just sitting down at the table for the Sunday midday meal. ' 'Ow yer've managed ter cope all on yer own is little short of a miracle ter me.'

'Well, I can't exactly claim that,' said Grace, who had already served up the meat and vegetables on plates in the scullery. 'If it hadn't been for Mickey, I don't know what I would have done.'

'So where *is* this fancy man er yours?' asked Hilda, in her usual sniffy way. 'Why ain't 'e joinin' us?'

'Mickey's not my fancy man, Auntie,' replied Grace tersely. 'He merely works for me. He eats his meals at his own digs round the corner. And, in any case, he doesn't come in on a Sunday.'

'Well, I must say,' added Stan, ' 'e keeps ol' Clapper spruce and tidy. Gus'd be pleased about that.'

'Yes,' said Grace, putting down a plate of meat and vegetables in front of him. 'Mickey loves horses. By the way he keeps Clapper groomed, you'd think he'd been working with them all his life. And he's such a marvellous help with the shop. All the tenants seem to like him.'

'Sounds like they're not the only ones,' added Hilda cuttingly.

'What *do* you mean, Auntie?' asked Grace.

'Well, just look at yer,' said Hilda. 'New 'aircut, an' all that war paint. Whose benefit is all *that* for, I'd like ter know.'

Grace immediately covered her lips with the back of her hand. 'It's for no one's benefit, Auntie,' she retorted defensively. 'I wanted a change, that's all.'

'Well, *I* like it!' said Viv, who was just coming in from the scullery carrying two more hot plates of meat and veg. 'And, in any case, Grace always looks good – with or without make-up.'

Hilda snorted. 'What's this s'pposed ter be?' she asked, turning her face up at the meal Viv was just putting in front of her.

'It's pork and red cabbage,' said Grace. 'I thought it would make a change from always having roast beef and Yorkshire pudding.'

'I prefer roast beef and Yorkshire pudding,' grumbled Stan, reluctantly picking up his knife and fork.

'Oh, stop complainin', Stan!' said Josie. 'It smells luvely.'

'This is all a mystery ter me,' protested Hilda. 'New 'airdo, new make-up, fancy food. Why?'

'Why not, Auntie?' asked Grace, refusing to be intimidated. 'Life can be very tedious if you only ever do the same things.'

'Hear! Hear!' exclaimed Josie.

Grace sat down at the table next to Viv, who flashed her a supportive smile. 'There's apple sauce on the table for anyone who wants it.'

'I like the cracklin',' said Stan, crunching the pork skin noisily.

Hilda glared at him.

Several minutes later, Grace finally plucked up enough courage to bring up the reason why she had asked them all to come there. 'Oh by the way,' she announced casually, and looking at no one in particular, 'I've decided not to sell the shop after all.'

Hilda looked up with a start. 'What's that?' she snapped.

'I said I'm not going to sell the shop, Auntie,' said Grace. 'I'm going to get it up and running again, so that I can pay off all Dad's debts.'

Now it was Josie's turn to be shocked. 'Debts?' she asked. 'What debts?'

'When Dad died, Auntie,' said Grace, 'there was nothing left in the bank. There were so many bills he hadn't paid, he was on the verge of being declared bankrupt.'

'I don't believe you!' growled Hilda.

' 'Ilda!' said Josie, reprimanding her. 'Don't say such fings!'

'Why shouldn't I?' insisted Hilda. 'I say this is all rubbish! Gus had fifteen 'ouses on 'is books. It doesn't matter 'ow many people were bad payers, 'e still 'ad plenty of money comin' in fer rents.'

'Oh yes,' replied Grace. 'The trouble was, the houses no longer belonged to him. When he first bought them, he bought them on a mortgage. He's been in default on the payments for years.'

There was a general feeling of disbelief around the table. Even Hilda felt the wind had been blown out of her sails.

Grace knew everyone was watching her, so she put down her knife and fork and looked calmly around the table. 'I hadn't intended letting any of you know about this,' she said, turning her attention specifically to Hilda. 'After all, the business belongs to me now, so it's my direct responsibility and no one else's. But after going through the books, I've decided that there *are* ways of my carrying on. Of course, it's going to need a lot of penny-pinching, a lot of reorganising, but I'm going to have a try. The reason I'm telling you all this is that Dad didn't leave a will, but even if he had, I'm afraid there would have been nothing left for him *to* leave.'

'Oh, Grace!' said Josie sympathetically, covering Grace's hand with her own. 'What a terrible shock for you. To think that you've been left with all these problems.'

'Wot the 'ell did ol' Gus fink 'e was playin' at?' asked Stan. 'Why didn't 'e tell us about all this long ago?'

'Precisely,' said Hilda, who, until now, had become quite withdrawn from the conversation. 'It seems my brother kept quite a lot from his family.' She threw a sly look at Grace, who had resumed eating.

'So if there's no money in the kitty,' asked Josie, ' 'ow're yer goin' ter get the business up and runnin' again?'

'At the moment, Auntie, I'm not quite sure,' replied Grace, eating her food. 'But I do have one or two ideas.'

'Is that why yer've bin goin' away at weekends?' asked Hilda, eagerly awaiting Grace's reaction.

Grace did no more than flick a quick glance at her. 'Where did you hear a thing like that, Auntie?' she asked.

Hilda grinned. 'Oh, you know, dear,' she replied mischievously. ' 'Ere an' there. I went ter Devon meself once. Yer gran 'ad a sister down there. It's a lovely place – 'specially down by the sea.'

Grace felt her stomach churn. The old witch knew. She knew *something*, but how much? Then she remembered her father telling her how Hilda always made a point of getting to know the rent-payers; even Jack Pertwee in Enkel Street had mentioned in passing how he had once met and talked with 'that nice relation of yours'. How should she respond, she asked herself. The first thing was not to panic. This was a battle of wills between herself and this wretched elder sister of her father. If Aunt Hilda was bluffing, then there was nothing to worry about, but if she knew something about The House on the Hill, then there could be only trouble ahead. 'I've never been to Devon, Auntie,' she found herself saying. 'I wouldn't know *what* it's like.'

Hilda's expression changed immediately. She was clearly

disappointed that Grace's answer was not the one she had been hoping for.

Fortunately, the family didn't stay for tea, which gave Grace the chance to put her feet up, and mull over all that had been talked about over the midday meal. What Aunt Hilda had said had really disturbed her. Could she really know about Grace's trips down to Dawlish, and why she was going there? If so, who could have told her? The thought that Aunt Hilda would find out about her father's inheritance worried her greatly. She was the last person in the world he would have wanted to benefit from his bequest.

Whilst she was trying to work out in her mind what to do next, there was a knock on the front door. When she went to answer it, she was surprised to find Uncle Stan there.

'Uncle?' she asked, opening the door for him. 'Is something wrong?'

'I won't come in, gel,' he said, remaining on the doorstep. 'The others've just gone on ter the bus stop, but I just wanted ter tell yer that if yer get yerself in any difficulty, I mean, if there's anyfin' we can do ter 'elp out, yer've got ter tell us – right?'

'Uncle . . .' said Grace, taken aback. 'I—'

Stan waved his hand to silence her. 'On the way ter the bus stop, me an' Josie was talkin' it over. You're Gus's gel. The least we can do is ter 'elp out.' He again prevented her from saying anything. 'Look,' he continued, 'we've got fifty quid stashed away for a rainy day. Part of it was fer Reg, but the way fings're goin' – well, who knows if we'll see 'im again. There'll be plenty left over fer Viv when we go, so – anyway, if yer need a lift up, it's there waitin' for yer. OK?'

Grace was not only taken aback, but deeply moved. 'Uncle,' she said, 'I don't know what to say to you. That's the nicest gesture anyone has ever made to me.'

'Don't give it anuvver fawt, Gracie,' insisted Stan. 'After all, that's wot relations are for, ain't they?'

Eric Tyler adjusted his tie and collar in the mirror, and tucked in his freshly ironed white shirt. He liked what he saw. After all, his good looks had helped him many a time when he took a fancy to a girl he liked. It had been like that when he first met Grace. He only had to comb his hair to get her to fawn all over him. That was part of the trouble. She had been just too eager. But she was different now. In those days she was little more than a silly little twenty-year-old, who went along with practically anything he said. But nowadays, she was more mature, more down to earth. And since her father had died, she had really changed her image, new hairstyle, make-up, clothes that were not old-fashioned, but above all, a whole new attitude. In place of the disapproving schoolmistress, what had emerged was a bright-eyed young woman who was stylish and feminine. Apart from the business she had inherited from her father, there was something more that Eric was beginning to like about her. Could it be that he was falling in love? He stopped to look at his alter ego reflected in the mirror. If that was the case, then it would be the first time it had ever happened. Actually *loving* anyone had never really figured in any of Eric's calculations, but when he thought about Grace, he felt – well, he didn't quite know *how* he felt.

He turned round and looked at his bedsitter; it wasn't exactly the place he'd want to bring a girl back to, especially a girl like Grace, who lived in a place like The Chapel. Of course he'd done so before, on more than one occasion, most recently with Grace's friend, Pauline, which had given him more than one sleepless night worrying about how much Pauline might tell Grace. But somehow he didn't see

Grace herself alone with him in the room. But as he continued to look into the reflection of his own eyes in the mirror, he did think about Grace. He thought about her a lot, about the touch of her lips, those full, smooth lips, the way she responded when he kissed them. He breathed heavily, and pulled himself together.

Tonight they were going out together for the first time since – since those unfortunate times when they were a couple. He had been looking forward to their meeting all day, not just because Grace had a lot going for her, but because he had begun to enjoy her company. He reached for a small bottle of eau-de-Cologne on his chest of drawers. It had been given to him by his soon-to-be-divorced wife, Jane, who liked to share it with him. The bottle was now almost empty, but he sprinkled the remains on his hands, and rubbed it over his face and neck. He took one last smile at himself in the mirror, collected his blazer from the back of a chair, and hurriedly left for his special night out.

Whilst Eric was on his way to pick up Grace, she was in the stable giving Mickey an off-the-cuff lesson in how to talk properly.

'No, Mickey,' she sighed, after repeating her correction for the third time. 'Try not to keep saying "ain't yer?". It's "aren't you?".'

'Aren't you?' Mickey repeated, correctly.

'That's better!' enthused Grace. 'Now you're getting the hang of it.'

'Sounds daft ter me,' said Mickey, scratching his head. 'Unnatural.'

'That's because you played truant from school so many times,' quipped Grace. She suddenly noticed that he looked stung by her remark. 'I'm sorry, Mickey,' she said. 'I didn't mean that. What I meant was—'

'It's all right, miss,' said Mickey. 'I *know* wot yer mean. I've got a lot ter learn.'

'You don't *have* to learn anything,' Grace assured him, 'if you don't want to.'

'But I do,' insisted Mickey. 'There's a lot I want ter learn, not just about 'ow ter talk, but 'ow ter work fings out fer meself.'

'I don't follow you.'

He collected a box of matches from a ledge, just above where Clapper was settling down for the night. 'Well,' he replied, 'I look at it this way. If yer walk around wiv yer eyes closed, yer miss an awful lot. When I'm wiv some of me mates up the pub in King's Cross, I watch 'em while they gab on about a whole lot er rubbish – usually gels they go out wiv, that sort er fing. It's all wind really. But then I get ter finkin', *why* do they 'ave ter boast about 'ow many gels they've bin out wiv, an' – if yer'll pardon the expression, miss – wot they do wiv 'em? Boastin's a funny fing, ain't it – I mean, isn't it? It's like tryin' ter impress someone, tryin' ter tell 'em 'ow good yer are at somefin'. I don't understand it meself – but I try.'

Grace watched him whilst he unclipped the paraffin lantern from a hook on the ceiling, and removed its glass globe. 'Don't *you* ever talk about girlfriends, Mickey?' she asked.

'Don't have any, miss,' he replied, striking a match to light the lantern wick. 'No, I lie. There *was* this gel I knew once up Chapel Market. But she got fed up, and ditched me fer someone else.'

'Her loss, I'd say,' said Grace.

Mickey liked what she'd said. 'Oh well, never seen 'er since. Found somefin' better, I reckon.'

For a moment, Grace watched him lighting the wick, which gradually produced a dazzling white glow across his face. It was a lovely face – not beautiful, if anything craggy and rough – but it was an endearing face, and for the first time she noticed that he had protruding ears, which stood out like cauliflowers from beneath his flat cap. She didn't know why, but she was feeling protective towards this man. In some funny way, he was crying out for attention, desperate to learn, to know about things. And he did have a lot to learn.

'I'd better be going,' she said with a smile. 'Eric will be here any minute.'

'Right yer are, miss,' said Mickey. He looked up at her. With the nights now drawing in and the stable in semi-darkness, he hadn't noticed that she was dressed to go out for the evening. 'Miss' looked beautiful. Her short hair was glistening in the harsh lamplight, and over her navy-blue three-quarter-length dress she wore a taffeta dust-coat which she said her father had bought for her birthday two years before, but which she had hardly ever worn. Now it took Mickey's breath away, and he had to struggle to avert his attention.

'What time will yer be settin' off for the rounds termorrer, miss?' he asked.

'Usual time,' replied Grace. 'I'll look forward to it.'

Mickey wanted to believe her, but somehow couldn't. 'Don't ferget yer promised ter take some shoelaces fer Mrs 'Obbs in Roden Street,' he reminded her. 'Though wot she wants 'em for, I don't know. 'Er ol' man's only got one leg.'

'Yes, I know,' replied Grace, with just a slight suggestion of a chuckle.

'An' that woman in Kinloch Street,' continued Mickey. 'Didn't she want some lino polish or somefin'?'

'Oh – yes,' groaned Grace. 'What's the matter with people? Why can't they remember to get these things when they're out shopping?'

'Yeah – I know,' agreed Mickey. 'Still, they're yer customers, ain't they? Sorry – aren't they?'

What Mickey said was obvious – but true. 'Yes, Mickey,' she replied, aware that she had been discreetly but wisely put in her place. 'You're right. They *are* our customers.'

Grace hadn't seen the bright lights of Piccadilly Circus since she was a teenager. The last time she had been there was when her mum and dad had taken her to the West End of London as a treat for her fourteenth birthday. What she remembered most about that day was going to feed the pigeons in Trafalgar Square, and watching the Changing of the Guard outside Buckingham Palace. She also distinctly remembered wondering why there were so many electric lights in Piccadilly Circus itself, when the backstreets of Islington only had lights that had to be lit by a lamplighter each night. That day was firmly in her mind as she and Eric strolled hand in hand around the Circus. It was an astonishing sight, with so many advertisements lighting up the night sky with multicoloured flashing signs.

Contrary to her expectations, Grace was actually enjoying her evening out. In fact, Eric was sweeping her off her feet. He was behaving impeccably, taking her first to a lovely meal of steak and kidney pie at Lyons Corner House in Coventry Street, followed by a long stroll down Whitehall to the Victoria Embankment by the River Thames, and then back again through Trafalgar Square and the Haymarket to Piccadilly Circus, stopping at the steps of Eros, where Eric bought Grace a single red rose from an old female flower-seller there. Grace responded by giving him a kiss, much to the delight of the flower-seller, and playful jeers from a group of passing teenagers. Although Grace felt quite self-conscious, Eric was completely oblivious to them all, and stood there for several moments, just staring into her eyes, extinguishing from his mind the flashing advertisement signs high above them on the other side of the circus, and the huge billboards of the London Pavilion theatre displaying a new revue with Jessie Matthews.

Grace loved the attention she was getting from Eric; in just those few hours it seemed to obliterate the painful memories of their former relationship. As the pubs were still open, Eric suggested they go for a drink to a place he knew just behind Lower Regent Street, and although Grace had never really liked going into such places, she agreed to go.

The Captain's Cabin was an old-established West End drinking house, small, cosy, and with an atmosphere different from what Gus and Georgie O'Hara had been used to in their beloved Nag's Head. There was only half an hour to go before closing time, and the place was packed with customers desperate to stay until they were thrown out. Whilst Eric was at the bar counter buying drinks, Grace felt a bit uncomfortable, for there were one or two over-made-up women sitting together there, who kept eyeing her with suspicion.

'I used to come here for a drink at lunch times,' said Eric, once he'd found his way back to Grace, who had managed to settle herself against a wall by the fireplace. He gave her the tonic water she'd asked for, and took a quick sip of his own whisky and soda. 'I did quite a lot of business around the Haymarket. I love the West End. One of these days I intend to buy a place of my own to live in round here.'

Grace took that remark with a pinch of salt. 'I prefer Islington,' she replied, taking a wary look around the strangely subdued customers in the bar.

'Why?' asked Eric, puzzled.

'I don't know really,' said Grace. 'Because I've spent all my life there, I suppose.'

'Sometimes it's good to make a change,' he said, 'do something entirely different. I think what you're doing now is terrific.'

'What d'you mean?' she asked.

'The way you're coping with things. Although I still think you should sell up and start a new life somewhere else. Preferably with me.' He leaned forward, and gave her a quick, light kiss on her forehead. 'D'you think you could ever forgive me, Grace,' he asked, his face almost touching hers, 'for the lousy way I behaved when we first met?'

This was a question Grace had hoped he would never ask, because she didn't know how to answer it. There was no doubt that she *was* growing fond of him again, but she still couldn't be certain whether love had anything to do with it.

'It was a long time ago, Eric,' she replied. 'Maybe we should take each day as it comes. Let's see what happens when your divorce comes through. Will you have to pay something to your wife?'

'Alimony, you mean?' he asked dismissively. 'Not if *I* can help it.' He took a gulp of his whisky. 'Anyway, I don't care about her. It's you I care about, Grace. I want to help you get through all your problems.'

Grace smiled weakly. She was only too aware that he had thrown one or two quick looks across at the two women sitting together on the other side of the bar.

'Tell me,' said Eric, leaning his hand against the wall above her head. 'Where do you go on these weekends?'

Grace gave him a surprised look. '*What* weekends?' she asked.

'Well – I bumped into your friend Pauline the other day,' he replied. 'I live in Ronalds Road, just round the corner from the library where she works. She was saying that you sometimes go off for the weekend, just to give yourself a break. I think it's a very sensible idea.' He paused to sip his whisky again, whilst asking casually, 'Where d'you go to?'

Grace hesitated before replying. 'I go to visit an old friend of my father and mother. They were devoted to her. She lives down by the sea, in Devon.'

'Devon?' asked Eric excitedly. 'I *love* Devon. Especially the rough cider. D'you know it's a hundred per cent proof down there.'

'Really?' said Grace, unsure of what he was trying to get at.

'We should go down there together sometime,' he suggested eagerly. 'Maybe put up at a B and B overlooking the sea somewhere.' He pressed close to her again. 'I want to spend more time with you, Grace. I want to try and make up for all the time we've been apart.'

Grace waited a moment before replying. 'I may not be going down there again, Eric,' she replied. 'The woman I go to see doesn't live there any more.'

Eric hesitated. 'Oh well,' he said with a persistent smile, 'we don't need an excuse to go *anywhere*. As long as I'm with you, that's all I care about.'

Once the pub had closed, the two of them again strolled hand in hand together through the dark backstreet between the Haymarket and Lower Regent Street. It was hard to believe they were so close to the bright lights of the West End, for, once the pub customers were on their way, the whole area became quite ghostly. Once he was sure the coast was clear, Eric gradually led Grace off into the shadows of a long dark back alley. Pressing up as close and tight to her as he possibly could, he took her in his arms, and kissed her passionately.

'One question,' he asked softly. 'Do you feel the same about me as I feel about you?'

'I don't know how to answer that,' replied Grace.

'I mean – do you love me?'

Grace waited a moment before answering. 'I – think I do, Eric.'

'Only *think*?'

'I've told you before,' she replied, 'I need time.'

This irritated him. 'For Christ's sake, Grace!' he snapped. 'How much time do you need? If two people love each other—'

'Before two people can love each other,' Grace reminded him, 'there has to be trust between them.'

'Are you saying you don't trust me?'

'No, Eric,' she replied. 'That's not what I'm saying. But this time, I want to get to know you, to *really* know you. I like you. I like you very much. And I want to go on seeing you.'

Eric went silent for a moment. As this was not going entirely as he had hoped, he changed tactic, and softened his stance. 'I'm sorry, darling,' he said. He gently lifted her chin with his hand, and moved his face so close that he could feel her breath against him. 'My trouble is that I'm so impatient. I want you so badly.' He kissed her long, and passionately.

She responded to him, and put her arms around his neck. She could feel the warmth of his body, and it excited her.

'Just one thing, though,' he said quietly, as he pulled away. 'That man – the one who's working for you – is he a permanent fixture?'

Grace was curious. 'I can't run the business without him, Eric,' she replied without apology. 'Now that Father's gone, I need a man around the place to help me with Clapper and in the shop.'

'You *have* a man to help you,' said Eric. 'I'll move in any time you like.'

Grace was disturbed by his remark. She was unsure how to answer it. 'You're different, Eric,' she replied. 'You're not an employee. I don't have to pay *you*.'

'I don't like him being there.'

Grace was aware of the coldness of his tone. 'I don't know what you mean?' she said.

'I don't like him being there in the house with you,' insisted Eric. 'I don't like the thought of you being alone with him.'

'He never comes into the house, Eric,' Grace replied. 'And the only time we've ever been alone together is when he's grooming Clapper, or we're out on our rounds.'

He drew closer to her, and whispered in her ear, 'Get rid of him, Grace. Do it – for *me*.' He kissed her again.

Whilst he was doing so, Grace could smell the lingering remains of the cologne he had put on before he came out that evening. She didn't like it. She didn't like it at all. It was stale – and sour.

Chapter 14

Georgie O'Hara hadn't seen Grace since her father had
died. No wonder. Ever since the drunken night he had
betrayed Gus's confidence by blabbering to Gert Jolly about
Grace's inheritance down in Devon, he had hardly slept a
wink. Time and time again he wanted to go up to see Grace
at The Chapel, but each time he had lost his nerve and kept
away from her. He hadn't even told his own missus what
he'd done; if he had, he knew only too well that he would
never have heard the last of it. But now it was two months
after that fateful evening with Gert in The Eaglet, and his
conscience was telling him that if he didn't own up to Grace
now, his ol' mate Gus would most certainly ensure that the
Lord High Guv'nor Himself would never let him through
those pearly gates. Even if Grace kicked him out and told
him that she never wanted to see him again, he had to clear
the air. By talking to Gert Jolly, he was talking to all of Gus's
customers and tenants. By now, the whole of Islington
probably knew that Grace had been left a very rich girl. No.
He couldn't go on like this any longer. He had to get it off
his chest once and for all. He knew exactly the time and
place where he could talk to Grace, and this time he
wouldn't run away from what he should have done a long
time ago.

Grace and Mickey were having a busy morning in
Annette Road. Although her father had taken on only two
properties there, the lower end of the road was in an area
that was always a thriving trade for groceries, mainly because

it was quite a walk to the nearest shops in either Seven Sisters or Holloway Roads. It was also a favourite spot for Grace, for it was very close to Shelburne Road, where she went to school. This morning there had been quite a run on spuds, especially the King Edwards, and Grace was only grateful that Mickey was on hand to lug the huge sacks around.

One of Grace's best customers was Kath Hamblin, a lovely young woman from nearby Caedmon Road, who was married to a porter up at the Royal Northern Hospital, but who had taken quite a fancy to Mickey.

'Wrap 'im up and put 'im under my Chris'mas tree any time,' she quipped, to gales of laughter from the other customers waiting to be served.

'I bet 'e could teach my ol' man a fing or two!' quipped one of the middle-aged customers.

Although Grace was a bit embarrassed by all this type of attention Mickey was getting, she quite understood it. With his muscles rippling as he lifted heavy sacks and wooden boxes, it was no wonder people tried to put two and two together.

'Lucky cow!' called an elderly customer, again to gales of laughter.

'So wot's all the larfter about gels?' called Mickey, as he struggled through the inside of the shop carrying a refill sack of carrots.

'Give us a kiss, darlin'!' yelled the elderly customer from the kerb, to more laughter.

'Sorry, mate!' he replied. 'Yer're a bit young fer me!'

The others laughed and cheered. They loved his repartee. Grace also loved it, and the way he got on so well with the customers. It seemed so effortless, which it was for Mickey, for he was a natural; he had no pretensions whatsoever. As she listened to the buzz amongst the customers talking about him, she couldn't help casting her mind back to what Eric had asked her to do. There was no way that she was going to get rid of Mickey. He was now an essential part of the business, and was showing a human face to the customers, just as her father had always done.

A short time later, Grace took Clapper and the shop off the road for their usual lunch-time stopover in the seclusion of the large goods delivery yard behind Jones Brothers department store. For the past few weeks she had taken to making sandwiches and a flask of hot tea for herself and Mickey, and this gave them all a chance to rest a while, and prepare themselves for the afternoon grocery round. The weather was beginning to look decidedly unsettled, with the threat of rain, and although the shop was crammed with provisions, they managed to find enough space to eat inside.

'Got a favour to ask, miss,' said Mickey, tucking into his cheese sandwich made with two thick slices of bread, which was how he liked it. 'Could yer teach me ter read?'

Grace flicked him a surprised look. 'Mickey!' she replied. 'Are you telling me you don't know how?'

Mickey, mouth full, shook his head. 'Can't write eivver. I got me neighbour, Ma Gremlin to write that letter I sent yer after yer dad died.'

The more she thought about it, the more she realised that, since it appeared he had rarely ever turned up at school, there was no reason why he should know how to read or write, or indeed have learnt anything. In fact, Mickey's request had suddenly made her understand why he had sometimes taken so long to collect a particular tin or jar or packet of something she had asked him for, even though he had always worked it out for himself in the end. 'Mickey,' she replied, 'you must stop me when I keep correcting you like a schoolteacher. As a matter of fact, you manage pretty well on your own.'

Mickey again shook his head. 'I like the way yer tell me 'ow ter say fings the proper way,' he assured her. 'It's funny, when I was a kid, I didn't care a frupenny bit wevver I knew about fings or not, but now I've got older I sometimes reckon I've missed out. It's fanks ter you I want ter find out 'ow ter catch up.'

For a moment, Grace thought about this. She put the remains of her sandwich back into the brown paper she had wrapped it in, and wiped her hands and lips on her handkerchief. 'It's not so hard when you set your mind to it,' she said. 'For instance,' she looked up at one of the shelves above her, 'which of those packets up there are tea?'

Mickey looked up to the shelf, and immediately spotted what she had asked for. 'Them!' he said triumphantly, pointing to several packets of Lipton's tea.

'How do you know that?' asked Grace.

Mickey was puzzled.

'What I mean is,' continued Grace, 'do you know what's in those packets because of what it says on the outside, or is it because you associate with what's inside?'

The last of Mickey's cheese sandwich disappeared as he gulped it down. 'Dunno wot yer mean, miss?' he replied sheepishly.

Grace reached up, and brought down one of the packets of tea. 'Here,' she said. 'Take it.'

Mickey wiped his hands on his work trousers, and took the packet.

'What does it say?'

'Tea, miss.'

'Where does it say that?' she asked.

Mickey scratched his head, and searched in vain for the word she had asked for.

Grace took it back from him, and pointed to the letters. 'T – E – A,' she spelt out, clearly and phonetically. 'That's the letter T, that's the letter E, and that's the letter A.'

Mickey repeated what she had said: 'T – E – A.'

'That's it,' said Grace. 'To be able to read and write, Mickey, the first thing you must learn is the alphabet.' She looked up at another of the shelves, and read out what she saw on the bottles, packets, and tins: 'Scrubb's Ammonia, Wright's Coal Tar Soap, Zam-buk.'

'That's that funny green stuff you get for that lady in Jackson Road!'

'That's right,' said Grace, 'but you didn't read the words, you just guessed.'

Mickey looked crestfallen.

'Don't worry,' Grace assured him. 'All you have to do is to learn the alphabet, then, as we sell things, if you really want, I'll get you to find them not by guessing, but by what the letters say. It'll all make sense in time.'

Completely baffled, Mickey's eyes looked up woefully, and scanned the products on the upper shelves.

'Grace.'

Both of them turned with a start to find someone peering into the back door of the shop.

'Mr O'Hara!' Grace immediately went to him.

'I'm sorry to trouble you, Grace,' he said edgily. 'I just wondered if yer could spare me a coupla minutes?'

'Of course,' she replied. 'I'll be back in a while, Mickey.' Georgie helped her down the steps of the van. 'Is anything wrong?'

'Could we go somewhere quiet?' he asked, conscious that he could be overheard.

'Of course.'

They strolled out towards the arcade leading to Holloway Road, which was busy with lunch-time shoppers.

'I've got somethin' ter tell yer, Grace,' he said, bringing them to a halt in a secluded spot by one of the shop windows. 'It's about your dad – and you. I've done yer both a terrible disservice.'

'Disservice?' asked Grace, puzzled.

'I should've told yer about this a long time ago,' he continued, his Irish brogue tripping off his tongue broader than ever, 'but I'm such a barmy ol' fool, an' I couldn't bear the thought of hurtin' yer.' He hesitated in his difficulty. 'Soon after your dad died, I went inter The Eaglet ter drown me sorrows. I couldn't bear ter drink in the Nag's Head, not after all those years him an' me . . .' Distressed, he paused. 'Anyways, quite by accident, I met up with ol' Ma Jolly – you know – Gert Jolly, one er yer dad's tenants.'

Grace nodded. 'I know her.'

'I was half cut, Grace,' he said, in a desperate attempt to explain before he had told her what he had done. 'Honest ter God, I didn't know wot I was doin', let alone wot I was sayin'.' He paused again, took off his flat cap, and ran his hands through his almost totally white hair. Then he looked her straight in the face. 'I told her everythin',' he said outright.

Grace hadn't the faintest idea what he was talking about. 'Told her what, Mr O'Hara?'

'About you,' he said, with real anguish. 'About what yer dad'd left yer – down in Devon.'

Grace was so taken aback, it took her a moment to grasp what he was saying. 'You told Mrs Jolly . . .' She hesitated to gather her thoughts. 'You mean, you know about—'

'I know *everythin'*, Grace,' said Georgie. 'I've always known. Yer dad used ter tell me everythin'. I know about the house in Devon, the money. I know about – about the little lady he knew down there.'

Grace found herself leaning her back against the shop window. Behind her, an ambulance was racing down Holloway Road. Its panicking alarm bell pierced the air, and caused heads everywhere to turn and watch it pass.

'Your dad was my friend, Grace,' continued O'Hara, desperately trying to avert her gaze. 'He trusted me, he confided in me. In all the years we knew each other, I've never breathed a word ter anyone of wot he told me – not even me own missus.'

Grace found it hard to take in what Georgie was telling her. Until this moment, she had no idea that, with the exception of Bernice Laurier, anyone in the whole wide world knew anything about her inheritance. Georgie's confession was shocking, not just for what he had said, but for its implications. If Gert Jolly knew about her financial affairs now that Gus had gone, then every one of her dad's tenants and customers would probably know too. It was an absurd situation to find herself in. How would she ever be able to continue pressing the tenants to pay up their arrears if they were under the impression that she was a rich woman? And if people like them knew, what about Aunt Hilda? What was it she had said over the Sunday meal only the week before: *Is that why yer've bin goin' away at the weekends?* She could hear Hilda's penetrating question ringing in her ears. She knew all right. She knew because by now the whole of Holloway must know.

And then there was the rest of the family. What could she, Grace, say to Auntie Josie and Uncle Stan? Would they, like Hilda, accuse her of trying to cut them out of her dad's inheritance? She cringed at the thought of how she was going to be able to deal with all this. And then she thought of Eric. Even though she had never told Pauline the exact reasons why she had been down to Devon several times, she surely must have put two and two together, and given Eric something to think about.

It started to rain. In Holloway Road, people were scurrying for cover, whilst in the goods yard, Grace could just see Mickey covering Clapper with a tarpaulin.

After a brief moment to compose herself, she turned to Georgie again. His face was crunched up, and tears were welling in his eyes. 'It's all right, Mr O'Hara,' she said reassuringly. 'These things happen. I know what Dad felt about you. I know that you would never have betrayed him – or me – intentionally.'

Georgie looked up at her. 'I hate meself, Grace,' he said angrily. 'All those years I kept his secret, an' after a few pints er bitter, I spill the whole thing out as though there was no termorrer. I'm tellin' yer, it's time they sent me off ter the knacker's yard.'

Grace smiled. 'No, Mr O'Hara,' she said to him bravely, trying to comfort him. 'You've got a lot of life ahead of you yet. You're not to worry. I'm not blaming you. I'm not blaming you for anything. What's done is done. What I've got to do now is to think again, think about how I'm going to deal with Dad's tenants, how I'm going to balance what I have, and what I don't have. But you've got to help me, Mr O'Hara. If you have any feeling for Dad at all, you've got to help me.'

They were interrupted by a deafening clap of thunder.

'Help you?' asked the distressed Georgie.

'Help me to get Dad's business on its feet again,' said Grace. 'I need all the support I can get.'

Georgie's eyes were glistening with tears, which he attempted to dab away. 'I'm an ol' man now, Grace,' he replied. 'There's not much *I* can do.'

Grace smiled, and put a comforting arm around his waist. 'Oh, but there is,' she replied. 'Dad trusted you in the past, and *I* trust you now. Forget all about Gert Jolly. Forget all about what happened in The Eaglet that night. Believe me, you've got far more to offer in this world than you think, dear friend. Dad knew it – and so do I.'

Hilda Barnet took cover from the rain in the Athenaeum Arcade at the junction of Holloway and Parkhurst Roads, just opposite the Nag's Head pub. It wasn't a place that she liked very much, because it usually stank of dog and fish food from the pet store just inside the main entrance. At night, the arcade was also a well-known knocking shop for young couples who'd picked each other up at the Irish dance hall in the same building, and so, to Hilda's way of thinking, it was no place for a lady like her to frequent during the day or night. However, as she had no wish to get soaked in the rain on her way to the post office just across the road, she had no option but to wait until it had cleared. What she hadn't anticipated, however, was a chance meeting with both Gert Jolly and Jack Pertwee, who had also been caught in the downpour on the way to the post office to collect their pensions.

'Gas masks?' spluttered Hilda incredulously, her crushed felt hat dripping with wet. 'Wot the bleedin' 'ell're yer talkin' about? We're not at war!'

'Gospel trufe, Mrs Barnet!' said Jack, always delighted to be the bearer of bad news. 'It's all over the papers. The government are goin' ter start issuin' gas masks to everyone – free er charge. It's a sure sign fings're gettin' worse over in

Germany. Our boys'll be back in khaki, you mark my words.'

'Gord 'elp us!' added Gert Jolly, who was trying to knock her brolly back into shape after it had been blown inside out in the wind. 'We've only just got over the last war.'

'That was nineteen years ago, Gert – believe it or not,' said Jack gloomily.

'Seems like yesterday ter me,' replied Gert.

Hilda left them alone to rabbit on, and moved to a more secluded spot away from the wind, which was blowing the rain right into the arcade. A few minutes later, Jack went off to the pet shop to buy some fish food for his goldfish, which gave Hilda the chance to bring Gert over for a private little chat. 'So wot's the latest?' she asked. 'About that rich young niece er mine?'

Gert suddenly went very quiet, and pulled her scarf tighter over her head.

'Wot's up then?' asked Hilda. 'Cat got yer tongue all of a sudden?'

'Look, Mrs Barnet,' Gert replied defensively, 'I've told yer before, I don't know nuffin' about your niece.'

'That's funny,' persisted Hilda. 'There were plenty of rumours goin' around that yer did.'

'Don't believe everyfin' yer 'ear,' said Gert spikily.

Hilda waited a minute whilst two people, who had been sheltering together out of the rain in one of the other arcade shops, moved on. 'I was just wondering if she was planning any more trips down ter Devon?' she asked.

Gert refused to answer.

'You're an intelligent woman, Mrs Jolly,' said Hilda, peering out aimlessly at the driving rain. 'You 'ave eyes an' ears, an' yer use them whenever yer want to. Whoever told yer about my Grace's good fortune must know a lot more – wouldn't you say?'

Gert swung her an angry look. 'I was told wrong!' she snapped. 'Grace 'Iggs is fightin' fer every penny she can get – just like all the rest of us. As a matter of fact, I've changed my tune about 'er. She's diff'rent ter wot she used ter be. She cares about us.'

'Diff'rent indeed,' added Hilda caustically. 'I wonder why.'

'People don't *'ave* ter 'ave a reason,' Gert replied. 'Since 'er dad died, she's gone out of 'er way ter make us feel as though she understands us. And *we* understand *'er*. At least – *I* do. As it so 'appens, I've managed to pay back over 'alf wot I owe already. Gus 'Iggs was good ter me, always was. It's the least I can do ter 'elp out 'is gel.'

'Wot if I told yer she doesn't need yer 'elp?' said Hilda, turning to her. 'Or *anyone's* 'elp.'

Gert again turned to look at her.

'Yes, Mrs Jolly,' said Hilda. 'My niece is a very clever gel. She knows she can 'ave 'er cake *an'* eat it. She also knows 'ow not ter share any of it wiv 'er own family.'

The rain was beginning to ease off, so Gert put up her umbrella and started to move off.

'Mrs Jolly,' called Hilda.

Gert stopped and turned.

'Don't get me wrong,' said Hilda. 'I loved my brother. I'd've done anyfin' for 'im. 'E was good, an' kind, an' considerate. I'd do anyfin' fer my niece too. The only fing is, she plays too many games wiv people's lives. It's not right. Wouldn't you agree?'

Gert sniffed, and left the arcade.

Hilda watched her go. She was worried about Gert's change of attitude. Only a few weeks before, she had been absolutely vitriolic about the way Grace was treating all Gus's tenants, and yet now, here she was defending the girl.

It was strange, truly strange. So why had Grace changed so much? There could only be one reason, and to understand that, she, Hilda, had to find out why her niece had been going to Devon so much. If Grace *was* keeping something from the family, then maybe it needed someone else to persuade her that she couldn't do so for much longer.

Soon after she got home, Grace received a telegram. It immediately made her stomach churn, for telegrams only ever seemed to bring bad news. She quickly ripped it open, and read the brief, typed message inside:

GRACE. REG MISSING IN ACTION. PLEASE COME OVER. UNCLE STAN

Grace felt quite sick, and after asking Mickey if he could stay with Clapper until she got home, she headed off to Stoke Newington.

Auntie Josie was utterly distraught and inconsolable. She, Uncle Stan and Viv were all crying; the news could hardly be worse.

'Who told you?' asked Grace, the moment she arrived at the house. 'How d'you know this has happened?'

'One of Reg's mates in 'is regiment come to see us,' said a grim-faced Uncle Stan. 'Spotty-faced little sod 'e is. Wot does a kid er that age know about politics? 'E should be 'ome playin' football wiv 'is mates, or chattin' up gelfriends.'

'He said Reg got caught up in a terrible battle in some place called Santander,' said a tearful Viv to Grace. 'It's in the north of Spain somewhere, on the Bay of Biscay.'

'They got ambushed,' said Stan, fighting back tears, and holding a sobbing Josie close to him. 'It was a real bloodbarf.'

'We don't know that, Dad,' said Viv. 'The boy said a lot of the other side got massacred, but he was on lookout on a bridge on the other side of the rocks.'

'Then how does he know what happened to Reg?' asked Grace.

'The last 'e saw of Reg,' said Uncle Stan, 'was when 'e went over the top wiv a whole lot of uvver blokes. Most of 'em got machine-gunned as they went in fer 'and-ter-' and fightin'.' He paused. 'Most of 'em didn't get back – includin' Reg.'

Grace went to Josie, and took over from Uncle Stan. 'You mustn't give up, Auntie,' she said, doing her best to comfort her. 'No one actually knows what happened to Reg. He's no fool. It's more than likely he got away. He's probably hiding out somewhere. If the worst came to the worst he might have been injured and been taken prisoner.'

Josie was not convinced. 'God knows *wot's* 'appened to 'im, Gracie,' she sobbed. 'All I know is 'e's my boy, an' I want 'im 'ome!' She collapsed into tears again in Grace's arms.

'Is there no way of finding out something more definite?' asked Grace.

'I went to the police station,' said Viv. 'They phoned some government place. I think it was the Foreign Office or something. All they said was it was totally illegal for Reg to have gone out to Spain in the first place, that because of the situation out there they had no way of checking whether he was dead or alive.'

Josie sobbed more intensely into Grace's shoulder.

There was a knock on the front door. Viv went to answer it.

'Let's not take any notice of what stupid people in the government say!' Grace said angrily. 'They don't know about people. They only know about rules and regulations.'

'Yeah,' added Stan, bitterly. 'An' they're far too busy suckin' up ter 'Itler an' Mussolini!'

'Wot's all this then?' called Hilda from the door. 'Reg missin'? Who said so?'

'One of his friends, Auntie,' said Grace. 'There's nothing we can do about it until we get confirmation.'

'Bleedin' Spaniards!' barked Hilda. 'I always knew they were savages. That's why they 'ave bullfights!'

Grace glared at her over Josie's shoulder.

Realising that she was in danger of distressing the others even more, Hilda quietly sat down in an armchair. 'Poor little bugger,' she said, with her first sign of sympathy. 'I'd 'ate ter fink anyfin's 'appened ter 'im. I was always very fond er that boy.'

Again Grace glared at her. 'The family must just stick together,' she said. 'Perhaps we should say a few prayers.'

'I'll say *anyfin'* if I can only get 'im back 'ome again!' sobbed Josie.

'Why do these kids 'ave ter do this sort er fing?' asked Stan, as if questioning his own conscience. 'This boy that come 'ere, when I asked 'im why *'e* did it, said, " 'Cos if yer don't believe in stoppin' somefin' yer know's wrong, then there's nuffin' ter live for." Nuffin' ter live for? When I fink er those kids lyin' out there on the ground in a foreign country, I wonder *why* they felt they 'ad nuffin' ter live for? Yes, I believe in 'elpin' uvvers who're in trouble, but I fink there comes a time when yer 'ave to remember where yer come from, *who* yer come from. When Mum an' I 'ad kids, I never fawt the day would come when one of 'em would go before us. Him up there give us the chance ter see an' 'ear all sorts er terrific fings. I'd 'ate ter fink one er me own didn't take that chance.' Stan sat down.

But for Josie's gentle sobbing, there was silence in the room.

Grace looked across at Hilda. Tears were now streaming down her face too.

It was dark by the time Grace got back to The Chapel. On the way home her mind had been pulverised by all the emotion of the past few hours. Auntie Josie was inconsolable, Uncle Stan was in the depths of gloom, and Viv had withdrawn back into her shell. The great surprise for Grace, however, had been Hilda, who had never seemed capable of being upset by anything or anyone. But Reg was different. For some reason or another, Hilda had always had a soft spot for her nephew, mainly because he was totally independent, just like herself. But to see her cry was a whole new experience for Grace. She had never seen her do such a thing before, and it was illuminating. At least it showed that somewhere there was a heart beneath that hard, grasping exterior. As for herself, she had been too busy trying to keep up the family's spirits to show how *she* felt. When she had left the house in Stoke Newington, she had wanted to grieve, but somehow the tears wouldn't come, and she couldn't fathom out why. But losing Reg was real enough. Auntie Josie and Uncle Stan had always fawned over him, and if anything had really happened to him, then it would devastate them to the end of their days.

Grace entered by the back yard gates. The first thing she noticed was that there was a light streaming from beneath the stable door, so she went straight across to let Mickey know that she was home. However, when she peered inside the stable, she found Mickey sprawled out fast asleep on the straw, his head resting on Clapper's stomach. It brought her first smile of the evening, so she crept out again quietly. But she had hardly reached the back door of the house when Mickey called to her from the stable.

'Is that you, miss?'

Grace turned, to find him coming towards her. The light from the stable cut across the yard, but all she could see was his silhouette. 'I'm sorry, Mickey,' she replied. 'I didn't want to wake you. Is everything all right?'

'Everyfin's fine, miss,' he replied. 'Wot about you?'

Grace sighed deeply. 'It's not good, Mickey,' she replied. 'The family are convinced my cousin is dead.'

'D'*you* fink 'e is?'

'I've no idea,' replied Grace. 'Unfortunately the authorities are no help at all when it comes to getting information about the British volunteers in Spain. They're only interested in the politics of the war over there. They're not much interested in what's happened to people's relatives and friends. Whatever you do, Mickey, don't go and fight someone else's battle unless you know what it's all about.'

'I'd never do that, miss,' replied Mickey, more serious than usual, his voice echoing in the dark. 'But if I had ter defend me *own* country, I would.'

'I hope you never have to,' said Grace.

'The way fings're goin',' said Mickey, 'I'm not so sure. If yer ask me, ol' Chamberlain's makin' a big mistake.'

Grace stared at him in the dark. Although she couldn't see his features, she could feel his presence strongly. 'I didn't know you knew anything about politics, Mickey,' she said, with some surprise. 'Especially as you can't read.'

'Oh, I don't 'ave ter read ter know wot's goin' on in the world, miss,' replied Mickey. 'I get all the info I need from me mates up the pub. They say Chamberlain should never trust 'Itler. They say 'Itler's the sort er bloke who'd stab yer in the back as good as look at yer.'

'But isn't it better to talk before going to war?' asked Grace.

'Depends, miss,' said Mickey.

'On what?'

'On who gets in first,' said Mickey. 'I mean it ain't no good fightin' back *after* yer dead, is it?'

Grace found Mickey's home-spun opinions disconcerting. In that respect he was just like every other man, young or old, who was currently worried about the Prime Minister's appeasement of the new, hostile regime in Germany.

'I must get to bed,' she said wearily. 'It's been a terrible evening. You get on home, Mickey. I can manage now. Thank you for staying on. Good night.' She turned to go.

' 'Night, miss.' Mickey went back to the stable, and blew out the lamp. ' 'Night, mate!' he called to Clapper, before bolting him in for the night. 'See yer in the mornin'.'

He made his way to the back yard gates, but just as he was getting there, he suddenly heard a sound coming from the back door of the house. 'Miss?' he called. 'Are yer all right?' Grace didn't reply, so he hurried across to find out what was going on. When he got to her, he found her quietly sobbing to herself. 'Miss! Wot is it? Wot's wrong?'

Grace was too upset to answer him, for all the tensions of the past few hours with the family were now being released, and tears were streaming down her face. 'Oh God, Mickey!' she cried. 'Sometimes, this can be such a rotten world!' In one sudden burst of uncontrollable emotion, she threw her arms around him, and kissed him full on the lips.

Mickey was taken completely by surprise. But he just stood there quite motionless, not knowing what to say or do.

Grace left her lips pressed against his for longer than she realised. But then gradually, she pulled away. 'Oh Mickey,' she gasped with a sigh. 'I'm so sorry. I'm so terribly sorry. I don't know why I did such a thing . . . I'm – so ashamed . . . I'm – so . . .' Flustered and disoriented, she rushed into the house.

For a brief moment, Mickey just stood there transfixed, hardly able to believe what had just happened. With the tips of his fingers, he gently touched his lips. They were still moist from Grace's kiss. It was a wonderful feeling, a feeling that he had not expected ever to happen to him. But he was glad it did. It was a moment he would never forget.

He turned, and quietly left the yard.

249

Chapter 15

Rose Marchmont was a woman of hidden depths. Grace first met her when she was a gangling adolescent, sent to Mrs Marchmont for piano lessons by her mother, Alice, who had hoped that her daughter would benefit from some kind of musical education. Unfortunately, it didn't quite turn out that way, for Grace soon showed that she had no ear for either rhythm or style, and was totally incapable of learning even the basic scales. However, what Grace *did* discover was that Mrs Marchmont possessed qualities that would make her a friend for life, and she had had no greater friend in that life than Grace's mother. Now in her late seventies, Rose lived in virtual seclusion on the ground floor of what had once been her elegant three-storey Edwardian house in Barnsbury Park, housebound for the past ten years after contracting a severe bout of polio, which was a recurrence of the same illness she had suffered from as a child in India, where her parents were stationed in the colonial service. However, although now confined to a wheelchair, Rose continued to present herself with dignity and style, for she would always dress beautifully, wear make-up and discreet pieces of jewellery, and wear her pure white hair in a way that was always a picture of sheer elegance.

Owing to her disability, Rose hadn't been able to get to Gus's funeral, which was why Grace hadn't seen her for some time. This was a pity, because 'Marchie', which had been Grace's nickname for her when she was young, had always been like a second mother to her, and when Grace's own mother died, it was 'Marchie' who had helped her get through the pain of losing her.

Marchie's large drawing room may not have been as elegant and well cared for as it used to be, but when Grace called on her, it seemed as though time had stood still, for there was Marchie in her wheelchair at the baby grand piano, playing Chopin with as much joy, vigour, and love as she had always done.

'See what you've missed,' called Marchie, the moment Grace entered the room. 'If only you'd practised your scales, you could have been the toast of the concert halls!'

Grace laughed. Her old friend and mentor hadn't changed a bit. And she was just as shrewd as ever, which she soon discovered once Rose's housekeeper, Mrs Snow, had brought in some tea.

'Come on then – out with it!' Marchie's eyes were bulging out of the sockets of a bony white face. 'You haven't come here just to listen to me playing Chopin. What's up?' She pointed to the settee facing her wheelchair.

Grace sat there. 'I don't know where to start, Marchie,' she said. 'So much has happened since I last saw you. I miss Dad so much – and I really need him to help sort out all the problems he's left me.'

She poured tea for them both, and for the next half an hour she told Marchie everything about The House on the Hill, the money her father had left her, and the woman with whom he'd had such a special relationship. She also told her about the problems she was having with her Aunt Hilda, and how, the way things were going, sometimes she even feared that the whole issue could end up in court. And then she talked about her relationship with Eric Tyler, her mixed feelings towards him, and her inability to know whether she loved him enough to want to spend the rest of her life with him.

Marchie smiled wryly. 'Bad as your mother,' she said. 'You spend most of your life hiding away from men, and then you can't make up your mind which one you want.'

Grace was startled to hear her old piano teacher talking about her mother in such a way. 'I don't know what you mean, Marchie. There was only ever one man in Mum's life.'

Marchie roared with laughter, and put down her cup and saucer on her small side table. 'Wishful thinking, my dear,' she said. 'Wishful thinking.' She manoeuvred her wheelchair over to her flip-top desk, and after rummaging through a drawer there, she took out an envelope. 'Here!' she said, turning round to offer it to Grace.

Grace got up from the settee, and took the envelope. 'What is it?' she asked with some trepidation.

Marchie shrugged. 'Take a look.'

Grace opened the envelope. Inside were several snapshot photographs of a young soldier in uniform. One or two of them were taken arm in arm with Grace's mother. Grace sorted through them, then looked up at Marchie, who was watching her with a certain amount of irony. 'Who *is* this man?' she asked sceptically.

'He was your mother's lover for four years,' Marchie replied. 'They met a long time before she married your father. She was – how can I say? – besotted with him. I won't burden you with his name – it's quite immaterial. But, as you can see, he was a very handsome creature. He asked your mother to marry him.'

Grace was now thoroughly confused. 'Then – why didn't she?'

'Because he walked out on her,' replied Marchie. She

turned her wheelchair away, and came to a halt with her back to the piano. 'There was someone else.'

Grace was in a state of total disbelief. Apart from knowing for the first time that her mother had had a relationship with another man, the coincidence of Grace herself having been jilted in the same way by Eric Tyler was almost impossible to grasp. 'What happened?' she asked, dazed.

'He found someone that he was more attracted to,' continued Marchie, 'not because she was more beautiful or intelligent or desirable than Alice, but because this other person found him utterly irresistible.'

'But – who *was* this other person?' asked Grace.

'It was me, my dear,' Marchie replied.

It took Grace a moment to take all this in. When she had recovered from the shock, she asked, 'You took this man away from my mother?'

Marchie nodded. 'Yes, Grace,' she replied. 'I'm afraid I did. The only consolation I have to offer is that it was the biggest mistake of my life. Of course, it wasn't easy to explain that to your mother at the time. For two years she hated the sight of me, until that is, our mutual friend did exactly the same to me. Fortunately for both me and your mother, we eventually met men that we loved, men whom we trusted enough to spend the rest of our lives with. Mind you, our "friend" hadn't quite finished with us. Some years later, after we were both married, he reappeared, and did his best to pick up where he had left off. But it didn't work. It didn't work for me, and it didn't work for Alice. But he tried.'

Grace found it hard to take in what Marchie had just told her, and her mind was buzzing with the parallel situation between herself and Eric Tyler. 'What happened to this man?' she asked.

'He died,' replied Marchie quite casually, swivelling her wheelchair around so that she was facing the piano. 'No one quite knows how or why. All we were told is that his body was found floating in the Thames near Blackfriars Bridge. It was sad but, for someone like him, inevitable.'

Grace returned her cup to its saucer. 'Marchie,' she asked. 'Why has it taken you so long to tell me all this?'

'Because now I don't want to see you making the same mistake,' replied Marchie. 'Some men can't help themselves. They see a woman as an object, a stepping-stone to things they want badly. You know there's always someone else waiting for you just around the corner, someone you may not have noticed before, someone who loves you, but hasn't the courage to tell you. Whoever he is, Grace my dear, he's worth waiting for.' Her fingers came to rest on the piano, and started to glide effortlessly over the keyboard. This time, however, the music was not Chopin, but the lilting strains of a popular current melody, 'I'll See You in my Dreams'.

Marchie's advice had given Grace a lot to think about, and she now knew what she had to do about Eric Tyler. It also made her realise that her relationship with Mickey Burke was something she could not afford to lose.

It was several days before Grace plucked up enough courage to mention to Mickey the impetuous kiss she had given him. 'I don't know what came over me,' she said, as Clapper led them and the shop down Caledonian Road towards the Nag's Head. 'I'd had such a terrible day. I was so upset, I suppose I must have just been bottling everything up inside.' She was tongue-tied, fumbling her words. 'I mean . . . it's not that I've ever been particularly fond of Reg, but he is, after all, my own flesh and blood, and – I couldn't bear to see my aunt and uncle so . . .'

'Yer don't 'ave ter apologise ter me about nuffin', miss,' said Mickey, who was at Clapper's reins. 'I knew 'ow yer felt. I just wish I could've done somefin' ter 'elp yer.'

'Oh, but you *did* help me, Mickey,' she assured him. 'The very fact that you were there . . .' Aware that she might be embarrassing him, she stopped what she was saying. 'What I mean is, I'm grateful there was someone I could talk to. You were so kind and understanding. I promise I won't do such a stupid thing again.'

Resisting the urge to turn and look at her, Mickey concentrated on the road ahead. He wanted to tell her so much, to tell her how he felt, and how that kiss had been one of the most wonderful moments of his life, but for the time being the words had to remain as forbidden as the feelings he had for her. 'Fink nuffin' of it, miss,' was all he would reply.

'Pull over to the side for a moment, please, Mickey,' Grace said quite suddenly.

Mickey swung a startled look at her. 'Miss?'

'Just for a moment,' she said. 'I want to talk to you.'

Confused, Mickey did as he was told. After signalling to a car behind to overtake, he tugged on Clapper's reins and brought them to a halt in Tollington Road. 'Miss?' he asked, turning to her.

'Mickey,' said Grace, 'if I do things during the coming few weeks that seem a little odd to you, will you promise not to take them too seriously?'

Mickey couldn't understand what she was trying to say.

'I think I'm beginning to see things more clearly,' continued Grace. 'I'm beginning to understand what I have to do, about the business, about my life. When my father died, I didn't know whether I wanted to carry on with what he had always done, or to give it all up and get away from it all. But thanks to your help, Mickey, my mind is now much clearer. I'm determined to make the business work. It's already showing signs of picking up. I don't know why, but the tenants are becoming much more co-operative, much more supportive. The arrears from the late payers are going down, Mickey. Once I've managed to balance the books, I intend to go to Mr Rumble – to the bank manager – I'm going to tell him that I want to pay off the mortgages on all the houses my father owned.'

Mickey was astonished that she was confiding in him so much. 'But where're yer goin' ter get all the money ter do that, miss?' he asked.

'From the money my father left me,' said Grace, who was really thinking aloud. After Georgie O'Hara's recent revelations she'd decided there was no point in keeping the truth from Mickey any longer and confided in him the day of Georgie's visit. 'Dad was wrong, Mickey. He shouldn't have left it to me – not all of it, anyway. That money is there to pay off our debts. It's also there for the family – *his* family. After all, they're *my* family too. It's not right that I should hang on to it all myself. I refuse to be greedy. I have obligations, Mickey, and I intend to carry them out.' She suddenly realised that he was looking at her with total bewilderment. She smiled. 'I'm sorry,' she said. 'I know I probably sound quite mad to you, but the fact is, that with you helping me, I think we can build Dad's business up again into something he'd be proud of. D'you understand what I'm saying, Mickey?'

Mickey scratched his head under his cap. 'Well – yes, miss,' he replied vaguely. 'I – *s'ppose* I do. But I dunno 'ow *I* can 'elp yer. I only look after Clapper and lift sacks!'

Grace shook her head. 'No, Mickey,' she replied firmly. 'You do much more than that. You give me confidence. You make me realise that there's more to running a business than collecting money.'

'Money?' asked Josie with very little enthusiasm. 'What *are* yer talkin' about now, 'Ilda?'

Hilda sat straight-backed at her sister's scullery table, eyes gleaming at her with defiance. 'Gus left Grace a fortune. I don't know exactly 'ow much, but from wot I 'ear, it's a tidy sum. An' that's not all. There's property.'

'Property?' asked Stan, who was smoking a fag at the back door.

'As far as I can make out,' said Hilda excitedly, 'it's an 'ouse or somefin' – a big'un. That's why she's bin goin' down ter Devon at the weekends.'

' 'Ow d'yer know all this?' asked Josie, who wasn't really taking it all in.

'Georgie O'Hara,' replied Hilda smugly.

'Georgie?' asked Stan. ' 'E was Gus's best mate.'

'Yes, 'e was!' retorted Hilda triumphantly. 'Apparently 'e knew *everyfin'* about Gus's business, which is more than any of us did.' Leaning across the table to Josie, she was getting more and more enthused. 'Anyway,' she continued, 'the week after Gus died, 'e got boozed an' told everyfin' 'e knew ter Gert Jolly – one of Gus's tenants. Then she passed it on ter some of the uvver tenants, and Bob's yer uncle! Of course, she denies it now. She says Georgie made it all up. But *I* know diff'rent!'

'Well, *you* would, wouldn't yer, 'Ild?' said Josie cuttingly.

Hilda ignored her sister's remark. A week ago she wouldn't have dreamt of confiding in her family about Grace's good fortune, but since Grace had told her that her father's business had nothing to do with any of her family, the only way she was going to get what she considered to be rightfully hers, was to gain the full support *of* the family.

'Just s'ppose Gus *did* leave all wot yer said,' asked Stan, 'wot's it got ter do wiv us?'

'I'll tell yer wot it's got ter do wiv us,' said Hilda, turning to him quite calmly. 'Equal shares.'

'Equal shares?' asked Stan.

'There was no will,' said Hilda. 'Whatever money Gus left ought ter be divided up amongst his relatives – 'is *close* relatives, that is.'

' 'Is closest relative is Grace,' Josie reminded her.

Her sister's comment irritated Hilda. 'We're entitled to equal shares!' she insisted.

'Who said so?' asked Stan, fed up with the constant pressure from his sister-in-law.

'The law!' growled Hilda, who was rapidly becoming a caricature of herself.

Josie looked up with a shocked start. 'The law?' she gasped. 'You've been ter see the law?'

'Not yet,' replied Hilda haughtily. 'But I intend to. I've heard there's a very good solicitor in Upper Street.'

'Are you bloody mad or somefin', 'Ilda Barnet?' snapped Stan, coming across to her. 'We've just lost Gus, an' now Reg, an' you go on about takin' one of yer own – ter *law*?'

Hilda lashed out at him. 'Wot's the matter wiv *you*, Stan Cooker?' she barked, her voice loud and shrill. 'Wot's the matter wiv boaf of yer? Are yer prepared ter let that gel get away wiv anyfin' she wants, ter get away wiv not even lettin' 'er own kith and kin know about wot's bin goin' on? Fer crissake, it was bad enuff wiv Gus 'imself. Never once did 'e 'ave the decency ter discuss anyfin' wiv 'is own family!'

'Why should 'e?' growled Josie, raising her voice in protest for the first time. 'Gus owed us *nuffin*'! 'E was a self-made man. Wot 'e 'ad 'e worked damned 'ard for, an' if 'e wanted ter leave it all ter 'is own daughter, then good luck ter 'im! I don't know wot's the matter wiv yer, 'Ilda. Yer've become tight an' graspin' an' greedy! I don't know yer any more. I don't *want* ter know yer any more. If you want ter go ter law, then you go right ahead, but don't fink *I'll* be there ter support yer – don't fink *any* of us'll be there – 'cos we won't!'

Hilda was stunned into silence. She waited a moment, collected her handbag from the table, and got up from her chair. 'Don't worry,' she said calmly. 'I won't be bothering any of you again.'

Stan went to the door, and opened it for her.

Hilda stopped briefly, and turned. 'But just remember,' she said icily, 'she who laughs last, laughs the longest.'

Considering it was now the end of September, it was still quite warm and humid, and the rain showers that had plagued commuters on their way home earlier that evening were still threatening to return. However, this didn't seem to bother Grace and her friend, Pauline Betts, who, at Pauline's request, had arranged to meet at Lyons Tea Shop opposite Charing Cross station, which had always been much revered because it remained open until the last bus left at night. As usual, the place was quite busy, for it was an evening meeting place for all kinds of weird and wonderful people, such as old tramps, both male and female, trussed up in several layers of second-hand clothes donated by the Salvation Army, spending their day's earnings begging on the streets on a cup of tea and a rock cake, theatregoers having a quick snack before curtain up on Shaftesbury Avenue, and rail passengers waiting for trains from the station just across the road. The air was thick with cigarette smoke, and the atmosphere buzzing with chatter, a perfect place in which customers could look back on their day. But for Pauline, it was different. She had a special reason for being there.

'I've seen Eric a few times,' she told Grace with some difficulty. 'The first time he was waiting outside the library for me when I came out for lunch. I didn't want you to know.'

Grace was curious, but not angry. 'Why not?' she asked casually.

'Well,' continued Pauline, pulling heavily on a cigarette in between sips of tea, 'I know how you and he are getting together again.'

Grace shrugged. 'Because I'm seeing him again doesn't mean I own him,' she replied.

Pauline lowered her eyes. 'Grace,' she said, 'you don't understand.'

At the next table, two elderly female tramps were counting out their day's takings on the table, their fingers protruding through their threadbare mittens, sorting out the farthings from the pennies and the ha'pennies.

'He had a special reason for wanting to see me,' continued Pauline. 'He wanted to know about you.'

Grace's expression changed. 'Oh yes?' she replied blandly.

'About why you've been going down to Devon. I said I had no idea. But I don't think he believed me.'

'What else did he want to know?' asked Grace.

Pauline took a moment to answer. 'About what you intend to do with the business.'

'He already knows that.'

'I think he wanted confirmation.'

'Did you give it to him?'

Pauline looked up with a start, just as the old female tramps burst into raucous laughter about something at the next table. 'Grace,' asked Pauline, once the noise had subsided, 'do you love Eric?'

'Who knows?' replied Grace evasively. 'He's very good-looking, even more so than when I knew him before.'

'That's not what I mean,' said Pauline. 'I mean do you *really* love him?'

Grace was watching her carefully. In all the years she had known Pauline, the one thing she could be certain of was that her best friend was totally incapable of hiding anything from her. She leaned forward across the table to her. 'Are you trying to tell me something, Pauline?' she asked directly.

'No, of course not,' replied Pauline edgily. 'Oh, for goodness' sake, Grace,' she cried, stubbing her cigarette out in a tin lid ashtray before she had finished it, 'there's never any privacy here. Let's get out of this place!'

A short while later, the two girls were strolling along the Victoria Embankment by the Thames. All the street gas lamps were now lit, and on the opposite side of the road by Scotland Yard, there were signs that electricity was gradually taking over from gas as the main form of street lighting. Every so often a tram rumbled out of the Kingsway Tunnel, and slanted at an eighty degree turn on to Westminster Bridge, almost knocking down Queen Boadicea's statue as it went. Although it was only half-past eight according to Big Ben across the road, there were very few people around, and those that were seemed to be in a rush to get home. Grace and Pauline finally came to a halt on stone steps overlooking the river, just alongside Cleopatra's Needle. The water down below was calm, and reflected the lights from the many offices in County Hall on the opposite side of the river. But the evening sky was dark, with the promise of rain from fast-moving clouds.

Grace was well aware that something was wrong with Pauline, for she was agitated enough to light another cigarette as soon as they had stopped. 'How much did you tell him, Pauline?' she asked, staring into the gently rippling tide in the water below.

Pauline looked at her with a start. 'Who?' she asked, unconvincingly.

'You *know* who, Pauline,' replied Grace, turning to look at her. 'Did you tell Eric about the house, the money, what I intend to do with the business?'

'Why would I do that?' asked Pauline, as though hurt by such an unjust question. 'He asked me a lot of things, but I told him that I . . .' She suddenly stopped, and clutched her forehead. 'Oh God, Grace!' she said, her anguish now out in the open. 'Whatever possessed us to get involved with someone like him?'

Grace looked directly at her. Her face was streaked with shadows cast by the flickering gaslight above them. 'What happened, Pauline?' she asked calmly.

Pauline hesitated before answering. 'That same night,' she started, 'he asked me out for a drink. He was – wonderful, kind, sweet – just lovely. You're right. He's so – good-looking.' She paused. 'He told me he'd always liked me, and if it hadn't been for circumstances . . .' She stopped again, and turned to look at Grace. 'He asked me back to his room,' she said, with real guilt. 'The awful thing is, I knew why he was doing it, and yet I let it happen.'

'Let *what* happen, Pauline?' Grace asked quietly.

Pauline hesitated, lowered her head, and started to gently cry. 'I didn't tell him *anything*, Grace. I swear to God I didn't!'

Grace put her arm around her waist, and waited for a taxi driver to pick up a fare at the kerb behind them. 'Look,

262

Pauline,' she said, once the taxi had pulled away. 'It doesn't matter *what* you told him. I know Eric. I know him only too well. Yes, I'm attracted to him too, but that's as far as it goes. Up until a week or so ago, I thought it was more than that. I actually thought I was beginning to love him, and in a bizarre sort of way, I think I probably do.'

'But I'm supposed to be your best friend, Grace,' cried Pauline, between sobbing. 'And I let you down. I slept with Eric. Don't you understand? I slept with him!' She was crying uncontrollably. 'How can you forgive me? How can you ever forgive me?'

Grace felt no anger, no bitterness towards Pauline at all. To Grace's way of thinking, any girl who was put in a similar position with someone like Eric Tyler would probably have done exactly the same thing. What she had now come to realise, however, was that after all Pauline had told her about Eric, the only person she could really trust was Mickey. Eric Tyler was shallow, dishonest and deceitful, and she now had to find some way to take her revenge on him. 'It doesn't matter, Pauline,' she said, squeezing her arm around Pauline's waist. 'What you did makes no difference to how I feel about Eric whatsoever. But I'm glad you told me. At least now I know exactly where I stand in his eyes too.' She turned Pauline around, and gently raised her chin. 'Look, Pauline,' she said softly. 'Would you do something for me?'

'Anything!' cried Pauline. 'Anything at all!'

Grace paused, and drew closer. 'Then just tell me where he lives. That's all I want to know.'

Eric Tyler lay back on his bed smoking a cigarette. He didn't smoke very often, but when he did, he liked to use the time it took to think about what was going on in his life, and how he intended to improve it. His first-floor bedsitter in Ronalds Road near Highbury Corner was modest enough, too modest after the way he had been living for the past few years with his wife in Sheffield, but for the time being it would have to do. As far as he was concerned, living in such cramped conditions was only temporary; he had plans that would change all that. That apart, something else was happening to him. He was falling in love with Grace Higgs, and the more he thought about her, the more he wanted to be in her company. What was more, he suspected she was feeling the same about him, for the last few times they had met, she had definitely showed a change in attitude, and when he kissed her, she responded so passionately that it sent his blood racing through his veins. Since her father had died, Grace had become so vivacious, so desirable. She had a way of making herself look beautiful just by how she wore a headscarf, or combed back her short hair so that it revealed her ears, her beautifully shaped ears that he had dreamt about many times, and had wanted to kiss and kiss again. Grace was no longer an immature twenty-year-old, she was a woman, and he longed to hold her in his arms.

His fantasy was broken by two knocks on the front door downstairs. With cigarette dangling from his lips, he leapt off the bed, and rushed to the window, but it was too dark, and he couldn't see who was standing in the shadows of the portico downstairs. He quickly placed his cigarette in a small china ashtray at the side of his bed, and rushed down to see who it was.

'Hallo, Eric.'

Eric could hardly believe what he was seeing. He had spent the past hour fantasising about Grace, and what he would like to do with her, and there she was, standing on his own front doorstep.

'Grace!' he spluttered in near disbelief. 'What are you – come in!'

'I hope you don't mind me calling on you,' said Grace, as she came into the narrow front passage, 'but I was longing to see you.'

Eric couldn't believe his good fortune. In the flickering light from the gas lamp on the passage wall, his eyes positively gleamed. 'Oh God, Grace!' he gasped. 'I've been longing to see you too.' He took her in his arms, and kissed her hard and long. He had no worries about his landlord, who lived on the ground floor, and had gone to stay with his sister in Streatham for a few days. 'But how did you know where to find me?' he asked, pulling away from her.

'Pauline gave me your address,' replied Grace.

Eric froze.

'She said she remembered seeing you come into this house one day – when she was on her way home from the library. I wanted to talk to you, so I took a chance that this was the right place.'

Eric breathed a sigh of relief. Thank God Pauline hadn't said more. 'This is the right place all right,' he said, taking her hand. 'Come on up.' He led her upstairs to the first floor.

As soon as she entered his room, Grace could smell the remains of his cigarette smouldering in the ashtray. She looked around the room, which was pleasant enough, with a jug, bowl, and washstand, a single brass bedstead, and a walnut wardrobe that looked in need of a good polish, but she imagined that it couldn't have been too easy for a future millionaire like Eric to live in such a confined space.

'I can't tell you what a wonderful surprise this is,' Eric said, taking her coat and putting it on the bed.

'Then you didn't mind my coming?' asked Grace wryly.

'*Mind?*' he replied, drawing the curtains at the window, and then returning to her. 'You've made my day.' He kissed her hard and long again.

Grace responded by throwing her arms around his neck, and letting him kiss her ears. 'I thought it was about time I shared some of my thoughts with you,' she said. 'About you and me, about what I thought we could do with the business once we're married.'

Eric pulled away with a start, and stared in disbelief at her. 'Married?' he said.

'You *do* want to marry me, don't you – darling?' she asked.

Eric was totally flustered. 'Well – of course,' he spluttered. 'Of course I do!'

'I know you have to wait for your divorce to come through,' continued Grace, 'but as soon as it does, I see no reason why we should wait any longer. After all, we've waited long enough – haven't we – darling?'

Eric was elated. 'Oh, Grace!' he gasped with desire. 'My dear darling. I can't tell you how much I've longed for this. I've wanted you so badly.' He pulled her to him, and held her tight against his body.

'And I've wanted you too, Eric,' she said. She put her arms around his neck, and allowed him to kiss her again. She didn't try to stop him as his hands gently cupped her breasts, which were firm and sensual. 'From now on, we don't have to worry about a thing,' she said. 'I have all the money you and I will ever need.'

Eric stopped what he was doing, but didn't look at her. 'Really?' he asked, trying to show as little enthusiasm as he could manage. 'I'm so happy for you.'

With her head resting on his shoulder, Grace smiled. His

adopted smooth city accent was showing definite signs of reverting to his East End roots. 'My father made quite sure that when he died, I'd have a good future for myself, *and* for the man I love. You *do* love me, don't you, Eric? You do want to come and live at The Chapel and help me run the business?'

'More than you'll ever know,' replied Eric, his face pressed into her shoulder. 'As long as I'm with you, that's all I care about.'

Grace squirmed as she felt him becoming aroused. 'Then that's settled,' she said quickly, pulling away from him, and holding him at arm's length. 'So then,' she asked, gently removing a lock of hair that had fallen across one of his eyes, 'how would you like a trip down to Devon?'

Chapter 16

Gert Jolly was very worried about the rising damp in her front parlour. She hadn't noticed it before, but after the recent heavy rain, she could see the wet patch quite clearly, halfway up the wall behind her settee, which she'd had since she married her late husband, Bill, over forty years ago. It wasn't the damp itself she was worried about, but the smell that hit her every time she went into the room. She had already discussed it with her neighbour, Molly Tebbit next door, who said the damp was affecting her side as well, for it was a party wall, and it was definitely the smell that was affecting her cat, Ginger, who had been sneezing quite a lot just lately. Knowing that she and Gus's tenants had never had any trouble in getting him to carry out repairs and maintenance in the past, Gert decided to mention it to Grace when she next called on her rounds. The only problem, however, was that the last time Grace came to collect the rent, she had indicated that, due to the fact that she needed to catch up on her book-keeping work, she and Mickey would be missing their rounds the following week. With that in mind, Gert decided to put on her best coat and hat, and pop along to see Grace up at The Chapel.

When she got there, she found Mickey up a ladder at the front of the house, painting the frames of the large arched windows on the first floor.

'You mind 'ow yer go up there!' she yelled. 'One slip an' yer'll be on yer way up the bone yard!'

' 'Allo, darlin'!' called Mickey, who immediately stopped

what he was doing, and came down to see her. 'Wot *you* doin' up in foreign parts? I like yer fevver! Did yer shoot the bird, or did it give itself up?'

Gert immediately adjusted the long pheasant's feather in the battered felt hat she'd had since the year dot. 'Don't you insult *my* bleedin' fevver!' she retorted with a scowl. 'It's seen me fru many a bad time!'

'I believe yer, Mrs J,' replied Mickey cheekily. 'Millions uvvers wouldn't! Wot can I do for yer?'

'I've come ter see yer employer,' replied Gert haughtily. 'Where is she?'

'I'm afraid she's out at the moment, darlin',' said Mickey. 'She's goin' away ternight, just fer the weekend. Anyfin' I can do?'

'It's a confidential matter,' said Gert grandly, 'concerning my property.'

'Ah, well then,' said Mickey, 'yer'd better come in an' wait fer the guv'nor. She shouldn't be too long. I'm just about ter brew up. 'Ow about a cuppa?'

A short while later, the two of them were sipping tea from enamel mugs, Gert sitting on a stool, and Mickey sitting cross-legged in the straw alongside Clapper.

'Risin' damp, eh?' said Mickey. 'Well, I'm not surprised, wiv all this wevver we've bin 'avin just lately. Sure sign autumn's on the way. Still, never you mind. The guv'nor'll soon sort it all out for yer – once she gets back from 'er weekend down Devon.'

Gert's ears pricked up. 'Devon?' she asked. 'She's goin' down there again?'

'Just till Sunday,' said Mickey, with a forced smile. 'She an' 'er gent.'

Gert was puzzled. 'Gent?' she asked suspiciously. 'Who's that?'

'Mr Tyler.'

'Who's *'e*?' asked Gert, shamelessly nosy.

'Guv'nor's gentleman friend,' replied Mickey glumly.

Gert was quickly mulling it over. 'Tyler, did yer say? I know that name from somewhere.' It suddenly dawned on her. 'Wait a minute. Ain't 'e that bloke she used ter knock about wiv years ago? Greasy 'air, real smarmer.'

Mickey shrugged. 'Couldn't tell yer, mate.'

'I'll bet 'e is,' persisted Gert, taking an agitated sip of tea. 'Yes!' she said, with a sudden flash of inspiration. ''E's that same bugger who's always 'angin' round The Eaglet – stands at the counter wiv 'alf a pint er bitter, chattin' up the reg'lars, never dippin' 'is 'and into 'is pocket not once all night. She's got that bugger in tow again, 'as she? Must be bleedin' mad!'

'Everyone ter their own choice, Mrs J,' said Mickey bravely.

Ever since Grace had told him about Eric Tyler going away with her for the weekend, he was beginning to worry about what he was doing staying on with her. After all, once that bloke of hers moved in, there would be no point for he, Mickey, to hang around any more. It was as clear as day that that fancy man of hers hated his guts, and much as he admired 'miss', and loved every moment he was with Clapper, as soon as the time was right, he'd move on. Trouble was, he felt something for 'miss'. He couldn't quite understand what it was – all he knew was that whenever he was in her company, she made him feel good, like someone more than just a skivvy. And when she kissed him that time, he realised that he was in love with her. He quickly pulled himself together, and swigged down his tea.

'So wot about *you* then?'

Mickey looked up to find Gert staring him out. 'Due wot?' he asked.

'You an' *'er?*' persisted Gert. 'I fawt you two was—'

'Well, yer fawt wrong, Mrs J!' snapped Mickey, getting up and taking his cup to wash it in a bucket of water. 'I work fer Miss 'Iggs – nuffin' more!'

Gert watched him closely. She was a shrewd old biddy, and she could see the problem he faced. 'That's not wot it looks like when I see the two of yer tergevver,' she said with due care and understanding. 'I've seen the way she looks at yer. I've seen the way you look at *'er.*'

Mickey threw his mug back into the bucket. 'Don't talk such bleedin' fodder, Mrs J!' he snapped angrily. 'I'm fond of my employer. I'm grateful to 'er fer all she's done fer me. But that's as far as it goes. She's my employer, so please don't try ter make somefin' of it.'

Gert got up, and took her empty mug to him. She was very aware of how touchy he was on the subject. 'Yer know somefin', Mickey,' she said, with more care and understanding than she had ever shown to anyone. 'Grace 'Iggs is a good gel. Up till the day 'er dad died, I didn't fink so, but I've changed me mind now. That's 'cos *she's* changed too. She's not a kid any more, she's grown up. These days, she's more like a woman, a woman who's got an 'eart, as well as a brain. But even a woman can make mistakes, Mickey. I know, 'cos I've made plenty in me own life. Wot I'm really tryin' ter say is, sometimes people 'ave ter *see* where they're goin' wrong. An' sometimes, it takes *uvver* people ter show 'em.'

Mickey slowly looked up at her. He smiled weakly, gratefully.

'Hallo, Mrs J!' Grace called from the stable door. 'This is a surprise.' She came across to her. 'To what do I owe the pleasure of your company?'

'It's me damp, Miss 'Iggs,' replied Gert stoically.

'Damp?' asked Grace, puzzled.

'Me risin' damp,' continued Gert. 'It's all up me parlour wall. It stinks ter 'igh 'eaven. I'm sorry ter intrude on yer, but I fink somefin' ought ter be done about it as soon as possible. I didn't fink I should wait tellin' yer till yer come round the week after next, just in case it gets worse. I mean, after all it *is* your property.'

'Oh dear,' said Grace, with a sigh. 'I'm so sorry to hear all this. But I shouldn't worry too much about it if I was you. I'm afraid I won't be able to get anyone round to look at it for a while.'

'I fink yer should,' said Mickey firmly, emerging from the shadows alongside Clapper. 'If it *is* risin' damp, it ought ter be dealt wiv as soon as possible. It's not good fer Mrs J's 'ealth.'

Grace was a bit taken aback by Mickey's intervention. 'Well, what do you suggest we do about it?' she asked him brusquely.

'First fing termorrer mornin', I'll go round an' take a look at it,' he replied. 'If it needs doin', you'll 'ave ter get the builder in ter give yer an estimate. Once 'e's finished, I can always do the place up meself. But yer can't leave it ter rot.'

Grace listened to him with some astonishment. She had never heard him talk to her like that before, especially in public. 'All right, Mrs Jolly,' she replied, really directing her irritation towards Mickey, 'we'll sort it out for you one way or another.'

'Fank yer very much,' replied Gert. She flicked a quick glance across at Mickey. 'Fank yer *boaf* very much.' She tottered across to the door. 'Cheerio then.'

'Bye-bye Mrs Jolly,' Grace called.

Mickey walked with Gert to the back yard gate. 'Good luck, mate,' she said quietly, with a parting wink. Then she left.

'So what was all *that* about?' asked Grace, who was quite cross.

'Due wot, miss?' asked a surprised Mickey, as they came together in the middle of the yard.

'Mickey,' she replied grandly, 'I don't like to be made to look a fool in front of my tenants.'

Mickey looked quite put out. 'All I said was, if it *is* risin' damp, it oughta be dealt wiv as soon as possible. It ain't good fer the ol' gel's 'ealth.'

'It may interest you to know, Mickey,' Grace replied, hopping mad, 'that I'm perfectly aware of that. I happen to have been working with my father for quite a long time. I do *know* how to deal with tenants' problems.'

'It din't sound like it ter me,' retorted Mickey.

Grace was totally taken aback. 'What did you say?' she demanded.

'I said,' replied Mickey defiantly, 'it din't sound like that ter me. You told Mrs J not ter worry. But if you was in 'er position, *you'd* worry. She ain't a kid, *Miss* 'Iggs. She's an ol' lady, an' like all ol' folk, she gets worked up.'

Grace couldn't believe what she was hearing. Not only was he telling her something that she already knew, but he was also addressing her formally for the first time since she had met him.

'Mickey,' she said haughtily. 'When I need your advice, I'll ask for it. Is that understood?'

'Anyfin' yer say, miss,' he replied. Without another word, he turned, and walked off briskly to the stable.

Grace watched him go with complete indignation. She couldn't believe the nerve of the man, the impertinence of talking to her in such a way. Enraged, she stormed off into the house. The moment she got into the scullery, she took off her coat, and threw it on to the back of a chair. She went straight to the window, and glared out towards the stable, just in time to see Mickey leading Clapper out for his early evening walk. She was seething with anger. Who did this fellow think he was, she asked herself. Hadn't she given him the chance of a lifetime to work for someone like her, to have a regular job where he knew that he was at least getting a regular wage each week? She didn't like his attitude. She didn't like it at all. He was getting above himself. If he wanted to move on, well he could do so. She didn't need him. She could manage perfectly well on her own.

But by the time Mickey had taken Clapper out into the street and closed the gates behind them, Grace had been struck by the most terrible realisation. Everything Mickey had said to her had been true. Of course Gert Jolly was an old lady, of course she had the right to be concerned about her rising damp. Grace cringed with disgust at her own behaviour. If anyone had been in the wrong, it was *her*, for although Mickey may have been a little tactless in the way he had scolded her, he was perfectly within his rights to draw her attention to Gert Jolly's dilemma. In fact, Mickey had shown more compassion than she was capable of herself. It was plain to see that he was no longer a boy, he was a man, and she'd been stupid not to have treated him like one. He had a mind of his own, a true sense of what was right and wrong. She made a sudden dash for the door.

'Mickey!'

Mickey was halfway down Pedlar's Way with Clapper when he heard Grace calling after him. He stopped and turned, to find her hurrying towards him.

'Mickey!' she said breathlessly, the moment she reached him. 'I'm sorry. I'm so terribly sorry. I can't think what came over me. You're perfectly right. I *should* have taken Mrs Jolly's anxiety seriously, especially as she'd come all this way to tell me. Do forgive me. My father always taught me to think first before saying something. I didn't do that. I just thought you were being too opinionated.'

'Is it wrong ter 'ave an opinion then, miss?' asked Mickey.

'No, Mickey,' she replied abjectly. 'As a matter of fact, it isn't.'

'Grace!'

They both turned. Eric Tyler, carrying a small overnight suitcase, was coming towards them from the Caledonian Road end of the street. The moment Mickey saw him, he turned Clapper around, and led him off in the opposite direction.

'Mickey,' called Grace.

Mickey threw a casual, glum look at her over his shoulder.

'Remember what I said. If I do things . . . that seem a little odd to you, please don't take them too seriously.'

Mickey shrugged. He still didn't know what she was talking about. ' 'Ave a good weekend,' he called sullenly as he went.

With a heavy heart, Grace watched him and Clapper go until they were well out of sight.

Georgie O'Hara hated being a pensioner. It seemed to him that having to give up work at the age of sixty-five years was the most stupid rule ever invented by man – or woman, or whoever it was. It was stupid because he felt just the same as he did when he was half his age – a bit slower perhaps, a few more aches and pains, but basically the same. Doing nothing all day but going shopping with the

275

missus, or doing the odd job around the house, or a bit of weeding in their tiny back garden in Hornsey Road was no stimulation for a man who had spent the best part of his life as a foreman in a milk bottle factory. For all those years he'd been in a position of responsibility and he'd worked with lots of different kinds of people – there was even a black man from the West Indies working on the metal tops line there just before he left – and Georgie's brain was active all the time. Since then, he had gone downhill fast, especially since his old mate Gus Higgs had died. He had nothing to look forward to, only a big hole in Finchley cemetery.

But quite suddenly, all that had changed. Thanks to Gus's girl, young Grace, he'd now got himself a job. True, it wasn't exactly well paid, but after the way he'd let Grace down by blabbering all about Gus's private business to Gert Jolly, if it hadn't been for Grace insisting, he would have been prepared to do the job for nothing. Best of all, it gave him back his self-respect, because it showed that Grace forgave him, and held no grudge against him. In return, all he had to do was, in Grace's own words, 'Keep your eyes and ears open, Mr O'Hara. If any of the tenants have a grouse about anything – anything at all – let me know.' It sounded easy enough, a kind of ears-against-the-wall job, but he soon found that some of Gus's tenants were awkward cusses, and were prone to grumble and complain about the slightest thing.

'Sounds like you're a Jack of all trades, and master of none,' said Sid Wilson, as he and Georgie drank together in The Eaglet that Friday evening. 'What d'yer 'ave ter do? Go round an' bang on people's doors just ter make sure they ain't got no gripes?'

'It's not quite like that,' replied Georgie in his cool Irish brogue. 'I'm just there as a kind er watchdog, ter keep an eye on wot's goin' on.'

'Yer mean you're a bleedin' spy?' said Sid, laughing at his own joke.

Georgie took down a gulp of his bitter. 'It's nuttin' like that,' he said. 'Nuttin' at all. I'd say it's kind er – public relations.'

'Due wot?' asked Sid, his quiff in danger of flopping over his forehead.

'Public relations,' repeated Georgie. 'Gettin' ter know people better, ter sort out any problems they've got.'

'Well, yer'd better start wiv 'Ilda Barnet,' said Sid critically.

Georgie did a double take. 'Hilda?'

'Gus's sister,' continued Sid. 'That's a right one, that is! Did yer know she's bin goin' round the tenants ter see if she can find out anyfin' about the money Gus left his gel?'

Georgie was shocked. He knew Hilda Barnet only too well, and had no illusions about her. Over the years, Gus had often talked about her, often stood in the public bar at the Nag's Head pub, shaking his head in despair about his sister's grasping ways, and how he feared for the things she might try to do once Grace was left on her own.

'Has she bin ter see you then?' he asked.

'Twice!' replied Sid. 'The first time was soon after Gus died. She said she was worried about Grace, an' 'ow she'd promised 'er bruvver that if anyfin' 'appened to 'im, she'd look after 'er.' He grinned. 'The real reason, er course, was she wanted ter know if Gus'd ever mentioned wot 'e was goin' ter leave 'er.'

'An' wot did yer tell 'er, Sid?' asked Georgie.

'I didn't tell 'er nuffin'!' Sid assured him. 'I told 'er Gus never discussed 'is personal affairs wiv me.'

Georgie hummed and hawed. 'Wot a woman,' he sighed.

'You ain't 'eard the best,' said Sid. Before continuing, he took a careful look around the bar to make sure that no one was listening. ' 'Ave yer 'eard about 'er goin' ter law?'

Georgie's eyes widened. 'Law?'

'The second time she come round,' said Sid, 'she tried ter get me ter say that Gus'd always wanted the business ter stay wiv the family, an' not just 'is daughter. She said 'er niece 'ad upset all the family by 'angin' on ter everyfin', and that they all wanted 'Ilda ter take 'er ter court, ter get wot they was entitled to.'

'Blimey!' said Georgie.

'Apparently, I'm not the only one she come to,' continued Sid. 'Jack Pertwee said she spent nearly 'alf an 'our tryin' ter get 'im on 'er side, and she tried the same with Mabel Buck up Kinloch Street.'

Georgie had a nasty feeling in his stomach, and for once it wasn't the booze. Things were getting unpleasant with Hilda Barnet, there was no doubt about that. Gus had always said that he found it hard to believe that she came out of the same place as him and his younger sister, Josie, but it seemed incredible that she would go to these lengths to further her own ends. What *was* the matter with the woman? She was no youngster; she hadn't got all that much time left ter play around with money. So what was she after? Was it that she was just trying to make hay while the sun shone, or was there some other reason why she behaved the way she did? Whatever it was, he had to do something about it. As soon as Grace got back from her weekend in Devon, he would have to warn her that she had a real battle on her hands.

* * *

The night train to Penzance seemed to take for ever. Grace envied those people who were rich enough to be able to afford to travel in a sleeper compartment, for they would get off the train in the morning at their destination fresh and ready to go. Not that she couldn't afford a sleeper herself, but as her travelling companion was Eric Tyler, she had no intention of spending any more money on him than was absolutely necessary. She had done this same journey now several times, but for her, this was clearly the worst, not just because the compartment they were in reeked of stale tobacco and pickled onions, but because the only light available came from a solitary low-voltage electric light bulb in the ceiling, which made her feel tired without actually letting her fall asleep.

In any case, sleep for Grace was impossible; she had far too much on her mind. As she took a cursory glance at Eric at her side, leaning on her shoulder fast asleep, she was only too aware that bringing him down to Devon with her was an act of madness. Soon he would know everything there was to know about her inheritance. She intended to tell him *everything*, about the money, the business, about The House on the Hill – *everything*. She could picture him now, picture his face as he walked into the house down in Dawlish for the first time, the look of awe as he walked into the hall and saw the golden future that was laid out before him. This was what he wanted, what he had always craved for, to be master of his own domain with no strings attached, to be someone whom people would have to look up to, because he had a house of his own that he would reluctantly share with a wife that, regardless of what he said or thought, he didn't really love.

She looked around the compartment. It wasn't full. Mercifully, the large lady and her husband sitting in the seat by the corridor window were fast asleep after gorging pickled onions with their saveloys and pease pudding, which they had probably bought from somewhere outside Paddington station before they boarded the train. Merciful also that the small baby cradled in its mum's arms sitting opposite them had also finally been rocked to sleep, after yelling its head off irritably all the way from Paddington to Slough. Yes, it was a long, late night journey that would not end until daybreak the following morning.

Grace finally dozed off, only to be woken again almost immediately by the roar of a passing train, the dim lights from its long trail of compartments flashing across her eyes like tiny illuminated darts. Once it had passed, her eyes gradually flickered and closed. Soon, she was miles away, back at The Chapel, in the stable. She could see Clapper, stretched out on the floor, head buried in the hay, and at his side, Mickey, leaning on Clapper's stomach, the two of them snoring away in unison, not a care in the world. For one brief moment, she felt her stomach crunch up inside, hating herself for how she had talked to Mickey just before she had left home. All the way to the station she had told herself time and time again that what Mickey had said to her was right, and she was absolutely wrong to put him down. She knew only too well what he must be feeling about her, seeing her go off for a weekend to Devon with Eric Tyler at her side. How could she tell him? How could she explain to him what she was doing – how she had warned Eric that she would only let him come with her on the trip if he promised not to force her into bed with him, at least not until after he had got his divorce? How could she tell Mickey that she had not slept with Eric at any time, even though he had reluctantly agreed to go along with her conditions? How could she tell him that, as long as there was life in her body, she would *never* sleep with Eric Tyler? As sleep gradually pulled her deeper and deeper into its dark web, she felt wonderful, quite wonderful, for it was Mickey she could see holding her in his arms, hugging her, protecting her, loving her. It was a strange, comforting feeling, which left her face with a faint, glowing smile as she drifted off into her dark, silent world . . .

Hilda Barnet had had a very disappointing day. The solicitor she had been to see in Upper Street had been no help, no help at all. Doddery old fool, she told herself. What did *he* know about family bequests and who was entitled to what? All he knew about was unimportant little crimes such as shoplifting, being drunk and disorderly, or petty pilfering. The cheek of sitting there and telling her that if she wanted a court to rule in favour of her being entitled to part of her brother's inheritance and business, then she hadn't a leg to stand on! She knew better, and if it meant spending a bit more money on consulting someone with more expert knowledge on such matters, then that's what she'd do. She had already told the nitwit solicitor that if she was put in the witness box, she would make a formidable case on her behalf. She had seen lots of pictures at the cinema in which there were court cases where the jury gasped at people just like her giving the performance of her life. But even she had to agree with the crusty old solicitor that real life was very different to the pictures.

It was the early hours of the morning, but, as so often happened with Hilda, she was still sitting up in her nightie at the table in her back parlour, curlers tightly clamped beneath her hairnet, sipping her second cup of hot cocoa. It was a hard job, deciding what to do next. Should she bide her time, at least until she had found a new solicitor, or should she go straight to Grace and give her one last warning that, unless she came clean about her father's estate and told the family about everything he had left, she would have no alternative but to take her to court? The trouble was, after the nasty scene she had had with Josie and Stan, there was very little chance of getting any help or support from *them*. She yawned. These sleepless nights were getting her down. But she couldn't give up now, not after having made her position so firm and clear. She turned down the gas lamp, lit a candle, and went up to her bedroom on the first floor. She blew out the candle and put it on the bedside cabinet, climbed into bed, and closed her eyes.

'Damn you, Gus 'Iggs!' she said out loud. She had hardly got the words out before she fell into a deep sleep.

Mickey Burke was also not getting much sleep. He had spent most of the night flicking through a newspaper he had bought earlier in the day, trying to make sense of the flood of words there. Without telling Grace, he had been doing this for some time now. After what she had told him, after all the times she had now pointed out words on grocery packets in the shop, he was gradually beginning to get the hang of it all. Of course, he still preferred the pictures, for they told a story without having to worry about words, but it was the words that were important, especially the ones about the war in Spain, and the dangers that faced the British people if Hitler didn't stop marching into other people's countries.

For quite a time, he stood in the yard outside, just staring up the back of the big house, the house where 'miss' lived, the house that he had vowed never to enter unless – unless she *wanted* him to.

Then he looked up at the sky. There weren't many stars tonight, for the night clouds were full of rain. But studying the sky gave him the chance to think things over. After having his first tiff with Grace before she left home earlier that evening, he felt very down in the dumps. She had never talked to him like that before, and despite her apologies and assurances that she could never run the business without his help, he wondered how much longer he could go on working for her. The situation wasn't helped by the fact that Eric Tyler was spending the weekend with her. Seeing the two of them go off like that together in a taxi when he and Clapper had got back to the house had upset him. He didn't know why. After all, 'miss' had a perfect right to a life of her own, and she could choose whomsoever she wanted to spend that life with. Even so, he still had that nagging feeling inside. Every time he thought about Grace, he wanted to be near her; he couldn't bear the thought that he wouldn't see her until Sunday night, and when he did see her, she probably wouldn't be alone. But as he stared aimlessly up at the sky, and the first light raindrops started to fall on his face, he had to admit that he was no competition for someone like Eric Tyler. Why would 'miss' want to hitch herself up to him, Mickey, a rough-and-ready, who had nothing to offer to anyone in the world except a bit of cheeky banter with Grace's tenants and customers? He was no match for class. He was no match for someone who could read and write, and talk about things that he wouldn't know about. And yet, what was it old Gert Jolly had said to him that very day: . . . *a woman can make mistakes, Mickey . . . sometimes people 'ave ter see where they're goin' wrong. An' sometimes, it takes uvver people ter show 'em.* The rain was coming down a little faster now, so he went back inside the stable.

The moment Mickey came in, Clapper raised his head from the straw where he was stretched out.

'Wot's all this then, mate?' said Mickey, bending down to give him a calming stroke on his mane. 'Can't sleep?' He chuckled. 'You an' me boaf, ol' son.' He stood up, and blew out the lamp. In the dark, he stretched out alongside Clapper, and covered himself with his blanket. In the silence that followed, he sighed. 'I don't know, ol' mate,' he said. 'We're a fine pair, ain't we? Like a couple er bleedin' orphans, lost in the storm!' He chuckled to himself again. 'But I've got ter do somefin', Clap. Can't go on like this much longer. Yer know 'ow I feel about 'er, don't yer, mate? If anyone knows, it's *you* all right.'

Clapper snorted in the dark.

'Yeah,' said Mickey. 'It's all right fer you, but I'm not stayin' round 'ere wiv that git in tow. Two's company mate, three's a crowd!'

Clapper snorted again.

'No, not you, yer stupid twerp!'

For a moment or so, the two of them lay side by side together, deep in thought. Clapper was restless, and rolled over on to his other side. Mickey stretched out his arm and rested it on him. 'Tell yer wot, Clap,' he asked quietly, in the dark, 'if I make somefin' er meself, d'yer fink I'd get a look in?'

Clapper didn't respond.

'Well, fanks fer yer 'elp, mate!' retorted Mickey. 'I'll do the same fer you some day!' He eventually closed his eyes and fell asleep, but not before having made up his mind that if he really did feel the way he was feeling about Grace, then he was going to have to go to battle for her.

The sun had only just broken through by the time the London train had pulled into Dawlish railway station. The pickled onion lady and her husband had already struggled along the corridor to have a quick wash in the toilet, and as they were staying on the train to another destination, they were now tucking in to a breakfast of bacon rolls and hot tea from a vacuum flask that they had brought with them. However, they were very quiet doing all this, so much so that the mother and her young baby were still asleep, and so was Eric Tyler. Grace also was still dozing, and as the train pulled to a sudden stop, she woke with a start, and after quickly wiping a clear space through the condensation on the compartment window, she saw the sign 'DAWLISH' repeated all the way along the platform. As she leapt up to start getting the luggage down from the overhead rack, Eric, who had been slumped against her in a deep sleep practically all the way from Paddington, woke up in a panic. 'What's up?' he spluttered.

'Come on, sleepy head!' she announced brightly. 'Time to see your new home. It's a lovely morning!'

As they stepped off the train on to the platform, the heavens opened, and it poured with rain.

Chapter 17

Number 22A Riviera Terrace wasn't exactly what Eric Tyler had in mind when Grace had asked him to come down to Dawlish with her. His bedroom was comfortable enough, with a nice bathroom right next door, but a four-storey Edwardian terraced guesthouse overlooking the main railway line and the sea beyond was not exactly The House on the Hill that Grace had told him so much about. And the famous Devon weather wasn't all that special either. It was now past ten o'clock in the morning, and it had not stopped raining since they arrived at daybreak. There was also a sea mist, which made it difficult to make out the beautiful red sandstone cliffs, which holidaymakers had loved so much over the years.

'It's quite unusual weather for the time of year,' said Mrs Darcy, the landlady, who spoke with a delightful West Country burr, and whose cheeks were rust-coloured from living all her life by the sea. 'September and October are usually very popular months for late holidays.'

'We often get Indian summers,' boasted her husband, Cyril, who seemed to do most of the chores.

Grace, who had booked rooms on separate floors for herself and Eric, smiled at Eric across the dining-room table, where they had just finished a slap-up bacon and egg breakfast, with grilled mushrooms, a grilled half tomato, two chipolata sausages, baked beans, and two slices of fried bread each. It was a genteel establishment, run by a warm-hearted landlady and landlord, and, when the weather was right, it had some of the best coastal views in the whole of the British Isles. Despite that, however, Eric still didn't understand why they were staying in such a place when Grace was the owner of a beautiful house of her own.

'And the one thing you can be sure of here, dears,' added Mrs Darcy as she cleared the breakfast things from the table, 'is peace and quiet.'

Even as she spoke, a train thundered along the railway line in front of the house, rattling the crockery in the glass-fronted china cabinet.

It took quite some time for the rain to stop, and when it finally did, just before lunch time, Grace and Eric made their way on foot along the promenade to the town, where the drains were having a hard time coping with the excess of rain water. Eric, wrapped up in his raincoat and trilby hat, didn't feel much like doing any sightseeing, for he was not only cold and fed up, but he was anxious to see Grace's house. However, Grace decided that in order to do that, he would have to work for it, and so, instead of taking a taxi directly up to The House on the Hill, she took him by foot up the long main road hill, which led to Smugglers' Inn.

The pub had only just opened when they got there, so the place was empty. Fortunately, Jackie was serving at the bar counter, and she was delighted to see Grace again. Once Grace had introduced Eric to her, and told her that he had never been down to Devon before, she waxed lyrical about The House on the Hill.

'Just wait till you see it!' she said in her lovely burr. 'You've got a real treat waitin' for you.'

This cheered Eric up no end, and he downed the brandy Grace had bought him in just a few gulps. By the time he had left, he had had another brandy, which for him was just one glass too much. But it certainly warmed him up, and brought a bright glow to his rather pasty cheeks. Grace felt good. This was just exactly the way she wanted him to get his first view of the house.

By the time they had gone down Smugglers' Lane and passed the cove, the mist had almost completely cleared, and the views of the sea and the 'spinning top' shaped rock just offshore were easy to pick out. Grace thought it quite funny that Eric found it a hard climb; he was certainly out of condition for someone of his age, and when he stopped to admire the spectacular scenery she knew it was just an excuse for him to rest. As she passed the stone statue of Josh in the distance, she could almost swear that the old smuggler's dog smiled and winked at her, clearly agreeing with everything she was getting up to.

Before she embarked on the journey down to Devon, Grace had already decided that she wanted to make as big an impression on Eric as possible, and so as they finally emerged from the copse at the top of the hill, she took him round to the front entrance of the house. Her instinct was right. For several moments, he marvelled at the grand sweep of the shingled drive in, and the imposing iron gates beyond.

'What a place!' he gasped. 'Imagine coming home to this every night.' Grace smiled, opened the front door of the house, and led him inside.

As she expected, the hall took Eric's breath away. 'This is fabulous!' he declared, wandering around excitedly, taking everything in. 'Mind you, the walls could do with a coat of paint, and I'll have to convert that chandelier to electricity, but by the time I've finished, you won't know the place.' He said much the same as Grace showed him around the rest of the house; he had it all worked out. This was the kind of place he had always dreamt of. This was what he wanted to do with the rest of his life, living in luxury with a woman he adored at his side.

'I think we should have two dogs,' he told her, as he looked from her bedroom windows out on to the back lawns.

'Dogs?' asked Grace.

'Great danes,' he replied confidently. 'Two of them. They'd be marvellous company for me when I go down for a drink at the pub. Do they have any shooting around these parts? I mean wild life – pheasants, grouse, rabbits – that sort of thing?'

'I wouldn't know,' replied Grace, who had perched on the edge of her bed, watching him with quiet amusement. 'I don't like killing things.'

'Oh, it's not actually *killing* things,' he replied, coming across to her. 'It's a sport, Grace, nothing more. And you can eat what you shoot. But, of course, if you wouldn't want me to do it, I never would. And in any case, they probably don't do that kind of thing down here.' Aware that he was talking too much, he perched down on the edge of the bed beside her. 'Oh Grace,' he said intimately, sliding his arm around her waist. 'I can't tell you how happy you've made me.'

'Have I really, Eric?' she replied, allowing him to stare with passion into her eyes. 'If *you're* happy, then so am I.' He leaned forward, hugged, and kissed her. But when he tried to lean her back on the bed to take things further, she resisted. 'No, Eric,' she said quite calmly. 'A promise is a promise.'

Eric stared hard and long at her. He didn't understand. He didn't understand at all. Reluctantly, he let her go.

Hilda Barnet felt as though she had been dragged through a tea strainer backwards. She had had a terrible night, lying awake churning over in her mind how much she hated that solicitor in Upper Street, especially as he had charged her two whole pounds just for the privilege of consulting him. Therefore, as soon as she had had her midday meal, she went back to bed for an afternoon snooze. No sooner had she done so, however, than she was woken by a loud knock on her front door downstairs. Growling and grumbling to herself, she got up, opened her window, and peered out.

'Who is it?' she yelled.

'It's me, Mrs Barnet,' called the man standing there looking up at her. 'Georgie O'Hara. I knew yer brother, Gus.'

'I *know* who yer are!' Hilda yelled back irritably. 'Yer'll 'ave ter wait a minute.' She slammed down the window and quickly put her dress back on. Grunting and grumbling to herself, she went downstairs and opened the door. 'Wot yer doin' round 'ere?' she asked ungraciously. 'Wot d'yer want?'

'A moment of yer time, dear lady,' said Georgie, the essence of courtesy. 'If I may?'

Hilda sighed deeply, and held the door back for him. 'Come on then,' she said grudgingly.

Georgie was shown into the back parlour, which, to his surprise, was small and sparsely furnished, with hardly anything on her dresser except a few cups hanging on hooks, saucers and plates fixed in place behind them, a teapot, and a pile of newspapers, which showed that Hilda was a hoarder. In other words, to say that the place was drab was an understatement.

'So – wot's this all about?' asked Hilda, sitting at one end of her parlour table.

'Ter be frank with yer, Mrs Barnet,' said Georgie, sitting opposite her, 'I'm worried.'

'Worried?' asked Hilda warily. 'Wot about?'

'Not *wot* about, Mrs Barnet,' replied Georgie, 'but *who*. It's your niece I'm referrin' to. Gus's girl.'

'Grace?' asked Hilda. 'Wot about 'er?'

'She's in trouble,' said Georgie, 'real, big trouble.' He leaned forward, with folded arms on the table. 'Yer've no doubt heard about the young thing's good fortune? Everyone else seems ter have done.'

Hilda shrugged with indifference.

'Her dad's fortune, and the house down in Devon?'

'I've 'eard rumours, nuffin' more,' said Hilda. 'Grace ain't very forward in tellin' her family about anyfin'.'

'Well,' said Georgie, 'someone's got their eyes on it.'

This really made Hilda sit up in her chair. 'On *wot*?' she asked, eyes darting across at him.

'On wot she's bin left.'

Hilda froze. 'Wot yer talkin' about?' she asked, shocked.

'It's this young lad she's taken up with,' he replied, now knowing that he had really got her hooked. 'Smarmy creature he is, just after one thing. Everyone seems ter know it except young Grace herself.'

Hilda sat bolt upright in her chair. 'It's that Tyler bloke, isn't it? I knew he was sniffing around her.'

'Afraid so, Mrs Barnet,' said Georgie, shaking his head gloomily. 'I'm afraid so.'

Hilda had a look of thunder. She remembered Eric Tyler. She remembered him well. When Grace had introduced him to her all those years ago, she thought then that he was devious, and had made a lot of snide assertions that if he was the best she could do, then she *must* have been hard up. To her way of thinking, Eric Tyler was a real go-getter, and was only after anything he could get out of a girl who would one day inherit her father's business. Why had she thought such a thing, she had asked herself so many times. Instinct.

She only had to look at a man's eyes to know what he was like. It was the same with her own husband, Bert Barnet. *He* had shifty eyes too, and she knew even before he married her that he would probably walk out on her. Oh God, she told herself, what a fool she had been!

'Tell me about this bloke,' she asked quickly. 'Are they still seein' each uvver regular?'

'At this precise moment,' said Georgie gleefully, 'they're down in Devon together.'

'What!' Hilda fell back in her chair with horror.

'Sure, it's not lookin' good, Mrs Barnet,' said Georgie with a look of grim foreboding. 'It's not lookin' good at all.'

Hilda thought for a moment, then thumped her fist on the table. 'Then we've got ter do somefin' about it!' she barked.

'Just my feelin's, Mrs Barnet.'

'We've got ter get rid of this menace, before that stupid niece er mine finds 'erself left wiv nuffin' at all!' Now highly worked up, Hilda got up from the table, went to the dresser, and without thinking what she was doing, picked up her large hairbrush that she always kept there. 'The fing is,' she continued, 'wot can we do ter stop 'im?'

Georgie jumped, as she thumped the hairbrush menacingly in the palm of her hand. 'That's why I come ter you, Mrs Barnet,' he said weakly. 'I knew you'd know wot ter do.'

Again Hilda thought carefully for a moment. Whilst she was doing so, her eyes darted all round the tiny room, as though Eric Tyler was there in every crevice in the walls. Grace hanging on to the family business for herself and refusing to share any of Gus's inheritance with her and Josie was one thing, but the thought that an outsider like Eric Tyler was in there with a chance was just too much to take. ' 'Ave yer said anyfin' ter Grace about this?' she asked.

'Not at all, Mrs Barnet,' replied Georgie, a little disconcerted that whilst she was talking to him, Hilda was winding down her washing from the ceiling on the drying rack. 'You know wot young Grace is like. Quite a firebrand when she wants; got a will of her own.'

'Well, so 'ave I!' snapped Hilda, dropping the rack so low that Georgie was in danger of being covered by her freshly ironed bloomers. 'I've 'ad just about all I can take from that gel. It's time she realised that she's got responsibilities, not only to 'erself, but ter *all* 'er family! It's bin on me mind ter take 'er ter court fer tryin' ter keep everyfin' fer 'erself, but this changes the situation! I don't need no court ter tell me 'ow ter deal wiv someone like Eric Tyler. If 'e finks 'e's goin' ter twist *my* kiff and kin round 'is little finger, 'e's got anuvver fink comin'!'

'Good fer you, Mrs Barnet!' said Georgie, struggling to free himself of Hilda's washing. 'Good fer you!'

'First fing Monday mornin', I'll be down there!' barked Hilda, wagging her finger at him. 'I intend ter tell that niece er mine that if she 'as any trouble from that lump of frozen cod, 'e'll 'ave *me* ter deal wiv!'

'Well said, Mrs Barnet!' cried Georgie triumphantly, removing a pair of Hilda's bloomers that had dropped down over his head. 'I knew I could count on you!'

Eric Tyler was having a funny old day. He had spent most of his time taking stock of The House on the Hill, making suggestions to Grace as to the type of improvements that could be made to the place after they were married, and strolling on his own around the grounds, imagining what it would be like when he took up residence permanently there, with his personal brass nameplate on the front entrance gates. Everything was ideal, but for one thing: Grace herself.

He just couldn't understand why she wouldn't let them stay in the house, instead of having to put up in a bed-and-breakfast guesthouse overlooking the railway line. Her excuse had been that she didn't want to use the house until after they were married, and they could start their life together at the beginning. But it didn't make sense to him, for if they were in love, then what was there to stop them from enjoying their time together to the full? One thing he *had* made his mind up about was that he would never run out on Grace again, not now, not with all this going for him. And in any case, everything had changed. The previous time they were together, he found her dull and tawdry, and couldn't wait to get away from her. Now, however, he was in love with her, truly in love. It wasn't just that she was rich, and that he would be able to live a trouble-free life, but because he found her attractive and desirable. He stood with Grace on a top-floor balcony of the house looking out towards the sea. What he saw was a paradise, a wonderful new world, a world that was so close, he could almost touch it. But not yet, not until he was quite sure what Grace had in store for them both.

'You still haven't told me what you're going to do with the business now,' he said, his arm firmly wrapped around her waist. 'I mean, surely there's no point any longer in taking a shop around the streets day after day?'

'I like the shop, Eric,' replied Grace. 'Those people were my father's tenants and customers. I'd miss them if I gave up. But I am going to buy the houses back from the bank.'

'Buy them back?' he asked, turning a puzzled look at her.

'My father bought them on a mortgage,' she replied. 'I thought I'd told you? He left a lot of debts, and the houses had to be handed over to the bank as part payment for the huge loan he'd taken out.'

'How did he manage to get such a loan if he had debts?' asked Eric, wanting to know more and more.

'Because of – all this,' Grace replied, scanning the spectacular scenery all around them. 'My father's bank manager knew about the inheritance. He understood the reasons why my father never wanted to touch it.'

'What reasons?'

She turned to look at him. 'Me, Eric,' she replied. 'He wanted me never to have to worry about money.'

'Clever chap.'

'Maybe,' said Grace. 'But money isn't everything. I'd swap it any day for happiness.'

Eric wrapped his arm around her shoulders. 'Well,' he said, 'I can't guarantee anything, but I'll try.'

Grace didn't reply. A flock of seagulls suddenly appeared from nowhere, a great flash of white wings, swooping off over the copse towards the shore below. The noise they made cracked the silence, and set off a chorus of dogs howling from back gardens on the other side of the hill. Grace looked up at an azure-blue sky, broken only by small puffs of restless white clouds galloping above the sea.

'I wonder what Dad would think if he could see me now?' she asked, partially thinking aloud.

'I'd say he'd be very proud of you,' replied Eric.

'You really think so?' asked Grace. 'Even though I'm spending all his money.'

Eric swung a startled look at her. 'Spending it all?' he asked, alarmed.

'Well, quite a lot of it,' said Grace, turning to look at him. 'Once I've paid off the mortgages on all the houses, I'm going to get the business on its feet again, probably employ some more staff and open a shop somewhere.'

Eric was getting worried. 'But – if you do all that,' he asked, 'surely you'll have very little left?'

'Out of fifty thousand pounds?' asked Grace.

Eric's eyes nearly fell out of their sockets. 'Fifty *thousand*?' he asked, flabbergasted.

'As near as damn it,' replied Grace. 'Give or take a pound or two. I reckon once I've paid off the mortgages, and built up the business the way I want it, I should still have a good twenty or twenty-five thousand pounds left over, and that doesn't include what this house is worth. The trouble is, I haven't the faintest idea what to do with all that money. Any ideas, Eric?'

Eric couldn't believe what he was hearing. That kind of money was an absolute fortune, enough to see them both through to the end of their lives. 'You – you must invest it,' he replied quickly, breathlessly.

'Invest?' asked Grace innocently. 'Oh yes, that's right. You invest money, don't you?'

'I could do it for you without any trouble at all,' he replied with tremendous enthusiasm. 'There are some wonderful projects you could invest in. You'd get some terrific returns for your money.'

'But I thought the economic climate was a little risky just now?' said Grace. 'Especially if there's another war.'

'Don't listen to that rubbish!' said Eric. 'Things are bound to get better sooner or later. You leave it to me, and you won't go wrong.'

'Really, Eric?' Grace asked, appearing to embrace his excitement. 'Oh, I knew you were the right person to talk to!' She looked up to the sky, as if addressing her father. 'You see, Dad,' she called. 'I told you you had nothing to worry about. I told you that Eric would know what to do, that everything was going to be all right. Thank you for trusting me.'

Eric grabbed hold of her and held her tightly. 'When your father put his trust in you,' he said quietly, in her ear, 'he knew exactly what he was doing.'

'D'you think so, Eric?' she replied softly. 'D'you really think so?'

'Oh yes,' said Eric. 'And d'you know why, Grace?'

'No?'

'Because he knows *I'm* here to look after you.'

Leaning on his shoulder, Grace smiled wryly to herself. 'Of course,' she answered. 'What a lucky girl I am.'

Mickey Burke had just about an hour to spare before the shops closed. When he left Clapper in the stable, he was fast asleep, no doubt dreaming of another of the long trots his mate Mickey would be taking him on around the streets later in the evening. Not that it was a shop that Mickey needed, for he would never have enough money to buy anything new. Saturday afternoon was always busy up the Cally, and, despite the fact that it was now getting chilly as the sun started to go down, today was no exception. As he made his way up the Caledonian Road, the barrow boys were out in force, with stalls containing some of the worst jumble ever seen, but even so, there were plenty of customers to buy it. Most of the traders along the kerb knew Mickey, and there were lots of calls of 'Wotcha, Mick!' and, to gales of laughter, ' 'Ere 'e comes, God's gift ter Savile Row!' Mickey took it all in good fun, and didn't mind being ragged about the rough-and-ready clothes he was wearing. In fact, that was the reason he was there – to do something about them. On the way, he passed Big Tim on his stilts, and in tailcoat and top hat, playing a penny whistle for his dancing dogs, and further along the road, old 'Mother Macree', the Irish toffee-apple seller, was also doing a roaring trade with the crowd of kids clustered around her bicycle barrow. 'One-eyed Max' was too busy picking up dog-ends from the pavement to notice Mickey passing by, but it looked as though by the end of the day he would have enough baccy to smoke himself to death. Mickey went straight to the barrow he was looking for.

' 'Allo, 'allo!' called Ed Firman from his second-hand clothes stand, which boasted in large scrawled letters a sign showing: QUALITY MEN'S CLOTHES AT ROCK-BOTTOM PRICES. 'Long time no see, ol' son?'

'Wotcha, Ed!' called Mickey, as he approached. He had known Ed and his missus since he was a kid, and Ed was the one person he knew along the Cally who would never twist him. Ed was also the reason why Mickey never shopped amongst the mass of stalls on the site of the old Islington cattle market. 'Fawt it was about time I gave yer some custom. Looks as though yer could do wiv it!'

Ed nearly had a fit. The last thing Mickey had bought from him was a flat, checked cap, which he was still wearing, and that must have been all of three years before. 'Wot yer after, mate?' he asked briskly, going through a dozen hangers containing the most impossibly unsuitable clothes for someone like Mickey. 'Wot about a nice tails,' he suggested, holding up a moth-eaten navy-blue tail coat. 'I could do a smart pair er striped long'uns ter go wiv it. Mind you, yer'll need some medals ter go wiv it. Yer'll probably get some er them up on Daisy's.'

Mickey laughed. He always loved Ed's humour; he loved all the barrow people's humour; to him they were the salt of the earth. 'Nah,' he said. 'I need somefin' a bit less classy than that, mate. White shirt an' navy-blue trousers – that's me limit.'

'Ah!' Ed said triumphantly. 'I must've known you was

comin'.' He went to the back of the stall. 'Just give me a coupla minutes, an' I'll be right wiv yer.'

Whilst he waited, Mickey sorted through the mountain of second-hand shirts, pullovers, vests and underpants, trying to find something that would make him feel good when he wore it in front of Grace. It had taken a lot of thought and consideration for him to come to the decision that if he was to have any chance at all with her, then he would have to smarten himself up a bit. He knew, of course, that on the money she paid him, he didn't have much to spare on togging himself up like Eric Tyler, but at least he could *try* to make himself look more presentable.

'Right, ol' son!' announced Ed as he returned to Mickey, holding up a well-creased pair of navy-blue trousers. 'Wot about this then? Fit fer a bleedin' duke!'

'I ain't no duke, Ed,' said Mickey, taking the trousers and holding them for size against his legs.

'Yer will be, if yer wear these!' retorted Ed, a smile splitting his huge round face with its two double chins. 'A pinch at one an' a tanner,' he said tapping the side of his nose, and leaning over to add softly, 'A bob to you, mate!'

Mickey was impressed. He reckoned Grace would go for these, because when they were once out on their rounds, she had remarked favourably about a man she saw passing in navy-blue trousers. 'Not bad,' he said. 'Not bad at all.'

'Not bad?' croaked Ed incomprehensibly. 'Who's the little gel *you're* tryin' ter chat up then?'

Mickey looked up with a start. ' 'Ow d'you know that?' he asked, a bit taken aback.

Ed came back at him quick as a flash. 'Come off it, mate!' he said. 'Men only buy cloves ter show off ter the gels. Then when they get 'ooked, it's the gels who do all the choosin'. I *know*! My ol' woman's bin pickin' my cloves fer me fer years!'

Mickey laughed, and held on to the trousers he'd decided to buy. 'So wot about a shirt?' he asked.

A short while later, he was on his way back down the Cally, clutching a pair of navy-blue trousers, white shirt, dark blue V-necked pullover, and pair of size nine black shoes, all of which Ed had reduced in price for his old mate. Five shillings and eight pence was more than Mickey had wanted to pay for clothes, especially as he had never had that kind of money to spend on such things in his entire life. But this *was* for something special. If he was going to compete with Eric Tyler, then he was going to have to fight him on his own ground. Bluff. That's what it was all about. Eric might talk smooth, but Mickey had qualities of his own. He wasn't quite sure what those qualities were, but he was certainly going to try to give Eric Tyler a run for his money. But as he made his way home, past stall after stall that was being cleared for the day, his confidence increasingly waned. How could he possibly compete against someone like Eric Tyler? It had nothing to do with how you looked, it was what you *were*. By the time he got back to The Chapel, he had already decided that he would never have the nerve to wear the clothes he had just bought from Ed's stall.

Viv got home late that evening. Josie and Stan had been in bed for hours, for it was now way past midnight. Viv didn't often stay out late at night, but this being a Saturday, her boyfriend, Alan, had asked her out to a dance at Hornsey Town Hall, and once everyone had turned out, there had been the usual scramble to get on buses, which always took for ever to turn up.

When Alan had asked her to go out, her first inclination had been to say no. The grief over Reg having been reported missing in action in Spain had cast a cloud of doom over the family, and it somehow seemed insensitive to enjoy herself when her parents were so deeply upset. She was upset too, for, in recent years, she and her brother had formed a close relationship, and she understood exactly what his feelings were about the suffering of people outside the family's own field of knowledge. But she was convinced that wallowing in misery was not what Reg would have wanted, so she resolved to resume as normal a life as she possibly could, and hope that her mum and dad would soon try to do the same.

On the way home from the bus stop, her journey took her past the main gates of Clissold Park, and, after the shocking incident when a girl was attacked by a man along the same stretch of road just over a year before, she was a little nervous of walking home alone, and didn't want to hang around for too long. To her distress, however, she had gone only a few yards past the gates when she had the uncomfortable feeling that someone was coming up behind her. She stopped and turned. To her irritation, the street gas lamps had still not been converted to electricity, and in the deserted road in front and behind her there were far too many shadows for people to hide in. However, she could see no one around, and after a quick, nervous look up and down the road, she hurried on her way. Once again she had only gone a few paces, when she thought she saw a shadow dart ahead of her, and disappear into a gap in the park railings. Fearing that someone might be stalking her, she made a swift movement to cross the road, but just as she was about to do so, someone leapt out on her from the shadows, and clasped a hand over her mouth. Terrified, she tried to break loose.

'No, Viv!' spluttered a man's breathless voice in her ear. 'Keep quiet! Quiet!'

On hearing her name, Viv stopped struggling, and allowed herself to be pulled into the shadows.

'Don't make a noise,' whispered the man, still holding on to her. 'If I take my hand away, will you promise not to make a noise?'

Viv nodded. She had recognised the voice. As the hand was removed from her mouth, she turned round to look. In the flickering light of the nearby gaslight, she could just make out the drawn features of a boy, who was now a man. It was her brother Reg.

Chapter 18

Grace was glad to be home. Although she loved going down to The House on the Hill, having to share her visit with Eric Tyler had taken away a great deal of the pleasure and relaxation she had been getting during her weekends down there. But it wasn't only that – something she hadn't realised until she was on her way home on the bus from Paddington station. It was the thought of seeing Mickey again, and the yearning she had felt inside her stomach ever since she had left him on Friday evening, the frustration of knowing that *he* was the only one with whom she wanted so badly to share the delights of Devon, and not Eric Tyler. None the less, the weekend for her had been a great success because she had achieved what she had set out to do. Eric Tyler had not only seen with his own eyes the magnificence of the house her father had left her, but now knew exactly what she was worth. As far as he was concerned, she was a real catch; he would make quite sure that from now on he would not put a foot wrong. Which was just the way Grace wanted it.

The moment she arrived home, Grace could see the amount of work Mickey had done around the outside of the house. Most of the window frames had now been painted white, he had patched up small holes in the brickwork with sand and cement, and he had even scrubbed away the black soot from the rims of the chimney-pots.

'You've done a marvellous job, Mickey,' she said, scarcely able to conceal her excitement at seeing him again. 'The least I can do is to ask you in for a good meal. I saved some cold chicken for us in the larder.'

'Fanks all the same, miss,' he replied, putting on his cap and working jacket in the stable, 'but my neighbours, the Gremlins, want me ter go in an' 'ave a drink wiv 'em. It's the old lady's birfday or somefin'.'

Grace was disappointed, and it showed in her face. 'Oh well, never mind,' she replied bravely, but uneasily. 'Some other time.' The reason she felt uneasy was because she wasn't sure whether he was still angry for the way she had talked to him before she and Eric had left for Devon. 'Anyway, we've got the whole week off to catch up on things,' she continued. 'I've got a lot I want to talk over with you about the business.'

Mickey was puzzled. 'The business, miss?'

'About all the plans I have in mind,' she replied. 'It's going to be quite exciting. I shall need all the ideas you can think of, Mickey.'

'Oh, you don't need me fer that, miss,' he replied, fidgeting with the cap on his head. 'I don't know nuffin' much about business. You need someone wiv more brains than me.'

Grace was disturbed by how subdued he was. Was he sulking, or just plain unhappy? 'Is anything wrong, Mickey? You don't seem yourself.'

'Bit tired, that's all, miss,' he replied. 'Bin a long weekend.'

'Grace.'

Mickey raised his eyes at her. 'Miss?'

'My name is Grace,' she said. 'If we're going to carry on working together, I think it's time we were less formal. Please call me Grace from now on.'

Mickey was embarrassed, and shrugged his shoulders without replying.

'Don't you want to?' she asked, watching carefully for his reaction.

'It's not that, miss,' he replied, fumbling for words. 'It's just that – well – you're my employer, and – I shouldn't really take liberties.'

Grace was astonished. She couldn't really understand him. 'Liberties?' she asked with incomprehension. 'Mickey. We're friends – aren't we?' She waited tensely for his reply.

Mickey shrugged. He took off his cap. 'You've *got* friends, miss,' he said boldly, 'friends er yer own type. They're the ones who should 'elp yer – not me.'

Grace didn't know whether to feel hurt or offended, but in the end she realised what he was getting at. Something inside told her that he was feeling the same way about her as she felt about him. The difficulty was, neither of them was capable of spelling it out to the other. She had no doubt that seeing her with Eric Tyler was affecting the way Mickey felt about her; he looked pained and hurt whenever Eric was around. There was no other way but to reassure him. But how? How could she tell him that what she was doing was the only positive way of getting rid of Eric for ever?

'D'you remember what I told you, Mickey?' she asked, moving closer to him. 'I told you a few weeks ago, and I told you just before I left for Devon on Friday evening.' To her surprise, he had a reply waiting for her.

'You said, "If I do things . . . that seem a little odd . . . please don't take them too seriously." '

'That's right, Mickey,' she said. 'And d'you know *why* I told you that? I told you because . . . I'm . . . fond of you, because I don't want to hurt you.'

'Why wouldn't you want to do that, miss?' he asked, painfully aware that she was standing so close to him.

'I think you know,' Grace replied, meeting his eyes.

Mickey stared her out for a moment, then averted his gaze. 'It's time I was gettin' 'ome,' he said with a sigh.

'Mickey.'

He stopped and turned to look at her.

'You know,' said Grace, 'you and I are no different from one another. Oh, we may come from different backgrounds, have different interests in life, but we're basically no different from anyone else. Don't ever think that you're not worthy of me because you are. You're more worthy than anyone I've ever known in my entire life. You know what I think our problem is? I think we both feel the same for each other, but we just don't know how to say it. But I'm going to say it now, Mickey. I love you, and I think you love me. Am I right – or am I wrong?'

Mickey finally struggled to look straight into her eyes. But when he did, once again his courage failed him. 'See yer in the mornin', miss.'

Grace smiled warmly at him. 'See you in the morning, Mickey.'

Mickey watched her leave the stable and return to the house. For several moments he just stood there, too confused to understand what had happened, or what she was trying to say to him. He turned round, and suddenly caught a fleeting glimpse of himself in a piece of broken mirror that he had fitted on one of the beams to use for shaving. He went across and looked at his reflection. His hand automatically reached up to feel the stubble on his face. He sighed as he remembered that he hadn't shaved that day. But as he stood there, he saw something else. He saw someone who was gradually coming to terms with the fact that he was no longer a boy, who could just amble through life with impunity, laughing and joking with his mates up the pub and down the market. He was now a man, who had feelings inside that told him how much he wanted, how much he needed love, *real* love. It was a new experience for him, and he had no intention of letting it pass him by.

Viv's message was urgent. Something very important had come up that would affect the entire family, and she was desperate to talk to Grace as soon as possible. This is where the telephone would have come in handy, Grace thought. When her father first suggested that they have one installed in the house, she was stupid enough to say that telephones were just a five-minute wonder, and a complete waste of money, but fortunately Mr Fitch the butcher was always willing to take any really urgent messages for her. However, regardless of all the work she had ahead of her during her coming week off from the rounds, she knew that Viv would only have made contact with her like this if it was something she couldn't deal with herself. The message said Viv would be coming up to The Chapel at ten o'clock, which meant that Grace had to delay working with Mickey on stocktaking. What she didn't anticipate, however, was an early morning visit from Georgie O'Hara, who brought the first smile of the day to her face when he told her about the plan he had hatched to stop Aunt Hilda from taking her to court.

Within a few minutes of Georgie's arrival, Hilda herself turned up. 'Are you mad or somefin'?' growled Hilda. 'After wot that feller did ter yer, an' yer wanna take 'im back again?'

'I know, Auntie,' said Grace. 'I must say, I *have* been having second thoughts about him.'

'Second thoughts!' Hilda looked as though she was about to burst a blood vessel. 'Eric Tyler's a bleedin' leech. 'E'll suck yer dry!'

'Yer aunt's right,' said Georgie, who had adopted a permanent look of foreboding for his performance. 'If this feller has his way, yer could have nothin' left in the kitty.'

'There!' said Hilda, in perfect agreement. 'I've told yer before, an' I'll tell yer again, wotever Gus left was not just fer you, it was fer *all* the family.'

'You're right, Auntie,' said Grace. 'I couldn't agree more.'

'Yes!' continued Hilda, who for one moment hadn't taken in what Grace had said. 'An' I'll tell yer anuvver fing—' She stopped dead. 'Wot did you say?' she asked, taken aback.

Grace smiled winsomely. 'I said, you're right, Auntie. I've decided that you and the rest of the family should get something of what Dad left.'

Hilda's jaw dropped. Even Georgie couldn't believe what he'd just heard.

'I've been working things out,' continued Grace. 'What with the house down in Devon, and the money he left, there should be something nice left over for you *and* Aunt Josie.'

Hilda took a gulp. 'Left over?' she asked, her expression fixed like stone.

'I have to pay off the debts first,' said Grace. 'I've told Mr Rumble that I intend to meet all Dad's commitments: the mortgages on the houses, the outstanding bills. Once I've taken care of all that, then we can sit down together, and see how much is left over for the rest of the family.'

Georgie didn't know whether he was coming or going. He sank back into the sofa in the front parlour like a deflated balloon.

Hilda sat upright in her straight-backed chair at the parlour table. She was in a state of shock. 'You're a very wise child, Gracie dear,' she said.

Grace smiled her appreciation.

'I always told yer dad that yer've got yer 'ead screwed on the right way,' said Hilda positively. She looked across at Georgie. 'Didn't I tell yer that, Georgie?'

Georgie was momentarily at a loss for words. 'Oh – yes,' he said finally. 'That yer did, Mrs Barnet. That yer did.'

'Good then,' said Grace. 'That's settled!' Aware that Viv would be turning up any moment, she got up quickly from her chair at the table.

'Not quite,' said Hilda, remaining seated. 'Yer still 'aven't decided wot yer goin' ter do about this bloodsucker bloke of yours.'

'Eric Tyler?' asked Grace. She sighed. 'Yes, I do see what you mean. He *could* be a bit of a problem, couldn't he?'

'*Could be?*' spluttered Hilda. ' 'E is right now. If yer don't get rid of 'im, yer'll lose the 'ole bleedin' lot.'

'So what do you suggest I do then, Auntie?' asked Grace demurely.

Hilda had no hesitation. 'Leave 'im ter me!' she bawled.

A few minutes later Hilda left The Chapel, having promised Grace her full support. Thanks to both Georgie's intervention and the knowledge that she would be getting something from Gus's inheritance, Hilda would at least give Grace a breathing space to get on with sorting out her future plans without the fear of constant threats and antagonism from a relative who, over the years, had been nothing to Grace but a pain in the neck. As for Aunt Hilda dealing with Eric Tyler, well that really brought a smile to Grace's face. In fact, if it wasn't for Grace's own plans for dealing with Eric, she would just love to be present at any confrontation between her aunt and Eric Tyler, for, in many ways, they were very similar: ruthless, and thoroughly determined to get what they wanted. However, Grace's immediate concern now was Viv, for it was now half-past ten, and she was beginning to worry about what was going on. To her relief, and embarrassment, Mr Fitch's errand boy turned up at the front door bringing a second message from Viv, who had called from the post office in Parkhurst Road, asking Grace to meet her in Lyons teashop at the Nag's Head.

'He's alive, Grace,' said Viv, breathlessly. 'Reg's alive. I've seen him. I've talked to him.'

Grace had hardly sat down at the table when Viv broke the news. 'Alive?' she asked. 'But that's wonderful news! When did he get home?'

'That's just it, Grace,' Viv said, passing her the cup of tea she had just bought her at the teashop counter. 'He's not at home. He doesn't *want* to go home.'

'What d'you mean?' asked Grace, puzzled, loosening the top button of her coat.

'I went to a dance with Alan at Hornsey Town Hall on Saturday night,' Viv said. 'When I was on my way back from the bus stop near the park, Reg was waiting for me.' Although she was clearly on edge, Viv was completely composed as she talked. 'At first I found it difficult to believe it was him. I know it was in the dark, but – oh, Grace, he's so different, so . . .' Now clearly distressed, she stopped for a moment to take a sip of tea. 'We walked around the corner to Church Street. We stood in a shop doorway where there was a bit of light. To tell you the truth, I didn't recognise him.'

Grace leaned across the table to her. 'Why?'

'Oh, you should have seen him,' replied Viv. 'He's aged. I mean he's two years younger than me, but his face looks more like someone much older. He's got a gash on his face. It's more or less healed up, but it's going to leave quite a scar. He says he got it from – from a bayonet.'

Grace shuddered. 'But why doesn't he want to go home?' she asked.

Viv waited a moment before answering. 'He can't face up to it, Grace,' she replied. 'He can't face up to telling Mum and Dad all the reasons why he disappeared from home the way he did. He doesn't want to tell them what he's been through, about the things he's seen, the death and destruction everywhere. Wherever he's been, whatever he's done, it's left a mark on his mind. I don't know how he'll ever get rid of it.'

Grace took a moment to think about what Viv was telling her. 'Viv,' she said, 'Reg is going to have to go home at some stage. Where's he living now?'

'I'd hardly call it *living*,' replied Viv. 'He's sleeping out rough – he won't tell me where exactly, but by some of the things he said, I have a feeling it's up in the West End somewhere. Anyway, he said he'd make contact with me again.'

Grace leant closer towards her across the table. 'That should tell you something, Viv.'

'What d'you mean?'

'It means that there's a part of him that doesn't want to be cut off from his family. He needs help.'

'I *know* he needs help,' said Viv with some irritation. 'But how do I give it to him if he won't come home?'

'Let me see if *I* can talk to him,' said Grace. 'I'm not as close to him as you are, and I'd probably do no better than you, but at least I'm far enough removed from your mum and dad to let him know that I won't be angry with him for what he's done.'

'That's a strange thing to say,' said Viv. 'If you saw him, you'd know that it's impossible to be angry with him. I doubt he can ever get over what he's gone through.'

Grace stretched her hand across the table, and placed it on Viv's hand. 'When he gets in touch with you again,' she said, 'tell him that I'd like to talk with him – not that I want to help him, just that I want to talk, nothing more.'

'And what if he says no?'

Grace sat back in her chair again. 'Then there's little we can do, Viv,' she replied. 'But at least we must try. If we don't, we may lose him for ever.'

Grace and Mickey hadn't discussed what they had talked about in Clapper's stable a few nights before, but there were clear signs of a warm, changing relationship between them. A couple of days later, Grace got Alf Cudlipp, the builder from Jackson Road, to go in and have a look at Gert Jolly's rising damp. After he'd confirmed that the trouble was indeed what Gert had suspected, Grace and Mickey called on her.

'Don't worry about a thing, Mrs Jolly,' said Grace reassuringly. 'I've already told Mr Cudlipp to go ahead with the work, and he's promised to get on to it as soon as possible.'

Gert breathed a sigh of relief. 'Oh, fanks so much, Gracie, me dear,' she said, pouring tea for them all at her back parlour table. 'I can't tell yer wot a load yer've taken off me mind. I 'aven't bin able ter sleep since I first found that damp.'

'Actually, you've raised a very good point,' said Grace. 'We must find somewhere for you to sleep whilst all this work is going on.' She turned to Mickey. 'Remind me to ask Mr Wilson if Mrs Jolly can use his spare room upstairs in his place until the work's done.'

'Not on yer nelly!' growled Gert. 'I ain't leavin' *my* 'ome, not fer no one! 'Ere I am, an' 'ere I stay!'

'But the smell would be ghastly, Mrs Jolly,' warned Grace.

'Yer can stay 'ere durin' the day, darlin',' added Mickey. 'But yer can't go on sleepin' 'ere wiv all that pong.'

'I can manage perfectly well, fank yer very much!' retorted Gert. 'I'll bring me bed back 'ere outside. It wouldn't be first time I've kipped down in the scullery.'

Grace and Mickey exchanged defeated looks. 'But Mr Cudlipp may not be able to start the work before the end of the month,' said Grace. 'By the time we get into November, it could start turning very chilly at night.'

'I don't care!' replied Gert adamantly. 'This may not be my property, but I've spent a good chunk er me life 'ere, an' I ain't gettin' out just 'cos of a bit er pong.'

Grace sighed. 'As you wish, Mrs Jolly,' she replied. 'But I know how you feel. You've always kept the place so spotless. My father used to say your doorstep was scrubbed so beautifully white he hated to step on it. If he'd had his way, he'd have given the property to you, to all his tenants.'

Grace's remark caused Mickey to look up with a start.

'Ha!' replied Gert. 'If I 'ad the crown jewels, I wouldn't wear 'em, but I'd keep 'em bleedin' clean!'

It wasn't until they were on their way back home, walking along Caledonian Road, that Grace realised how little Mickey had said to her since they had left Gert Jolly's place. 'You're very quiet, Mickey,' she said. 'Is anything wrong?'

'Huh?' said Mickey, snapping out of his thoughts. 'Oh – nah – nuffin',' he replied. 'Sorry about that. I was just finkin', that's all.'

'Oh yes?' asked Grace. 'What about?'

'About wot you said ter Mrs J,' he replied. 'About 'ow if yer farver 'ad 'ad 'is way, 'e'd've given away all the properties to 'is tenants.'

'It's true,' said Grace. 'I was always telling him what a rotten businessman he was. Sometimes I think he thought he was Lord Rothschild!'

'Is it such a bad idea?' asked Mickey, bringing them to a sudden halt.

'What?'

'Givin' all the tenants their own properties?'

Grace roared with laughter. 'You're just as bad as him!' she said, walking on.

'No, I mean it!' persisted Mickey, hurrying along after her. 'I don't mean ter actually *give* 'em the properties, but ter give 'em all the chance ter *buy* 'em.'

Again Grace came to a halt. 'Mickey!' she said. 'Are you mad? Do you honestly think that any one of those tenants could actually afford to buy their own house? As it is, a lot of them can't even find the money for the rent.'

'I *know* that!' retorted Mickey, who was really smitten with his own idea. 'But s'ppose yer asked 'em ter pay it off in instalments? I mean, it wouldn't cost 'em much more than what they pay fer their rent now.'

'So what's the point of getting them to buy?'

'Pride,' answered Mickey quite straightforwardly. 'Give 'em the responsibility of lookin' after their own place. They can do their own repairs and maintenance, and not keep waitin' ter ask you ter do fings for 'em.'

Grace's expression was no longer dismissive. To her surprise, she was suddenly listening to every word he said. In the stiffening breeze, she could hear the flapping of flags and bunting that were still left over from the coronation in May, and even though the weather was warming up again, there was the first premature smell of smoke coming out of a chimneypot on the roof of one of the houses further down the road.

Aware that Grace was now listening, Mickey began to elaborate on what he was suggesting. ' 'Ow much does it cost you on runnin' repairs, miss?' he asked. 'Paintin', decoratin', drains, wear 'n' tear – must cost yer a bomb? Right?'

Grace nodded.

'So if yer added up the cost of all that, an' put it against wot yer get in rents, I bet there ain't much profit left at the end of it?'

Grace, now a captive listener, agreed.

'So if yer got all those 'ouses off yer 'ands,' continued Mickey with intense eagerness, 'get the tenants ter buy an' look after their own places, just fink wot yer'd save?'

'That's all very well, Mickey,' said Grace, finally speaking, 'but you've forgotten one thing. These are my father's tenants. They were his friends. I don't want to wash my hands of them and say goodbye as though they never existed.'

Mickey looked hurt. 'Yer've got me wrong, miss,' he said. 'I'd never suggest a fing like that. All I'm sayin' is that this would be the best fing fer you – *an'* them. After all, yer could carry on seein' 'em whenever yer want, and in any case, yer could still go on wiv the shop.'

Grace thought for a moment. 'It's an idea, Mickey,' she said, without commitment. 'Let me think about it.'

Mickey shrugged. 'Fine by me, miss.'

They walked on. It was a lovely afternoon, with the sun winning its struggle to dominate the sky, and a cool breeze that by evening would turn chilly again. In the distance, workmen were feverishly putting finishing touches to the new Mayfair Cinema, which was now scheduled to open in December, and as Grace and Mickey walked, the first leaves of autumn were beginning to flutter down on to the pavements.

Grace thought hard about Mickey's suggestion. In some strange way, it made sense, because there was no doubt that the properties her father had left her *were* now becoming a burden. All of the houses were built long ago, and therefore needed constant repair and attention. It wasn't that she resented her responsibilities, but since her father died she had dreamt about developing the grocery business, which offered so many opportunities.

However, it wasn't just Mickey's idea she was milling over in her mind, it was Mickey himself. For the past few weeks he was beginning to show how capable he *really* was, not only with the way he had helped Clapper to recover from the loss of the one person in the world who really adored him, but the way he had gently steered Grace into calmer waters. Each day she was discovering new things about Mickey, each day she was impressed with the way he was helping her to build up the trust between herself and Gus's tenants and customers. But what she noticed most was that Mickey was losing his boyish ways. He was now a force to be reckoned with in his own right. She knew he cared for her too, but how she longed to hear him tell her so. However, she had done her best to make her own feelings known to him. From now on, it was up to Mickey himself. After all that had happened the other evening, all she could do was wait.

When they got back to The Chapel, they found Eric Tyler sitting on the front doorstep, smoking a cigarette. He was none too pleased to see the two of them together.

'Eric!' said Grace, greeting him brightly. 'What are you doing here?'

'I said I'd be coming round this afternoon,' Eric replied sourly, getting up to meet her. He glared at Mickey. 'Clearly you've forgotten.'

'I'm so sorry,' said Grace, not too apologetically. 'Come on, let's go in.' She quickly retrieved her key from her coat pocket, and went to open the door. 'Thank you, Mickey!' she called. 'I'll talk to you about that later!'

For Eric's benefit, he tipped his cap to her, and went off to the back entrance.

'Talk to him about what?' asked Eric, as he followed Grace into the house.

'Oh, nothing important,' she replied vaguely. 'Mickey's always coming up with foolhardy ideas. I don't take any notice of them.'

Eric left the house soon after dark. He had wanted to stay on, but Grace made the excuse that she had a lot of work to get through before she resumed her rounds the following week. However, as soon as he had gone, she went out to the stable to see Clapper. She hadn't expected to find Mickey still there, for he usually went home in the early evening, so she was surprised to find him stripped to the waist, drying himself after a wash-down in a cold bucket of water.

'Isn't it time you were getting home?' she asked casually.

'I've only just got back,' replied Mickey, quickly putting on his shirt. 'Me an' Clap've just bin out fer a bit of a trot.'

'It's a bit late for that, isn't it?' asked Grace.

'It makes the night shorter fer 'im,' Mickey replied. ' 'E spends a lot er time cooped up 'ere on 'is own. Anyway, I wasn't doin' anyfin' special. I didn't fink yer'd notice, seein' as 'ow yer 'ad a visitor.'

Grace took his point, and stood in the open doorway whilst he finished dressing. 'I don't think Eric will be around too much longer,' she said. 'I have a feeling he doesn't like your being here.'

'Oh really?' replied Mickey dismissively.

'I've told him several times that you're going to be here for as long as you want,' she said pointedly. 'I've told him that I need you, and want you.' She stared hard at him. 'In fact, you've no idea how *much* I want you.'

Mickey stopped what he was doing, and looked across at her.

'I've given your idea a lot of thought, Mickey,' she said, coming over to him. 'I think there may be something in it. We'll have to talk more.'

'Anyfin' you say, miss,' he said, watching her carefully and playing along with her game.

'Thank you for all you're doing for me, Mickey,' she said. 'You've no idea how grateful I am.' She turned to leave.

'You're welcome – Grace.'

Grace stopped and turned. The look she gave him was of pure astonishment. 'What did you say?' she asked.

'I said – you're welcome, Grace.' He went to her, took her in his arms, and kissed her.

A few minutes later, they went back inside the house together. It was the first time Mickey had ever done so.

Chapter 19

Charing Cross was not particularly the best place to be in the middle of the night, especially beneath the arches of Hungerford Bridge. Here the street people huddled together to while the night away, lost souls in a world they had forsaken either through ill fortune or in a lack of confidence in their ability to be able to cope with the everyday problems of life. They were a sorry lot, most of them elderly, military veterans of the Boer War or the Great War, others simply cast-offs from society, who were forced to live out rough, to beg on the streets for a few coins to keep alive during the day, and sleep on newspapers and old moth-eaten blankets on the cold pavements by night. Theirs was an aimless existence, their futures as precarious as life itself.

Grace and Mickey found it a depressing place to be wandering around in the dark. The only reason they were there was that, despite the promise he had made to his sister, Viv, Reg Cooker had not made contact with her since the night they had met in the dark outside the gates of Clissold Park. With no clue as to his whereabouts, Grace had taken it on her own shoulders to search every seedy part of the West End of London where the street people were known to spend their nights. She and Mickey had already searched, without success, Hyde Park, Green Park, and St James's Park, but the nearest they got to finding out about Reg was a vague reference to 'young Scarface', who, only a few weeks earlier, had apparently got into trouble with one of the other cast-offs for trying to muscle in on his 'pitch'. Eventually, however, Grace's trail led her to Charing Cross, but if it hadn't been for Mickey at her side, she was convinced that she would never have had the courage to pick her way in the dark through the sleeping, heaving bodies beneath the bridge.

'Viv said I probably wouldn't recognise Reg even if I see him,' whispered Grace, trying desperately to pick out the grubby faces in the beam from Mickey's torch. 'She said he looked as though he hadn't shaved for weeks, and the only thing to look out for was the scar on his forehead and down his cheek.'

'It's all right,' replied Mickey reassuringly. 'We'll find 'im, but we've got ter be careful we don't upset any er this lot. They could turn nasty if they wake up 'an find us nosin' around.'

For as long as they dared, they searched amongst the sleeping mounds, the grunts and snores echoing in the hollow sound beneath the dripping arches. But suddenly a cracked voice called to them in the dark, 'Who yer lookin' fer?'

Mickey swung his torch beam round to the crumpled, lined face of an elderly woman tramp, swathed in what looked like several layers of grubby clothes. 'Leave this ter me,' he whispered to Grace, keeping her behind him. ' 'Allo, Ma,' he said in a barely audible voice, crouching down beside the old woman.

'Who yer lookin' fer?' repeated the woman irritably.

'Young bloke,' replied Mickey. 'Bin sleepin' rough fer the last few weeks. 'Ave yer seen 'im?'

'I might,' replied the old girl. 'An' I might not. If I 'ad a fag, I might remember.'

Although Mickey didn't smoke, he had deliberately brought a packet of cigarettes with him for just such bribes.

' 'Ere yer are, mate,' he said, taking out a couple of cigarettes and giving them to her.

The old girl snatched them from him feverishly. 'There're plenty of young blokes sleepin' out rough,' she croaked, quickly hiding her booty as though they were diamonds. 'Why should I remember this one?'

' 'Is name's Reg,' pressed Mickey.

The old girl grunted dismissively.

' 'E's got a big scar on his face.'

The old girl looked up with a start. '*That* one?'

Mickey leaned down closer to her. ' 'Ave yer seen 'im?' he asked eagerly.

'Try the doss,' replied the old girl, laying her head back on her makeshift newspaper cushion.

'Rowton 'Ouse – up Farringdon Road?' he asked. 'We've bin up there.'

'Not there!' snorted the old girl. 'The Army. Up the Castle.'

'Which one, Ma?' pressed Mickey. 'D'yer mean the Elephant?'

Despite giving the old girl a gentle prod with his hand, she had gone back to sleep as quickly as she had woken up.

Mickey reluctantly got up. 'Let's get out of 'ere,' he whispered urgently.

'What does she mean?' asked Grace anxiously. 'The Army? The Castle?'

'I don't know, Grace,' replied Mickey. 'But it could be a Salvation Army 'ostel up the Elephant an' Castle somewhere. Let's go over ter the cop shop an' see wot we can find out.'

After a quick trip across the road to the reception desk at Scotland Yard, the two of them hopped on an all-night bus that took them to the Elephant and Castle, on the south side of the river. Following the directions given to Mickey by the police sergeant on duty at the Yard, they soon found their way to a small backstreet. There they found a run-down-looking building which they eventually discovered was a Salvation Army hostel for down-and-outs. Grace was nervous about going in, so she kept as close to Mickey as she possibly could.

'Reg Cooker, you say?' The small, plump-faced, rather severe-looking Salvation Army woman on the reception desk was not altogether welcoming, which was hardly surprising with the number of unfortunates who drifted into the hostel for shelter each night. 'I'm sorry. But I've got no one registered by that name here tonight. Mind you, most of them don't seem to have a name, or if they do, it's a false one. What's this cousin of yours look like?'

Grace again went through the whole business of trying to describe Reg to her.

'Can't say it rings a bell,' said the Salvation Army woman. 'We've got a few young chaps in here, but he could be any one of them. Or on the other hand, he may not be here at all. Have you tried St Martin-in-the-Fields up in Trafalgar Square? They sometimes take in poor souls for the night.'

Grace nodded.

'We was over there just after midnight,' said Mickey. 'No luck, I'm afraid.'

'Well, I'm sorry I can't help you,' said the Salvation Army woman, putting on her spectacles again, and returning to her paperwork.

'If you should happen to come across him,' pleaded Grace, 'could you please tell him to get in touch with his cousin? My name's Grace Higgs.'

The woman nodded without looking up from her work.

Grace and Mickey started to leave, but before she left

Grace called back, 'You can't miss him. He's got a big gash on his face.'

The Salvation Army woman looked up with a start. 'A gash, you say?' Her eyes darted back at Grace above her spectacles. 'On his forehead . . .' she pointed to her own face with one finger, 'down here . . . down his cheek?'

'Yes, yes!' replied Grace, eagerly going back to the counter. 'Have you seen him?'

'Well, if it *is* the one you're looking for,' replied the woman, 'his name's not what *you* call him.'

'Can I see him?' begged Grace. 'Please – just let me see him. If I can just talk to him . . .'

'It's all men up there,' the woman replied sternly. She turned to Mickey. 'If *you* want to go up, he's in the last bed on the right-hand side just by the window.' She turned back to Grace. 'I'm sorry, young lady,' she said. 'I'm afraid you'll have to wait down here.'

Mickey hurried up the narrow wooden staircase, leaving Grace to sit on a bench with her back leaning against a bare plastered wall. The entrance area was a very bleak place, where the smell of cocoa from the community dining room seemed to be fighting a duel with the stench of urine from the toilets, and the sour fragrance of carbolic soap from the washrooms.

Grace felt as though she had been waiting for hours. It had been such a long night, and she was now drained and weary. She leaned her head back against the wall, closed her eyes, and tried to pretend that none of this was happening. She found it difficult to believe that she would find Reg in a place like this. War, and everything it implied, was cruel and unnecessary. It claimed not only life, but also heart and soul. She was nervous at the prospect of seeing Reg again. After what Viv had told her, he seemed to be wandering alone in a desert of uncertainty, unable to trust *anyone*. Sitting there with no one to talk to, she felt cold, so she turned up her collar. As each minute passed, her anxiety grew. Suppose Mickey *did* find Reg upstairs? How would he react to being found in such a place, to being found at all? Would seeing Grace, a member of his own family, do more harm than good? Her mind was full of apprehension. But then she thought how lucky she was to have Mickey at her side, supporting her, giving her the strength to go to all the places she would never expect to see in an entire lifetime.

The moment she thought about Mickey, she felt the warmth seep through her veins. She was still in a whirl about how they had finally come together, two people from totally different backgrounds, but united in the strongest desire to be together. What had happened the night before between them had changed her entire feelings towards men, at least to *this* man, for Mickey *was* a man, a man who wanted nothing more from her than her love. It was a whole new experience for her, and she was elated that this was a relationship she could cherish.

'Grace.'

Her eyes sprang open to find Mickey standing in front of her. He moved to one side. Behind him was the strange, bedraggled figure of a man who seemed to have stepped right out of her worst nightmare. 'Reg!' she cried. She opened her arms, and made a move towards him, but he flinched, and pulled back.

Mickey signalled to her to take things carefully.

Reg, with unkempt hair flowing over his shoulders, and a shaggy beard that tried hard to conceal the monstrous gash on his face, stared at her with piercing, frightened eyes, like a wild rabbit caught in a trap.

'If you want to talk,' said the Salvation Army woman,

'you can go in the reading room there. There's no one around. You won't be disturbed.'

Grace hesitated and went across to the room indicated by the woman. Mickey waited for her to go in, gave a reassuring nod to Reg, then let him go in behind her.

'I'll wait for yer outside,' said Mickey, closing the door.

Grace was now alone with Reg, and for a brief moment she stood looking at him. She found it distressing to see the condition he was in, the defeated look on his face.

'It's good to see you again, Reg,' she said, smiling bravely.

Reg didn't answer, just stood where he was, head bowed. She went to the reading table in the middle of the room, and sat there. 'Won't you come and sit with me for a few minutes?' she asked tentatively.

'Who's that bloke?'

Reg's sudden blunt question took her by surprise. 'That's Mickey,' she replied. 'Mickey Burke. He's my friend. You'd like him, Reg.'

Reg remained where he was, hands clasped together in front of him.

Grace waited a moment before continuing. 'We've missed you, Reg,' she said softly, gently. 'All the family.'

'Family?' he asked, his face crushed with what seemed like puzzlement. '*Wot* family?'

'Viv,' replied Grace. 'Your mum and dad . . .'

Reg turned to go.

Grace immediately got up and went to him. 'Reg!' she pleaded, gently taking his arm.

'Why did yer come 'ere?' asked Reg. 'Did *they* send yer?'

'No, Reg, no,' insisted Grace. She had suddenly come face to face with him, and she could see the dreadful enormity of the bayonet scar, the way it had changed his features so dramatically. 'Your mum and dad know nothing about this. They don't even know you're here. They think you're dead.'

'Good!' replied Reg, pulling his arm away.

'Why, Reg?' asked Grace, soft and sensitively. 'Why are you doing this? Why are you hurting them – *and* yourself?'

Reg refused to answer.

'When they heard about what happened to you,' continued Grace, 'they were heartbroken. They couldn't understand. None of us could understand. Won't you tell me, Reg – please?'

She watched him deep in thought for a moment. Without so much as a passing look at her, he turned, went to the table, sat there, reached into his trouser pocket for a flat tobacco tin, and took out a cigarette that he had rolled himself. It was strange for Grace to watch him, for every movement he made was slow and methodical, and as she waited for him to light the cigarette, she realised that, until this moment, she had never seen him smoke before.

He inhaled and exhaled deeply. 'There are some fings yer just can't ignore,' he began, his voice much deeper and huskier than Grace remembered. 'I knew wot was goin' on over there. I knew that if people like me didn't try ter help, there'd be no termorrer fer the people over there. I met some great blokes. Some of them were my best friends. They weren't all from England, but we all felt the same way about wot we was doin'. When I first got out there, I got the shivers. I got scared, not just 'cos I knew I'd soon be riskin' my life in a war, but 'cos I was away from 'ome fer the first time in me life, I was away from me own family, the people who'd brought me up ter be just like them, ter close my eyes ter anyfin' that 'ad nuffin' ter do wiv me. Suddenly, I was learnin' ter do fings fer meself, ter scrap around fer food, ter eat anyfin' I could lay me 'ands on. Me an' my mates used ter kill rats, and roast them over a bonfire.' He shook his head. 'It wasn't all that much diff'rent from Sunday roasts back 'ome.'

Grace lowered her eyes in horror.

'Injustice, Grace,' he continued. 'D'yer know wot that means?' He didn't wait for an answer. 'It means takin' away people's rights, poor people's rights, forcin' 'em ter give in ter men who 'ave the power to dictate the way yer live yer life, wevver it's right or wrong.' He took a deep puff of his cigarette. 'The trouble was,' he continued, 'wot I didn't realise was the country I went to was all one people. OK, they all come from diff'rent backgrounds, from all round the place, but still – they're really just one country. And yet, there they were, fightin' each uvver. The more I saw, the more I couldn't understand. All I knew was that everyone 'ad the right ter 'ave a diff'rent opinion of 'ow they wanted ter live. But it didn't 'appen that way. They fought an' killed each uvver.' His eyes suddenly darted a look up at Grace. It was a chilling look, cold and angry. 'Yer see this?' he asked, reaching up with the tip of his finger to outline the scar on his face and forehead. 'I got this from a bayonet. It was this man – grey 'air, grey moustache, face lined and thick with gunpowder smoke. 'E was too old ter be fightin' in a war that was killin' 'is own bruvvers and sisters and 'is own kids. An' yet, there 'e was, chargin' at me wiv a rifle an' bayonet. When 'e come at me, I froze. I was so scared, my finger couldn't pull the trigger of me own rifle. All I remember was 'im yellin' out at me in Spanish – I didn't know wot the 'ell it was. Then 'e slashed at me, an' I felt all this wet rushin' down me face. I was in so much pain, I wanted ter scream out, but I couldn't! All I could do was ter stand there, an' wait fer 'im ter run me through. But 'e didn't get the chance.' He paused for another deep puff of his cigarette. 'I could see the steel from 'is bayonet above me 'ead. The sun was shinin' on it. An' then suddenly – it wasn't any more. The ol' boy yelled out in Spanish: "*Dios! Dios!*" – God! God! Then 'e fell forward, flat on 'is face on the ground right in front er me. 'E 'ad a ruddy great knife stuck in 'is back.' With some difficulty he hesitated. 'When I saw who shoved it there, I couldn't believe me eyes. It was a gel, a young gel – she couldn't've bin more than sixteen years old or so. She smiled at me, and then rushed off.' He hesitated again. 'All I remember after that was falling down and blackin' out. The next fing I knew I was lyin' in someone's bed in a tiny 'ouse in a village.'

Once he had finished there was a long silence. Grace had been unable to watch him whilst he relived what had happened to him.

'I'd 'ad enuff, yer see,' continued Reg, stubbing his cigarette out in a mug on the table before he had finished it. 'All I wanted ter do was ter get 'ome, get back ter Mum an' Dad and all the family. But on the way, I kept finkin' about them all. I kept finkin' wot they'd say when I told 'em why I went all that way to 'elp fight somebody else's battle. And yer know wot? All I could 'ear Dad sayin' was, "Why did yer 'ave ter go an' upset yer mum like that, son? Yer shouldn't've done it." ' He shook his head. 'I just couldn't face up to it.'

Grace sat in silence for a moment, then got up and moved to a bench table on the other side of the room, where several of the day's newspapers were scattered around. The head-lines were much the same as they had been for weeks on end, about Nazi Germany's territorial ambitions in Europe, the Japanese invasion of China, and the bloody civil war conflict in Spain. After the graphic way in which Reg had described what he had been through, Grace did her best not to look at any of the newspapers. She slowly turned round to look at Reg. He was still again, like stone, his eyes fixed grimly on the table in front of him.

'There's nothing you want to hear from me, Reg. I know that,' said Grace. 'All I can say is that I admire what you've done.'

She flinched when he swung round on her. 'I don't need admiration!' he snapped. 'I'm not a hero. I didn't come all the way back 'ome ter 'ear people tell me 'ow sorry they are fer me.'

'I'm *not* sorry for you, Reg!' retorted Grace, coming straight back at him. 'In fact, I think you've been a damned fool! And d'you know why?' She slowly made her way back to him. 'Because you thought of everyone else except the people who care for you, the people who *really* care. All right, so it's good to know that you have a conscience – everyone's entitled to have *that*. It's good to care for the less fortunate of this world. It's good to fight their battles.' She came and stood over him. 'But it isn't right to think that you're the only person who matters, that all your family and friends are irrelevant, that they have no feelings that you should even consider. A few moments ago you talked to me about rights, about taking away people's rights because they had an opinion of their own. Well, your mum and dad have rights too, Reg, and so do your family. We have the right to worry about you, to care about you, to grieve if anything happens to you. That's not a political statement, it's about human frailty. What I'm trying to say, Reg, is, there's nothing to be ashamed of in accepting help from those who love you, even if we don't understand what you're trying to do.' She leaned her hand on the table, and talked close to him. 'Go home, Reg,' she pleaded softly. 'Your mum and dad need your help too.'

A short while later, Grace left the room, and came out

into the reception area where Mickey was waiting for her. He could see that she looked tense and upset.

'Wot's 'appenin'?' he asked apprehensively.

Before Grace could reply, Reg came out of the room and, without looking at either of them, slowly made his way back upstairs.

The coming week brought mixed fortunes for Grace. Her meeting with her cousin Reg had deeply depressed her, for despite her assurances that she and Mickey would help him in any way that they could, she came away from the Salvation Army hostel with no promise that he would return home. Inevitably, Grace convinced herself that by trying to help, she had only made matters worse. 'If anything happens to him,' she told Mickey, 'I'll never forgive myself.'

'If anyfin' 'appens to 'im,' Mickey reassured her, 'it'll be *'is* fault, not yours.'

Grace loved the way Mickey had become so protective. It was also refreshing to have someone who seemed to take no interest at all in how much she was worth, unlike Eric Tyler, who, in the short time they had spent away in Devon, had managed to get everything out of her about her father's inheritance, and talked at length about how he intended to help her spend it when they were married. Marriage to Eric Tyler, however, was, as far as Grace was concerned, nothing more than a figment of his imagination. But for the time being, it suited her purpose to let him think otherwise.

Her blossoming relationship with Mickey was another matter. Despite the fact that they had decided not to live together yet in The Chapel, there was now no doubt in Grace's mind that Mickey was gradually coming out of his shell, and that was something she wanted to encourage, not only for their personal relationship, but for the sake of the business.

Each day, Mickey was showing more and more initiative in the way he was talking to her about her plans for extending the grocery side of the business, and she was giving more and more thought to his suggestions about selling off her properties to her father's tenants who lived in them. Unfortunately, however, Eric Tyler also had plans of his own as to how Gus Higgs's business should be run, and, to Grace's disquiet, when he turned up unexpectedly at The Chapel over the following weekend, he had some rather unsettling news to convey to her.

'The divorce is going through,' he announced jubilantly. 'Jane's agreed to get the whole thing out of the way as soon as possible. With a bit of luck we could be in and out of the court by the New Year.'

Although Grace knew that Eric's divorce was pending, she was still shocked to hear his news. 'The New Year?' she asked, with little enthusiasm. 'Isn't that a bit quick? I mean, I thought these things took much longer.'

'There are ways,' replied Eric, who had plonked himself alongside her on the settee in her front parlour. 'The solicitor said if both parties agree, and there are no kids involved, there's no reason why we couldn't come to some arrangement with the judge for a quick divorce.' He slid his arm around her shoulders and hugged her. 'Isn't it wonderful, darling?' he said. 'It won't be long now before I can *really* carry you across that threshold.'

Out of the corner of her eye, Grace caught a glimpse through the window of Mickey leading Clapper out for his evening exercise. This prompted her to get up immediately. 'We've got a lot of things to do before that,' she replied.

Eric was puzzled. 'Things?' he asked. '*What* things?'

'Well . . .' replied Grace, floundering, 'there are our two families to think about. Your mother and father . . .'

'To hell with my mother and father!' snapped Eric, leaping up from the settee and going to her. 'I couldn't care less whether they like you or not!'

'Well, *I* do,' said Grace firmly. 'It's important to get on with one's in-laws.'

Eric was too thick to realise that she was hedging. 'Look, Grace,' he said, turning her round to face him. 'My parents would love you.'

'How d'you know that?' she asked.

'Because they hated Jane,' he replied adamantly. 'When I parted with her, they said that she was nothing but a snooty little tart.'

'That's a bit unkind, isn't it?' suggested Grace, surprised. 'I mean, you must have found something in her that you liked. After all, you *did* marry her?'

'Grace,' said Eric, forcibly holding her close, 'it's *you* I love. I want to try and forget the mistake I made. I want us to go forward together as though I'd never ever met anyone else in my whole life.'

'But you did,' Grace reminded him.

He looked at her. 'It's over, Grace,' he said, desperately trying to reassure her. 'From now on, it's just you and me. I love you. Can't you understand that?'

Grace hesitated, then smiled at him. 'Of course you do, Eric,' she said emptily. 'And I promise I'll make up to you all the time we've spent apart.'

Eric's face lit up. He kissed her. 'Thank you, darling,' he said. 'There's just one thing, though,' he added falteringly. 'Before I can go ahead with the divorce, I need some help.'

Grace raised her eyebrows. 'Help?'

'This divorce,' he continued. 'It looks as though it could be quite expensive. Mind you, I've got plenty of money owing to me, so I could pay you back . . . that is . . . if you could see your way to lending me . . . it wouldn't be too much.'

Grace smiled wryly to herself. 'How much?' she asked.

Eric went across to her. 'I think – fifty pounds would see me through. Of course, if you don't have it at this precise moment, I could wait . . .'

'No need to worry, Eric,' said Grace, giving him a reassuring, comforting look. 'As you know, I have plenty of funds. It'll be no problem to me at all. I'll go to the bank first thing Monday morning.'

The relief on Eric's face was overwhelming. 'Oh . . . my darling!' he spluttered, again taking her in his arms. 'What *have* I missed all this time?'

'Yes, Eric,' replied Grace, with irony, 'what *have* you missed?'

Clapper was making heavy weather of his evening exercise. Ever since Mickey had led him out of the back gates of The Chapel he had seemed unwilling to keep a steady pace, and every time Mickey tried to move him on, he stubbornly refused. Something was clearly causing the animal to behave like this, so Mickey turned him round and headed back towards home.

On the way, Mickey kept thinking about why Eric Tyler had called on Grace, and how she would be dealing with him. He now knew what Grace was determined to do about him, because she had told him. When a girl wanted revenge, there was no holding her. Even so, he still couldn't understand why she just didn't tell the bloke what she thought of him, and then kick him out. But then Grace had quite a lot of funny ways. She did things that he would never understand, would never try to understand. All he knew was that she was the first person in his entire life that he had actually loved, and it made him feel good. What had happened between them a few nights before had absolutely amazed him; in his wildest dreams he had never thought that such a thing would be possible. When he first saw her that Sunday morning, taking Clapper for his exercise in Stock Orchard Crescent, he thought that she was a right little madam who looked down on the likes of him. But how wrong he had been; she had turned out to be one of the most amazing girls he had ever set eyes on: warm-hearted, understanding, but sure and steady on her feet, ready to take on anyone who put on her. In some ways, he pitied Eric Tyler, because he didn't know what he was up against. When Grace set out to do something, she did it. That's why her dad's business was coming together – not just because he'd left her a house in Islington, a posh house by the sea, and a load of cash, but because she wanted to make a go of things.

As they turned the corner into Caledonian Road, Clapper snorted, and came to an abrupt halt.

'Wos up now, mate?' asked Mickey. 'Too much exercise for yer? It's about time I cut down on yer treats. No more sugar from the customers. Right?'

Clapper snorted again, and bucked his head up and down as though he was trying to tell Mickey something.

'Mickey!'

Grace was calling and waving to him from a short distance down the road. He waved back.

'Eric's just gone,' said Grace, as she approached. 'He's so damned persistent. I just couldn't get rid of him.'

'I don't blame 'im,' retorted Mickey, a touch sourly. 'I 'ope 'e didn't try nuffin' wiv yer?'

'Well, as a matter of fact,' replied Grace, teasing him, 'he *did*.'

Mickey's expression immediately turned to anger.

'Oh, it's all right,' Grace assured him. 'Not in the way you think. He wants to borrow some money from me. Fifty pounds.'

'Wot!' exclaimed Mickey, outraged. 'Wot for?'

'To pay for his divorce,' said Grace. 'He's been told that he can get one by the New Year. By which time he'll be free to marry me.'

Mickey looked as though he was about to explode. 'That dirty little tyke!'

His reaction made Grace laugh.

'It's not funny, Grace!' he snapped. 'You're not goin' ter give it to 'im, are yer? Fifty quid?'

'It'll be worth every penny,' replied Grace, still amused. Regardless of the fact that people were passing by in the road, she threw her arms around him, and hugged him. 'Don't you see, Mickey?' she said. 'The sooner he gets his divorce, the sooner we can be free of him. But don't worry, he'll soon find someone else.'

'Get rid of 'im, Grace,' pleaded Mickey, who looked decidedly uncomfortable. 'Just tell 'im ter bugger off!'

'D'you know something, Mr Burke?' she asked, staring into his eyes. 'I do believe you're jealous.'

'You bet yer life I am!' spluttered Mickey angrily.

She kissed him, but as she did so, Clapper let out a terrible whinnying sound, rose up on his hind legs, and tried to break loose.

'Clapper!' cried Grace in alarm. 'What is it, boy? What's the matter?'

Fortunately, Mickey was still holding Clapper's reins, but he had to use all his strength to keep the animal under control. In the road nearby, a car driver, alarmed that Clapper was going to bolt in front of him, skidded his car to a halt. Then, several passers-by stopped and held back, terrified that he was having some kind of a fit.

'It's all right, mate!' said Mickey, tugging on Clapper's reins, struggling to hold him down. 'You're all right, Clap,' he said, trying to stroke Clapper's nose. 'Take it easy, boy . . . take it easy . . .'

Grace managed to get a hold of Clapper's halter, and between them they gradually managed to calm him down. 'Clapper,' said Grace, gently smoothing his mane. 'Poor old boy. What is it? What's wrong?'

Mickey got close to the animal, and tried to talk softly into his ear. 'It's all right now, mate,' he said. 'Don't worry. We'll soon get yer 'ome.'

'Mickey!' gasped Grace, looking in horror at Clapper's mouth. 'Look!'

What Mickey saw shocked the daylights out of him, for Clapper was foaming at the mouth.

Chapter 20

Clapper's sudden illness was causing great concern. Once Mickey and Grace had got him back home to the stable, Mr Pudney, the vet, was immediately called in, but before he had even got there, Clapper's breathing became deep and heavy, his nose started running, and his eyes closed.

After checking the animal's temperature the vet asked with some anxiety, 'Has he had a cold? A touch of the flu, or any breathing problems?'

'Not that I've noticed,' replied Mickey, who was kneeling alongside Clapper, gently stroking the creature's shoulder whilst the vet examined him. 'As far as I know, this is the first time anyfin' like this 'as ever 'appened to 'im.'

'What is it, Mr Pudney?' asked Grace, who was kneeling down on the far side of Clapper, gently wiping the sweat off his face with a damp rag.

'I'd say he's got a touch of pneumonia,' said Pudney, raising Clapper's eyelids for a closer look with his torch.

'Pneumonia!' Grace exchanged a frantic look with Mickey.

Clapper suddenly coughed and snorted. He was clearly in distress.

'It's all right, mate,' said Mickey, trying to soothe Clapper. 'We'll take good care of yer.'

'So what can we do, Mr Pudney?' asked Grace urgently. 'Is it dangerous?'

The vet stood up. 'It will be unless we move quickly,' he said. 'I need bandages and a bucket of cold water.'

'Bandages?' asked Mickey, flicking a puzzled look across at Grace.

'Horse bandages,' said the vet, swiftly taking off his jacket and hanging it on a hook behind the stable door. 'I've got plenty back at the surgery, but we need them right now. If you don't have them, you'll have to tear up some sheets.'

'I'll fetch them!' said Grace, without a moment's hesitation, getting up and rushing back to the house.

'The first thing to do,' said the vet urgently, 'is to keep this place well ventilated.' With Mickey's help he pulled back both stable doors. 'The water, please, Mickey!'

Mickey did as he was told immediately, and rushed off to fill a bucket of water from the tap in the yard. When he returned, he found the vet gently examining the back of one of Clapper's hind legs. 'Touch of bog spavin too, by the looks of things.'

'Say again?' asked Mickey, bewildered, plonking the bucket of water down nearby.

'It's a distention of the capsular ligament . . . the hock joint . . . here.' He indicated to Mickey what he was concentrating on.

Mickey, totally out of his depth, could only scratch his head.

The vet elaborated. 'It's an ailment that's not uncommon to carthorses,' he explained.

'Clap ain't no cart'orse,' replied Mickey huffily.

'Come off it, man!' snapped the vet. 'He pulls a ruddy great shop around most of the time! From now on this animal is going to need a great deal of rest.'

Grace returned with three old white sheets and a large pair of scissors. 'Will these do?' she asked briskly.

'Cut one of them up into strips,' Mr Pudney called, whilst frenziedly rummaging through his medical case. 'We'll need the others to cover him, and if you've got a couple of blankets, we could do with those too.'

Mickey went straight to the bed he occasionally slept in, and pulled off his own two blankets.

Meanwhile, the vet had brought out a large tin, which he practically slammed across to Mickey. 'Get that open!' he demanded brusquely, without ceremony.

'Wot is it?' asked Mickey, dropping the blankets.

'Green tar,' replied the vet, rolling up his shirtsleeves. 'I need to get his legs dressed with it as soon as possible.' After putting on surgical gloves, he then got out a bottle of liquid and a measuring spoon, unscrewed the cap, and dropped the equivalent of a tablespoon of the liquid into Clapper's bucket. 'Nitrate of potash,' he said, more or less to himself. 'We'll have to get him to drink as much of this as he can. Got to get the temperature down.'

Grace, opening out one of the sheets ready to be cut, watched what the vet was doing with a mixture of admiration and anxiety. She was scared. It was a soul-destroying experience for her to see poor old Clapper lying there, covered in sweat, small swills of foam still dripping from the ends of his mouth. She couldn't bear to think what she would do if anything happened to him. For so long, Clapper had been such a part of her life, the closest friend her father had ever had. With her handkerchief she wiped the sweat off her own forehead, and looked upwards. She prayed that her father was there, watching over Clapper as the poor creature fought for his life.

With great difficulty, Mickey had managed to prise open the lid of the tin the vet had thrown at him. The vet grabbed it, took a handful of the thick green tar, and started applying it to Clapper's hind legs. 'Hurry up with those strips!' he demanded.

With Mickey's help, Grace was feverishly cutting one of the single white sheets into roughly two-inch strips. As they toiled, the bright white lights from the two overhanging oil lamps were throwing frantic shadows on to the timber panelling of the stable walls, and the box where Clapper was stretched out was unbearably hot and claustrophobic.

'Get one of those strips over here, fast as you can!' called the vet, his voice calm and composed, but firm.

Grace and Mickey did as they were told.

'Wrap up the leg,' he said, moving back slightly to let Grace and Mickey bandage Clapper's hind leg that was now covered with green tar. 'Not too tight!'

The whole procedure was repeated on Clapper's other hind leg. When it was finished, the vet stood up, took off his surgical gloves, turned them inside out, and dropped them into one of the thick paper bags he had retrieved from his medical case. 'Now we have to get some of this down him,' he said, picking up the bucket containing the cold water mixed with nitrate of potash. 'Just support his head a moment.'

With Mickey on one side of Clapper and Grace on the other, between them they started to raise his head.

'Take it easy now!' said the vet.

Clapper was wheezing badly, his eyes glazed with panic as Grace and Mickey gently raised his head enough for the vet to prise open his lips and teeth. It was a frantic few moments, for Clapper was too frightened to co-operate. Time and time again the vet tried to pour just a few drops of water from the bucket into Clapper's throat, but each attempt was unsuccessful.

'Nothing we can do,' announced the vet, abandoning his efforts to get Clapper to drink. 'Our best hope is that he'll drink for himself when he's desperate enough. Just leave the bucket here by his side.' He got up, went to Mickey's wash-basin and poured some water from a jug into it.

'How long will this go on, Mr Pudney?' asked Grace. 'I mean, is he going to get better?'

'We shall soon find out,' called the vet, washing his hands in the basin. 'If his temperature doesn't go down during the night, then it won't look good. It'll probably peak sometime in the next few hours. If it doesn't, you'd better get back to me right away.' Mickey threw him a towel, and he dried his hands. 'But I tell you this much,' he continued, 'his days of dragging your shop around are over.'

Grace exchanged a shocked look with Mickey. 'But – Clapper's not an old horse, Mr Pudney. He's hardly six years old.'

The vet shook his head. 'Whether he is or whether he isn't,' he replied, 'his working days are over. The best thing for this old boy is to turn him out to grass.'

Mickey put a comforting arm around Grace. He knew how badly she would take this news.

Once the vet had left, they went to Clapper and crouched down beside him. It was a gloomy prospect for them all, for Clapper seemed to have no life left in him. What was worse, the poor creature didn't want to respond to any of their approaches. All he could do was to just lie there, wheezing, breathing heavily, the sides of his stomach moving gently up and down, his one exposed ear every so often flicking away an imaginary fly. Grace and Mickey wanted nothing more than to be with him.

Rose Marchmont hated sitting in a wheelchair all day. She found it boring not to be able to do what she wanted or go where she wanted, without having to rely on someone to help her. But that's how it was, and that's how it would be to the end of her days. What rankled her most, however, was that because of her interfering neighbours, she was forbidden to play her piano before nine in the morning, and after eight in the evening. It was such an intrusion on her personal liberty! Although it was now hardly ten o'clock at night, her housekeeper, Mrs Snow, had already been in to change Rose into her nightdress. Ten o'clock at night, and here she was all trussed up and ready for bed! How she yearned for the good old days, when she was young, when her evenings didn't start until ten o'clock, when music and dancing were such a major part of her life. Her life? What sort of a life was it to be cooped up all day in a few rooms in Barnsbury Park? It was just as well that that life would soon be over, if she was to believe her doctors' latest prognosis. And when it *was* finally over, what would she have to show for it – a happy marriage, yes, but a short one, and no children or grandchildren to come and visit her? How she longed for company, someone to talk to, someone who could talk her own language: music, the theatre, the opera, the ballet – oh how wonderful it would be to keep in the swing of things, to keep up with the times and know what was going on in the world other than people killing each other all the time.

As good as Mrs Snow was, she couldn't talk about anything except how she needed some more furniture polish, or a new recipe she'd discovered, or how her granddaughter was only interested in herself and her boyfriends. And, in any case, Mrs Snow was a bully: she wouldn't let Rose play the piano during the forbidden hours, she wouldn't let her try to get out of her wheelchair to see if she could walk, she wouldn't let her smoke, she wouldn't let her do *anything*! Rose was so frustrated she felt like opening the window and screaming her head off. But what good would that do? The police would probably just come round and tell her to 'be a good girl', and then she'd lose her temper and be bound over by some doddering old magistrate to keep the peace.

Sitting there alone in her wheelchair in her ground-floor bedroom, waiting as usual for Mrs Snow to come in and turn down the gas lamps, then tuck her into bed for the night, she thought of all sorts of mischief she would like to get up to. There were two things in life that she loved: putting people's backs up, and secrets. Rose had had so many secrets in her life. In her time she had kept a lot of them, some her own, some of them other people's. The best one of all, of course, for her at any rate, had to be the one passed on to her by her dear departed friend, Alice Higgs. She chuckled to herself when she remembered the look on young Grace's face when she told her about her mother's fling with that young unmentionable before she married Gus Higgs. But the more Rose churned things over in her mind, the more she knew that there was still one burning secret that she just couldn't take with her to her grave.

'Oh yes, I will!' she said to herself out loud, as though answering some invisible image in the room. 'Damn it – I *will*!' As impetuous as ever, she firmly gripped the wheels of her chair, spun round, and made for the door.

Not caring whether Mrs Snow heard her or not, Rose threw open the door of the adjoining drawing room, and charged her wheelchair straight in. She made directly for her flip-top desk, struggled to roll back the lid, then feverishly rummaged through the various tiny compartments until she had found what she was looking for. It was a jewellery box, no bigger than a matchbox, but just the right size to contain a small locket and chain.

'Ah!' she sighed, her face beaming. 'There you are, my darling!'

She carefully removed the locket from the box and, with some difficulty, finally managed to click open the clasp. As she had left her spectacles in her bedroom, the minute, hand-coloured sketch of the person squeezed inside the locket was no more than a blur to her. But she needed no eyes to recall the image of the young boy's portrait. In her mind, she could see him as clearly as if he was right there with her in the room. He was so handsome, so irresistible. Just like his father.

Grace and Mickey snuggled up together on a makeshift mattress in the straw next to Clapper. Although it was well past midnight, neither of them had slept, for they were listening to every little sound Clapper made, hoping against hope that his breathing would eventually start to sound less laboured. The moment the vet had left, Mickey had said that he would not leave Clapper's side, so there was no need for Grace to lose a night's sleep. But she would have none of it. She was determined to see this crisis through, whatever the outcome. Mickey had no complaints; sleeping with Grace was a wonderful way to share something with her, even if they had both agreed not to make love until the time was right. In some way, the warmth of their two bodies gave them both the will to face up to the very real possibility that Clapper might not survive the night.

'I just can't believe it,' whispered Grace, tucked up in Mickey's arms. 'To think that Clapper might have to be turned out to grass seems absurd. He's had so much life in him.'

Mickey sighed. 'Better than 'avin' ter 'ave 'im put down,' he whispered back.

'Oh God, Mickey!' gasped Grace, turning with a start towards him. 'D'you think that might happen? D'you think all this we've done is a waste of time? D'you think Mr Pudney was just trying to prepare us for the worst?'

'No, Grace,' Mickey assured her, though not too convinced in his own mind. 'I fink Mr Pudney knows wot 'e's doin'. If 'e didn't fink Clap 'ad a chance, 'e'd've told us.'

'But turning Clapper out to grass sounds so – final,' she said, close to tears. 'I don't know what we'd do without him. We'll have to give up the business, Mickey.'

'Now stop jumpin' ter conclusions, Grace,' he insisted. 'We may not be able ter keep Clap as a work 'orse, but we can find uvver ways of gettin' the shop on the road again.'

'How?'

Grace's swift blunt question took him by surprise. 'I dunno, Grace,' he replied, floundering. 'Except there's always a motor van.'

'A what?'

'A motor van. Everyone's goin' in fer 'em these days. The way fings're goin', there won't be any more 'orse-drawn carts on the roads. Mind you, I'd 'ave ter take drivin' lessons.'

Grace turned away from him. 'It sounds a terrible idea,' she sighed. 'How can you replace someone like Clapper with a motor van?'

Mickey leant over her. 'Yer can't replace Clap wiv anyfin',' he said, kissing her gently on her ear. 'But if we can find somewhere 'appy fer 'im ter spend the rest of 'is days, then at least we know we've done our best fer 'im.'

'That's all very well,' replied Grace. 'But *where*?'

As she spoke, Clapper suddenly became restless and grunted. In a flash, both of them got up and went across to him. Some of the sheets and blankets they had covered him with had been tossed off, and so they replaced them as fast as they could.

'Is he all right?' Grace asked frantically. 'Has he drunk the water?'

Mickey unhooked the lamp from the ceiling, and held it over first Clapper, and then the bucket of water containing the nitrate of potash. He sighed, and shook his head.

'Not even a little?'

'Don't look like it.' Mickey knelt down alongside Clapper, and felt his nose. ' 'E's still burnin' up. Come on, mate,' he said, stroking Clapper's shoulder. 'You can do it. 'Ave a little drink fer me.' He suddenly realised that Grace behind him had started to sob quietly to herself. He got up immediately, and threw his arms around her. 'Hey!' he said, hugging her. ' 'E'll be all right. Take my word fer it. Don't yer go upsettin' yerself now.'

Grace took a hard swallow. 'I can't believe I'm doing this,' she sobbed in frustration. 'To think that I'm actually getting upset over a stupid animal!'

Mickey looked back at Clapper over his shoulder. 'Clap ain't no stupid animal, Grace,' he said. ' 'E's our mate.'

Grace collapsed in tears in his arms.

By the early hours of the morning, both lamps in the stable had run out of oil. But as the sun was gradually squeezing its way through the clouds, a long shaft of dazzling light shot through the open stable doors and came to rest across Grace and Mickey's two faces. Although it was now day-break, they were both fast asleep. Mickey was first to wake. Carefully casting off the blanket on his side of the mattress, he got up quietly, and went across to look at Clapper. As he knelt down beside him, Mickey's first reaction was of deep despair. In the semi-dark, Clapper was quite still. Mickey put his hand under the blankets and sheets covering him;

there was no moisture, no sweat. Mickey's hand trembled as he slowly reached up to feel Clapper's nose.

'Mickey!'

Mickey turned with a shocked start to find Grace standing behind him. 'He's drunk it!' she bellowed ecstatically, holding out the empty bucket. 'He's drunk every drop – look!' She turned the bucket upside down. It was completely dry.

Bewildered, Mickey turned back to Clapper to feel his nose, but before his hand could get anywhere near, Clapper's head shot up, and he let out an invigorating whinny.

Grace, delirious with relief, laughed out loud as Mickey fell back into a pile of straw. Then she rushed across to make a fuss of Clapper, but he was still very exhausted, and slumped his head back. 'Oh, Clapper!' she exclaimed. 'Please don't do this again!'

Mickey recovered himself, and joined her. The two of them gently stroked the horse's mane and shoulder, then replaced the blankets covering him.

'Don't rush 'im,' warned Mickey. 'Yer've got a bit er catchin'-up ter do first, ain't yer, mate?' he said to Clapper.

Clapper snorted, and closed his eyes again.

Rose Marchmont sat in the back of the taxi with Mrs Snow. It wasn't very often that she got a treat like this, and when it happened it was usually a trip to the hospital to see a bunch of dreary doctors. But this was different. This was an afternoon out that she had insisted on, despite Mrs Snow's angry objections. When they left Barnsbury Park, it had taken Mrs Snow and the poor taxi driver nearly ten minutes to fold up Rose's wheelchair and lift her into the taxi. Obstinate as ever, she was determined to call on the daughter of her best friend as soon as possible; she had one more secret to pass on to Grace, and she wanted to ensure that she had fulfilled her pledge to her old friend Alice before she herself passed on.

'Are yer goin' ter be able ter get up them front steps, lady?' asked the dubious taxi driver, once he'd pulled up in front of the main entrance of The Chapel.

'Of course I'm not!' bellowed Rose through the open door of the taxi. 'There are plenty of people who can lift me!'

The taxi driver groaned.

Irritated beyond speech with the behaviour of her impossible employer, Mrs Snow, a woman of ample proportions herself, struggled to get out of the taxi. 'If there's no one at home,' she grumbled, 'all this will be an absolute waste of time.'

'Good!' Rose called to her, thoroughly enjoying all the fuss she was causing. 'That's what I pay you for – to waste your time!'

Mrs Snow was not amused, but had learnt over the years not to try to banter with her irascible employer.

Rose waited in the taxi, watching with some amusement as poor Mrs Snow struggled up the steps to the front door of the house. She breathed a sigh of relief when Grace appeared at the door, and came hurrying down to meet her.

'Marchie!' Grace exclaimed, bleary-eyed after a long night without sleep. 'What a wonderful surprise! What are you doing here?'

'Well you may ask!' grumbled Mrs Snow, red in the face and out of breath.

'I could do wiv a bit of 'elp, lady,' groaned the taxi driver, getting Rose's wheelchair out of the vehicle, and setting it up.

Once Grace had called Mickey, it was only a matter of

minutes before he and the taxi driver were lifting Rose out of the taxi, and up the front entrance steps into the house. Having swiftly dispatched Mrs Snow to the kitchen to help Mickey make a pot of tea, Rose settled down into her wheelchair, and looked around the place as though she owned it.

'Well, at least you've got someone to help you,' she said, once Mickey had left the room. 'I hope he's worth what you pay him.'

'Mickey's worth more than money to me, Marchie,' replied Grace, sitting in an armchair opposite her. 'He's very special.'

Marchie's face lit up. 'Ah!' she cried mischievously. 'So that's *him*, is it?'

Grace nodded.

'He's not much of a looker,' sniffed Marchie, ruining everything. 'But he has to be better than that other creature.'

'*Much* better, Marchie,' said Grace, who had learnt never to be offended by anything her mother's old friend had to say. 'But you didn't come here to talk about Mickey?'

'No I didn't!' replied Marchie firmly. 'As a matter of fact, I came to bring you a present.'

'A present?' asked Grace, watching the old lady rummaging through her handbag. 'It's not Christmas yet, is it?'

Marchie retrieved the small jewellery box she had taken from her desk the previous night. 'Before I hand this over to you, however,' she said, enjoying Grace's wary look, 'you should know that it was the last thing I promised your mother.'

'What?' asked Grace. 'Another secret?'

Marchie grinned. 'Just – one more,' she replied. 'The last one. You remember I told you about your mother's relationship with the man she met before she married your father?'

'How could I forget it?' asked Grace wryly.

'Well,' continued Marchie, '*this* is what I *didn't* tell you.'
She held out the jewellery box.

Grace looked at it suspiciously. 'What is it?' she asked.

'Stop being so inquisitive, child!' snapped Marchie. 'Take it!'

Grace quickly took the box. 'You know, Marchie,' she said before opening it, 'you're always so full of surprises. It's no wonder you and Mum got on so well together.'

'Open the box!' growled Marchie.

Grace did so, and looked at the locket inside. 'It's beautiful,' she said, carefully taking it out of the box. 'I never saw my mother wearing this. Did it belong to her?'

Marchie nodded. 'Oh yes,' she replied knowingly. 'Open it up.'

Grace had to use her fingernail so delicately to prise open the clasp. Once she had done so, she found herself looking at the coloured portrait of what appeared to be an adolescent boy. 'Who is he?' she asked.

'A relation of yours,' replied Marchie, teasingly.

'Oh, really?' asked Grace. '*What* relation?'

'Your brother,' replied Marchie wickedly.

Grace looked up with a shocked start.

'Your *half*-brother, to be precise,' added Marchie. 'His name's Thomas. Most people called him Tommy.'

Although she was completely taken aback, Grace understood immediately. Her eyes flicked back down to the portrait in the locket.

'He didn't arrive until after his father had run out on Alice,' said Marchie. 'She had a difficult time bringing him up.'

'But what did *my* father say?'

'Gus?' asked Marchie. 'Oh, he never knew anything about Thomas.'

'What!' Grace's eyes shot up at her in horror. 'Are you saying Mother never told him that she had a child by this man?'

'Yes,' replied Marchie. 'It was a strange, stupid thing to do – I told your mother so over and over again. But that was Alice. She didn't want to lose someone she *really* loved. Thomas was nearly six years old when Gus and Alice married.'

'But if my father didn't know anything about this boy,' asked Grace, 'where did the boy live all that time?'

'With me,' replied Marchie. 'I brought him up until he was eighteen, until he went to live with my brother in Canada. He must be over thirty now. I'm told he's doing rather well, works for a newspaper or something. He has two children of his own – two girls, your half-nieces, I presume.'

Grace was too shocked to say anything. She just stared in utter amazement at the small portrait squeezed inside the locket. Her mind was already crammed with so much, but now this! As she looked at the tiny, crudely coloured picture, she couldn't help wonder what this boy was like, what he had been thinking about all those years, with no father to turn to, and a mother who kept him locked away from the man who *really* loved her, and, if only told, would have been the one person who would have embraced her son into his family. Grace suddenly became consumed with frustration that she hadn't known about this boy – this man – all these years. She had always craved to have either a brother or a sister. It seemed incomprehensible to her that her mother could have kept such a secret from her all those years. Secrets, secrets, secrets! Both Gus *and* Alice Higgs were indeed the most extraordinary parents!

'So you see, I kept my promise,' said Marchie, taking out

a long cigarette holder from her handbag, and then a packet of Abdullah cigarettes. 'I promised that when the time was right I would give you that locket and tell you everything that she should have told you herself.'

'But why now, Marchie?' asked Grace, utterly bewildered. 'Why wait until now to tell me all this?'

Marchie smiled, and fixed one of her cigarettes into the holder. 'Because if I wait very much longer, I'd be taking your mother's little secret to my own grave.'

Grace's whole expression changed. 'Marchie . . .' she said, crushed by what Marchie was implying and, knowing how ill she had been, shocked to see her smoking.

'Come, come now, Grace!' Marchie said, delicately lighting her cigarette. 'The last thing I want is for anyone to mimp and moan about me. As a matter of fact, I'm looking forward to seeing all my old friends again – especially your mother. I intend to give Alice Higgs quite a piece of my mind – she's caused me a great many problems over the years.' She inhaled and exhaled with tremendous enjoyment.

'Oh, Marchie,' said Grace, distressed, getting up from her chair, and going to crouch in front of her. 'Marchie . . .'

Marchie smiled down at her. 'What are you getting so upset about, you silly girl?' she said. 'I've thoroughly enjoyed my life – except for the last few years, that is. As I'm always saying to that terrible Mrs Snow, we're all here today and gone tomorrow. If we don't move over and make room for someone else, the place is going to get awfully crowded.'

Chapter 21

November was turning out to be quite a dreary month, with fog and drizzling rain leaving a carpet of depression over a nation that was becoming increasingly nervous about the possibilities of a war with Germany. With this in mind, the House of Commons introduced an Air Raid Precautions bill, which only underlined the dangers that might lie ahead. The news elsewhere was equally disturbing. Earlier in the month, the former Labour Party leader, Ramsay MacDonald, died at sea on his way to South America on a quest to improve his health; in the Japanese-Chinese war, Japanese troops captured Shanghai, and in Spain the civil war between the Republicans and the Falangists was getting more bitter and ferocious, with an enormous number of deaths not only amongst the indigenous population, but also amongst the foreign volunteers.

Grace was deeply saddened that her cousin Reg had still not returned home. Ever since she had met him at the Salvation Army hostel that evening, she had prayed and hoped that he had at least listened to something of what she had had to say, but, much to her regret, he had clearly chosen to keep away from his family.

With Clapper's working days at an end, Grace had no choice but to follow Mickey's advice: that if she wanted to continue the grocery rounds then she would have to buy a motor van. For Grace it was a reluctant decision, especially as she had always been nervous and suspicious of motor vehicles, but once Mickey had taken driving lessons from one of his mates in the Caledonian Market, and got through a fairly simple driving test up at Hendon, the business soon resumed where it had left off. However, as far as some of Grace's tenants and customers were concerned, Gus Higgs's grocery business would never be the same without Clapper.

'Nasty, smelly fing!' complained Gert Jolly, who hated the smell of petrol fumes popping out of the new van's exhaust pipe right outside her front doorstep. 'Give me an ol' 'orse any day. At least they don't make all that noise!'

'Never mind, Mrs J,' said Mickey, teasing her. 'At least yer don't 'ave ter feed the van sugar an' carrots!'

Gert grunted. 'So 'ow's poor ol' Clapper now?' she asked, handing over her rent book to Grace. 'Does this contraption mean we ain't goin' ter see 'im no more?'

'I'm afraid so, Mrs Jolly,' replied Grace, marking in the rent book the half-crown Gert was handing over to her. 'Thank God he's fully recovered and back on his feet again, but the vet says that from now on he needs plenty of rest. So we're building a stable and paddock for him down at the house in Devon.'

'Ah!' sighed Gert with relief. 'I'll miss the ol' boy, but I reckon 'e'll be far better off down there. 'E deserves a good time. 'E's served you an' yer dad well all these years.'

'Indeed he has, Mrs Jolly,' replied Grace, handing Gert back her rent book. Then she took the half-crown from her. 'How's the rising damp now?' she enquired.

'Marv'llous!' said Gert with real enthusiasm. 'Took that builder no time at all.'

'No pong?' asked Mickey, grinning.

'No pong – fank Gord!' replied Gert. 'I feel like a duchess livin' in a bleedin' palace.'

Grace beamed. 'I'm so glad,' she said, 'because I've got

something to talk over with you that I want you to think about.'

Gert pulled a face. Whenever anyone asked her to think about anything, it usually spelt trouble. 'Oh yes?' she asked suspiciously. 'D'yer want ter come in?'

'No, no,' replied Grace. 'Just a quick question: how would you like to own your own house?'

Gert's eyes widened. What sort of a question was that? 'Own it?'

'Be yer own guv'nor, Mrs J,' added Mickey. 'You know – make yer own decisions wivout 'avin' ter ask Grace all the time.'

Now Gert was really suspicious. Were they having her on, a poor woman who had to balance out every penny of her pension each week to make ends meet? And as she looked from one to the other of them, how come Mickey Burke was now calling his employer by her first name? Unless Grace was planning to make her a present of her house, it was a cruel game to play on her. 'I don't know wot yer're talkin' about,' she replied.

'I'm offering you your own house, Mrs Jolly,' explained Grace. 'For you to buy.'

'Ha!' snorted Gert. Now she knew they were mad. 'An' where d'yer fink an ol'-age pensioner like me's goin' ter find money like that?'

'With this,' replied Grace, holding up the half-crown Gert had just paid for her rent. 'Instead of paying me something each week for rent, give me whatever you can afford until you've paid off the price I'm asking for the house.'

'An' 'ow much is that, may I ask?' asked Gert through eyes squinting with deep suspicion.

'A hundred pounds.'

Gert roared with laughter.

'A 'undred pounds ain't much, Mrs J,' Mickey assured her.

'Good!' retorted Gert. 'Then *you* pay it!'

'No seriously,' persisted Mickey. 'Yer wouldn't get an 'ouse like this anywhere fer that kind er price. Property's goin' up all over the place. In a few years' time the 'ouses along this street'll probably go fer 'alf a grand.'

' 'Alf a grand?' Again Gert let out a dismissive laugh. 'You're tellin' me that people'd be willin' ter fork out five 'undred quid on a place like this?'

'Yeah,' insisted Mickey. 'And in times ter come, a lot more, you mark my words!'

'Bunkum!' scoffed Gert.

'Look, Mrs Jolly,' said Grace quietly, reasonably. 'I'm not asking you to do anything you can't or don't want to do, but I do want you to consider that having your own property does have certain advantages.'

'Such as?' asked Gert curtly.

'Well, for a start,' continued Grace, 'if you want to change anything in the house, knock something down, build something, you don't have to ask my permission.'

'An' where would *I* get the money ter do fings like that?' Gert asked, not unreasonably. 'I barely 'ave enuff money left over from me pension each week ter buy me pint er milk.'

'That's not the only advantage,' continued Grace. 'I'd have no objection if you wanted to sublet the top two floors. That way you could make a small additional income, and put it towards paying off the price of the house. You wouldn't need to touch your pension any more than you're doing now.'

Gert went quiet. For the first time she showed a glimmer of interest. Then, after a moment's thought, she asked, 'Does that mean I could 'ave two lots er tenants?'

'As many as you want, Mrs Jolly,' replied Grace. 'As many as you can cope with.'

'Give yer a second lease er life, Mrs J,' quipped Mickey. 'Yer wouldn't know wot ter do wiv all that luvely loot!'

'Oh, yes I would!' growled Gert, with a sneaky smile.

This made Grace and Mickey laugh. But as she watched Gert turning things over in her mind, Grace realised only too well what a bombshell this must be for the old lady. For years most people in this walk of life had never even considered the idea of being property owners. This was mainly because money was hard to come by, and it was bad enough trying to eke out a bread-winner's meagre wages to fork out for rent each week; renting a place was all they had ever known, would probably *ever* know. But these were also people with pride and great inner dignity, and even though the property they lived in didn't belong to them, most of them looked after their homes as though they were palaces, constantly painting up their front and back parlours, their bedrooms, their sculleries, scrubbing, cleaning, and polishing, tending their tiny back gardens with loving care so that the summer blooms could add a riot of colour to their humdrum daily lives. Like people in every backstreet all over London, Grace's tenants deserved the chance to be independent, to feel that they owned something of their very own.

'Wot about the uvvers?' asked Gert, eyes darting back to Grace like a ferret. 'Are yer goin' ter ask the uvver tenants if they want ter buy too?'

'I already have,' replied Grace. 'Everyone is giving the idea very serious thought.'

'All except 'er next door!' grunted Gert. 'Molly Tebbit ain't capable of 'avin' a serious fawt about anyfin'!'

Grace and Mickey stifled a laugh.

Gert crossed her arms and pursed her lips. 'Well,' she said, 'all I can say is I'll fink about it.'

'Thank you, Mrs Jolly,' said Grace. 'We can't ask for more than that.'

'But yer needn't 'old yer breff,' she added caustically. 'Money don't grow on trees, yer know!'

'Not unless yer've got green fingers, gel!' quipped Mickey.

Gert dismissed him with a wave of the hand, and closed the door. But she opened it again almost immediately. 'One more question!' she bellowed to Grace and Mickey as they were going through her front-yard gate. 'Does this mean yer're movin' out – givin' up 'Olloway?'

Grace stopped and smiled back at her. 'Oh, no, Mrs Jolly,' she called. 'You can't get rid of the chandler's daughter as easy as that.'

Eric Tyler was feeling on top of the world. The fifty pounds Grace had loaned him had secured him a court hearing for the quick divorce his wife, Jane, was bringing against him. With luck, he would be a free man by the New Year, free to marry Grace and live like a country squire for the rest of his life. However, there were still one or two hurdles for him to overcome. Despite the fact that he really was now in love with Grace, he was frustrated by her stubborn refusal to let him move in with her. He just didn't accept her argument that he should do nothing to jeopardise his chances of getting a divorce; as far as he was concerned *that* was a foregone conclusion. He also thought she cared too much about what her family, tenants, and customers thought about her living with a man before getting married. Grace was a single woman, and she lived alone. She was entitled to have the support and protection of a man who loved her. Therefore, he decided that his most important task now was to gain the support of Grace's family. With them behind him, Grace would have no more excuses. And so, he asked himself, who better to start with than Auntie Hilda?

'Eric Tyler?' growled Hilda, standing in the doorway of her house in Berriman Road. The last person in the world she had expected to see standing on her own doorstep was the pig-head who had walked out on Grace all those years ago, the same pig-head who was now hanging around again, waiting to see what he could drain out of Grace's inheritance. Her first inclination had been to slam the door in his face, but she had promised Grace a few weeks before: 'Leave 'im ter me!'

'It's very good of you to see me, Auntie,' said Eric, as she showed him into her back parlour. 'Grace has told me so much about you.'

' 'As she now?' asked Hilda, plonking herself down in her usual place at the table. Little did Eric know that he had instantly put her back up by presuming on a relationship that didn't exist. Auntie indeed! she growled inside. I'll bleedin' Auntie 'im!

'Oh yes,' said Eric, sitting opposite her without invitation. 'She's always said that you're her favourite aunt, and how she's always come to you whenever she's wanted help or advice.'

Hilda felt sick. 'Funny,' she replied caustically. 'She's never mentioned it ter me.'

'Oh yes,' insisted Eric. 'That's why I came to see you. After all, you're head of the family now. I want to get your blessing before Grace and I tie the knot.'

'Tie the knot?' asked Hilda, sceptically. 'D'yer mean – gettin' married?'

Eric nodded coyly.

'I fawt yer already 'ad a wife?'

Eric was a bit taken aback by that remark. It was clear that Auntie Hilda was not going to be the walkover he had hoped for. He had to think fast. Grace had often referred to Hilda as the 'old dragon', and if he was going to win her over, then he was going to have to find a way of charming her. 'My divorce comes through in the next few weeks,' he said sheepishly. 'After that, Grace and I can't wait to get together. In fact . . .' he lowered his voice, 'we're kind of *together* right now – if you get my meaning?'

'No, I don't get yer meanin',' replied Hilda, with a smile that could kill. 'Unless yer mean that you're sleepin' tergevver?'

Although Eric was astonished by her frankness, he lowered his eyes guiltily. 'Grace and I are very much in love, Auntie,' he replied. 'I'd do anything for her.'

'Is that so?' asked Hilda. 'Then why did yer walk out on 'er the last time?'

Eric looked up with a shocked start. He was thunderstruck.

'Yer could've ruined 'er fer life, yer know that, don't yer?' she asked. 'In fact, yer very nearly did. Don't yer care about people's feelin's? Yer walked out on that gel becos yer found someone who could offer yer somefin' better, an' now that's not worked out the way yer wanted, you're back fer anuvver try – especially knowin' 'ow Grace's fortunes 'ave changed.'

'That's not true!' insisted Eric firmly. 'I know I've not behaved well towards Grace in the past, but I now know I love 'er.'

'Wonderful!' cried Hilda mocking him. 'At long last yer've discovered 'ow much yer love 'er!'

'I *do* love her,' insisted Eric. He held up the palms of his hands. 'So help me God!'

'Yes, *'e* might 'elp yer,' said Hilda wryly, 'but millions wouldn't!'

Eric got up from the table. 'I'm sorry, Auntie,' he said. 'I think you've got me wrong. I only came because I wanted to get to know Grace's family, to get you to know me.'

'Wot's there ter know about yer, son?' asked Hilda.

Eric shrugged. 'That what I'm telling you is genuine.'

'Genuine?' Hilda gently eased herself up from her chair. 'If you're genuine, then yer'd better find a way ter prove it.'

Eric was puzzled. 'I don't know what you mean?' he asked.

'I'll tell yer wot I mean,' said Hilda. 'If you want ter prove ter Grace that yer love 'er fer 'erself an' not fer wot she's worff, then go an' tell 'er so. Tell 'er that before yer even get married, yer'll sign a bit er paper ter say that yer'll 'ave absolutely no claim on anyfin' she possesses.'

Eric's expression was of concern and disbelief. 'Why should I put a thing like that in writing?' he asked. 'If we're going to marry, a husband and wife should trust each other.'

'I quite agree wiv yer, young man,' said Hilda. 'But trust is somefin' quite speshull. There ain't much of it around these days. In fact, I don't fink there ever 'as bin. I should know. I 'ad a 'usband of me own once, an' I never trusted one single fing 'e ever said ter me.' She paused, went to the parlour door, and opened it. 'If yer take *my* tip, young man,' she said, holding the door open for him, 'yer'll prove yer word, or else lose out ter someone else.' She grinned knowingly. ' 'Cos I'm tellin' yer, there are plenty more fish in the sea.'

Finsbury Park was covered in a thin layer of white. Delicately patterned webs of frost had formed on practically every tree and drooping plant from the Seven Sisters Road entrance to Endymion Road in Harringay, and as the sun fought its way through the early morning fog, the world took on a magic all its own. It was a riot of creation. Despite the seasonal November weather, however, the usual amateur football match took place on the field not far from the park gates, with hordes of local kids there to cheer on their mates, whilst on the bridge overlooking the LNER railway track nearby, waiting for the fog to clear, several train spotters were already in position to take down the registration numbers of any of the train engines that passed below on their way back and forth to the north of England and Scotland. Amongst the young, and not so young enthusiasts, was one solitary figure who was no more than a shimmering dark image, peering down on to the track below, almost invisible in the stark blanket of white. But as the sun gradually gained strength and burnt the fog away, the figure emerged as a man of indeterminable age, wrapped up in a heavy woollen pullover and khaki topcoat, with a tattered haversack thrown across his shoulder, and a rough woollen cap that succeeded in covering only part of his long flowing brown hair, which met with an equally long shaggy moustache and beard, and the scar of a gash that had clearly only recently healed. It was Reg Cooker.

Soon after the excitement amongst the train spotters had passed, with the first train of the morning roaring off into the distance, Reg tucked his hands into his pockets, and moved on. A lot had happened to him since the night Grace had found out he was staying in the Salvation Army hostel. He had been in one or two lodgings around town, but in the main he had slept rough on the streets like so many of his comrades who had returned from the Spanish Civil War to find that it was impossible to exist in the life they had once lived. *Comrades?* Over these past few months he had had plenty of time to work out the meaning of the word. Friend, associate, companion? Or did it mean a member of an elitist political organisation, a band of brothers who were not afraid to take the troubles of the world on their shoulders? Whatever it meant, those people *were* his comrades, and, despite the sacrifices he had had to make with his own family, he was proud to have served alongside them. However, after months of anguish and deep soul-searching, he had reluctantly come to the conclusion that he couldn't go on the way he was for ever. A decision had to be made, and he was now ready to take it.

He strolled on at a snail's pace, the laces of his Spanish army boots trailing on the frosty path as he went, mittened hands tucked deep into his topcoat pockets, shoulders stooped, eyes fixed firmly on the ground ahead of him. The gradually approaching smell of urine slowly brought him to a halt. He was aware that he was standing outside the entrance to the park's public lavatories. After a moment's consideration, he went in. It was a dirty, seedy place, used by every drunk who was able to crawl through a hole in the fence after being kicked out of any of the local pubs. Even the floor was covered with an overflow of flushing water from the urinal stalls, and the walls covered with unmentionable sexual graffiti. He went straight to the grubby washbasin, and took a glimpse at himself in the one piece remaining of the broken smeared mirror on the wall above.

It was a sight he had carefully avoided ever since he left Spain, a sight he couldn't even bear to look at in passing. He stared at his own eyes. To him they seemed grey and doleful. In those eyes he could recall all the horrors he had seen, the bloodshed, the suffering, the waste of human life. He quickly shut his eyes, and then, almost immediately, opened them again. He finally took his hands out of his pockets, and cold as his fingers were, slowly, methodically unbuttoned his topcoat. Satisfied that the place was deserted, he dipped into one of his inside pockets, and took out what he was searching for. It was a pair of scissors. Taking a long, hard look at them, he put two fingers through the handles, pointed the tips at his wrist, and gripped as hard as he could. Then he took one last look into the mirror, prepared now for what he knew he *had* to do.

Grace was so proud of Mickey. He was everything she had hoped he would be – supportive, protective, loving, caring, and, despite his lack of education, had a sense of basic intuition that was proving invaluable to the business. She now had no hesitation in taking him along to meet the family. Sitting with him in the front seat on the top of the bus, amused that she had got him to carry an obscure potted plant for her, she bristled with affection for him, especially as he had put on clothes she had never seen him in before, a white shirt and navy-blue trousers, a navy-blue V-necked pullover, and a flat cap and raincoat which he had bought from his mate Ed up the Cally market. He looked *so* smart. What she loved even more was the fact that he had consistently refused to let her buy any of his clothes, insisting on doing it with his own money that he had earned since working for her. And as she snuggled up to him on the bus seat, she smiled to herself when she recalled helping him to knot his tie, something he had never had in his entire life. Oh yes, she was proud of him all right, and she was dearly looking forward to showing him off to the family.

Auntie Josie's birthday this year was a very low-key affair. Ever since the night Reg had disappeared, all the life seemed to have gone out of her. She didn't sleep well, and when she did, it was only after she lay awake crying.

To Josie, being fifty-five years old was no different to being fifty-four years old, or ninety years old. In fact there were times when she had wished that she *was* ninety years old, because that would mean that her life was at an end, a life that in recent months had brought her nothing but pain and misery. However, she had to make an effort if only for the sake of her family. She was even willing to forgive Hilda for all the terrible things she had said about young Grace's inheritance. It was what Gus would have wished, and she had loved him with all her heart. Josie loved Grace too, had always loved her, and now that she was bringing a new young man to meet the family, she at least had an incentive to cheer up, if only temporarily.

'Auntie,' said Grace, soon after she and Mickey had appeared on the front doorstep of the house in Stoke Newington, 'I want you to meet Mickey.' She turned a ravishing smile towards him. 'Mickey. This is my Aunt Josie.'

Mickey beamed, and offered his hand. ' 'Allo, Aunt Josie!' he said brightly. ' 'Appy birfday!' Much to his relief, he was at last able to hand over the potted plant.

Josie was a bit taken aback by his cheeriness, but it did bring a smile to her face. ' 'Allo, Mickey,' she returned, shaking hands with him, and taking the plant. 'Fank yer very much.'

'And this,' continued Grace, as they progressed into the front parlour, 'is my Uncle Stan. Uncle, this is Mickey.'

' 'Allo, son,' said Stan, getting up from his armchair to greet Mickey with his usual firm handshake.

' 'Allo, Guv'nor,' replied Mickey, returning the handshake with a beaming smile.

Stan then turned to Hilda, who was sitting bolt upright in her usual hard-backed chair. ' 'Ave yer met my sister-in-law?'

Mickey grinned. 'No,' he replied, 'I 'aven't 'ad the pleasure. 'Allo, darlin',' he said, offering his hand for her to shake. ' 'Ow are yer?'

Without getting up, Hilda gave him a stiff, disapproving look. 'I'm perfectly well,' was all she would say, as she reluctantly shook hands with him.

Grace grinned, and turned away. From that moment on, with Mickey around, she knew that Auntie Hilda had met her match.

A short while later, they were joined by Viv, but as she and Mickey had already met briefly at The Chapel, there was no need for any further introductions. Although Josie's birthday had come on a Sunday, she had opted for a tea party rather than the family's former regular Sunday roast, and as Josie herself had been unwilling to mark the event at all, Viv and Grace between them prepared most of the food, which consisted mainly of cold ham and salad, a bowl of cockles, thickly sliced bread and butter, fresh Cheddar cheese, fruit trifle, buttered crumpets, and Chelsea buns and rock cakes, with the ladies drinking tea, while Stan and Mickey stuck to a couple of glasses each of bitter.

Stan also was very down, and, as much as he enjoyed Mickey's company, he was finding the celebration a pointless event without his son being there. Grace, however, was enjoying the afternoon more than she expected, mainly because she was enjoying the sight of Mickey sitting next to Aunt Hilda at the table, where, without Hilda realising it, she was being teased mercilessly by someone who not only had a natural humour of his own, but who used it with such inestimable charm. During the meal, Viv and Grace cleared some of the used plates away, and took them off to the scullery, giving Grace a chance to have a few words with her cousin.

'Any word from him?' asked Grace apprehensively, as she and Viv piled the plates up on the draining board by the sink.

'From Reg?' returned Viv. She shook her head. 'Nothing, I'm afraid. I don't know why, but I thought he'd have made an effort for Mum's birthday. He was always far better at remembering it than I've ever been.'

Grace sighed. 'I blame myself,' she said. 'I should never have thought I could do more than you. Going to him that night was the wrong thing to do. The fact that Mickey and I had found him clearly made him worse.'

Viv shook her head. 'As much as I love Reg,' she replied, 'I have to admit he's always been the sort of person who hates to think that somebody else can work things out better than him. Once he's made his mind up to do something, no one can persuade him otherwise.'

'What about your mum?' asked Grace. 'Has she given up hope of seeing him again?'

Viv shook her head vigorously. 'Oh no,' she replied firmly. 'She'll never do that till the day she dies. She even leaves the front door unlocked morning, noon, and night.'

'Isn't that a bit dangerous?' asked Grace, concerned. 'I mean, anyone could just walk in.'

'I know,' replied Viv, whose voice was beginning to falter. 'But she insists that when her boy comes home, he'll never find the door barred to him.' She was now finding it difficult to talk. 'Dad's no better. He carries on as though Reg's dead and buried. I just can't bring myself to tell him that he *isn't* dead, that he's alive and just doesn't want to see his family again. It's too much, Grace! I'm telling you, it's all too much. I don't know how much longer I can stand this . . .' She broke down in tears on Grace's shoulder.

Grace threw her arms around her and held her tightly.

'It's all right, Viv,' she said, trying to reassure her, and at the same time concerned that Aunt Josie might walk through the door at any moment. 'It's all right . . .' For one fleeting moment, she felt anger towards Reg for the pain and suffering he was causing his family. She had never seen her cousin Viv like this before. During the past few months, Viv had become a very down-to-earth type of girl who had that rare quality of being able to understand both sides of an argument. It was distressing to see her like this. 'Don't you worry,' said Grace. 'One of these days Reg *will* come to his senses, and when he does, he'll walk through that front door and realise just what a silly ass he's been.'

Viv, tears streaming down her cheeks, slowly looked up at her. 'You don't understand, Grace,' she said, voice cracking. 'It's not like that. On the night I spoke to Reg in that shop doorway, he told me . . . he told me . . . he said he wished he'd been one of his mates who'd been left to die in a field out in Spain. He said, "There's nothin' left 'ere fer me, Viv. Once I've worked fings out, I'm only 'angin' around till it's time ter go." '

Grace felt a cold chill down her spine. 'He – he didn't mean anything, Viv,' she said, voice low. 'He *couldn't* have meant anything. He said that to scare you.'

'Why should he want to scare *me*?' snapped Viv angrily, pulling away from her. 'I haven't done anything to him. I haven't tried to stop him becoming the saviour of the world! I believed in what he was doing. I believe that it was right what he was doing. But to do away with himself is wrong, totally wrong!'

'He's *not* going to do away with himself, Viv,' insisted Grace.

'I'm telling you he is!' retorted Viv, close to breaking point. 'For all we know, he's probably already done it!'

'But how can you say that?' pleaded Grace. 'How can you even *think* such a thing?'

'Because he *told* me!' Viv insisted, no longer trying to keep her voice down. 'He told me that as soon as the time was right, he was going to kill himself!'

In the next room, Mickey was doing his best to prevent Josie's birthday party from turning into a wake. Fortunately, Hilda seemed to be getting on well with him, and even cracked her normally severe expression with a raucous laugh.

'Bleedin' rubbish!' she bellowed. 'You ain't never seen no bird wiv three legs!'

'Excuse me, madam!' retorted Mickey, with mock pretence. 'Are you accusin' me of bein' a sprucer?'

'Yes I am!' came Hilda's emphatic, chuckled reply.

'Had it ever occurred to you, madam,' said Mickey, leaning close to her, 'that all birds carry a spare leg round wiv 'em?'

'Oh, yes?' replied Hilda, playing along with him. 'Now why would they do that?'

'Well, it's obvious, ain't it?' quipped Mickey. 'If they lose one leg, they don't wanna fall down!'

Hilda screeched with laughter. Josie and Stan tried hard to join in, but their hearts just weren't tuned in to enjoying themselves.

' "Happy birthday to you, Happy birthday, dear Josie . . ." '

Grace, singing as she came in, returned carrying a birthday cake for Josie. Viv followed behind with tea-plates, doing her best to conceal the fact that her eyes were still puffed from crying. Mickey, grateful to be relieved of his funereal duties, sang along, and then applauded. 'Good ol' Aunt Josie!' he called, standing up. ' 'Appy birfday!'

Everyone was now standing, and looking towards Josie,

who remained seated. Grace put the cake and knife down in front of her. 'No candles this year, Auntie,' she said brightly. 'Once we get past twenty-one, we stop counting.'

Josie smiled weakly, and looked at the cake on the table in front of her.

'Come on, Mum,' said Viv bravely. 'Cut the cake.'

Mickey applauded, and tried to urge the others to do the same. Josie took hold of the knife, but just as she was about to stand up and cut the cake, Grace spoke out.

'Hang on a moment please, everyone,' she announced. 'Before Auntie cuts the cake, I want to say something to you all. It's a bit of a speech, so you'd better sit down again.'

Puzzled, everyone did as they were told. Once they had settled down, Grace began.

'As you all know,' she said in a clear and firm voice, 'this has not been an easy time for the family. Losing Dad was not only totally unexpected, but hard to take – *very* hard to take.'

Murmurs of agreement from around the table.

'And then,' she continued, with a passing, concerned look at her aunt, 'what with Reg, and all that followed . . . it's left us all in a state of – oh, I don't know – I suppose you could call it a kind of depression. Unfortunately, however, there are some things that you can't put right. You can't turn the clock back, and you can't bring time to a standstill. None the less, there is something *I* can do – well, partially do – to raise our spirits.' She paused briefly to glance at Mickey, who, knowing what she was about to say, gave her an encouraging smile. 'I know you're all aware that when Dad died, he left everything in the world he had to me, and, as it turned out, the inheritance was, to say the least, substantial. I want you to know that at the time I knew absolutely nothing at all about any of this. I knew that he wanted me to carry on with the business when he died, because he'd discussed it with me.' She turned a quick look at Aunt Hilda. 'He made it quite clear to me that whatever happened, the business was to remain in *my* hands, and in no one else's. The properties Dad owned, and the grocery business, which he loved so much, were never part of the family.'

Hilda looked away, but found herself staring straight into Mickey's face, which was smiling cheekily at her.

'I know some of you think that I was just trying to upset you,' said Grace, 'to hold on to something that wasn't by rights mine to hold on to. But the facts are that the business *does* belong to me, and, with the help of Mickey, I intend to go on running it in one way or another for as long as I can.'

Everyone threw a cursory look at Mickey, with the exception of Hilda, who swung a look of sheer disbelief at him.

'However,' continued Grace, 'Dad's business wasn't the only thing he left me. I'm sure you all know that he was a man of quite a few surprises – to say the least. The first big surprise was to discover that he had a house – a magnificent house – in a place called Dawlish, in south Devon. It's a beautiful place. In fact I've never seen anything quite like it. I've been down to see it several times, and I find it hard to believe that it actually belongs to me. It's vast – six bedrooms, a couple of bathrooms, kitchen, sitting and dining rooms. It also has a beautiful garden.' She paused briefly. 'It's a perfect place for a family – a family – just like ours.'

There was dead silence around the room.

'Oh, yes,' continued Grace. 'I almost forgot – the money.'

This made Hilda look up with a start.

'Dad left fifty thousand pounds,' said Grace, waiting with fascination for Aunt Hilda's reaction. 'It was deposited in a separate account in Devon, but Mr Rumble, our bank manager here in London, assured me that, as Dad's only legal heir, in the absence of a will, I inherit *that* money too.'

Hilda took a deep breath, and steeled herself.

'However,' continued Grace, 'I've been doing a lot of thinking about all this, and I've come to the conclusion that, since Dad himself inherited all that wealth from someone else, I don't think he'd disapprove if I said that at least a chunk of it should be shared by the family. And that's exactly what I propose doing. Out of the fifty thousand pounds, I intend to repay the vast debts owing on Dad's properties and business. By the time I've done that, I shall make arrangements with the bank that each one of you receive a fair share of what's left over. I shall keep my share as well, of course, but I think you'll find that you'll be more than satisfied with what each of you will receive.'

She looked around the table. Aunt Josie's hands were in her lap, her eyes fixed firmly, aimlessly on the birthday cake in front of her, and both Stan and Viv were staring at different parts of the wall. The only two people looking towards Grace herself were Mickey, who was overawed by the way Grace was passing on her intentions, and Aunt Hilda, who seemed to be locked in time, like a sleeping statue.

'Oh, yes,' continued Grace. 'There's just one thing more.' She paused. 'The house,' she said, 'the house in Devon. As I told you, it's vast – too vast for just one or two people to live in. So I want you to know that it's there, and that it's there for all of us to use whenever we want. Dad probably never knew what I really wanted, but somehow I think he would have approved of what I'm doing.' She smiled round the table. 'It's a wonderful place for a holiday – especially when the weather's good. We can take turns.' She turned a brief glance at Mickey. 'And I can't wait for Mickey to try the cider!' She paused again, and took another look around the table. Nobody stirred. 'So,' she said, 'that's about all I have to say. Happy birthday, Auntie!' She sat down quietly.

For several moments, no one said anything. The silence throughout the room was only broken by the gentle, uncharacteristic sobbing of Aunt Hilda, who had covered her face with her hands. Then Viv got up, went to Grace, put her arms around her shoulder from behind, and gently rubbed cheeks with her. Suddenly, Stan looked up, but past the table to the door. Without saying a word, eyes wide, he rose up from his chair. Almost simultaneously, everyone around the table, with the exception of Josie, did the same, their heads all turned in the same direction.

Josie looked up, bewildered, baffled. In the split-second silence that followed, she had no time to turn round and see what everyone was looking at, for someone was already behind her, arms outstretched, hugging her.

A voice whispered into her ear, 'Happy birthday, Mum.'

Her face crumpled up. It wasn't necessary to be told who was there. All she could do was to laugh and to cry.

Her boy had come home.

Chapter 22

Eric Tyler was now becoming a real problem for Grace. Since the end of November he had taken to calling on her unexpectedly at The Chapel, despite Grace's warnings that being seen together might jeopardise his chances of getting the type of divorce that would favour him. An added complication for Eric now was the possibility that if his wife, Jane, really wanted to get her own back on him, she might want to go back on her offer not to claim for alimony in return for a quick divorce. If that happened, he had no idea how he would find the money, especially as Jane's father was also keen to retrieve all his funds that Eric had used for some of his own ill-fated investments.

Much against her will, and against Mickey's advice, Grace agreed to spend an evening out with him. With Christmas and the New Year just around the corner, Grace was determined to see Eric go the same way as he had so ruthlessly dispatched her.

Dog racing had never appealed to Grace. The thought of a whole lot of poor greyhounds being forced to chase after a stuffed, mechanical hare seemed to her to be an utter waste of time, and the fact that people actually gambled money on the race seemed to her to be quite pointless. 'A sucker's game!' her dad had once told her, which was why neither he nor she had ever set foot in the Harringay Greyhound Stadium. None the less, it was a popular sport, especially for people like Eric, who, after betting threepence or sixpence at the tote, watched the madcap race with frenzied excitement. And if the event itself wasn't bad enough, standing in the cold for a couple of hours was agony. Grace longed for it all to be over so that they could get away and find somewhere to have a hot cup of cocoa.

However, Eric's plans did not include cocoa; what he was dying for was something much stronger. He had always been a pub crawler, and Green Lanes in Harringay was the perfect place to find any number of pubs to cure his alcoholic appetite. The place they chose was inevitably called The Dog and Hounds, and by the time they got in there the place was buzzing with both male and female customers waving their hands in excited conversation about the form of each of the dogs they had just seen racing.

'That's Harry Foster over there,' said Eric, nodding towards a skinny-looking individual with a pencil-thin 'tache, and togged out in a bowler hat, pin-striped suit, and a heavy navy-blue overcoat that was much too large for him. 'He knows more about dogs than anyone else in the country. I bet he's had more wins than I've had hot dinners.'

Grace wasn't at all impressed. Pressed against the bar counter by a surging mass of supporters who were still pouring out of the stadium nearby, in the absence of a hot cup of cocoa, all she longed for was the glass of ginger wine Eric was trying to order for her. It was impossible for her to see what the pub looked like, because there didn't seem to be one single person in the place who didn't have a fag in their mouth. And she couldn't hear anything either, because someone, she couldn't see who, was thumping out unrecognisable tunes on a piano somewhere, and whilst a group of men were playing darts over in the corner, a deranged woman's shrill voice was taunting the pub landlord's poor caged parrot with endless cries of: 'Pretty Polly! Pretty Polly!'

Once Eric had managed to get the drinks, both he and Grace decided that there was more room to breathe outside, despite the cold. And it *was* cold, bitterly cold. The tips of Grace's fingers were numb in her thin kid gloves, and she was certain that only the ginger wine flowing down her throat was saving her from complete hypothermia. Taking shelter from the biting wind in a shop doorway next door to the pub, Grace was interested to see how many punters Eric knew; practically every customer going in or out of the pub greeted him with a nod or a wink.

'Darling,' said Eric, sipping his usual whisky and soda, and sliding his other hand around Grace's waist. 'I've got something I want to suggest to you. It's about Christmas.'

Grace steeled herself. 'Christmas?' she asked.

'Why don't we spend it together?' he continued. 'Just the two of us – you and me. We could go down to the house together. Nobody would know me down there – nobody who's going to get back to Jane and tell her. Just think of it.' He snuggled up close, and leant his head on her shoulder. 'Lying together on the rug in front of a huge log fire, planning what we're going to do as soon as the divorce comes through.'

'I'm afraid that won't be possible, Eric,' said Grace.

Eric looked up with a start. He couldn't see her features too well in the dark. 'What d'you mean?' he asked.

'Christmas is always the time when I get together with my family over at Stoke Newington,' replied Grace. 'Especially so this year. My cousin has just come back from fighting in Spain.'

Eric was clearly disappointed. 'You mean, you have to be with them for the *whole* of Christmas?' he asked.

Although she was lying through her teeth, Grace knew she had to make her story sound convincing. 'What usually happened,' she replied, 'was that Dad and I went over to my Aunt Josie's for Christmas Day, and they all came over to us on Boxing Day. It's been like that ever since I can remember. A kind of family tradition, I suppose.'

'A bit repetitive, isn't it?' suggested Eric, sourly. 'The same thing every year?'

'It won't be the sáme this year without Dad,' she replied.

Eric suddenly realised he'd been a bit tactless. 'Of course,' he said guiltily. 'I'm sorry, darling.' He leant forward and kissed her gently on the forehead. 'Never mind, we'll make up for it in the New Year. As soon as the divorce comes through, we'll have a celebration. Don't worry – it'll be on me!'

'Wonderful!' said Grace, tongue-in-cheek. 'I can't wait.'

Encouraged by what she had said, Eric pressed his body hard up against hers. Grace desperately wanted to back away, but for the time being she didn't want him to know exactly what she felt about him.

'There's no one else, is there?' he whispered into her ear.

'What d'you mean?' asked Grace.

'You *know* what I mean,' he replied. 'If there *was* someone else, you'd tell me – wouldn't you?'

Grace heard what he was saying. She heard it loud and clear. It took her back to that night on King's Cross station, that soul-destroying night, when she waited for the boy who, only hours earlier, had told her that she was the only one who mattered in his life, that he would sooner die than lose her. 'But I've got *you*, Eric,' she replied softly. 'Why would I want anyone else?'

'That's my girl!' he replied, pushing harder against her. 'That's what I like to hear.' He hurriedly undid his raincoat belt and buttons, and wrapped the coat around her.

She knew that he was aroused, but as she felt his body

377

pressing hard into her, she had nothing but revulsion for what he was attempting to do. He was making her feel like a common street girl, and she hated him for it. In a determined effort to stop him going any further, she dropped the half-finished glass of ginger wine she was still holding. The trick worked, for the sound of glass smashing on the ground pulled Eric up with a jolt, and he pulled away from her.

'Damn!' she spluttered. 'I'm so sorry! What a clumsy fool I am!'

'It doesn't matter!' returned Eric irritably, quickly buttoning up his raincoat again. 'But it's the last time I'll ever let a broken glass come between us.'

The following evening, the ground-floor hall of Pakeman Street School proved a perfect place for Gus Higgs's tenants to have a meeting about Grace's offer for them to buy their own houses. The headmaster, Mr Piper, had readily given his permission for them to use the hall, which during the day was the domain of the school infants, whose nursery paintings adorned the walls of the teachers' platform and all the classroom doors around. Unperturbed by a large children's play sandpit behind them, the tenants chatted about the whys and wherefores of owning their own properties.

'In one way,' said Sid Wilson, who had to be back on duty at Finsbury Park station within the hour, 'it makes a lot er sense. I mean, I'm always patchin' up me scullery and wallpaperin' the front room. In all the years I've bin doin' it, I've never asked Gus ter contribute anyfin' ter any of it. So I can't see it makes any diff'rence if I own the place.'

'If yer look at that letter at the back of yer rent book,'

Mabel Buck reminded him, 'it tells yer that any interior work is yer own responsibility.'

'But not risin' damp!' added Gert Jolly, with some current knowledge on the subject.

'Not risin' damp, nor any uvver major structural work,' insisted Mabel.

'I know when I ever 'ad anyfin' wrong wiv my geezer,' said Gert's neighbour, Molly Tebbit, 'it took ages fer Gus ter get it fixed fer me.'

'Well, er course it did!' snapped Gert at her. 'Gus never 'ad anyfin' ter do wiv geezers!'

Jack Pertwee from Enkel Street chipped in. 'The fact that 'e got it done at all, Molly,' he told her, 'was becos 'e was doing yer a favour.'

'Was 'e really?' asked Molly, who, to the others, seemed to be living on a different planet from them.

'I agree with you, Jack,' said Letty Hobbs from Roden Street. 'Gus wasn't like any other landlord. He had a heart of gold.'

Her husband, Oliver, agreed. Although Oliver was an inarticulate man, he spent a lot of his time deep in thought, and the idea that he and Letty could own their own house had already given him a few sleepless nights. 'If I 'ad the money,' he said, 'I'd buy *my* place termorrer.'

'Me too, Olly mate,' agreed Sid Wilson. 'Trouble is, money's 'ard ter come by. I've never bin in debt in me life, and I wouldn't want ter start now.'

'But Grace isn't askin' us ter get in debt, is she?' asked Molly.

Everyone turned to look at her.

'Well, she isn't,' insisted Molly, who wasn't quite as simple as her neighbours thought. 'All she's sayin' is that we could turn our rent money into weekly payments. If I could let my top-floor rooms an' the attic, I could probably make enough to cover the cost.'

'That's true,' said Letty Hobbs. 'We asked Gus years ago if we could let our top floor, and he had no objections. It hasn't brought much in, but it's been more than enough to pay our rent. The only thing is . . .' she took a quick look at her husband, 'Olly's got to have another operation on his leg in a few weeks' time, and I'm not sure we want to start playing around with our outgoings until that's over.'

'I still fink it's a good idea,' added Oliver.

Everyone started chatting things over amongst themselves.

'There's just one question I'd like to ask, though,' said Jack Pertwee, bringing all the chatter to a halt. 'Does Grace mean that our properties will still belong ter 'er until we've paid 'em off, or is she sellin' 'em ter someone else?'

This brought the first prolonged silence to the hall. There was a worried look on everyone's face, including those tenants who hadn't really contributed to the conversation.

'D'you fink she's sellin' us off?' asked Gert Jolly, breaking the silence.

'Grace'd never do that,' said Sid Wilson.

'No, but Jack's got a point,' said Letty Hobbs anxiously. 'Another landlord might not be so tolerant as Gus or Grace.'

Once again, the hall was plunged into silence. Quite suddenly everything was not quite as clear-cut as it had seemed when they had all met up earlier. Everyone had something to think about, and it wasn't just the exciting prospect of owning their own home, but the thought of what would happen if Grace *should* sell to a third party. The circle they were sitting in was becoming restless, and even though the men had agreed not to smoke in the infants' hall, they were all becoming frustrated for a fag. It was a real dilemma. Nobody wanted to offend Grace, who had shown such consideration to them all since her dad had died, and nobody wanted her to think that they didn't trust her, but this was a big step for any of them to take. Ownership of their own place was big time, and they had to know all the facts before they made any firm decisions.

'I've got an idea,' said Jack Pertwee, getting up from his chair and breaking away from the group. 'What say we tell Grace that we like 'er idea in principle, but we don't want ter make up our minds till we know if we'll still be dealin' wiv 'er alone?'

There was a rumble of indecisiveness around the circle.

'I suppose that wouldn't be a bad idea, Jack,' sighed Letty. 'I mean, for all *we* know, Grace may be givin' up the business altogether, and going off to live in Devon.'

'I don't think that's true,' called Sid Wilson, who had slipped out to have a crafty quick fag in the open front door of the hall. 'I 'eard Grace 'as put down a deposit on a shop round Seven Sisters Road.'

Everyone swung a startled look at him.

'Wot's that, Sid?' called Gert Jolly, her voice echoing across the hall. 'She's givin' up the shop?'

Sid corrected her. 'Givin' up the van, Gert,' he returned. 'Since ol' Clapper got sick, she's wanted ter settle down, and run a normal nine-ter-six grocery shop.'

A buzz of speculation from everyone.

'Anyway,' said Jack, taking a handful of sand from the children's sandpit. 'We've got ter make up our minds one way or anuvver. We can't just let this chance slip through our fingers.' Symbolically, he did so with the handful of sand.

'Well, I've made up *my* mind!' announced Gert, easing herself up from her chair. 'I'm too old ter be spendin' me 'ard-earnt money on sticks and stones. As far as *I'm* concerned, I shall tell Grace that I'm grateful fer the offer, but there's no way I can accept it.' Without further ado, she called back as she tottered off, ' 'Night all!'

Nobody turned to watch her go, but the words she left lingered behind for quite some time.

Grace and Mickey looked around the empty shop in Seven Sisters Road, which Grace had already chosen to be the new home for the grocery and provisions side of the business. Formerly a shoe shop, it wasn't a very big area, but Mickey was very enterprising in the ideas he had for using the space in the best, most sensible way.

'It's still a shame we won't be doin' fruit and veg no more,' he said, calling down from the top of a stepladder where he was taking from the wall some price tickets for shoes, left behind by the previous occupiers. 'No more trips up Covent Garden.'

'I know,' replied Grace, 'but with Hicks the greengrocers just down the road, it would be far too much competition. As it is, we'll have to be careful about the name we put outside. "Higgs" and "Hicks" are a bit too similar. I think I'll call it, "GUS HIGGS, CHANDLER".'

'Chandler?' asked Mickey, puzzled. 'Wos that?'

'It's what Dad was in the Merchant Navy,' replied Grace, who was holding on to the base of the stepladder, which was a bit wobbly. 'It's someone who sells grocery provisions, a shopkeeper, that sort of thing. I want to get a good supply of candles in. We've always done a good trade in them with our tenants, especially when they run out of gas.' She looked up at the bare electricity bulb dangling down from the ceiling. 'And in any case, I don't trust electricity lighting. I don't think they've perfected it yet for home-users.'

'Got quite a bit of plasterin' ter do up 'ere,' said Mickey, coming down the steps with the price tickets.

'Oh Lord, is there?' asked Grace.

'Don't you worry,' he replied. 'Won't take me long ter patch it up. I'll go fru this place wiv a brush an' paint like a dose er salts!'

Grace sighed with affection and admiration for him. 'Oh, Mickey,' she said, putting her arms around his waist. 'It's going to be so wonderful once you've moved in. For me, sharing this place with you will be a dream come true.'

'Sharing wiv me *an'* the kids,' insisted Mickey.

'Kids!' exclaimed Grace.

'I want at least six!' teased Mickey.

Grace laughed, and pretended to ignore him. 'We've got to make this place different,' she said, walking around, working out things in her mind. 'It's no use trying to sell the same old things that people can buy anywhere else along the road. You can get practically anything in Seven Sisters and Holloway Roads. We've got to concentrate on all sorts of things.'

'Such as?'

'Oh, I don't know – knick-knacks.'

'Knick-knacks?' asked Mickey, scratching his head. 'A knick-knack shop!'

Grace laughed. 'No, you daft thing!' she replied. 'No – actually you're not daft, Mickey,' she said, quickly correcting herself. 'As a matter of fact you've had some very good ideas for this place, especially for selling a few second-hand clothes. The only thing that's worrying now is whether we're going to need some help to run the shop.'

'We can manage,' Mickey said confidently.

'I'm not so sure,' said Grace. 'What happens when we go down to Devon to be with Clapper?'

At the mention of Clapper's name, Mickey went silent. He was trying to put to the back of his mind the fact that his old mate was being taken off the following day for the start of his new life in Devon.

Grace went to him. She knew exactly how he felt, because she was feeling that way herself. 'I know, Mickey,' she said, slipping her arm round him again, and leaning her head on his shoulder. 'But he'll be better off down there. Those people on the farm near Teignmouth have promised to look after him well until we've had a chance to build a stable and paddock at the back of the house.'

'I know,' said Mickey, trying to put a brave face on it, 'but I'll miss 'im. Why the stupid ol' git 'ad ter go an' get ill I just don't know.'

They were suddenly interrupted by a tapping on the shop window.

'Blimey!' gasped Mickey. 'We've got a visitor.'

Grace turned with a start to find a woman peering through the window, her face lit up by the electric light bulb. 'Aunt Hilda!' she gasped, rushing across to open the door. 'Auntie!' she said, letting her in and pecking her on the cheek. 'What are *you* doing here?'

'Well, yer told me yer'd got this shop,' she said, her cheeks flushed with the cold. 'So I fawt I'd come round an' take a gander at it. Didn't know you'd be 'ere, though.' Her face lit up when she saw Mickey. ' 'Allo, young man,' she said coyly.

' 'Allo, Auntie, darlin'!' said Mickey, also pecking her on the cheek.

Grace exchanged a wry smile with him over Hilda's shoulder.

'So this is it, is it?' said Hilda, blowing her nose on her hanky as she looked around. 'Bit big, ain't it?'

'Actually, we were thinking just the opposite,' replied Grace. 'It's going to be a bit of a squeeze to get everything in.'

'You're not goin' ter sell fruit an' veg, are yer?' asked Hilda knowingly. 'Yer can't compete with ol' 'Icks down the road.'

'We know that, Auntie,' Grace assured her.

'An' it's no use sellin' dried peas and beans an' broken biscuits, not when yer've got Lipton's practically next door.'

'We know that too, Auntie,' sighed Grace.

'So wot *are* yer goin' ter sell?' she demanded.

'Knick-knacks, darlin'!' said Mickey.

'Knick-knacks?' growled Hilda. 'Wot's that s'pposed ter mean?'

'You name it, we'll get it!' explained Mickey. 'From a jar of bee's 'oney to a pair er knickers.'

Hilda's scepticism was halted dead in its tracks as she giggled at Mickey's cheeky reply. 'Well, if yer need any 'elp,' she said, 'yer know where ter come.'

Grace exchanged a puzzled look with Mickey. 'What d'you mean, Auntie?' she asked.

'Wot I said,' replied Hilda. 'I know I'm not wot I used ter be, but I did once work in a shop yer know – before *an*' after I was married. I'm used ter dealing with the public. I get on well wiv 'em.'

Grace smiled bravely.

'Mind you,' continued Hilda, 'I don't want ter interfere. I know it's your business, an' nuffin' ter do wiv the family, but if yer want some time off, like when yer go down ter Devon or anyfin', I'll always fill in for yer.'

For the first time since she had known her aunt, Grace suddenly felt a surge of warmth for her. 'That's very thoughtful of you, Auntie,' she said. 'We'll remember that, won't we, Mickey?'

'Absolutely!' replied Mickey, going to Hilda, and putting a friendly arm round her shoulders. 'We'd get on like a 'ouse on fire, wouldn't we, darlin'?'

Hilda smiled back eagerly at him. She was so taken aback to be treated so warmly by both him and Grace, she seemed close to tears. 'Besides,' she continued softly, 'I don't get out as much as I used to. It'd give me somefin' ter do, somefin' ter keep me mind occupied. I wouldn't want any wages,' she said, shaking her head, 'especially since you're givin' me and the rest er the family a bit er money.'

Grace could hardly believe this change of attitude, could hardly believe this was the same Aunt Hilda who had been the plague of her life – of everyone's lives – for so many years. Was this really an attempt to be a nicer person, to stop quarrelling with her relations, as happened in so many families, or was it just a way of getting herself involved in the business? Only time would tell. At least, Aunt Hilda was showing a vulnerable side to her nature, and that could only be a good thing.

'Once we've moved in here, Auntie,' said Grace warmly, 'we'll see how things go.'

Hilda flicked a grateful smile at her, but smiled winsomely up at Mickey.

Despite the cold, frosty morning, Clapper was enjoying his final trot around the backstreets with both Grace and Mickey. As the sun was only just up, the streets behind Caledonian Road were empty, and Clapper's hoofs echoed on the hard cobbled roads as he went. Grace and Mickey had not slept a wink all night. Once they had got back from the new shop they had been looking over the previous evening, neither had slept a wink, bedding down together in the straw as close to Clapper as they could get. It was the longest night either of them could remember, not only because they both knew what the morning would bring, but because they had the strangest feeling that Clapper did too.

Matters were made worse when various neighbours came out to bid farewell to their favourite drayhorse, who had been such a regular sight on their streets for so many years. It was difficult for them to understand why he had to go, but they realised that being turned out to grass would at least ensure that he had a comfortable retirement, albeit a premature one. Mickey even brought Clapper to a brief halt just outside the shed that had been his own home for such a long time, and which he still refused to leave until he knew what the future held for him and Grace. It was an emotional time too for him and Grace when they led Clapper around Stock Orchard Crescent, where his head bucked gently up and down as he trotted, almost a final farewell to the place where he had brought his master and mistress together for the first time just a few months before.

When they finally got back to the house, the horsebox van that was being used to take Clapper to his temporary new home in Teignmouth was already parked just outside the stable yard gates. The driver was the farmer himself, to whose farm Clapper was going. He was a likeable, middle-aged man, a real country squire type, whose Devon burr was only slightly more pronounced than that of his young wife, who had come along as her husband's passenger to help out on the journey back home.

'Better not hang around too long, Miss Higgs,' the farmer said. 'I don't care much for your weather up here in London. By the looks of things, we shan't get back much before dark this evening.'

Once Mickey had brought out the last of Clapper's

equipment, he and Grace were allowed just a moment or so to say farewell.

'Won't be fer long, mate,' Mickey, voice cracking, whispered into the animal's ear. 'Just fink, yer'll be 'avin' the best 'oliday yer could possibly 'ave. Just wait till I tell yer mates up the Cally. I'm tellin' yer, they're goin' ter be green wiv envy.'

Whilst Mickey stroked and stroked Clapper's ear, Grace pressed her face against the side of his neck. 'Go safe, old friend,' she said, voice low and close to tears. 'Don't worry, Dad'll be there to take care of you.'

A few minutes later, Mickey was about to lead Clapper up the ramp into the rear of the horsebox, when he and Grace suddenly noticed a small silent group of Grace's tenants and customers watching and waiting for Clapper's departure on the other side of the road.

' 'Ang on a minute!' called Gert Jolly, who broke away from the others and came across carrying a large carrot. 'You 'ave this on the journey, mate!' she said, stroking Clapper's nose. 'Yer've got a long way ter go.'

The farmer's wife smiled as Gert handed her the carrot. Then the farmer took the reins from Mickey, led Clapper up into the horsebox to tether him, then returned to raise the ramp, and close the rear entrance of the vehicle.

As Gert Jolly returned to her neighbours across the road, Grace was clearly finding these parting few moments difficult to take.

'See you at the weekend,' said the farmer, shaking hands with both Grace and Mickey.

'Yes,' returned Grace, barely able to speak.

The farmer's wife also shook hands with them. 'Don't worry,' she said reassuringly. 'We'll take good care of him.'

Grace smiled gratefully, and nodded.

A moment later, the horsebox pulled away from The Chapel, and turned off up Caledonian Road. It was a cumbersome departure, thought Grace. Clapper himself would have done the journey much better than a motor van. Mickey held her tightly round the waist, and she leaned her head on his shoulder.

'Isn't it ridiculous?' she said, with tears streaming down her face. 'All night I've been telling myself that when this moment came, I wouldn't be sentimental, I wouldn't be stupid. But you know what, Mickey? I don't care if I am!'

Mickey held on to her, and hugged her. But as they turned to go back inside the back yard, they noticed that, without saying a word, the small group of tenants had gone, and were already making their long, silent way home on foot.

Chapter 23

The House on the Hill was covered in snow. Against a deep blue December sky, the sun crept up over the sea and turned it and the entire landscape into a blinding scarlet wonderland. At every window of the house, long icicles were beginning to drip in the gathering warmth of morning, and the snow that had settled on the red tiled roof was holding on for grim death. Every tree and every plant was drooping with the weight of the previous night's fall, which had turned to ice, making it difficult for any wildlife to nibble on the leaves. Rabbit holes everywhere were covered over, and the first robin of the day left its little footprints in the snow as it searched around desperately for something to eat.

Mickey couldn't believe his eyes. Not only had he just travelled on a train for the first time in his life, but he was also looking at a house that looked big enough to accommodate about ten families.

'You're not kiddin' me, are yer, Grace?' he asked, as he stood on the main doorstep looking around, waiting for her to open the front door. 'This really *does* all belong ter you?'

'Every square inch,' replied Grace. 'I'll take you on a tour later. You'll get some idea how enormous the place is.' She loved the look on his face as he stepped out of the taxi with their overnight luggage at the front entrance of the house. In fact this had been a moment she had been waiting for, bringing him to Devon and seeing the expression on his face as he looked at the house where, she hoped, the two of them would in future years spend so much of their time together.

Inside the house, Mickey's eyes scanned the vast hall; he was overawed by everything he saw. The huge crystal chandelier hanging down from the ceiling scared the daylights out of him, his first thought being what would happen if he slammed a door accidentally and the whole thing came crashing to the stone floor. He felt the same when Grace took him into the sitting room, with all the fine antique furniture, rich tapestries and upholsteries. In the dining room, he peered out through the great arched windows on to lawns that, to him, looked to stretch for miles.

'I've often wondered about the people who used to live here,' said Grace, showing him into the dining room. 'They must have been sublimely happy.'

'Yer fink so?' asked Mickey, looking around sceptically.

Grace swung him a surprised look. 'Well – don't *you*?' she asked.

Mickey shrugged, delicately running the tips of his fingers over the highly polished dining table. 'I dunno,' he replied uneasily. 'Can't've bin much fun fer that poor ol' boy who left this place to yer dad.'

Now Grace was really puzzled by his strange reaction. 'What d'you mean, Mickey?' she asked.

'Well,' he replied, 'livin' in a great big place like this all on 'is own, no family, no relatives.'

'He must have had friends,' Grace pointed out. 'After all, he must have thought something of my father to leave him all this.'

'Doesn't mean a fing, Grace,' replied Mickey, looking up at one of the many Victorian portrait paintings that were hanging around the walls. 'OK, yer can 'ave friends, but if yer lock yourself away in a place like this an' only see 'em once in a while, then – well, I don't see no point.'

'I'm so sorry you feel that, Mickey,' replied Grace haughtily, getting irritated with him.

He swung round to her. 'Don't get me wrong, Grace,' he said. 'This is a – an amazin' place. But it needs people, lots er people, a family or somefin'.' He looked around the room, then wandered out into the hall again. 'If *I* lived in a place like this,' he said, his voice echoing right up to the ceiling beams, 'I'd probably get lost even tryin' ter find me way ter the lav!'

Now he was really getting on her nerves. At least when Eric Tyler had seen the place he had appreciated what he saw. He might have had delusions of grandeur about all the plans he was concocting, but he certainly didn't have some kind of guilt complex about living in such grand surroundings. Grace was already beginning to wish she had taken Mickey and herself off to at to stay at the B and B guesthouse in Riviera Terrace. 'D'you want to see any more of the house?' she asked curtly.

Mickey turned to look at her, and could see that she was hurt. He went to her, and put his arm round her. 'Of course I do!' he said affectionately, giving her a quick kiss.

However, Mickey's reaction to the upstairs rooms turned out to be much the same as to what he had already seen. It was a feeling he couldn't describe; he just felt uncomfortable in such a place, as though hundreds of pairs of eyes were watching them with disapproval, telling them that they had no right to occupy such a place all on their own. In the main bedroom on the first floor, where Grace had taken to sleeping during her weekend visits, Mickey perched himself timidly on the edge of the bed, and looked around. All he could think about was his own tiny bedroom curtained off in the shed back home near Caledonian Road. To him something was wrong about this place.

Grace was standing by the window, arms crossed, looking down sadly, aimlessly into the back gardens below. She felt thoroughly shattered by Mickey's reaction to the house; it was so unexpected. She didn't know what to do. Should she take them both straight to the B and B until they could catch the train back to London the following morning, or should she have it out with Mickey here and now, telling him that he was an ungrateful young man, and that he was lucky to have someone like her who had more to offer him than he had had in his entire life? She clutched her forehead with her hand. How on earth could she even think such a thing? She didn't love Mickey for what she could give him, and he certainly didn't love *her* for what he could get from her. She suddenly felt ashamed of herself. Mickey had every right to say what he thought. He had a mind of his own, and if she ever tried to influence it, she would lose him. If he didn't like the house, then she should do nothing to persuade him otherwise. None the less, Mickey's reaction was something she had not predicted. It showed that he was capable of working things out for himself, of having his own opinions that did not necessarily agree with her own. As she stood there, she felt him come to stand beside her. His arm slowly slid round her waist.

'I'm sorry, darlin',' he said softly, in a voice so different to the cheeky way he joked with the tenants back in Holloway. 'Yer mustn't take too much notice of *me*. I've got a brain not much bigger than a pea-pod. I don't know very much about fings. Maybe it's 'cos er who I am, where I come from – who knows?' He leaned his head on her shoulder. 'It's just that – oh, I dunno – this place, fantastic though it is, well – it seems more like an 'ouse than an 'ome. It don't seem right that just the two of us should live 'ere.'

'I've told you, Mickey,' she replied without rancour.

'We're not going to live here. We've got The Chapel. We've got a place to live in back in Islington. This place is for all my family. It still belongs to me, but they can use it whenever they want. It'll be marvellous for them to have holidays.'

' 'Olidays ain't enuff, Grace,' he replied. 'An 'ouse ain't just bricks an' stones. It needs ter be lived in. It needs a life of its own. It needs ter be loved.'

She turned to look at him. 'What makes you think I can't love it?' she asked. 'What makes you think that both of us can't love it – together?'

'That's not wot I'm sayin', Grace,' he said. 'Wot I'm sayin' is that an 'ouse shouldn't be left on its own fer so long, especially a big 'ouse like this. Oh, I know yer've got people ter look after it when yer're not 'ere, but – well, yer've only got ter feel 'ow cold it is. It's got no 'eart. It's got no blood flowin' fru its veins. Don't worry, I'll soon get some fires goin' – but it won't be the same. This ol' 'ouse needs somefin' more than someone kippin' down in it fer a few weeks each year. It needs someone ter take care of it, I mean *really* take care of it. It needs somefin' it doesn't seem to 'ave 'ad before. It needs people, Grace. People.'

Reg Cooker was looking a totally different person. In the short time he'd been home, he had had a proper haircut, shaved off his moustache and long beard, and discarded all the grubby handed-down clothes he had been wearing since he got back from his traumatic time in Spain. On Grace's advice, his mum and dad never mentioned Spain, never asked any questions about his experiences in the civil war there that had left him with such a terrible bayonet scar on his face that would be with him for the rest of his life. Much to Auntie Josie's frustration, Grace had also advised against pampering the boy too much, because a major part of Reg's rehabilitation with his home life was that he should be made to feel that he was completely independent, capable of making a go of things on his own.

Another important change for Reg was that although his dad, Stan, was not much of a talker, he had done his best to touch on subjects other than sport, which brought the two of them much closer. It also made it much easier for Reg to ask his dad if he could go with him to watch an Arsenal-Spurs football match at the Arsenal stadium on Saturday afternoon, which brought Stan undiluted joy, for the two of them had not done such a thing since their regular Saturday afternoon visits to support their home team, Arsenal, when Reg was a small boy.

However, things were to take yet another unexpected turn, as Josie, Stan and Viv soon discovered when Reg and Stan got back from the game, and sat down for a hot tea-time meal.

'Goin' away again?' asked Josie, her whole expression crushed and anxious. Until this moment it seemed as though she was coming back to life. Having her son sitting at the same table as herself had given her, and Stan, the chance to make amends, to see where they had gone wrong in their relationship with Reg, but now everything was about to fall apart again.

'Why?' asked Stan, ashen-faced, mouth full of Reg's favourite stew. 'Wos up now?'

'Nuffin's up, Dad,' replied Reg, sitting opposite him. 'Well – not really. It's just that, I don't want ter live in London any more.'

Josie feared the worst. 'Yer mean,' she said, barely audible, 'yer don't like livin' at 'ome any more.'

'No, Mum,' replied Reg, putting down his knife and fork. 'It's got nothing to do with home. It's got nothing to do with all the fings I said to you before I went to Spain, fings I used ter lie awake wishin' I'd never said 'cos I never meant 'em. It's London,' he said, desperately trying to qualify what he was saying. 'Since I came back to England, since I came back to the big city, it's bin as though I can't breave. It don't matter where I walk, where I look, there're people everywhere. I can hear 'em, see 'em, smell 'em, touch 'em – they're everywhere I go.' He sighed. He found it almost impossible to put into words what he was thinking. 'I just want ter get away somewhere, somewhere more natural, where I've got time ter think, ter 'ave time to appreciate fings I've never 'ad time ter notice before.'

Josie exchanged looks of total anguish with Stan. Neither of them had the faintest idea of what he was trying to say to them. All they could hear was that he wanted to get away from *them*, because he couldn't take living with them any more.

'I think I know what Reg is trying to say,' said Viv, flicking him a supportive glance. 'After what he's gone through, it takes time for more than the body to heal.'

Reg gave her a faint smile of appreciation.

'But – where would yer go, son?' asked Stan, totally confused.

'I dunno,' replied Reg, opening his tobacco tin, and taking out one of his rolled fags. 'Somewhere quiet, maybe in the country – I just dunno. But wherever it is, I'd still see yer. I'd come back an' see you fer visits. It's just that, I wouldn't 'ave ter keep pushin' me way through crowds, and crossin' busy roads.'

Josie tried hard to work out what to say to him. 'Well,' she said, after a long agonising pause, 'I s'ppose all birds 'ave ter leave their nests sooner or later, but – won't yer be lonely, livin' all on yer own?'

Reg hesitated before replying. 'No, Mum,' he said, slowly looking up at her. 'I won't be lonely – 'cos I won't *be* on me own.' He lit his fag and got up from the table. 'I've bin waitin' ter tell yer since I got back, but – well, the fact is, I've met someone, someone I like very much.'

All three turned with a start to look at him.

'A gel?' asked Josie. 'Yer've got a gelfriend?'

'Yes, I 'ave, Mum,' replied Reg confidently.

'But that's wonderful, son!' spluttered Josie with relief, getting up from her chair and going straight to him. 'Who is she?' she asked eagerly. 'Wot's 'er name?'

' 'Er name's Sandy,' replied Reg, embarrassed.

'But that's a lovely name,' persisted Josie. 'Where did yer meet?'

'In a hostel,' replied Reg. 'In a hostel fer people like me – livin' rough out on the streets.'

Josie shut up immediately, and clasped a hand to her mouth in horror.

Stan swung round in his chair to get a better look at his son. 'She's a – down-and-out?'

'Those are *your* words, Dad,' Reg said reprovingly, 'not mine.' He looked across to Viv for support, but as he hadn't discussed this with her in advance, she was too taken aback herself to be of much help. 'As a matter of fact,' he continued, 'Sandy was one of the staff at the hostel. She was on duty most nights for the soup queues. We got talking, and found we had a lot in common.' He came back to the table, but didn't sit down. 'She's a lovely girl. She's got sandy-coloured 'air. That's 'ow she got 'er name. It's not 'er real name, though.' He paused. 'I'm in love wiv 'er.'

Feeling some relief that at least he had found himself a girlfriend of sorts, Josie returned to her chair at the table. But she was too bewildered to eat.

'Where does Sandy live, Reg?' asked Viv.

'Edmonton,' he replied. 'Silver Street.'

'Got a mum an' dad, 'as she?' asked Stan, trying to put a good face on it.

Reg paused before answering. 'Yes, Dad,' he replied wryly. 'She's got a mum an' dad.'

'Oh, well,' continued Stan cheerily, 'can't be much wrong if that's the case. If *you* like 'er, I'm sure she's a lovely gel. Once yer've got ter know 'er a bit, who knows – yer might even like 'er enuff ter get married.'

'We've already decided that, Dad,' replied Reg.

'Wot d'yer mean?' asked Josie anxiously.

Reg sat down at the table again and took a puff of his rolled-up fag. 'We've decided that as soon as I've found a decent job somewhere, we're goin' ter get married as soon as possible.'

Although the wind was taken out of his sails, Stan took the news with great calm. 'Well – that's – lovely, ain't it, Jose?'

Josie sat back in her chair. She was too confused to say anything more than, 'Yes – lovely, dear.'

'Yer must bring 'er over sometime,' continued Stan. 'Sooner we get ter know 'er the better. I'm glad this 'as 'appened, son. Like yer mum an' me, I'm sure yer'll find that married life 'as a way of sortin' out all yer problems. Yes, son. Bring yer young lady over ter meet us as soon as yer like.'

'I will, Dad,' replied Reg. 'As a matter of fact, I've asked 'er over ternight. She'll be 'ere any minute.'

The winter moon was so clear and close, it looked as though it would drop into the sea at any moment. The walk from Teignmouth along the footpath by the railtrack was straight and easy, but once the sun had gone down it had become quite treacherous underfoot, with early evening frost promising to turn to ice at any moment. But it was a truly spectacular evening, and Grace and Mickey were determined to make the most of it, wrapped up warmly against the biting cold, arms round each other's waists, picking their way carefully along the frosty path, the red sandstone rocks alongside them dazzling white beneath the luminous moon, and the 'spinning top' rock just offshore spinning wildly in an imaginary eye.

Although they had put their previous disagreement over the house to one side, Grace was still disappointed to think that Mickey had reservations about the place. How could she fill the house with people if people didn't want to live there? She understood his sentiments, but not the practicality of getting a whole lot of people to live there. And yet she was interested in his idea to offer the place to her father's tenants for holidays; she could just see people like old Gert Jolly sleeping in a huge double bed, and eating fish and chips off the dining-room table! No. The only solution would be to employ someone to take the place of Bernice. At least then there would be *someone* to properly care for the house, even if it wasn't, as Mickey had said, a real home.

'When you look out there,' said Mickey in reflective mood, bringing them to a halt, 'it's 'ard to imagine that in a few days' time it'll be Chris'mas. I mean, just look at that – one moon in the sky, an' anuvver one in the water. If someone'd told me a few years back that one day I'd be standin' 'ere in the middle of December, I'd've told 'em they're bonkers.'

'Anything's possible in this life, Mickey,' said Grace, leaning her head on his shoulder. 'When I was young, I used to be terribly scared by the thought that Father Christmas always came down the chimney, especially as there were always so many burglars around. I often used to lie awake until the early hours, but you'll be sad to know that I never saw him.'

Mickey chuckled, and they walked on.

'But I'm glad Clapper's settled in at the farm,' she said. 'At least *he'll* have a good Christmas. Did you see that huge Christmas tree in the stable yard?'

'Of course,' replied Mickey. 'When we took ol' Clap out for a run 'e gave it a good ol' sniff!'

'And there was another one in the farmhouse,' continued Grace. 'I've always loved Christmas trees. When Dad was alive it was the one thing he always insisted on having. We used to get a huge one from the market, and put it in the front parlour for when the family came on either Christmas or Boxing Day. And there were so many candles, I was convinced that one day we'd set the whole place on fire!' She sighed. 'I'm going to miss Dad so much at Christmas,' she said forlornly. 'No tree this year.'

'Why not?' asked Mickey, again bringing them to a halt.

'Well, it wouldn't be the same, would it?' she asked. 'Not without him.'

'Come off it now, Grace,' said Mickey, his voice accompanied by the gentle lapping of waves on the shore in the distance. 'Yer can't stop livin' 'cos one person ain't around no more. I din't know yer dad, but I'd bet a bob to a shillin' that 'e'd want you ter go on gettin' yer Chris'mas tree just like every uvver year. So wevver yer like it or not, when we get back, the first fing I'm goin' ter do next mornin' is ter go ter see my mate 'Arry Maitland up the market, and get you the biggest Christmas tree yer've ever 'ad!'

'Oh, Mickey!' she sighed, snuggling up to him. 'And

d'you know what I'm going to do for you – but not until after Christmas?'

'No?' asked Mickey, mystified. 'Wos that?'

'I'm going to take you to the pictures.'

'The wot?'

'The pictures!' she growled. 'You *do* know what the pictures are, don't you? Talkies, movies, or whatever they like to call them.'

'I know wot they are, which is more than *you* do!' he retorted. 'You said yer ain't bin ter the pittures since you was a kid.'

'Ah!' replied Grace. 'But these are very special pictures. I've got tickets for you and me to go to the opening of the new cinema in Caledonian Road – the Mayfair. It's mainly by invitation only, for local people and the builders who worked on the place. There's going to be a speech by the Mayor of Islington, and – wait for it – who d'you think's going to do the official opening?'

' 'Aven't the faintest,' replied Mickey.

'Gracie Fields.'

'Wot!' gasped Mickey. 'Yer've got ter be jokin'? I presume yer mean Our Gracie, and not *my* Gracie?'

Grace laughed. 'I'm not famous enough for that,' she replied. 'But it should be a wonderful evening. A lot of singing, and two films as well. But we'll have to make sure we dress up. It's quite an occasion, you know. A lot of people would give their right arm to go to an event like that. And with a personal appearance by one of the most famous film stars in the country – or at least, that's what it says on the invitation.'

'Blimey!' said Mickey, who immediately started singing Gracie Fields' most popular song, 'Sally'.

A few minutes later, they climbed into the caves down at

Smugglers' Cove. As it was low tide, and the moon was acting like a huge spotlight, they were able to climb over the rocks inside the cave without too much difficulty. None the less, Grace was a little ill at ease to be in a place that was once frequented by a bunch of dangerous cutthroats.

'Don't let's stay too long,' she said, her voice echoing around the dark, bleak stone walls. 'I should think this place is terribly haunted.'

'Don't worry,' Mickey assured her. 'I'm far more scared of the livin' than the dead. Listen.'

Grace immediately panicked. 'What?' she gasped, quickly snuggling up to him.

'Nuffin',' he replied, keeping his voice low. He slipped his arm around her waist, and held her close. 'Can't yer 'ear it? Nuffin' at all.'

It wasn't quite true, for the gradually returning tide was gently flowing up from the shore, and trickling over the rocks in the cave. Even so, Mickey's calm reassured her, and she held on to him with total confidence. For a few moments they just stood there, and despite the intense cold, they felt warm in each other's company.

'D'yer know wot terday is?' said Mickey, finally breaking the silence. 'It's exactly five munffs ter the day that I first set eyes on you.'

'Really?' asked Grace. 'You made a note of it?'

'You bet I did!' he replied.

'And did you think *this* would happen?'

'Not in a million years.' He pulled her even closer. 'I fink somebody up there must've bin keepin' a lookout for me.'

'For me too,' said Grace.

It was some time before they spoke again. Both stood there letting their imaginations take over. Mickey reckoned he could hear the sound of men's voices, pulling in the small boats that carried their smuggled goods, and Grace shivered when she remembered all the bloodthirsty things young Billy had told her about the murders that had taken place in the cave, in the very place where they were standing right now.

'Did yer bring Eric Tyler down 'ere?' asked Mickey.

Grace was snapped out of her thoughts by his sudden question. 'Are you mad?' she asked. 'I'd no more come down here with Eric than the man in the moon. Knowing the sort of person he is, he'd have done what he liked with me – or at least he'd have tried.'

'D'yer fink 'e'll ever let go?' asked Mickey. 'I mean, when 'e finds out about us, d'yer fink 'e'll accept it?'

'Mickey!' said Grace, turning round to face him. 'You and me are a fact of life. I don't care what Eric Tyler accepts and what he doesn't. I love you, and that's all that matters. When his divorce comes through after Christmas, he's in for a nasty shock. I've waited for this moment for a long time.'

'I wish yer wouldn't,' Mickey said, again right out of the blue.

Grace was puzzled. 'What d'you mean?'

'I wish yer wouldn't do what yer goin' ter do,' he replied. 'Eric Tyler ain't worf it. 'Is type are a dime a dozen.'

'Mickey!' protested Grace, her voice bouncing off the walls in the hollow cave. 'Have you any idea what that man has done to me? If it hadn't been for you coming along, he could have destroyed my life – once and for all.'

'I know that,' said Mickey, 'but gettin' yer own back on someone, especially in the way you're plannin' ter do it – well, *I* fink it puts you in the same category as 'im. Any'ow, that's the way I see it.'

'Mickey!' Grace said, pulling away from him. 'How can you say such a thing?'

'Grace – listen ter me,' he said, pulling her back so that his face was so close, the condensation from his breath was darting out in small spurts. 'I never said you're like ''im, ''cos yer not. You're one of the nicest, most lovin', understandin' girls in the 'ole wide world. That's why I love yer, Grace – not 'cos you're someone who wants revenge, who wants ter get 'er own back by destroyin' someone's life, but becos you're a woman who cares – cares about me, cares about quite a lot er people. All I'm sayin' is, yer've done all yer need ter do. Yer've told ''im everythin' about wot yer dad left you, you've brought ''im down 'ere an' let ''im see wot 'e'll never 'ave. But that's enuff, Grace. I know 'ow yer feel about ''im, an' I know wot yer plannin'. But don't do it, Grace, 'cos if yer do, yer'll never be the same person again.'

Reg had chosen well. His girlfriend, Sandy, was quite lovely – thin, lithe, a funny little pointed nose, in height only an inch or so shorter than Reg himself, and with light brown eyes and shoulder-length sandy-coloured hair that was tied behind her head. But the moment she walked through the front door, Josie knew something was wrong, for Sandy had arrived with a holdall, and a haversack thrown over one shoulder. Reg knew it wasn't going to be easy. Sandy wasn't a very talkative girl at the best of times, even though she had a smile to kill for. However, she was immediately made welcome, especially by Viv, who put her at ease by showing her the Christmas paper decorations that she and Reg had been sticking together that morning. To Josie's surprise, the girl was ravenously hungry, and when she was offered some hot beef stew left over from tea, she ate it as though she hadn't eaten for several days.

'Reg tells us yer live up Edmonton way?' asked Josie,

watching Sandy swallowing her last mouthful of stew. 'Is that where yer was born, dear?'

Sandy wiped her lips with the back of one finger. 'No,' she replied. 'Actually, I was found in a dustbin.'

To say that Josie and Stan were shocked was an understatement. 'A dustbin?' asked Stan, practically choking on his fag.

The girl nodded shyly.

'Sandy's an orphan,' said Reg. 'She was found abandoned when she was just a few munffs old. She was taken inter care.'

'Oh,' gasped Josie. ' 'Ow terrible!' This somewhat unfortunate information immediately warmed Josie to the girl. ' 'Ow could a woman do such a fing to 'er own child?'

'It 'appens quite a lot,' replied Sandy. 'There were four uvvers like me in the 'ome where I was brought up. It took a long time ter get adopted.'

'Fank God there was *someone* ter love yer,' added Josie, with genuine sympathy.

Sandy exchanged a pointed look with Reg.

'So wot about yer mum an' dad?' asked Stan. 'I mean yer *new* mum an' dad. 'Ave they looked after yer OK?'

'Oh yes,' replied the girl casually. 'They've given me everyfin' I've wanted. I've no complaints.'

The girl's reluctance to elaborate on her home life left moments of awkward silence. Reg looked to Viv for support.

'Reg says you're planning to get married,' said Viv, quickly changing the subject. 'Have you any idea when?'

'Gotta get some money first,' Reg replied quickly, sitting beside Sandy at the table. 'I'm lookin' fer a decent job.'

'Any ideas wot?' asked his dad.

'Anyfin',' replied Reg. 'I 'ear they need some casual labour up the Town 'All – snow clearin'.'

Josie threw an anxious look at her husband.

Stan smiled bravely at the boy. 'That's not much of a job, son,' he said. 'I'm sure yer can do better than that.'

'Not durin' the Chris'mas 'olidays,' said Reg. 'There's nuffin' about. I need ter start earnin' some cash as soon as I can.'

'Well,' said Josie, 'I'm sure yer dad an' I can keep yer goin' till yer find somefin' better than snow clearin'.'

For some reason this remark irritated Reg, and he sprang up from his chair. 'I've told yer, Mum!' he snapped. 'I need to earn some money now – right now – my *own* money!'

Josie tensed. After all that had gone on over the recent past, the last thing she wanted to do was to upset the boy. It wasn't easy. Reg was very touchy, and she had come to realise only too well that saying the slightest wrong thing could jeopardise his relationship with her and Stan all over again. 'I understand, son,' she said timidly, sitting back in her chair.

After an awkward silence, Stan asked, ' 'Ave yer fawt about goin' back ter yer ol' job down the paint shop?'

Reg shook his head. 'I wouldn't want ter do that, Dad,' he replied. 'Not after walkin' out on them the last time.'

Stan scratched his head. 'Well, if yer like, I could always 'ave a word wiv my foreman. The company's buildin' a new office block up Fetter Lane. They're goin' ter need a few extra labourers. Won't be till after the 'olidays, though.'

'Wot about *you*, dear?' Josie asked the girl. 'Reg says yer on the staff of the – the place where 'e stayed.'

'I was,' replied Sandy. 'Till last night.'

Josie looked to Reg for some kind of explanation.

'Sandy's just been made redundant,' said Reg.

'That's not true!' snapped the girl. 'I got kicked out! They didn't want me no more.'

Josie's heart sank.

'Why's that, Sandy?' asked a grim-faced Stan.

Sandy suddenly wished she could have bitten off her tongue. She looked to Reg for help.

'There are so many people being made redundant these days,' said Viv, once again coming to Reg's rescue. 'I think it's got a lot to do with people's worries about the threat of war.' Viv got up quickly, and started to clear the table. 'Anyway,' she said brightly, 'we mustn't keep cross-examining Reg and Sandy. They've got a lot to talk over, to work out—'

'Mum an' Dad,' asked Reg, cutting straight through what his sister was saying, 'can Sandy stay wiv us?'

Josie's stomach churned. Although she had expected something like this, Reg's request still came as a bombshell. 'Stay here, dear?' she asked. 'Yer mean – fer ternight?'

'Fer as long as it takes.'

Josie exchanged a panicked look with Stan. 'Well – we've only got the Put-u-up down here, son,' she said apologetically.

'She can stay wiv me,' insisted Reg. 'I've got plenty er room.'

Josie seized up. She had no idea how to deal with this.

'Wiv respect ter boaf of yer, son,' said Stan, 'that wouldn't be very proper, would it?'

'Why not?' demanded Reg bluntly.

Stan was in a quandary. He had never had to talk like this to his son before, especially in front of Josie, and he found it difficult to find the words he was looking for. Passing on the facts of life to their kids may have been easy for some parents, but not for Stan Cooker. 'Well, let's face it,' he spluttered, 'livin' tergevver ain't the done fing before yer actually married, now is it? I mean, if it gets around—'

'Who the 'ell cares if it gets around?' growled Reg. 'Sandy's my gel, an' as soon as we can do it, we're goin' ter get married. So wot diff'rence does it make if we sleep tergevver now or later?'

'It makes a lot of diff'rence, son,' replied Stan reluctantly. 'To yer mum an' me.'

Reg paused just long enough to take in what his dad had said. 'Come on, Sand,' he said quite suddenly, impetuously, pulling back her chair to let her get up. 'We'll find somewhere.'

'Wait!' Josie sprang up from her chair. 'If that's wot yer want, son,' she said with immense courage, 'if *you* want Sandy to stay 'ere, then it's – all right wiv me.'

Stan swung her an astonished look. 'But why?' he then asked the girl, trying his best to be as reasonable as he was capable of. ' 'Ow will yer mum an' dad feel about this? Won't *they* be upset?'

Sandy looked to Reg to provide an explanation. 'As far as Sandy's concerned,' he replied, 'she ain't got no mum an' dad any more. They kicked 'er out.'

Dreading the worst, Josie clamped her hand over her mouth.

'But – why, son?' asked Stan. '*Why?*'

Sandy's eyes were lowered. Reg looked at her, and then back at his father. 'Need you ask?' he replied.

Chapter 24

For Grace, Christmas morning brought mixed blessings. It was not only the first time she had woken up in her own bed knowing that her father would not be downstairs waiting to greet her with a present under the Christmas tree, but it was also the first time that she had woken up in her own bed on a Christmas morning with the sweet, loving sound of a man's voice whispering in her ear, 'Merry Chris'mas, miss.'

She turned over, and was engulfed in Mickey's arms. 'Merry Christmas, Mickey Burke,' she replied. 'I love you.' And she *did* love him, more than she would have ever thought possible, and despite the fact that she would never be able to bring herself to do what he had asked her to do about Eric Tyler. As far as she was concerned, she could never let Eric get away with the lies and deceit that had nearly brought her life to a standstill. Only two days to go now before she would take her revenge once and for all, but until then she still had time to convince Mickey that her plan had to be carried out.

A short while later, the two of them were sipping tea by the huge Christmas tree in the front parlour that Mickey had bought for a song from his mate up the Cally market. The room was snug and warm, for Mickey had been up early that morning to light the fire in the front parlour. There was great excitement when they both opened presents from each other, a toolbox for Mickey, which he had seen in a hardware shop in Caledonian Road and desperately wanted, and, to Grace's absolute surprise, a fountain pen for her, which she had been promising to buy for herself. But the highlight of the morning came before breakfast, when the postman brought a stack of Christmas cards, some of them from friends of Grace's father, others from Josie, Stan and the family, and Auntie Hilda. There was also a delightful card in French from Bernice, who had now returned to her home in Normandy, and even cards from some of Grace's tenants and customers, which touched her enormously. However, the most intriguing card had a Canadian stamp on the envelope. Once she had ripped it open, she was absolutely astounded to read the warm Christmas greeting there, together with the short letter with an address in Toronto that accompanied it. Puzzled, she read out the name on the card. 'Tom Marchmont?' And then the penny struck. 'My God!' she gasped. 'It's from my half-brother in Canada!'

With Mickey listening intently, she read out the letter.

Dear Grace,

I know this will probably come as a shock to you, but my adopted mother, Rose Marchmont, wrote to tell me that she had finally told you about the real mother that you and I share. This, of course, I knew about years ago, but when Rose explained the situation, and the reasons why it all had to be kept from you, I respected her wishes not to make contact with you. But with the passing of your father, Gus Higgs, for which I send you my deepest condolences, I guess the time has come when we should put the record straight, and get to know each other. Rose has told me so much about you, about who you are and what you do, and I can't wait to meet you. That's really why I'm including this in with my card. The fact is, I'm coming over to England on business in a few months' time, and I was wondering if there was some way we could get together? I shall be bringing my wife, Ellen, with me, also our two lovely children, Mary (who's 8) and Buzz (who's 6), and we're all dying to meet you. We've got a hell of a lot of catching up to do, and I just hope you're as eager to do so as I am.

Hope to hear from you, but in the meantime, I hope that you, and those you love, have a great Christmas and a wonderful New Year.

Love from your half-brother,
Tom Marchmont

Grace slowly put down the letter. She was in a daze. 'Marchie never told me she'd given him her name,' she said. 'I can't believe he actually exists.'

'Sounds a nice bloke,' said Mickey. 'Nice ter know yer've got more family than yer fawt!' He paused a moment to let her take it all in. 'Wot yer goin' ter do about it?'

Beaming, she swung a look at him. 'What do *you* think?' she cried. 'I shall write straight back to him!' She sighed. 'Oh, Mickey,' she said, stretching out for his hand. 'This is going to be such a wonderful day, I know it is! I'm so grateful to you. You've made everything so perfect for me.'

'It would be Grace,' said Mickey, with an anxious sigh, 'if it wasn't fer Eric Tyler.'

Grace's expression changed. It was a smile of some sort, but one that revealed the only real gulf between them. 'Please, Mickey,' she pleaded. 'Don't let's talk about that again – not on Christmas Day.'

'But we 'ave ter talk about it, Grace,' persisted Mickey, holding on to her hand, which she had tried to pull away. 'If we don't it's going ter come between us, an' that's the last fing I want. Look,' he said, drawing closer. 'Eric's got 'is divorce this week. You know as well as *I* do that any minute, 'e's goin' ter be round 'ere *wantin'* yer, expectin' yer ter be waitin' for 'im. When 'e comes, fer your sake as well as 'is, yer've got ter tell him that it's all over wiv 'im an' you, that yer never wanna see 'im again.' He gripped her hand once more as she tried to pull away. 'If yer don't, Grace, if yer try ter do this same fing that 'e did ter you, it'll be – well – cruel.'

'Cruel!' Grace pulled away and got up. 'And what about me? How d'you think *I* feel? How d'you think I've felt all these years? No, Mickey – you're wrong. The only time that Eric Tyler will ever understand what he's done to me – and to others – is when he's waiting for me at that railway station. What I want for him is not revenge, it's justice.'

'An' *you* fink that by sendin' 'im packin', wivout turnin' up at that station ter tell 'im why, you fink that's goin' ter make any diff'rence to 'im?'

Grace hesitated. 'Maybe not to *him*, Mickey,' she replied. 'But it will to *me*.'

It was mixed blessings too for Josie and Stan. The slap-up Christmas party they had planned for Reg's return home had turned out not quite as they had hoped. Despite the turkey and all the trimmings, despite the Christmas tree, the booze, the decorations, and Aunt Hilda getting a little tipsy, Sandy's presence, and the reason she was staying with Reg under the same roof, was casting a long, dark shadow over the celebrations.

Grace hadn't heard the news until after she and Mickey had arrived at the house and were introduced to the girl, but apart from the embarrassing sly grin and wink Mickey gave Reg when he heard about the baby, Grace took it all in her stride. However, it was left to Viv to explain to Grace the real problems that lay ahead for Reg and Sandy, and she did this whilst the two of them were serving up the Christmas pudding in the scullery, which everyone was eagerly awaiting next door in the front room.

'The trouble is,' said Viv, 'Reg can't get a job. There's very little work around at this time of year, and about the only thing he can do is snow clearing for the Town Hall.'

'When's the baby due?' asked Grace.

'Oh, not for some time – thank God!' replied Viv, easing the pudding out of the saucepan. 'End of August, I think.'

Grace could see why her Auntie Josie and Uncle Stan were getting themselves all worked up. It was not going to be easy for them to face up to the neighbours and everyone else when the baby arrived, apart from the fact that they would have to juggle things around in the house to accommodate not only their son and daughter-in-law, but a baby as well.

'The funny thing is,' continued Viv, 'I think Mum will probably enjoy having a baby around the place – it'll give her something to do with her days. No, it's Reg I worry about. In his present state of mind, I'm not sure how he's going to be able to cope with finding enough money to look after a wife and kid. What do *you* think, Grace?'

Grace snapped out of her thoughts. 'Oh – yes,' she replied. 'I do see the problem. Tell me, though, d'you think Reg is serious about this girl? And does she feel the same way about him?'

'Oh, I think so,' replied Viv. 'Of course, you never can tell, but they're always together, always seem happy in each other's company. Why d'you ask?'

'Well,' replied Grace, unscrewing the top of the half bottle of brandy to pour over the Christmas pudding, 'I've just had a thought. It may not work, but it may be a solution to everyone's problems.'

Much to Mickey's amusement, Hilda, now well oiled, cheered and hugged him as Viv came back into the front room with Grace, carrying the flaming Christmas pudding on a serving dish.

'I won't 'ave any pud,' giggled Hilda. 'I'll just 'ave the brandy!'

'Well said, darlin'!' agreed Mickey, allowing himself to be dragged over for a slobbery kiss from Hilda at his side.

Sandy sniggered. She was clearly enjoying herself no end. But Josie was a bit embarrassed by the way her sister was behaving; she was cross with Stan for giving Hilda too much to drink before the meal had been served.

Once Grace had passed around the last plate of pudding, she resumed her place next to Sandy. The two of them were getting on quite well. In the short time since they had met, Grace had heard a lot about the traumatic upbringing Sandy had had, the feeling of being unwanted by both her real, unknown mother, and also by the two people who had adopted her, and now turned their backs on her. When Grace had first heard about the situation with Reg and Sandy, Auntie Josie had given the impression that the girl was only using Reg for her own selfish purposes, that she had trapped him into fatherhood. But after talking with Sandy both before and during the Christmas meal, Grace wasn't so sure. She had an idea that she wanted to put to both Reg and Sandy, but first she wanted to sound them out.

'Auntie says you want to move out of London, Reg?' she asked. 'Is that true?'

'Absolutely!' replied Reg, mouth full of Christmas pudding.

'Where d'you want to go to?' asked Grace.

'Anywhere,' replied Reg, 'as long as it's out in the country somewhere.'

'What about you, Sandy?' asked Grace. 'D'you feel the same way?'

'Oh yes,' replied Sandy, who seemed quite gooey-eyed even at the thought. 'I can't imagine what it'd be like ter 'ave peace an' quiet.'

'Some people find it boring,' suggested Grace. 'Even threatening. Nothing to look at except birds and trees and plants.'

Sandy shook her head. 'Not me,' she said. 'When I lived at 'ome, there was this tree just outside my bedroom window. Every time I did somefin' wrong an' my mum locked me in, I used ter climb out the window at night in the summer an' sit in that tree. It was funny 'cos though we lived near a main road, all I could ever 'ear was the sound er frogs in our back yard, an' when I woke up in the mornin', there were always loads er birds up on the branches all round me. They used ter kick up a 'ell of a noise, as though they was tellin' me off fer cashin' in on their territory.' She smiled to herself. 'When my dad found out wot I was doin' each night, 'e cut down the tree, and put a lock on my window. But it didn't make no difference, 'cos when I go ter sleep at night, I often dream that I'm still up in that tree.'

Grace was impressed and touched by Sandy's story, and it made up her mind to say what she had been thinking ever since she had arrived that morning. 'D'you like horses?' she asked right out of the blue.

Sandy swung a puzzled glance at Reg.

'Yer know I do,' said Reg, replying for both of them. 'Yer remember 'ow I used ter take Clapper fer a walk wiv Uncle Gus when we came down ter The Chapel on Sundays? Why d'yer ask?'

'Because now Clapper's been turned out to grass in the country, he needs someone to look after him,' replied Grace. 'And if you feel you're up to the job, it's yours.'

Both Reg and Sandy sat bolt upright in their chairs. Their faces were a picture. '*Us?*' asked Reg in disbelief. 'Look after Clapper?'

'Why not?' asked Grace. 'Mickey and I have been talking it over, haven't we, dear?'

Mickey was nonplussed. She hadn't mentioned a word of it to him, but he agreed wholeheartedly. 'Too true!' he replied, beaming.

'It just so happens that we've been looking around for someone to do the job,' continued Grace, 'so as far as we're concerned, you and Sandy would fit the bill perfectly. It won't be a huge wage—'

'You don't 'ave ter pay us nuffin'!' said Reg excitedly. 'Right, Sand?'

Sandy shook her head excitedly.

'It won't be a huge wage,' continued Grace, overriding them. 'But it'll be enough to get you on your feet, especially as you'll have your own place to live in.'

Stunned, both Reg and Sandy looked first at his mum, and then his dad, both of whom were totally taken aback.

'It's a kind of gamekeeper's cottage,' continued Grace. 'But it's very nice – right on the edge of some woods. Mind you, it's not only a question of looking after Clapper. One of the main reasons for being there is to look after the old house too. In fact, whenever you and the baby want a holiday, all you have to do is to move across! After all –' she took a lingering glance across the table to Mickey – 'a house should never just be a house. It should be a home.'

Mickey responded to her look with a huge smile of love and admiration.

Reg and Sandy couldn't take their eyes off Grace. They were too full of emotion.

'The place is called The House on the Hill,' said Grace. 'It's very quiet and secluded down there. And there are some lovely walks down by the sea. By the time you've lived there a few months, you'll have forgotten that such a place as London even exists.'

On the opposite side of the table, Auntie Josie's eyes were full of tears. Beneath the table, Stan, also clearly very moved, reached for her hand, and squeezed it gently.

'So,' asked Grace, directing her attention exclusively towards Reg and Sandy. 'Your own place in the country, a weekly wage, and looking after dear old Clapper. Do we have a deal?'

Reg and Sandy stared hard at one another, got up from their chairs, and embraced. Then Reg turned back to Grace. 'Fanks a lot, Grace,' he said simply. 'We've got a deal.'

That evening, a Christmas party was in full swing. It was just like old times, with Hilda, tipsy as she was, playing the upright piano, her fingers going in between the notes instead of on them, Josie and Stan singing their heads off with all the others in one medley of popular tunes after another, Viv making sandwiches and endless cups of tea, and, to Grace's amusement and joy, Mickey leading her around the tiny front parlour in a madcap dance in which he likened them to Fred Astaire and Ginger Rogers. There were musical chairs, a game of charades in which nobody seemed to guess any of the right answers, and three rowdy bashes of 'Knees Up Muvver Brown', in which, to Josie's embarrassment, Stan and his son repeatedly sang the dirty version of the words. Tired and exhausted, in the early hours of the morning everyone collapsed into chairs and, with the brightly decorated Christmas tree serving as an appropriate background, the festivities concluded with a lulling chorus of 'Silent Night'. After that, everyone went to their respective bedrooms, leaving Grace and Mickey to sleep on a mattress that had been put in front of the fire.

Auntie Josie was too full to say much, but the grateful and loving hug she gave Grace was sufficient to tell her what she felt, and when Uncle Stan retired for the night, albeit a little unsteady on his feet after quite a few pints of bitter, he was really only capable of stuttering, 'Fank yer, gel. Ol' Gus an' Alice knew wot they was doin' when they 'ad *you*.'

The only ones who didn't go to bed straight away, were Reg and Sandy. After saying an emotional thank you and good night to Grace and Mickey, they were too excited for sleep, and hand in hand, left the house for an early morning stroll along the frosty streets outside. As for Aunt Hilda, well she very nearly had to be carried up to the room she was sharing with her niece, but as it was Mickey who was supporting her up the stairs, she went to bed a very happy, if tipsy woman.

Last to go was Viv, who, after bidding Mickey good night with an affectionate peck on the cheek, turned to Grace and hugged her tight. 'You're quite an amazing person,' she whispered into Grace's ear. 'Did you know that?'

Grace smiled. 'It's our family that's amazing, Viv,' she replied. 'Not me.'

It had been a long night, but one that Grace and Mickey were not likely to forget for a long time. It had been an odd feeling for Grace, leaving Stoke Newington that morning, leaving behind a household that, when she and Mickey had first arrived on Christmas Day, was so full of family gloom that she had wanted to turn round and go straight back home to The Chapel. However, by the time everyone had come downstairs for a late Boxing Day breakfast, the atmosphere was somewhat different, with the whole company discussing their plans for the future: Josie and Stan in animated conversation with Reg and Sandy about how they could help them to get settled in to their new home in Devon, Viv looking forward to promotion at the Labour Exchange, and Aunt Hilda sobering herself up with several strong cups of tea, and talk of how she intended to help Grace and Mickey out in the new shop. As she mulled it all over in her mind, Grace couldn't help feeling a sense of achievement, of being able for the first time in her life to solve a family problem on her own. Her dad would have been proud of her.

Mickey was proud of her too. On the journey back home on the top of the bus, he spent most of the time just looking in wonderment at her. How she had changed, he told himself. How she had changed in these past few months since he had first met her. At that time, she seemed to be thinking of herself grandly as 'her father's daughter', a remote figure who had been so damaged by a personal relationship that her only escape was to disguise her true feelings and present herself as someone who could stride through the world without care, without heart. But not now. Now, Grace Higgs was someone to be reckoned with. She was not only a woman who cared, but a woman who cared about being loved. However, she had one serious weakness – Eric Tyler. If she still decided to go ahead with her plan to repeat what Eric had done to her six years before, to make an arrangement for them to go away together, and then not turn up at the railway station, then, reluctantly, Mickey would be unable to go along with it. It was the one issue that divided them, but it was important enough for it to prey on his mind.

When they got off the bus in Caledonian Road, Mickey said that he would have to go back to his 'pitch' to take a bath and change into some clean clothes. Grace asked why he couldn't just come back with her and do all that at The Chapel, but he assured her that it was something he had to do, *wanted* to do.

'Isn't it about time you moved in with me for good?' she asked sadly, as they stopped briefly at the street corner before he made his way off in a different direction home. 'After all, if we can sleep on a mattress together at Auntie Josie's and Uncle Stan's, I don't see what's wrong with sleeping permanently in our own bed?'

Mickey smiled as best he could at her. 'I dunno about that, Grace,' he replied awkwardly.

'We *could* do something about it,' she replied, averting his gaze, '*if* you want to?'

Mickey took a moment to take that in. With one hand, he gently raised her chin, and looked into her eyes. 'I always fawt it was the feller who does the proposin'.'

'That's old-fashioned,' replied Grace, with a mischievous grin. 'We girls have to assert our rights, you know.'

Despite the deep affection and love he felt for her, he lowered his eyes guiltily.

Grace noticed this. 'Did I say something wrong?' she asked.

'No, Grace,' he replied, giving her a quick, bland kiss on her lips. 'You din't say nuffin' wrong. But I've got ter get back. I'll be round later.' He gave her another last, hurried kiss, then went.

For several minutes, Grace watched him go without moving from the spot where they had stood. She had a strange feeling inside, a feeling that, unless she could find a way to overcome the one remaining gulf between them, then their relationship could go no further. She moved on. As always, Boxing Day was the day after, a time for everyone to pick themselves up after the hectic build-up to the Christmas festivities. For this reason, the streets were still deserted, and although it was the middle of the morning, the sun was having a difficult time melting the thick frost that had formed on the pavements overnight. She looked up briefly to take in the main Caledonian Road she was walking along. Even though it was now nearly seven months since the coronation of King George and Queen Elizabeth, there were still lots of flags and bunting hanging out from people's windows in the long rows of terraced houses. Grace could still hear the shouts and cheers and excitement of the residents who had blocked off so many of the backstreets for their open-air tea parties. It was such a joyous, such a happy time, the start of a new monarch's reign after the shock of King Edward VIII's abdication. And this got her to thinking about marriage, and the sacrifice a man would be prepared to make for the woman he loved. Would Mickey be prepared to make sacrifices? Would he be prepared to understand that seeking justice from Eric Tyler was not the sin he tried to make of it?

A few minutes later, she let herself into the stable yard by the back gate, and for a moment or so stopped to take a look at the cobblestone surface, now covered in a thin layer of frost. She had intended to go straight into the house, but something made her change her mind, and she went instead to the stable itself. Inside, everything was much the same as when Clapper had left, except that the place was bare and deserted. The main thing that was missing, of course, was Clapper himself, and it took Grace some time to accept the reality. Try as she may, she could not erase the memories, the endless happy memories of times past, times when she had come into this very stable and heard her father talking to Clapper as though he were a real person. But then, to Gus Higgs, Clapper *was* a real person, as real as any human being he knew. She also remembered the times when she had talked to Clapper herself, invariably scolding him for not keeping still whilst she tried to groom him. She looked around the stable; it was now nothing more than a gloomy barn, a dismal reminder that nothing could ever quite be the same again.

With one last forlorn look around, she turned and made for the door. But before she could go more than a few steps, she suddenly found herself clasped in Eric Tyler's arms, his lips pressed firmly against her own.

'Eric!' she gasped, finally managing to pull away. 'What are you doing here? I told you, my family are coming over here today.'

'I'm free, Grace!' he blurted ecstatically, like a man just released from prison. 'I've finally got rid of her! Don't you understand, darling? From now on, it's just you and me!'

'That's – wonderful, Eric,' said Grace, smoothing her hair, which he had just ruffled. 'You must be very relieved.'

'Relieved?' he exclaimed, drawing as close to her as he could. 'I'm over the moon! D'you realise what this means? It means that you and I can move in together without caring a damn for anyone any more. It means that we can go wherever we want, and do whatever we want. It means that I've got you once and for all – for the rest of our lives!'

Grace steeled herself. Although she knew this moment would come sooner or later, she felt she wasn't entirely prepared for it. 'So – where do we go from here?' she asked apprehensively.

He held her around the waist, and looked deep into her

eyes. 'I want to move in with you, Grace. Now, right now – this evening!'

Grace shook her head. 'No, Eric,' she insisted. 'That won't be possible.'

Eric pulled back slightly from her. 'What d'you mean, it's not possible? Is this another excuse? Why do you have to keep making excuses, Grace?'

'I'm not making excuses, Eric,' she returned.

'Then what's to stop us?'

'What I've told you before,' she said. 'Before we – get together – I want us to be married. I know it probably sounds old-fashioned to you, but marriage is important to me. It's the way I was brought up. I *believe* in marriage.'

'So do I, for chrissake!' cried Eric, who was getting rattled. 'I'll marry you as soon as the divorce is final. I can't say more than that!'

She turned her back on him and looked out through the open stable door. 'But you *do* want to marry me, Eric?' she asked. 'I mean, you're quite sure about that?'

He went to her, and turned her round. 'Of course I do, you silly thing,' he replied, becoming more conciliatory. 'I don't think you realise how much I love you. I've waited for this moment for so long, and now it's actually come, I want you so badly.'

'All right!' she said, in a moment of firm decision. 'You can move in with me, at least for a few days.'

Eric beamed with excitement. 'Oh – darling . . .!'

He went to kiss her, but she moved aside. 'But not here,' she said. 'Not here in The Chapel.'

Puzzled, Eric watched her pacing up and down. 'Well – *where*?'

'The House on the Hill,' she replied when he had hardly finished speaking. 'Let's go down to Devon. We can take a train first thing tomorrow morning. The *Cornish Riviera Express* leaves at ten. Let's meet up there – say, fifteen minutes before.'

'My God, Grace!' gasped Eric. 'D'you mean it? D'you really mean it?'

'Of course I mean it!' she snapped. 'I wouldn't say it if I didn't!'

'But what about the business, the shop?' he asked. 'Can you afford to be away for so long?'

'So long is only a few days, Eric,' she replied. 'I'm in charge of the business, remember. I pay someone to take care of things whilst I'm away.'

Again Eric's face lit up. He had never heard Grace talk like this before. She was so assertive, so determined to show that she was not going to be a walkover for the pea-brain who worked for her. 'So it's true,' he said. 'He really *is* just an employee?'

Grace stopped and glared at him. '*Who?*'

He nodded towards the door. 'The casual labour.'

'Please don't say things like that to me, Eric,' she replied curtly. 'Mickey Burke is a good, solid worker, and I have a lot to be grateful to him for. To suggest he's anything else to me is, to be frank – offensive.'

Quick to retract what he had implied, Eric went to her. 'That's *not* what I meant, darling, I promise you,' he said, wishing he had never said it. 'It's just that I worry for you, worry that anyone can take advantage of you. You're far too precious to me to allow that to happen.'

'The more time we're together, Eric,' she replied, 'the more you'll realise that I'll never allow *anyone* to take advantage of me.' To his surprise – and delight – she leant forward and kissed him gently on the lips. 'Now go home, Eric,' she said with a sweet, loving smile, gently removing a lock of hair that had fallen across one of his eyes. 'From tomorrow, things are going to be so different between us. Life's a funny old thing, isn't it? It has a way of turning people's lives upside down.' He made a move to kiss her again, but she resisted it. 'A quarter to ten at Paddington station tomorrow morning. I'll have the tickets waiting. Don't be late. Whatever you do, Eric, this time – don't be late.'

Mickey lay on his tiny bed in the cramped space of his 'pitch' just around the corner from Pedlar's Way. Although he'd left Grace an hour before, he still hadn't had the bath he'd used as an excuse to be on his own for a while. He had so much on his mind, so much to trouble him, a decision so great that every time he thought about it he became depressed. How could he break away from Grace now, he had asked himself over and over again. After all she'd done for him, and despite everything she had ever meant to him – and *still* meant to him – how could he let her think that he would marry her knowing that there was one fundamental disagreement between them that, unless tackled head on, would mean the end of their relationship? Who was right, and who was wrong? If Grace was determined to go ahead with what he had described as an act of revenge, how did he know that *she* wasn't right, that she had a right to treat Eric Tyler in the same shabby way that he had treated her? And Eric *had* treated her badly – there was no doubt about that.

Mickey had told himself so many times that there were unscrupulous characters like Eric Tyler in this world, who would stop at nothing to get what they wanted, even though their actions could destroy a life both physically and mentally. But revenge was not justice. Revenge was spite, and to Mickey's way of thinking, Grace was above all that.

But then, suppose he, Mickey, had got it all wrong? A lot of people would agree with Grace that justice *should* be done, if only to stop Eric from doing such a thing again. But *would* it stop him? Would it *ever* stop someone like that? Eric Tyler was sick, and revenge was no cure.

He suddenly leapt up from his bed. In deep despair, he went to his jug and basin, and took a long, agonising look at himself in his shaving mirror. He had never liked what he saw, and at this very moment, he liked it even less. As he started to fill his shaving mug, the only thing he was trying to work out now was what would happen if he went back to Grace that evening, and gave her an ultimatum? How would she react if he told her that what she was going to do to Eric Tyler was too much for him to take, that unless she pulled back from it, they could no longer go on seeing one another? He slammed down his mug. What sort of a big-head was he? he asked himself. But as he calmed down again, he had no answer. He only hoped that he would have by the time he saw Grace again that evening, because if he didn't, how would she be able to forgive him, how would she not know that he was no better than Eric Tyler himself?

It was a night for decision, and he was absolutely dreading it.

Chapter 25

Even though it was the morning after Boxing Day, the Christmas decorations everywhere had a jaded look about them. For most people it was a pretty gloomy time, for it meant going back to work after a lot of celebrating, but it also meant that there would now be no more bank holiday until Easter, which felt an awful long way away. For Grace, however, 27 December meant something quite different. This morning she had an appointment to meet Eric Tyler at Paddington station, where he would be waiting in great excitement and anticipation to catch the *Cornish Riviera Express* with her to Dawlish. But Grace was determined that he should wait in vain; never again would he be able to walk out on her, never again would he be able to tell her that he loved her, whilst at the same time sleeping with any woman who took his fancy. For Grace, this was her day of reckoning. Unfortunately, she knew only too well that it could also mean the end of her relationship with Mickey.

Much to Grace's despair, Mickey hadn't returned to The Chapel the previous evening. But then, after the few terse words they had exchanged when he left her on that street corner to go back home to his 'pitch' to get changed, she was not entirely surprised. As Mickey had got it into his mind that what she was doing to Eric Tyler was wrong, she knew there was nothing she could do to persuade him that *he* was wrong. Her mind was made up. She had waited six years for this day, and now that it had come, she would teach Eric Tyler a lesson – once and for all. None the less, turning her back on Mickey was not an easy decision to take. For these past few months, he had been her backbone, and she had relished the advice and support he had given her. The trouble was, she also loved him deeply, and if she lost him because of her own pride and vanity, it was possible that she would regret it for the rest of her life.

The first thing she did when she woke up was to look at the clock on her bedside table. It was half-past seven. She had done exactly the same all through the night, tossing and turning, dreaming of Eric Tyler waiting at the platform, smoking one cigarette after another, and cursing Grace with every fibre in his being. But, at the start of the day itself, it wasn't Eric she was thinking about, it was Mickey.

Mickey arrived at the back door of the house soon after the postman had brought some late Christmas cards, and a few more letters. He looked decidedly awkward.

'Sorry I couldn't get back last night,' he said glumly. 'My neighbours, the Gremlins, asked me in ter 'ave a drink wiv 'em. I usually do so every Chris—'

'It's all right, Mickey,' said Grace letting him in. 'There's no need to explain. I was very tired anyway. I went to bed quite early. Would you like a cup of tea? The kettle's boiling.'

'Fanks,' said Mickey, following her in to the scullery. Grace's lack of a warm greeting upset him.

'We've got two more buyers amongst the tenants,' she said, pointing to the small pile of letters on the table. 'Jack Pertwee and Sid Wilson have both said yes, but Mrs Jolly said a firm no, and the Hobbses said they couldn't say yes until they knew what was going to happen after Oliver has had the next operation on his leg – poor man.'

'So 'ow many does that make now who wanna buy?' asked Mickey.

'I haven't counted them,' replied Grace, 'but it's about

fifty-fifty I think. Anyway, I'm going to see Mr Rumble at the bank tomorrow, to see where we go from here.'

Whilst she was at the stove pouring hot water into the teapot, Mickey came up behind, and clasped his arms round her waist. 'Fanks fer a wonderful Chris'mas, Grace,' he said, kissing her ear. 'You made it the best one I've ever 'ad.'

Grace smiled sweetly over her shoulder. She wanted to hug him to her, but no matter how hard she tried, something inside stopped her from doing so. 'You're welcome,' she replied.

Mickey waited for her to put the kettle back on the stove, then swung her round to face him. 'Don't let's fight, Grace,' he pleaded, his eyes filled with anguish. 'We've got so much goin' fer us.'

'Have we, Mickey?' she asked.

Mickey was stung. 'Well – ain't we?'

'I don't know, Mickey,' replied Grace. 'Honest to God, I don't know. This time yesterday morning, I thought the whole world belonged only to you and me. I thought nothing could ever come between us, now or forever. But clearly it has.' She paused a moment, then looked up straight into his eyes. 'Eric Tyler came here last night,' she said.

Mickey slowly eased his arms away from around her waist.

'I told him I want us to go down to the house together, just him and me. I arranged to meet him this morning at a quarter to ten at Paddington station. But I have no intention of turning up.'

Mickey's whole expression changed. He felt as though she had suddenly punched him in his stomach. He turned away, and sat at the kitchen table.

Grace joined him. 'I'm sorry, Mickey,' she said. 'I can

only follow my instinct, and my instinct is telling me that this is what I have to do.'

' *'Ave* to?' he asked. 'Yer mean yer instinct is more in charge than wot's right?'

'How can you say that, Mickey?' she asked, overwrought by his reaction. 'When it comes to a situation like this, what makes you so sure that *you're* right, and I'm wrong?'

'I don't know, Grace,' replied Mickey. 'Maybe it's the same as you an' your instinct: it's a gut feelin'. But wot I would ask yer ter do is ter try an' imagine wot it's goin' ter be like fer that bloke, sittin' at Paddington station, and watchin' the train leave the platform. So many fings'll be goin' fru 'is 'ead. Maybe 'e'll be wonderin' wevver 'e's got the wrong time, the wrong day, or the wrong place. So wot'll 'e do? Will 'e just call it a day, an' just ferget about the 'ole fing, or will 'e be so angry that 'e's been made ter look a real Charlie that 'e'll come stormin' after you up that street outside, an' give yer merry bleedin' 'ell?'

'I don't *care* about Eric Tyler's feelings, Mickey!' insisted Grace. 'I don't *care* what he might or might not do. Don't you understand, I'm not frightened of him?'

Mickey considered this for a moment. 'Well, I'm sorry about that, Grace,' he said, getting up from his chair. 'I'd sooner yer was frightened of 'im than fillin' yerself wiv so much – hate. Yer see, it's the effect all this is goin' ter 'ave on *you* that I worry about. An' also the effect it'll 'ave on *me*. It means I'd 'ave ter look at yer in a diff'rent light. Instead of the person I've come ter know an' love, a person who's capable of so much love and fair play, wot I'd see is someone who doesn't know 'ow ter fergive.'

'Forgive?' asked Grace calmly, but unable to look up into his eyes. 'I'll never be able to forgive someone who deliberately set out to destroy me.'

Mickey shrugged. 'Fair enuff,' he said, with obvious pain. 'Then I reckon that's that.' He turned, and made for the door. But he stopped briefly without looking back. 'Don't worry about the tea,' he called. 'I'll make one when I get 'ome.'

Grace watched him leave the room, then heard the back door open and close. She wanted to get up and see him go out across the stable yard, but she was too upset to do so. She also wanted to cry. Although losing Mickey was the last thing in the world she wanted to happen, crying would only be admitting that she was wrong – and she wasn't. Distraught though she was, she got up from the table, and poured herself a cup of tea. As much as she loved Mickey, nothing he said had convinced her to prevent Eric Tyler from getting what was coming to him. Her eyes flicked up to the clock on the wall above the cooker.

It was half-past eight.

The hands of the big clock over the cafeteria at Paddington station were pointing restlessly at seven minutes to ten; one more tiny quiver and there would only be six minutes left to the departure time of the *Cornish Riviera Express*. No one was more aware of that than Eric Tyler, who was pacing up and down anxiously near the platform ticket barrier, smoking his umpteenth cigarette, and scanning the station concourse for any sign of Grace. It was a frustrating, aggravating time for him; if there was one thing he deplored more than anything else in this world, it was people being late for appointments. Punctuality had been the hallmark of his life, and as this was one of the most important events of his life, he was running out of patience.

He had arrived half an hour before Grace was due to

turn up, his small smart suitcase packed and ready for his entry into a grand new world of respectability. As he sat in the cafeteria nervously gulping down one cup of tea after another, smoking almost as many cigarettes in that time as he had done during the whole of Christmas Day, all he could think about was freedom, freedom from a little slut who used to call herself his wife, and the freedom to move on to an horizon blazing with sunlight. Ever since that moment when he had met Grace outside the bank after breaking with her all those years before, he had not once looked back. Oh, he had been involved with many girls and women in his time, but he never imagined the day would come when he would actually fall in love with someone. Grace was everything he wanted in this life; this time he was not going to lose her.

At five minutes to the hour, he was jolted into absolute panic by the voice over the Tannoy of the station announcer: 'The train standing at platform one is the *Cornish Riviera Express* leaving at ten o'clock, and calling at Exeter, Plymouth, and Penzance. Change at Exeter for Dawlish, Teignmouth, Paignton, and Torquay. Platform one for the *Cornish Riviera Express*, departing at ten o'clock.'

Eric looked up at the big clock over the cafeteria, and checked it with his own watch. 'Damn!' he growled, face glowing red with rage. 'Stupid cow! Where are you?'

'Eric.'

He swung with a start. Grace was there behind him. 'Grace!' he gasped breathlessly. 'Where've you been? Come on, we've got to hurry!' He took another frenzied look up at the station clock. 'The train's leaving any minute. Where's your suitcase?' But he was stopped dead in his tracks when he looked at her.

Grace was shaking her head. 'No, Eric.'

'What d'you mean, no?' he asked quickly, very agitated. 'What're you talking about?'

'I said no,' she repeated. 'We're not going to Dawlish.'

'But the train!' he blurted excitedly, pointing to the train standing at the platform, smoke already billowing from the funnel of its engine. 'It's going!'

'Don't you understand, Eric?' repeated Grace calmly. 'We're not going to Dawlish. We're not going *anywhere*.'

Eric stared at her in disbelief, then slowly put down his suitcase. 'What's this all about?' he asked.

'It's about *me*,' replied Grace. 'It's about *us*. I don't want to marry you, Eric. I never have, and I never will.'

Stunned, completely taken aback, Eric stared right into her.

'I'm sorry,' she continued, having to raise her voice above the bustling activity surrounding the train's impending departure, 'but that's the way it is. I could never forgive you for what you did to me all those years ago; it was so cruel, so unnecessary. If you hadn't wanted me, you should have told me so, not led me to believe something so totally different. And yet, in some ways, I have a lot to thank you for. I loved you. I *thought* I loved you with all my heart. But the moment you came back into my life again, I realised that there was nothing between us, and never had been.'

'And you've waited all this time to tell me?' he asked bitterly.

'You left me no alternative,' replied Grace. 'I'd hoped . . . I'd hoped that things might have been different, that you'd changed. But you *haven't*. You haven't changed at all.'

'How can you say that?' he persisted. 'You don't know me. You've never given me the chance to show how I *really* feel about you.'

'Oh, I know you, all right, Eric,' said Grace. 'I know who

you are and what you want, about the people you mix with, the people you *need*. When we've been together, Eric, I haven't walked around with my eyes closed. The more I kept them open the more I knew that I never wanted you to be a part of my life. When I got up this morning, I had every intention of just leaving you standing here on the platform, just the way you did to me six years ago. I wanted revenge, Eric, a chance to show you that I can be just as ruthless as you. But the fact is, I can't.'

The air was suddenly pierced by the sound of a train guard's whistle.

'You're wrong,' pleaded Eric, his attention torn between her and the departing train. 'Give me time! Just give me time to prove that we can make a go of things. I love you, Grace! Why can't you understand that I really do love you?'

Grace hesitated, lowered her eyes and raised them again. 'Then I'm sorry for you,' she replied. 'Goodbye, Eric.' She turned to leave.

'Close the doors, please!' The train guard's voice boomed along the platform, and the atmosphere was fractured by the slamming of compartment doors.

Eric watched solemnly as Grace started to walk away. Behind him came the shrill call of the train engine's whistle, followed by the noisy building up of steam. Gradually, the train pulled away from the station, accompanied by the distant farewell calls of people who had come to see off their friends and relatives.

'Grace!'

Grace came to an abrupt halt, as Eric hurried to join her.

'Don't do this to me, Grace,' he pleaded. 'You need me. Things are changing for you. You're going to need all the support you can get.'

Grace smiled appreciatively. 'Thank you, Eric,' she

replied. 'But that's one thing I *don't* have to worry about.' She turned, and held out her hand to Mickey, who was waiting nearby. He joined her, took her hand, and without either of them saying another word, they slowly strolled off arm in arm together.

The new Mayfair Cinema in Caledonian Road was decked out proudly in bunting and flags, and the road outside was thronged with hundreds of people, all waiting to catch a glimpse of the famous British film star who was about to perform the opening ceremony. Bricklayers, carpenters, plasterers, electricians and many other workers had been toiling away for weeks leading up to the great occasion, struggling to get the place ready for the cinema's first customers.

As the opening ceremony was due to take place at twelve noon, Grace and Mickey only had enough time to rush back home to The Chapel to get changed into their swanky clothes, which they had bought especially for the occasion. Mickey was bowled over when he saw Grace in her new flaming-red three-quarter-length woollen dress, which she wore beneath a stylish black topcoat and black and red bobble hat. Grace was equally impressed when Mickey togged himself up in the new three-piece brown suit and brown moccasin shoes that he had bought, even though she had to once again help him to knot his tie. Nervous and excited, they left The Chapel together, full of joy and anticipation, both of them relieved that the tensions that had threatened to keep them apart were now a thing of the past.

'Wot you did terday,' said Mickey, as they hurried along, arm in arm, 'was just about the most sensible fing I've ever known.'

'Oh yes?' replied Grace, grinning at him. 'You mean because it was *your* idea?'

'No ways!' insisted Mickey. 'Becos it was the right fing ter do, becos someone like you could never've done anyfin' else.'

'Oh, I don't know, Mickey,' replied Grace wistfully. 'I'm not so sure. But despite all I said to Eric, I still feel he could do the same thing to someone else.'

' 'E will,' Mickey assured her. 'But it won't be so easy for 'im next time. Next time, 'e'll fink again before 'e climbs on someone else's back.'

Grace sighed. 'I do hope you're right,' she replied.

As they neared the Mayfair Cinema, they could hear the sound of a brass band playing in the street, and as they approached the front entrance, some pearlies amongst the crowd of spectators on the other side of the road had started doing a knees-up. The merriment was infectious, and soon everyone was joining in with every song the band played.

A few minutes later, a great roar went up from the crowds lining the road, as Gracie Fields, the star guest, turned up in her chauffeur-driven car, to be met by the beaming Mayor of Islington, who welcomed her to the borough, and invited her to open the cinema. Gracie duly obliged, and after treating the crowds to a bit of her homespun Lancashire humour, and cutting the magical red ribbon, she launched straight into an impromptu rendering of what was probably her most famous song, 'Sally'.

Bubbling with excitement and happiness, Grace and Mickey settled back into their plush red seats in the stalls, and whilst they waited for the celebrations on stage and screen to begin, Grace couldn't help enthusing about all the wonderful things they could look forward to during the coming year: about Reg and Sandy going down to look after dear old Clapper at The House on the Hill; about her dad, and how he would have loved to be sitting there with her and Mickey right now; about the new shop; about Auntie Josie and Uncle Stan and Viv and Auntie Hilda. Grace thought about her tenants and customers and what owning their own property was going to mean to some of them, but above all she thought about herself and Mickey, and what the future held for the two of them.

'It's not going to be easy,' said Grace, over the general hubbub amongst the rest of the audience. 'Especially if we get involved in another war. I couldn't bear it if they called you up.'

Despite an irritating grunt from someone sitting behind them, Mickey put his arm around Grace's shoulders. 'Don't worry,' he assured her. 'Fings're diff'rent now. If there's a war, you mark my words – it'll be over in five minutes.'

Grace sighed. 'I hope you're right, Mickey,' she said. 'I hope to God you're right.'

Once the Mayor came on stage to thank Gracie Fields for her presence, and then praised the local workmen who had succeeded in building such a magnificent new cinema, there was a lively half-hour of dance music from a famous radio band, but before the first double-feature film programme commenced on the brand-new screen, 'Our Gracie' launched into a selection of her most famous songs, including, 'Walter, Walter, Lead Me to the Altar', and a reprise of 'Sally'.

Together with everyone else in the audience, Grace and Mickey joined in with gusto the chorus of the final song, 'Sing As We Go', especially Mickey, who had waved to and cheered his heroine Gracie Fields as though she was one of his own mates. Then, without pausing for breath, he leaned back to his very own Grace, and out of sheer enjoyment kissed her.

'I dunno 'ow yer did this, Grace,' he yelled over the rousing audience sing-song, 'but I'm 'avin' the time er me life!'

Grace roared with laughter. 'Me too!' she called back. 'Aren't you glad you're marrying a chandler's daughter?'

A Perfect Stranger

Victor Pemberton

The advent of the Second World War changes everything. So, when Tom, home on leave, asks Ruth to marry him, she agrees. After all, once Tom returns to the front, who knows if they'll ever see each other again? But months go by and Tom's letters dry up. Ruth is forced to get on with her life and starts to enjoy the attentions of another man. It is this temptation which will alter her life for ever. And when the war is finally over she will find the battle for her own personal freedom and safety has just begun . . .

A Perfect Stranger is a deeply emotional, evocative and gripping account of the difficult decisions facing women left on their own.

Praise for Victor Pemberton's wartime sagas

'A wonderfully detailed and involving study of a community surviving the destruction of war' Barry Forshaw, *Amazon*

'A potent mix of passion and suspense' *Evening Herald*

'A vivid story of a community surviving some of the darkest days in our history . . . warm-hearted' *Bolton Evening News*

'A real treat' *Peterborough Evening Telegraph*

'Warm and entertaining . . . brimming with the atmosphere of wartime London' *Coventry Evening Telegraph*

0 7472 6653 0

headline

Better Days

June Tate

Despite living in the shabby docklands of Southampton, in 1954 Gemma Barrett has much to be thankful for. She has a good job in a big department store, a best friend with whom she shares her hopes and dreams, and a blossoming romance with Nick Weston, a first officer with Cunard. Life would be great if it wasn't for her mother, Eve, who likes more to drink than is good for her. And when Gemma's dad walks out and Eve starts bringing strange men home, Gemma doesn't know where to turn.

Desperate to escape, she seizes the opportunity to be a stewardess on the *Queen Mary*, voyaging to and from New York, and when she discovers that Nick is also on board, it seems an affirmation that she made the right decision. But a chance encounter with Vince Morelli, a gang boss in the New York docks, looks set to jeopardise her newfound happiness. Vince has friends in high places and is used to getting what he wants – and when he sets his sights on Gemma, the results could be devastating.

June Tate's previous novels, *For the Love of a Soldier*, *Riches of the Heart* and *No One Promised Me Tomorrow* are available from Headline:

'Excellent and gripping . . . compelling' *Sussex Life*

'Her debut book caused a stir among Cookson and Cox devotees, and they'll love this' *Peterborough Evening Telegraph*

0 7472 6324 8

headline

Now you can buy any of these other bestselling books by **Victor Pemberton** from your bookshop or *direct from his publisher*.

FREE P&P AND UK DELIVERY
(Overseas and Ireland £3.50 per book)

A Perfect Stranger	£5.99
Leo's Girl	£5.99
Goodnight Amy	£5.99
My Sister Sarah	£5.99
Nellie's War	£5.99
The Silent War	£5.99
Our Rose	£5.99
Our Street	£5.99
Our Family	£5.99

TO ORDER SIMPLY CALL THIS NUMBER

01235 400 414

or visit our website: www.madaboutbooks.com

Prices and availability subject to change without notice.

News & Natter is a newsletter full of everyone's favourite storytellers and their latest news and views as well as opportunities to win some fabulous prizes and write to your favourite authors. Just send a postcard with your name and address to: *News & Natter*, Kadocourt Ltd, The Gateway, Gatehouse Road, Aylesbury, Bucks HP19 8ED. Then sit back and look forward to your first issue.